SONIC
SAGA SERIES

THE DARK MIRROR

WELCOME TO SONIC'S COMIC BOOK
ADVENTURES -- A WORLD UNIQUE
AND BEYOND WHAT YOU KNOW
FROM THE SEGA GAMES! WHERE
SONIC THE HEDGEHOG AND THE
HEROIC FREEDOM FIGHTERS WORK
TO SAVE THE WORLD FROM THE
FORCES OF EVIL!

SONIC™
SAGA SERIES

IAN FLYNN
SCRIPT

TRACY YARDLEY
SONIC THE HEDGEHOG #190-194

JONATHAN H. GRAY
"FATHER AND SON"
- SONIC THE HEDGEHOG #192
"SLEEPLESS IN NEW MEGAOPOLIS"
- SONIC THE HEDGEHOG #194
PENCILS

JIM AMASH
INKS

JOSH RAY
SONIC THE HEDGEHOG #190-194

JOSH & AIMEE RAY
SONIC THE HEDGEHOG #192
"SLEEPLESS IN NEW MEGAOPOLIS"
- SONIC THE HEDGEHOG #194
COLORS

JOHN WORKMAN
SONIC THE HEDGEHOG #190-192

TERESA DAVIDSON
"FATHER AND SON"
- SONIC THE HEDGEHOG #192
SONIC THE HEDGEHOG #193-194
LETTERS

COVER BY
TRACY YARDLEY
& JASON JENSEN

SPECIAL THANKS TO
TYLER HAM &
ANTHONY GACCIONE
AT SEGA LICENSING

ARCHIE COMIC PUBLICATIONS, INC.
JON GOLDWATER, publisher/co-ceo
MIKE PELLERITO, president
VICTOR GORELICK, co-president, e-i-c
ROBERTO AGUIRRE-SACASA, chief creative officer
HAROLD BUCHHOLZ, senior vice president of
publishing and operations
ALEX SEGURA, senior vice president
of publicity and marketing
PAUL KAMINSKI, exec. director of
editorial/compilation editor
JONATHAN BETANCOURT, director - book sales
and operations
VINCENT LOVALLO, assistant editor
STEPHEN OSWALD, production manager
JAMIE LEE ROTANTE, editorial assistant/proofreader

SONIC SAGA SERIES, Book Seven: The Dark Mirror, 2015. Printed in Canada. Published by Archie Comic
Publications, Inc., 325 Fayette Avenue, Mamaroneck, NY 10543-2318. Originally published in single magazine form
in Sonic the Hedgehog #'s 190-194. Sega is registered in the U.S. Patent and Trademark Office. SEGA, Sonic The
Hedgehog, and all related characters and indicia are either registered trademarks or trademarks of SEGA CORPORATION
© 1991-2015. SEGA CORPORATION and SONIC TEAM, LTD./SEGA CORPORATION © 2001-2015. All Rights Reserved.
The product is manufactured under license from Sega of America, Inc., 350 Rhode Island St., Ste. 400, San Francisco,
CA 94103   www.sega.com. Any similarities between characters, names, persons, and/or institutions in this book and
any living, dead or fictional characters, names, persons, and/or institutions are not intended and if they exist, are purely
coincidental. Nothing may be reprinted in whole or part without written permission from Archie Comic Publications, Inc.
ISBN: 978-1-61988-950-7

TABLE OF CONTENTS

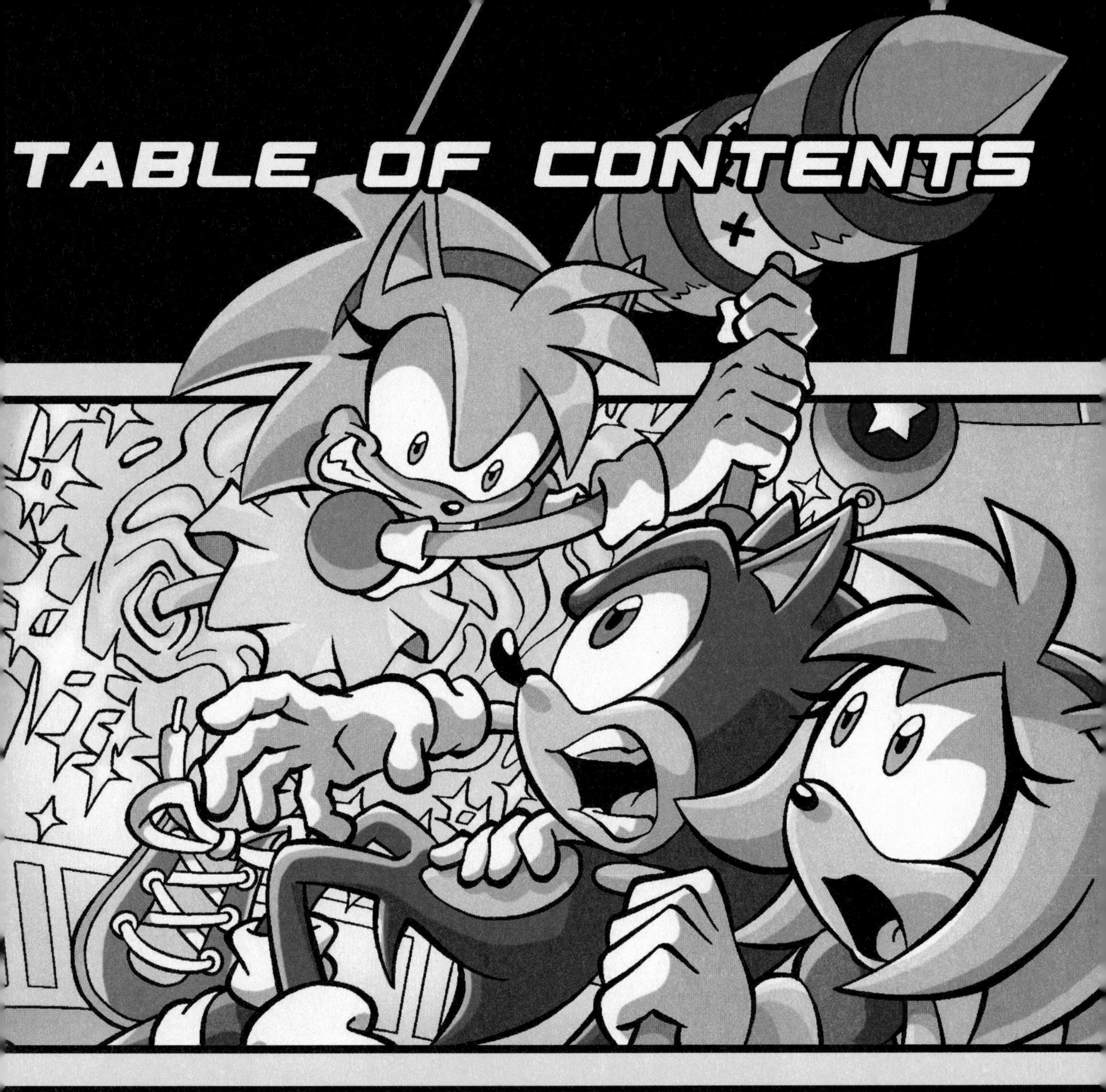

CHAPTER 1

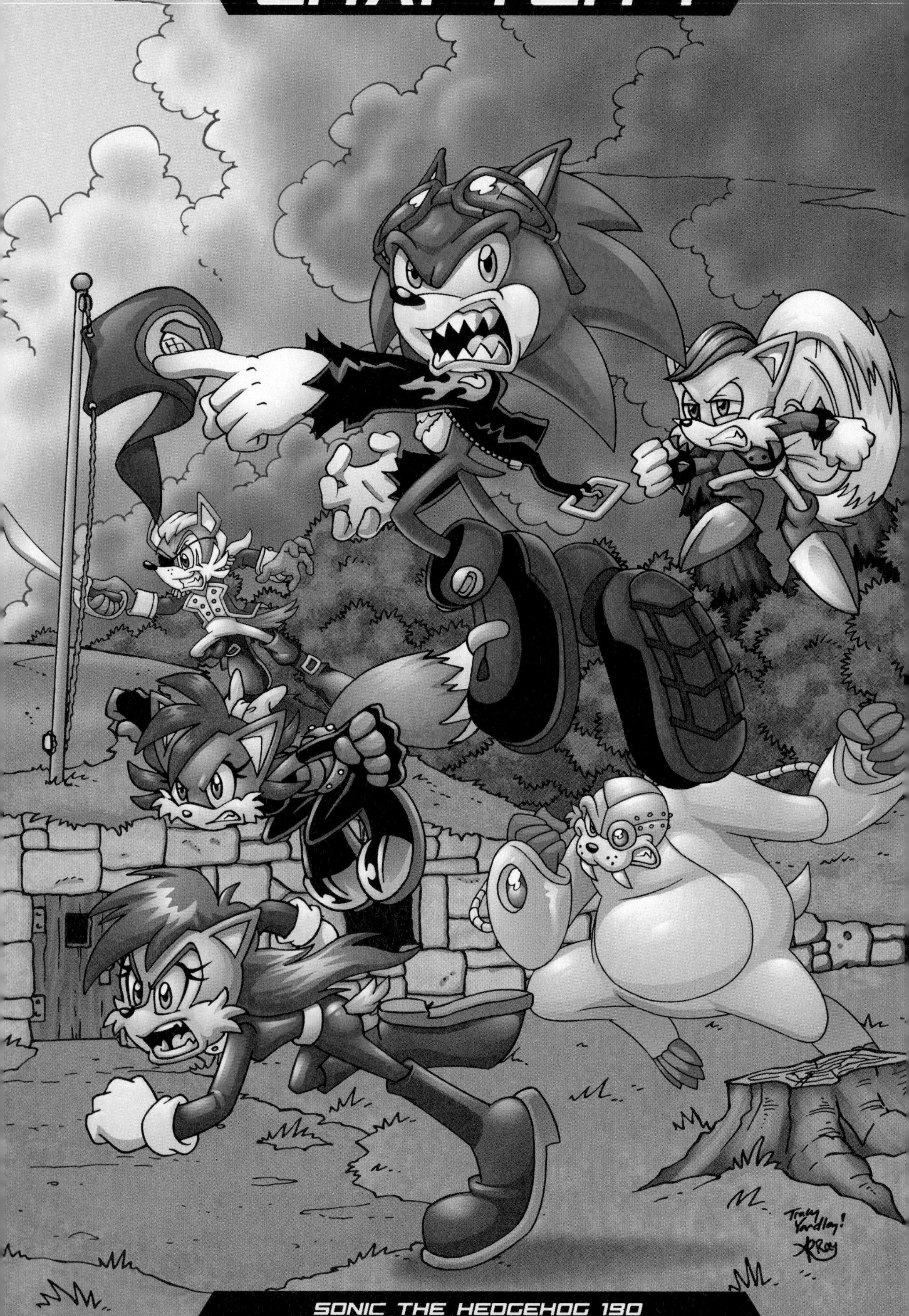

SONIC THE HEDGEHOG 190
COVER BY TRACY YARDLEY AND JOSH RAY

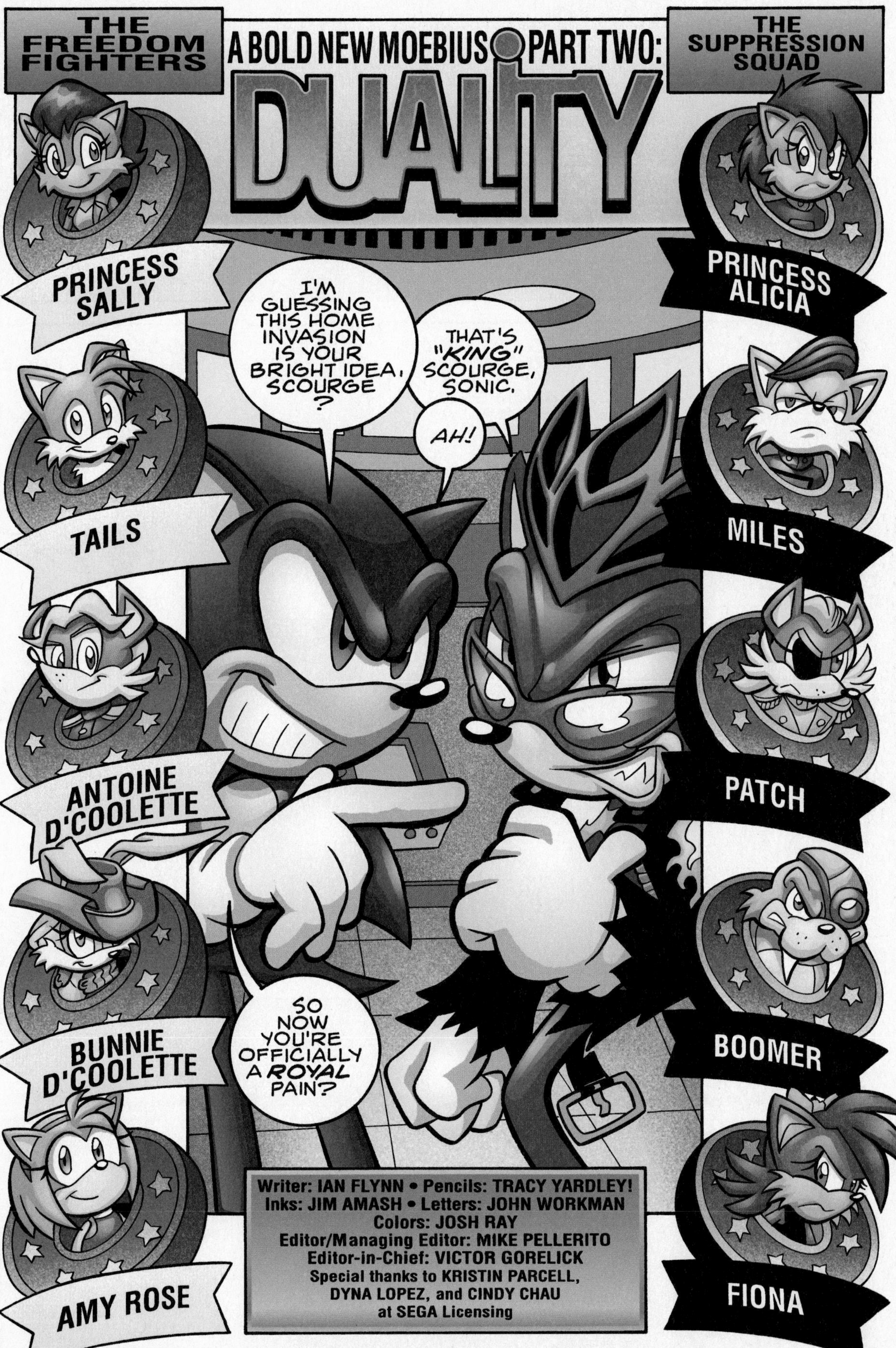
THE FREEDOM FIGHTERS
A BOLD NEW MOEBIUS PART TWO:
DUALITY
THE SUPPRESSION SQUAD
PRINCESS SALLY
PRINCESS ALICIA
I'M GUESSING THIS HOME INVASION IS YOUR BRIGHT IDEA, SCOURGE?
THAT'S "KING" SCOURGE, SONIC.
AH!
TAILS
MILES
ANTOINE D'COOLETTE
PATCH
SO NOW YOU'RE OFFICIALLY A ROYAL PAIN?
BUNNIE D'COOLETTE
BOOMER
AMY ROSE
FIONA
Writer: IAN FLYNN • Pencils: TRACY YARDLEY!
Inks: JIM AMASH • Letters: JOHN WORKMAN
Colors: JOSH RAY
Editor/Managing Editor: MIKE PELLERITO
Editor-in-Chief: VICTOR GORELICK
Special thanks to KRISTIN PARCELL, DYNA LOPEZ, and CINDY CHAU at SEGA Licensing

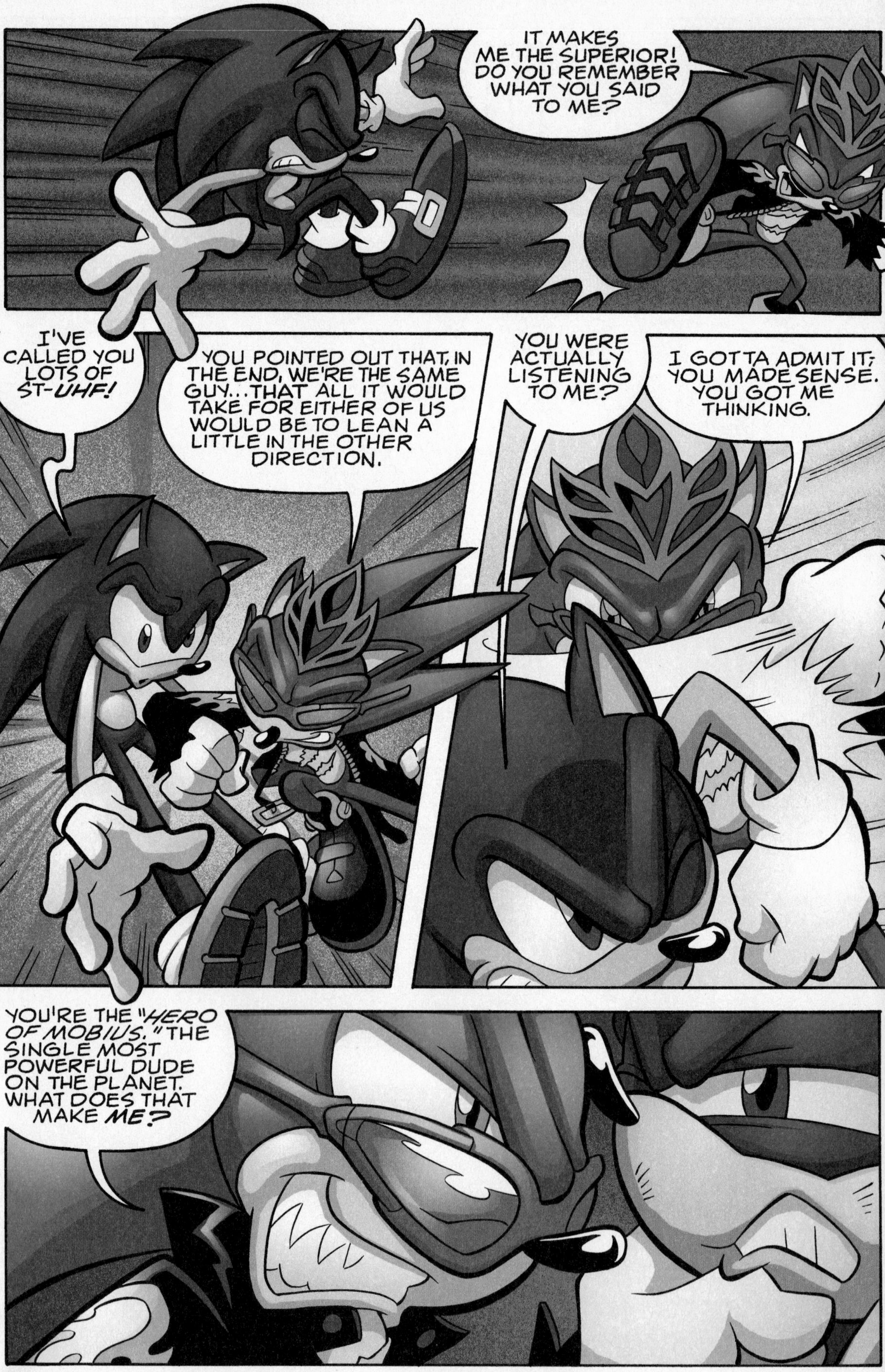
IT MAKES ME THE SUPERIOR! DO YOU REMEMBER WHAT YOU SAID TO ME?
I'VE CALLED YOU LOTS OF ST-*UHF!*
YOU POINTED OUT THAT, IN THE END, WE'RE THE SAME GUY...THAT ALL IT WOULD TAKE FOR EITHER OF US WOULD BE TO LEAN A LITTLE IN THE OTHER DIRECTION.
YOU WERE ACTUALLY LISTENING TO ME?
I GOTTA ADMIT IT; YOU MADE SENSE. YOU GOT ME THINKING.
YOU'RE THE "*HERO OF MOBIUS.*" THE SINGLE MOST POWERFUL DUDE ON THE PLANET. WHAT DOES THAT MAKE *ME?*

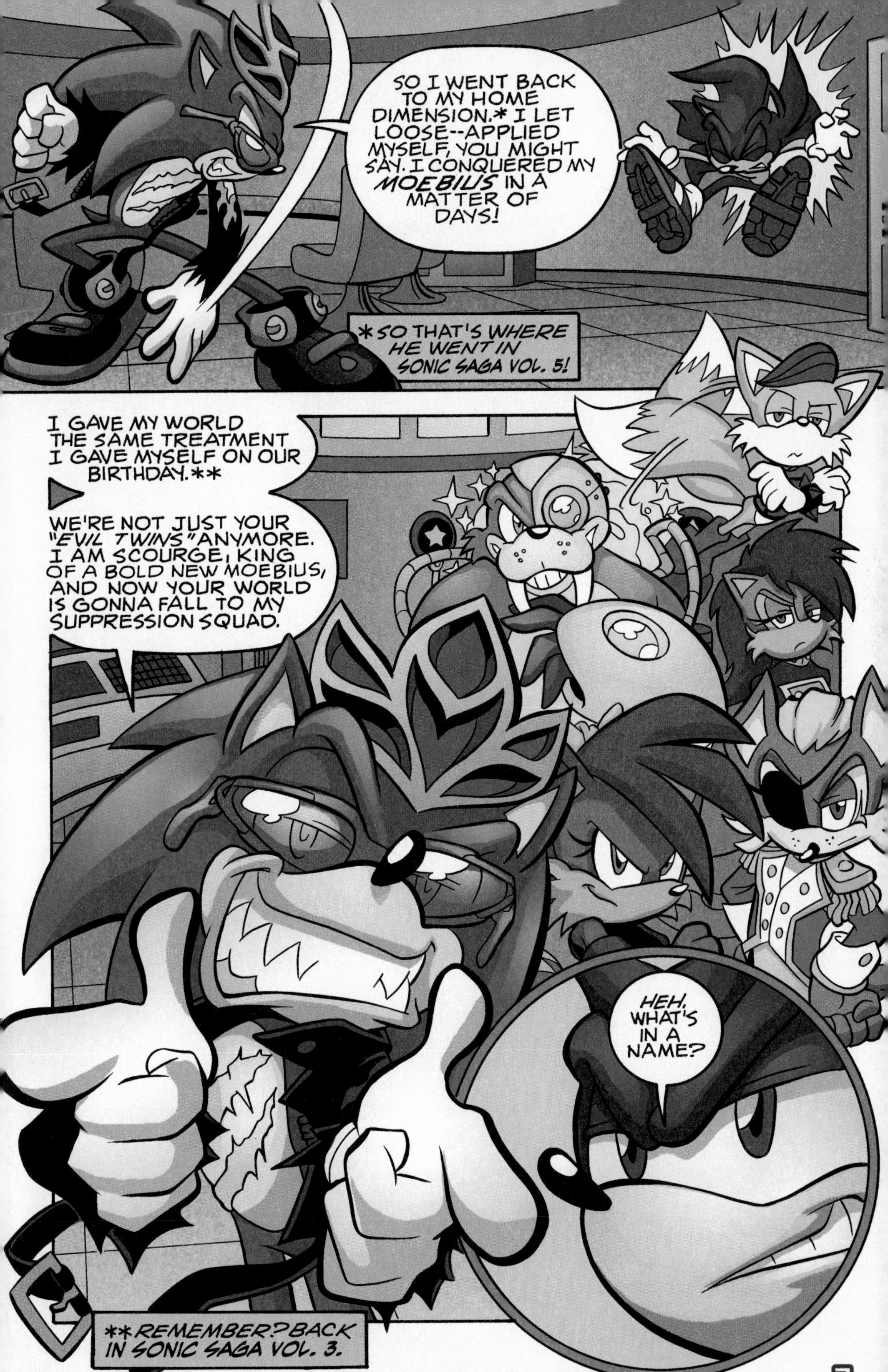
SO I WENT BACK TO MY HOME DIMENSION.* I LET LOOSE--APPLIED MYSELF, YOU MIGHT SAY. I CONQUERED MY MOEBIUS IN A MATTER OF DAYS!
*SO THAT'S WHERE HE WENT IN SONIC SAGA VOL. 5!
I GAVE MY WORLD THE SAME TREATMENT I GAVE MYSELF ON OUR BIRTHDAY.**
WE'RE NOT JUST YOUR "EVIL TWINS" ANYMORE. I AM SCOURGE, KING OF A BOLD NEW MOEBIUS, AND NOW YOUR WORLD IS GONNA FALL TO MY SUPPRESSION SQUAD.
HEH. WHAT'S IN A NAME?
**REMEMBER? BACK IN SONIC SAGA VOL. 3.

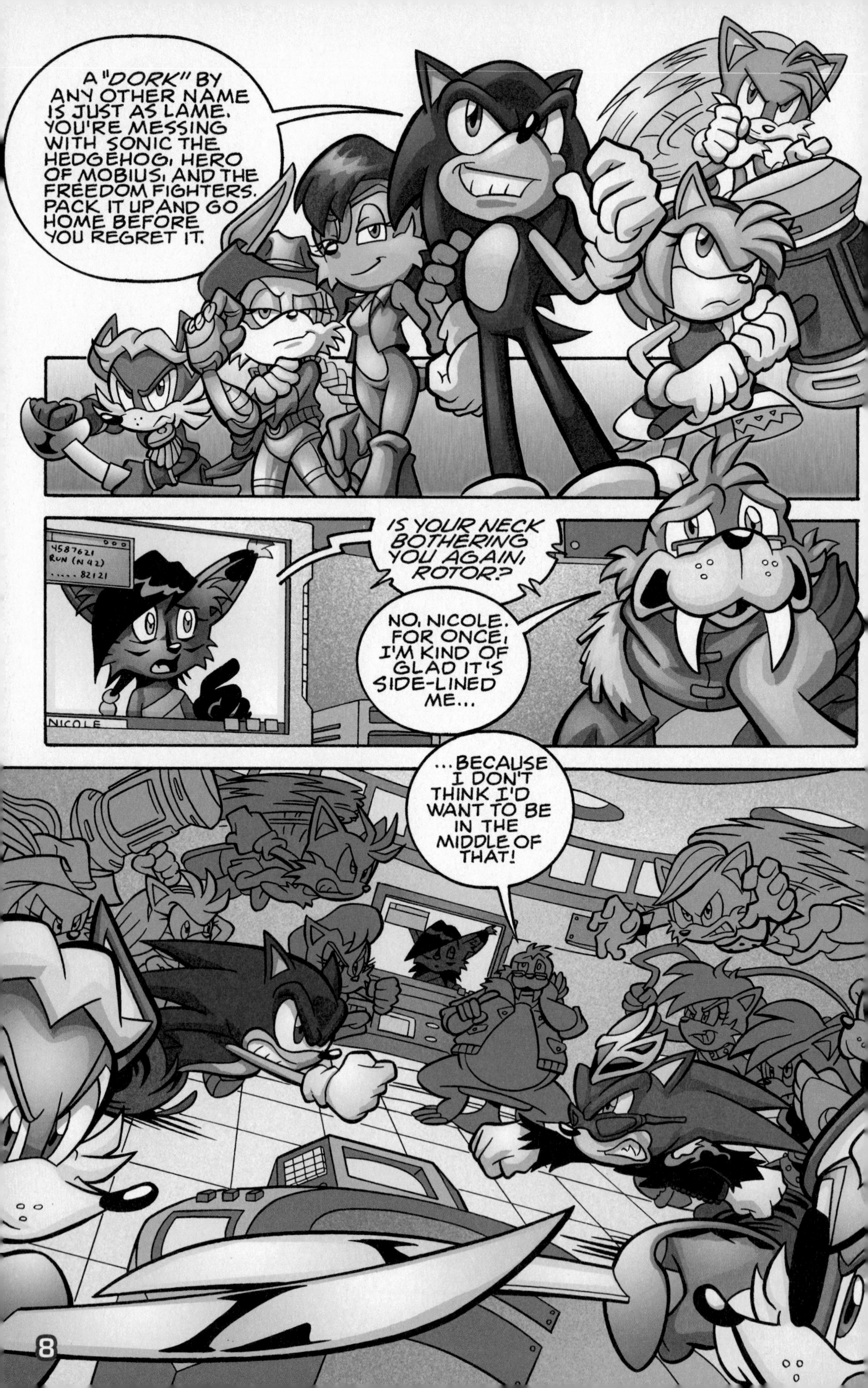
A "DORK" BY ANY OTHER NAME IS JUST AS LAME. YOU'RE MESSING WITH SONIC THE HEDGEHOG, HERO OF MOBIUS, AND THE FREEDOM FIGHTERS. PACK IT UP AND GO HOME BEFORE YOU REGRET IT.
4587621
RUN (N 42)
..... 82121
NICOLE
IS YOUR NECK BOTHERING YOU AGAIN, ROTOR?
NO, NICOLE. FOR ONCE, I'M KIND OF GLAD IT'S SIDE-LINED ME...
...BECAUSE I DON'T THINK I'D WANT TO BE IN THE MIDDLE OF THAT!

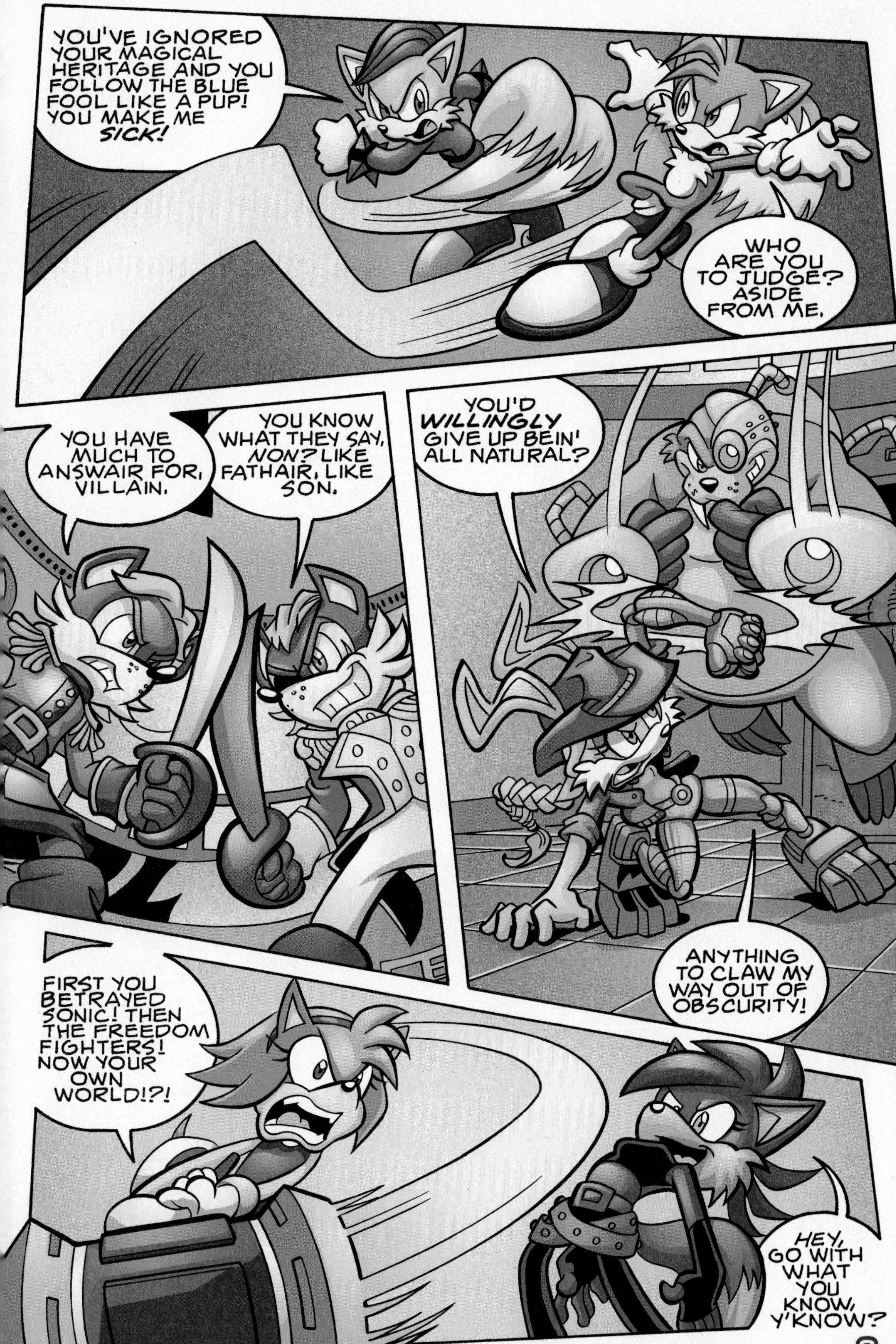
YOU'VE IGNORED YOUR MAGICAL HERITAGE AND YOU FOLLOW THE BLUE FOOL LIKE A PUP! YOU MAKE ME SICK!
WHO ARE YOU TO JUDGE? ASIDE FROM ME.
YOU HAVE MUCH TO ANSWAIR FOR, VILLAIN.
YOU KNOW WHAT THEY SAY, NON? LIKE FATHAIR, LIKE SON.
YOU'D WILLINGLY GIVE UP BEIN' ALL NATURAL?
ANYTHING TO CLAW MY WAY OUT OF OBSCURITY!
FIRST YOU BETRAYED SONIC! THEN THE FREEDOM FIGHTERS! NOW YOUR OWN WORLD!?!
HEY, GO WITH WHAT YOU KNOW, Y'KNOW?

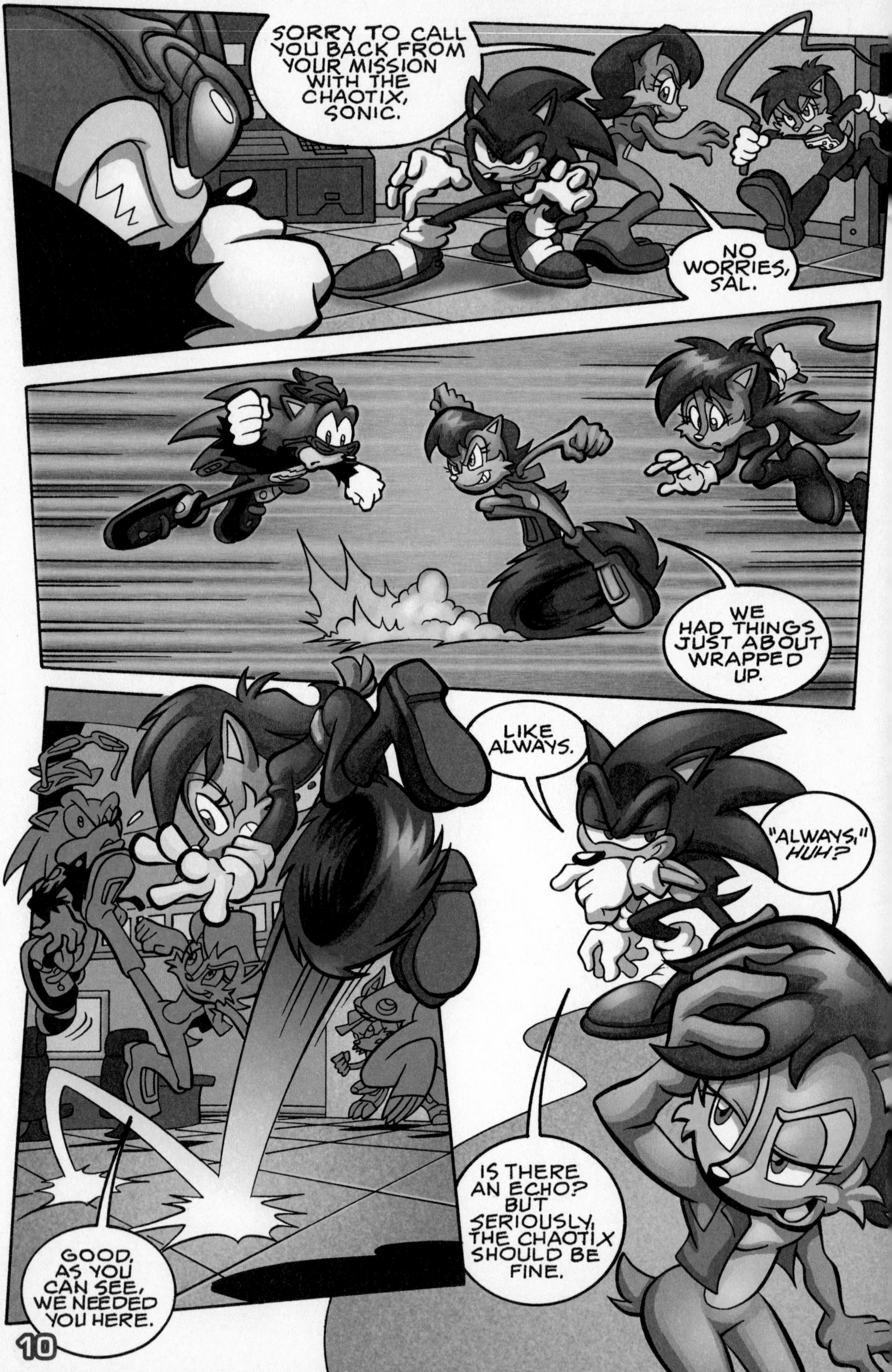
SORRY TO CALL YOU BACK FROM YOUR MISSION WITH THE CHAOTIX, SONIC.
NO WORRIES, SAL.
WE HAD THINGS JUST ABOUT WRAPPED UP.
LIKE ALWAYS.
"ALWAYS," HUH?
IS THERE AN ECHO? BUT SERIOUSLY, THE CHAOTIX SHOULD BE FINE.
GOOD, AS YOU CAN SEE, WE NEEDED YOU HERE.

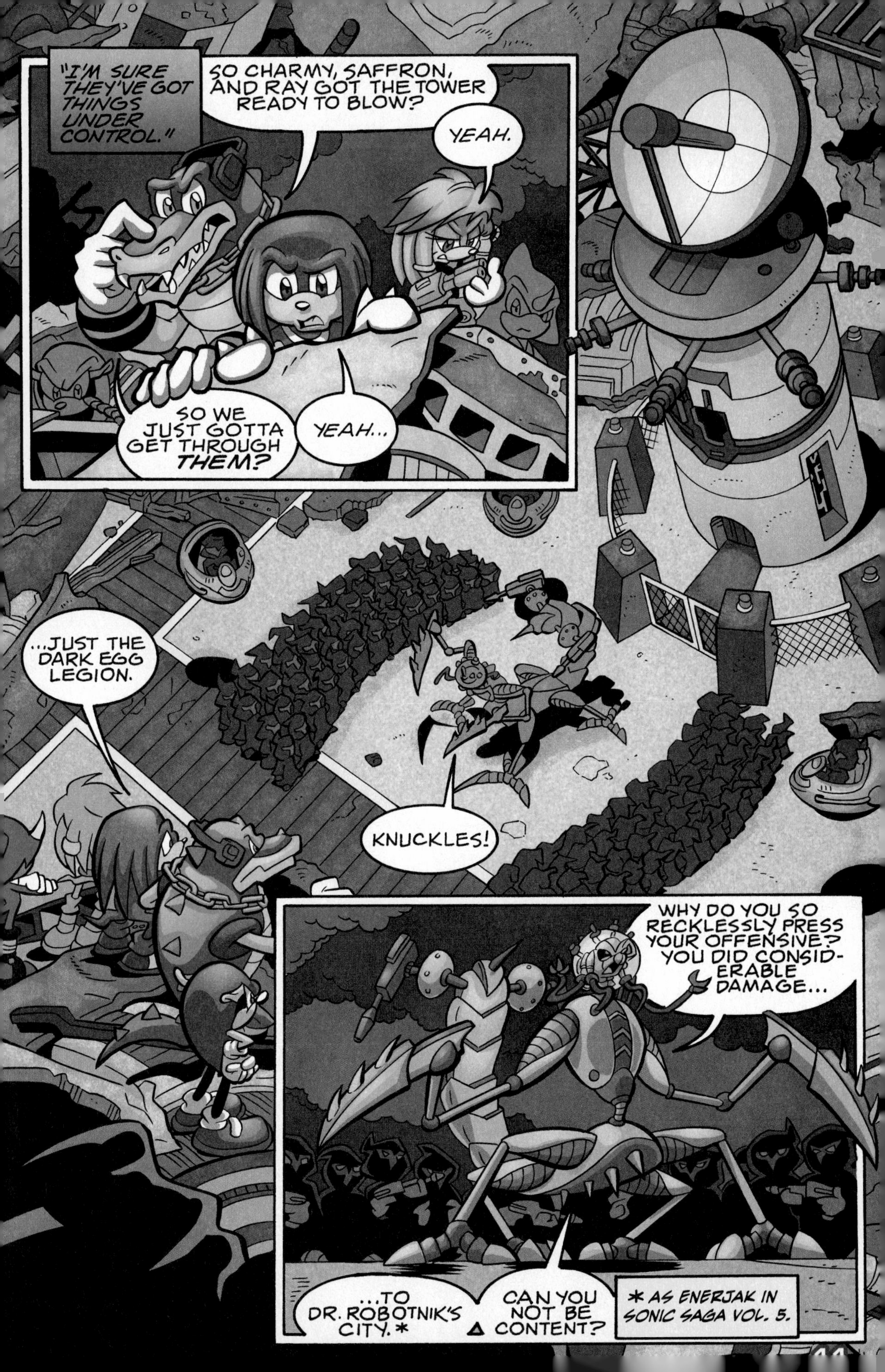
"I'M SURE THEY'VE GOT THINGS UNDER CONTROL."
SO CHARMY, SAFFRON, AND RAY GOT THE TOWER READY TO BLOW?
YEAH.
SO WE JUST GOTTA GET THROUGH THEM?
YEAH...
...JUST THE DARK EGG LEGION.
KNUCKLES!
WHY DO YOU SO RECKLESSLY PRESS YOUR OFFENSIVE? YOU DID CONSID-ERABLE DAMAGE...
...TO DR. ROBOTNIK'S CITY.*
CAN YOU NOT BE CONTENT?
*AS ENERJAK IN SONIC SAGA VOL. 5.

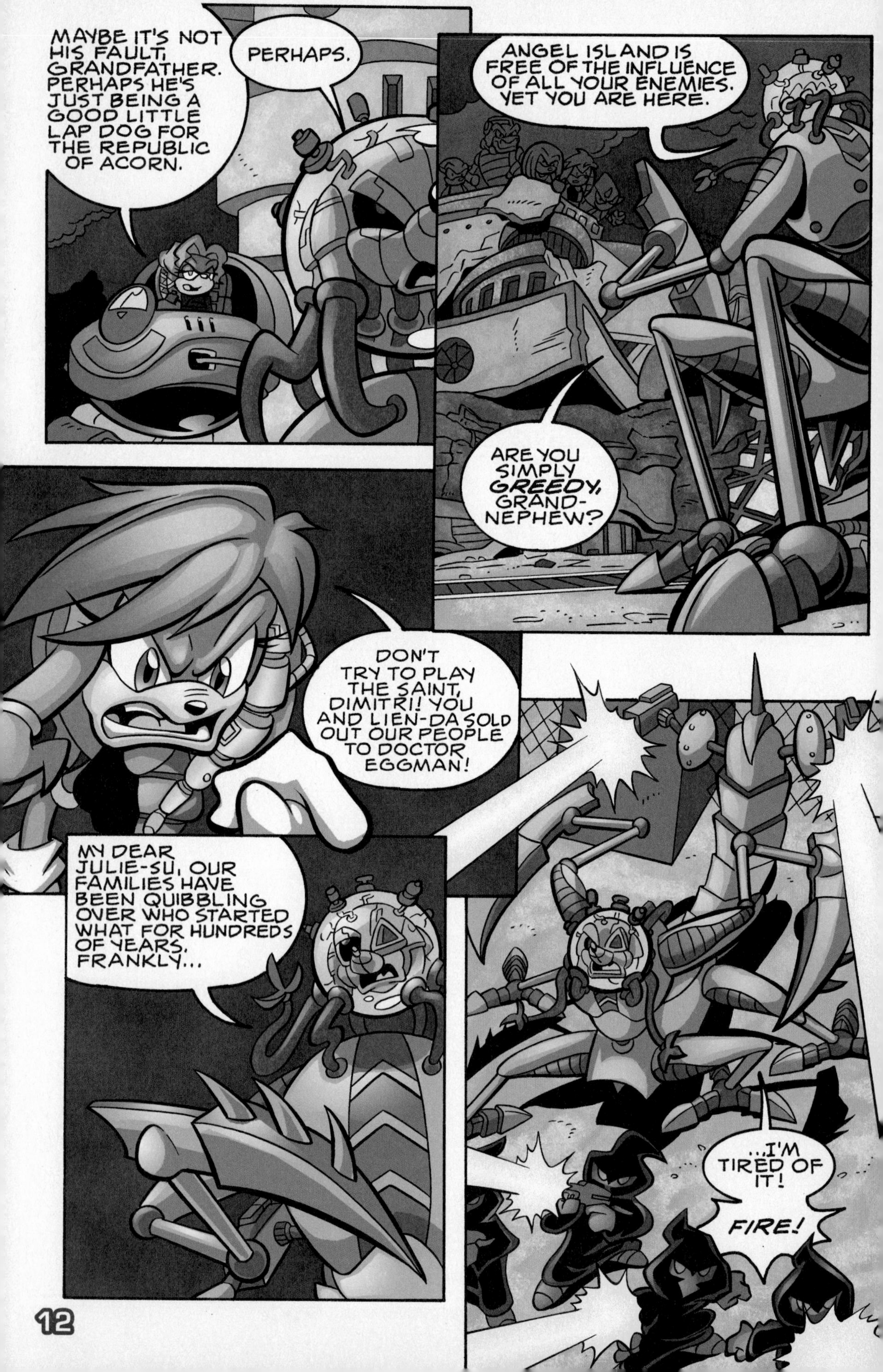
MAYBE IT'S NOT HIS FAULT, GRANDFATHER. PERHAPS HE'S JUST BEING A GOOD LITTLE LAP DOG FOR THE REPUBLIC OF ACORN.
PERHAPS.
ANGEL ISLAND IS FREE OF THE INFLUENCE OF ALL YOUR ENEMIES. YET YOU ARE HERE.
ARE YOU SIMPLY *GREEDY*, GRAND-NEPHEW?
DON'T TRY TO PLAY THE SAINT, DIMITRI! YOU AND LIEN-DA SOLD OUT OUR PEOPLE TO DOCTOR EGGMAN!
MY DEAR JULIE-SU, OUR FAMILIES HAVE BEEN QUIBBLING OVER WHO STARTED WHAT FOR HUNDREDS OF YEARS. FRANKLY...
...I'M TIRED OF IT!
FIRE!

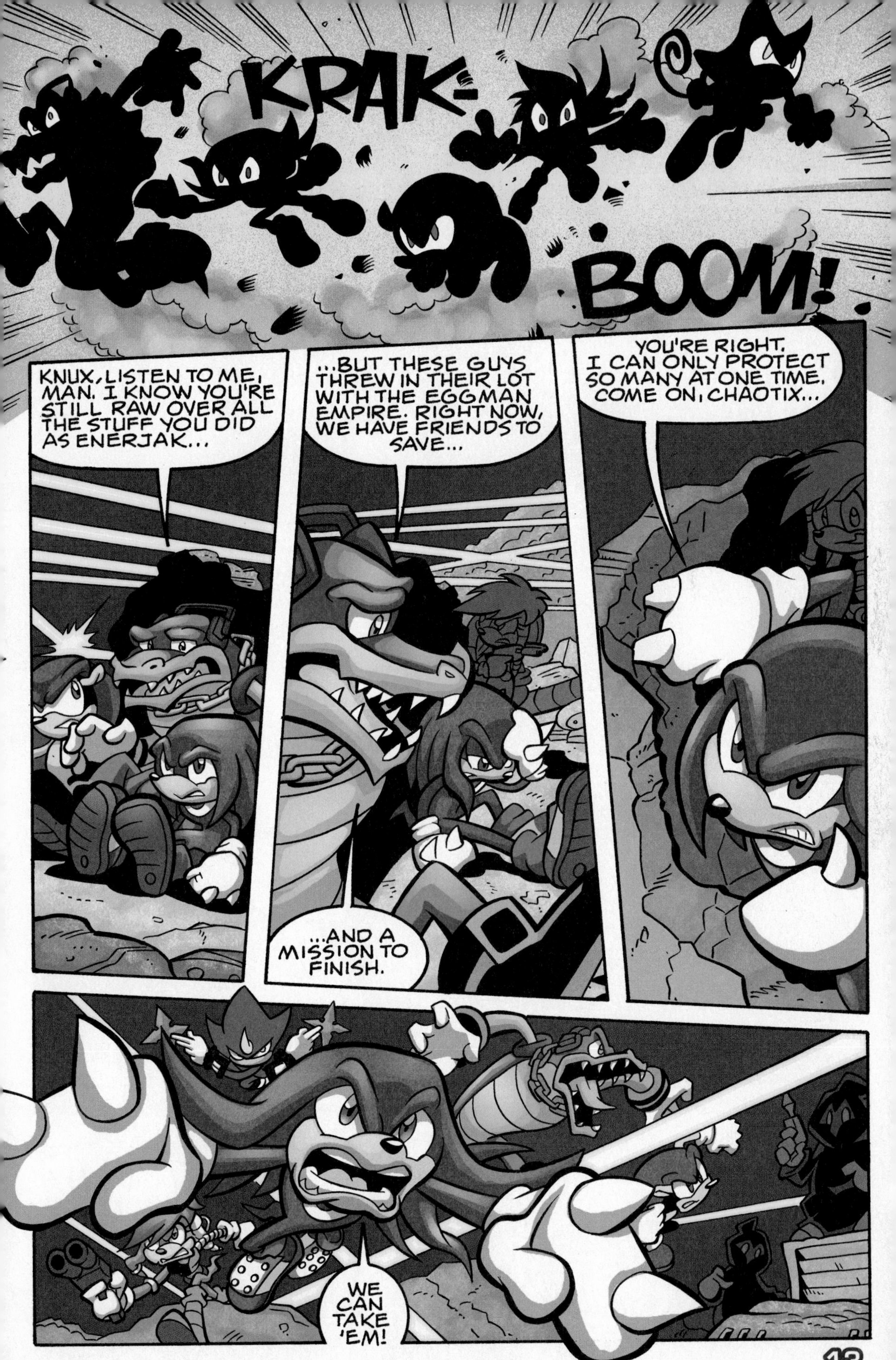
KRAK-BOOM!
KNUX, LISTEN TO ME, MAN. I KNOW YOU'RE STILL RAW OVER ALL THE STUFF YOU DID AS ENERJAK...
...BUT THESE GUYS THREW IN THEIR LOT WITH THE EGGMAN EMPIRE. RIGHT NOW, WE HAVE FRIENDS TO SAVE...
...AND A MISSION TO FINISH.
YOU'RE RIGHT. I CAN ONLY PROTECT SO MANY AT ONE TIME. COME ON, CHAOTIX...
WE CAN TAKE 'EM!

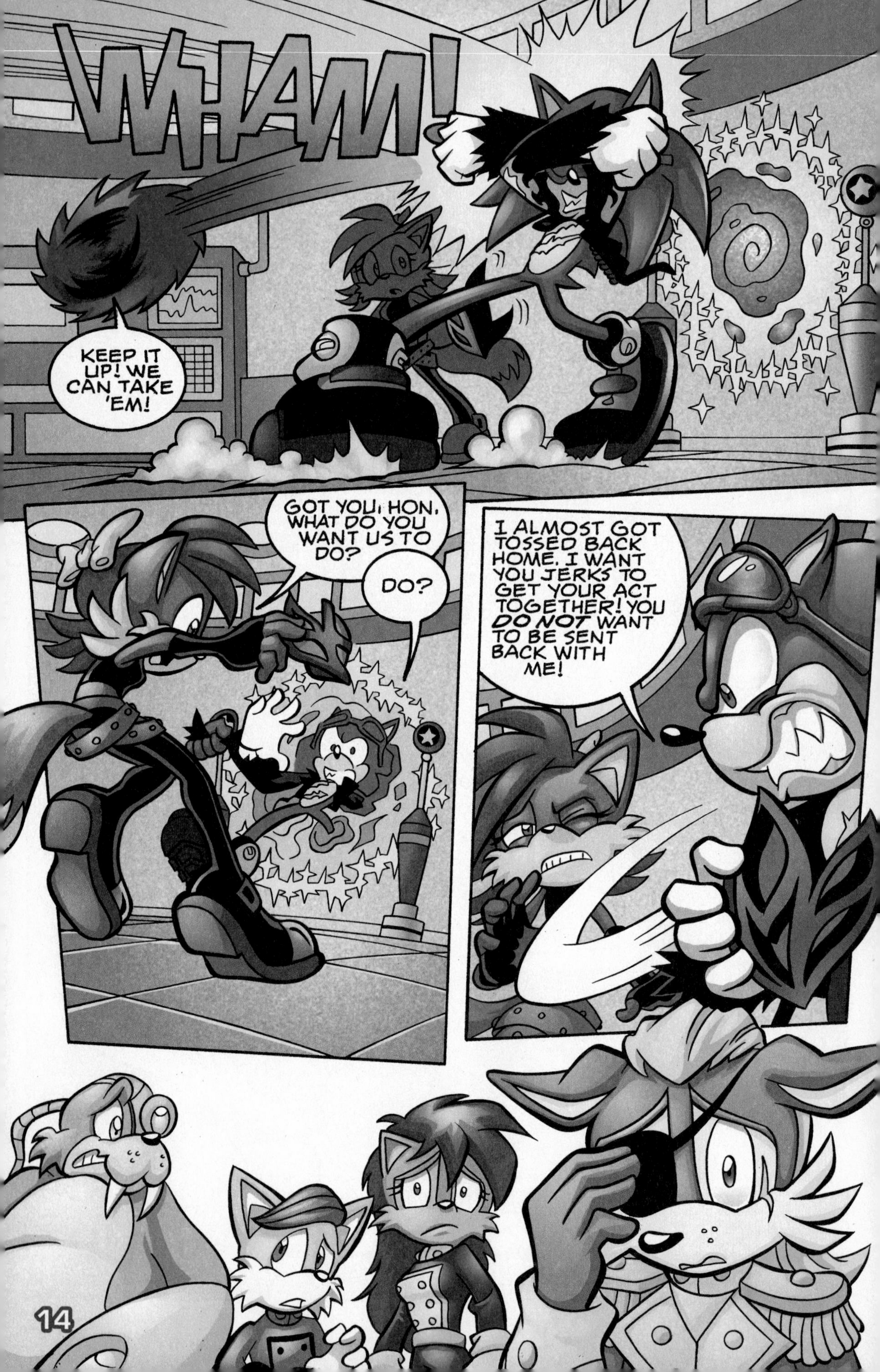
WHAM!
KEEP IT UP! WE CAN TAKE 'EM!
GOT YOU, HON. WHAT DO YOU WANT US TO DO?
DO?
I ALMOST GOT TOSSED BACK HOME. I WANT YOU JERKS TO GET YOUR ACT TOGETHER! YOU *DO NOT* WANT TO BE SENT BACK WITH ME!

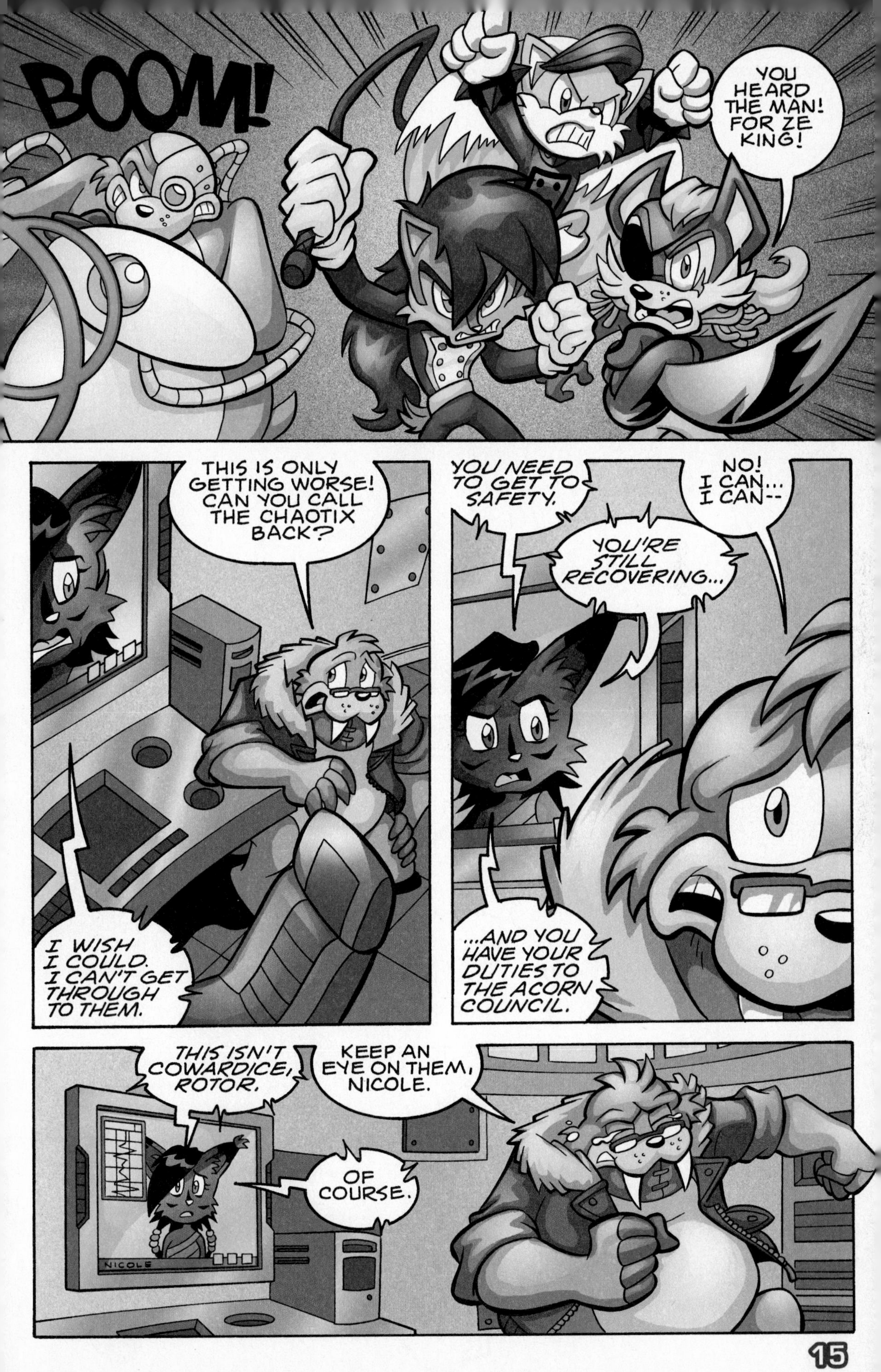
BOOM!
YOU HEARD THE MAN! FOR ZE KING!
THIS IS ONLY GETTING WORSE! CAN YOU CALL THE CHAOTIX BACK?
I WISH I COULD. I CAN'T GET THROUGH TO THEM.
YOU NEED TO GET TO SAFETY.
YOU'RE STILL RECOVERING...
NO! I CAN... I CAN--
...AND YOU HAVE YOUR DUTIES TO THE ACORN COUNCIL.
THIS ISN'T COWARDICE, ROTOR.
KEEP AN EYE ON THEM, NICOLE.
OF COURSE.
NICOLE

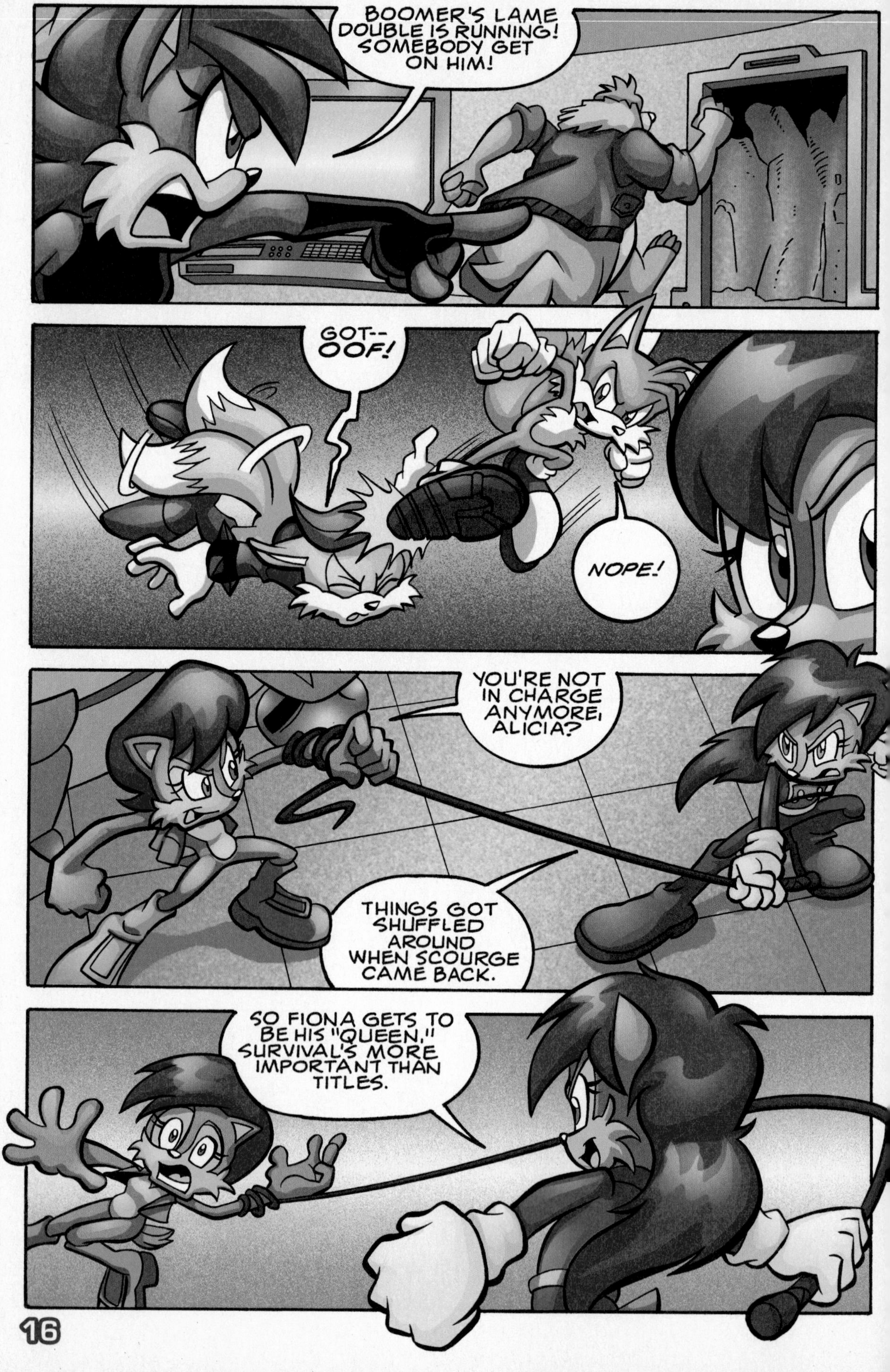
BOOMER'S LAME DOUBLE IS RUNNING! SOMEBODY GET ON HIM!
GOT-- OOF!
NOPE!
YOU'RE NOT IN CHARGE ANYMORE, ALICIA?
THINGS GOT SHUFFLED AROUND WHEN SCOURGE CAME BACK.
SO FIONA GETS TO BE HIS "QUEEN." SURVIVAL'S MORE IMPORTANT THAN TITLES.

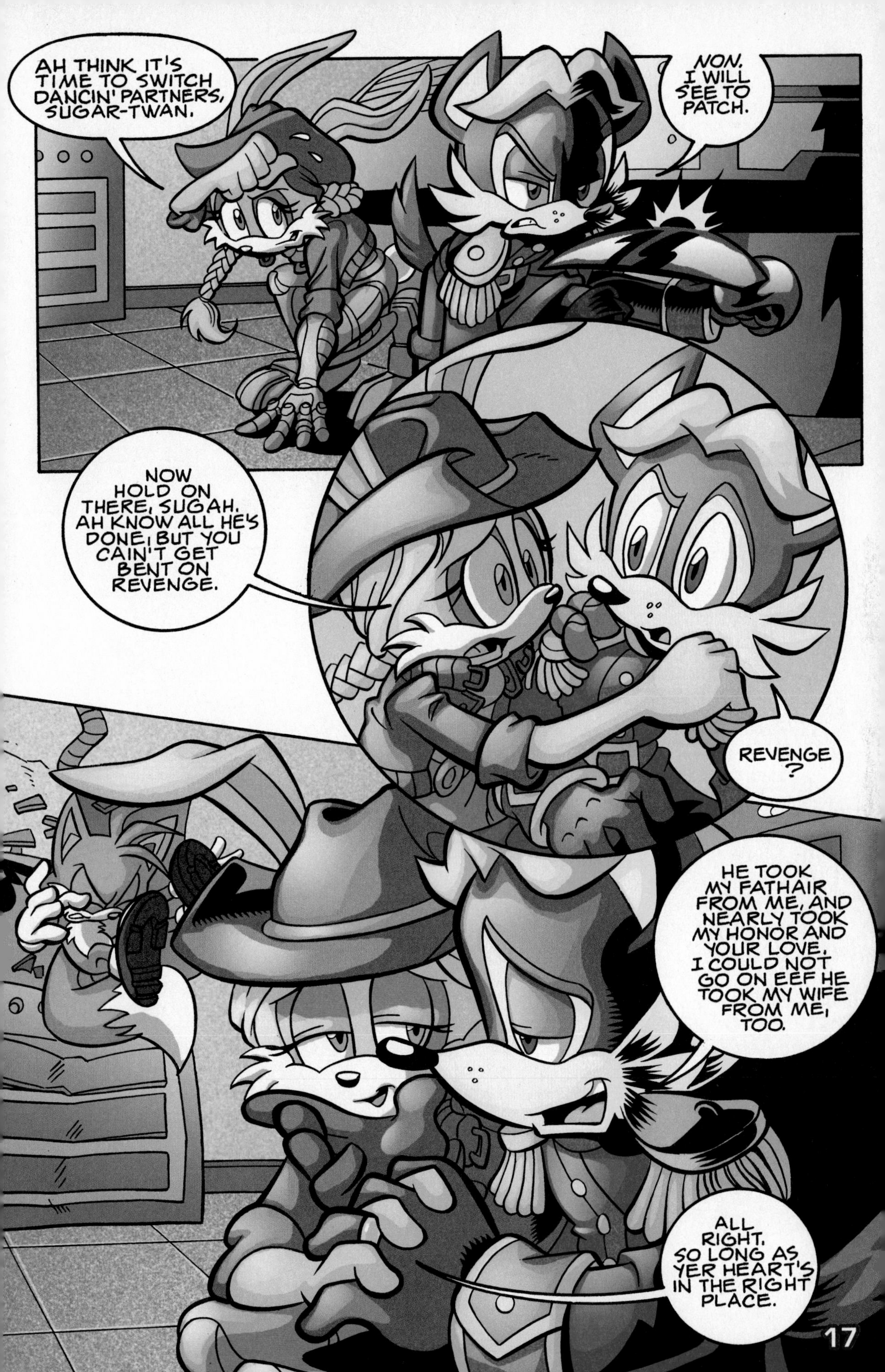
AH THINK IT'S TIME TO SWITCH DANCIN' PARTNERS, SUGAR-TWAN.
NON. I WILL SEE TO PATCH.
NOW HOLD ON THERE, SUGAH. AH KNOW ALL HE'S DONE, BUT YOU CAIN'T GET BENT ON REVENGE.
REVENGE?
HE TOOK MY FATHAIR FROM ME, AND NEARLY TOOK MY HONOR AND YOUR LOVE. I COULD NOT GO ON EEF HE TOOK MY WIFE FROM ME, TOO.
ALL RIGHT. SO LONG AS YER HEART'S IN THE RIGHT PLACE.

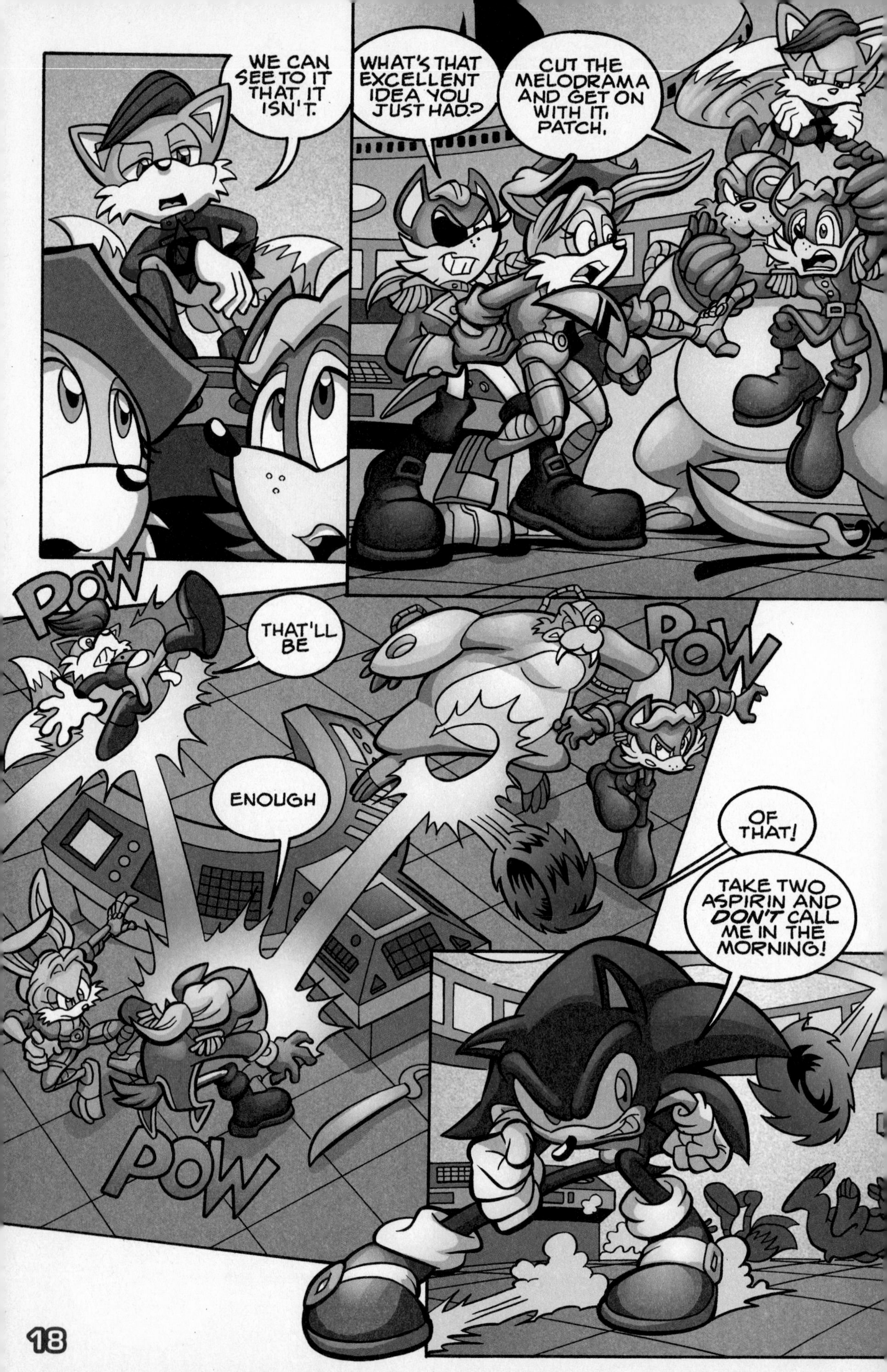

WE CAN SEE TO IT THAT IT ISN'T.
WHAT'S THAT EXCELLENT IDEA YOU JUST HAD?
CUT THE MELODRAMA AND GET ON WITH IT, PATCH.
POW
THAT'LL BE
POW
ENOUGH
OF THAT!
TAKE TWO ASPIRIN AND DON'T CALL ME IN THE MORNING!
POW

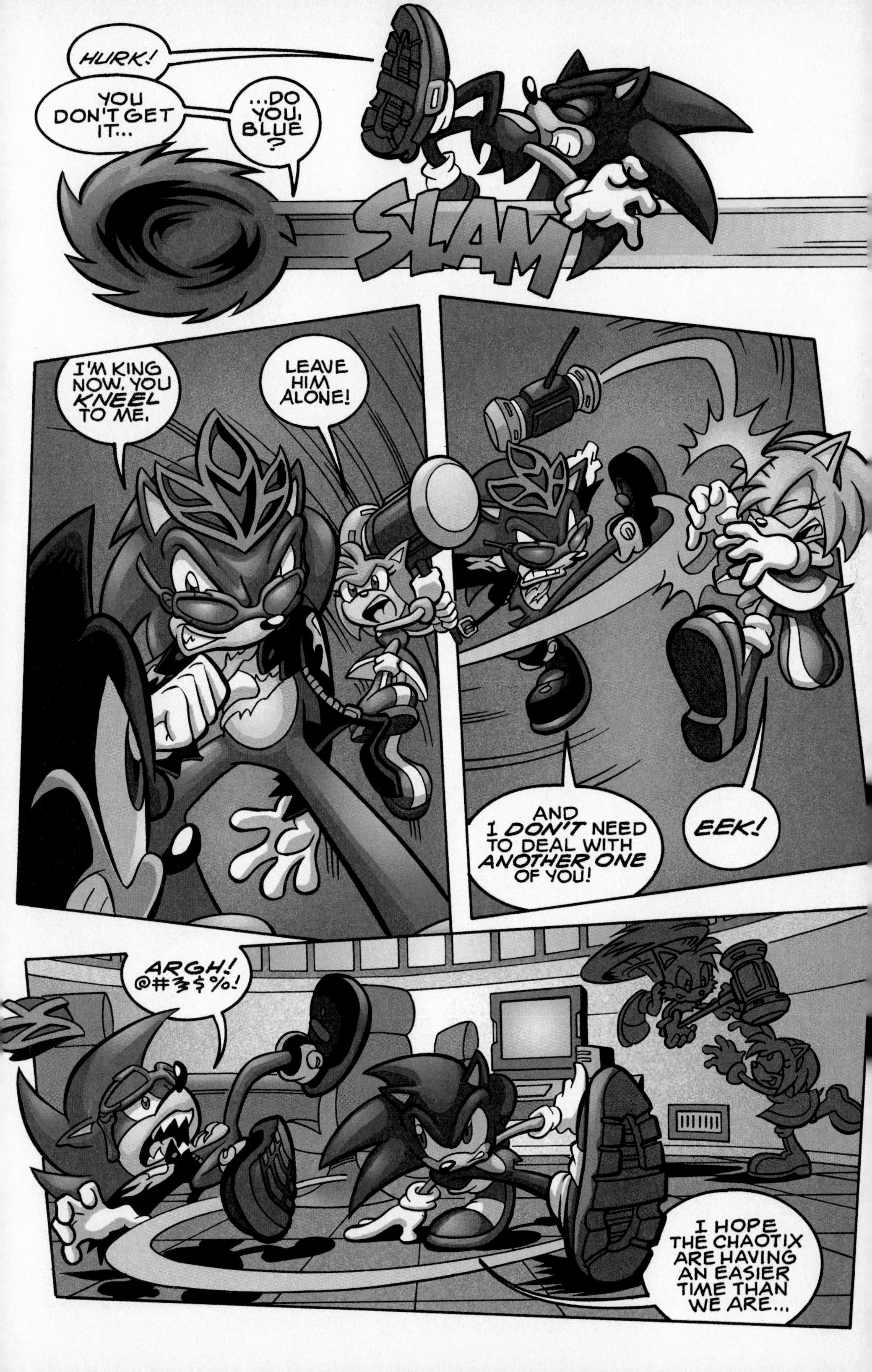
HURK!
YOU DON'T GET IT...
...DO YOU, BLUE?
SLAM
I'M KING NOW. YOU KNEEL TO ME.
LEAVE HIM ALONE!
AND I DON'T NEED TO DEAL WITH ANOTHER ONE OF YOU!
EEK!
ARGH! @#3$%!
I HOPE THE CHAOTIX ARE HAVING AN EASIER TIME THAN WE ARE...

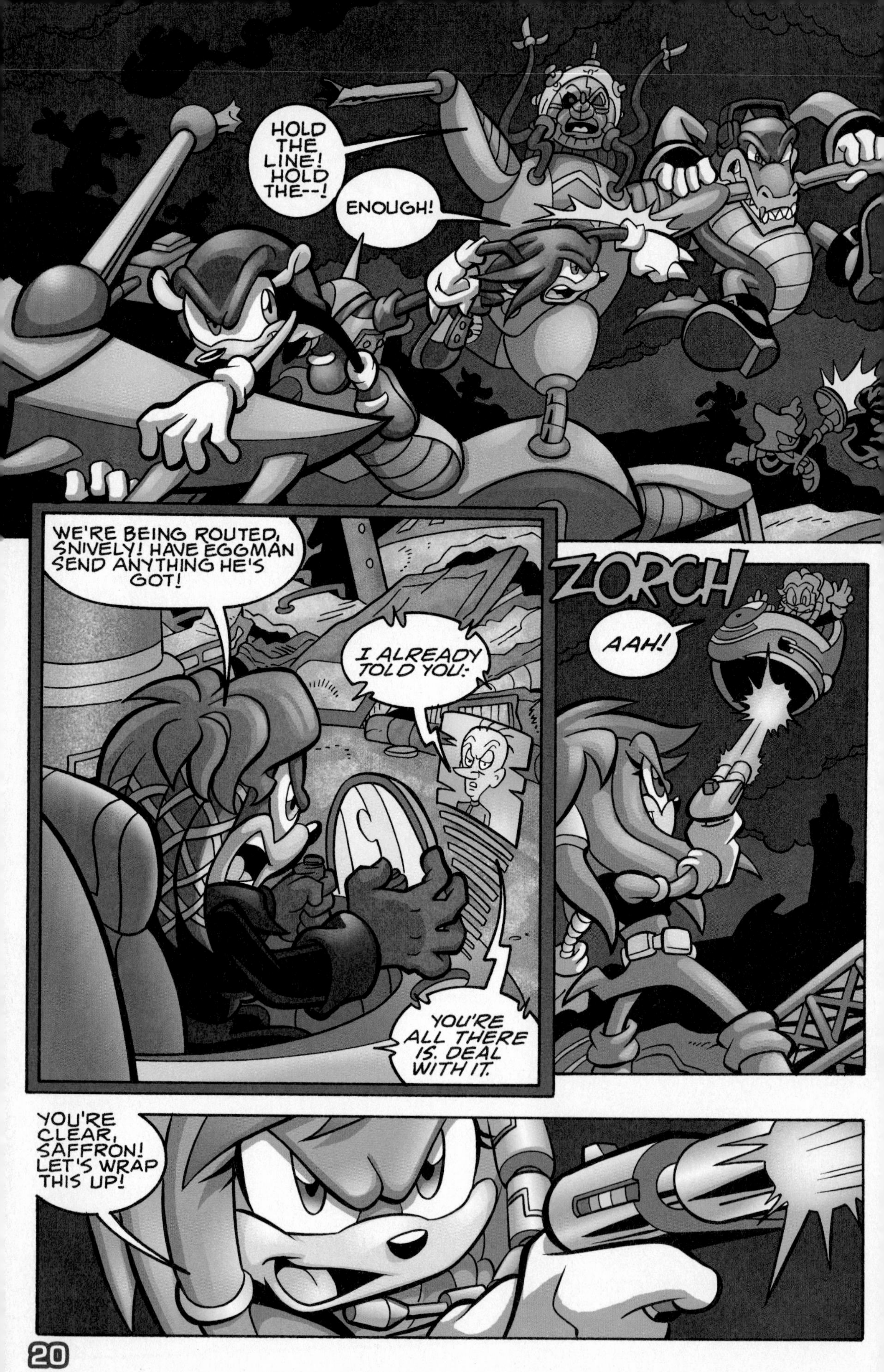
HOLD THE LINE! HOLD THE--!
ENOUGH!
WE'RE BEING ROUTED, SNIVELY! HAVE EGGMAN SEND ANYTHING HE'S GOT!
I ALREADY TOLD YOU:
YOU'RE ALL THERE IS. DEAL WITH IT.
ZORCH
AAH!
YOU'RE CLEAR, SAFFRON! LET'S WRAP THIS UP!

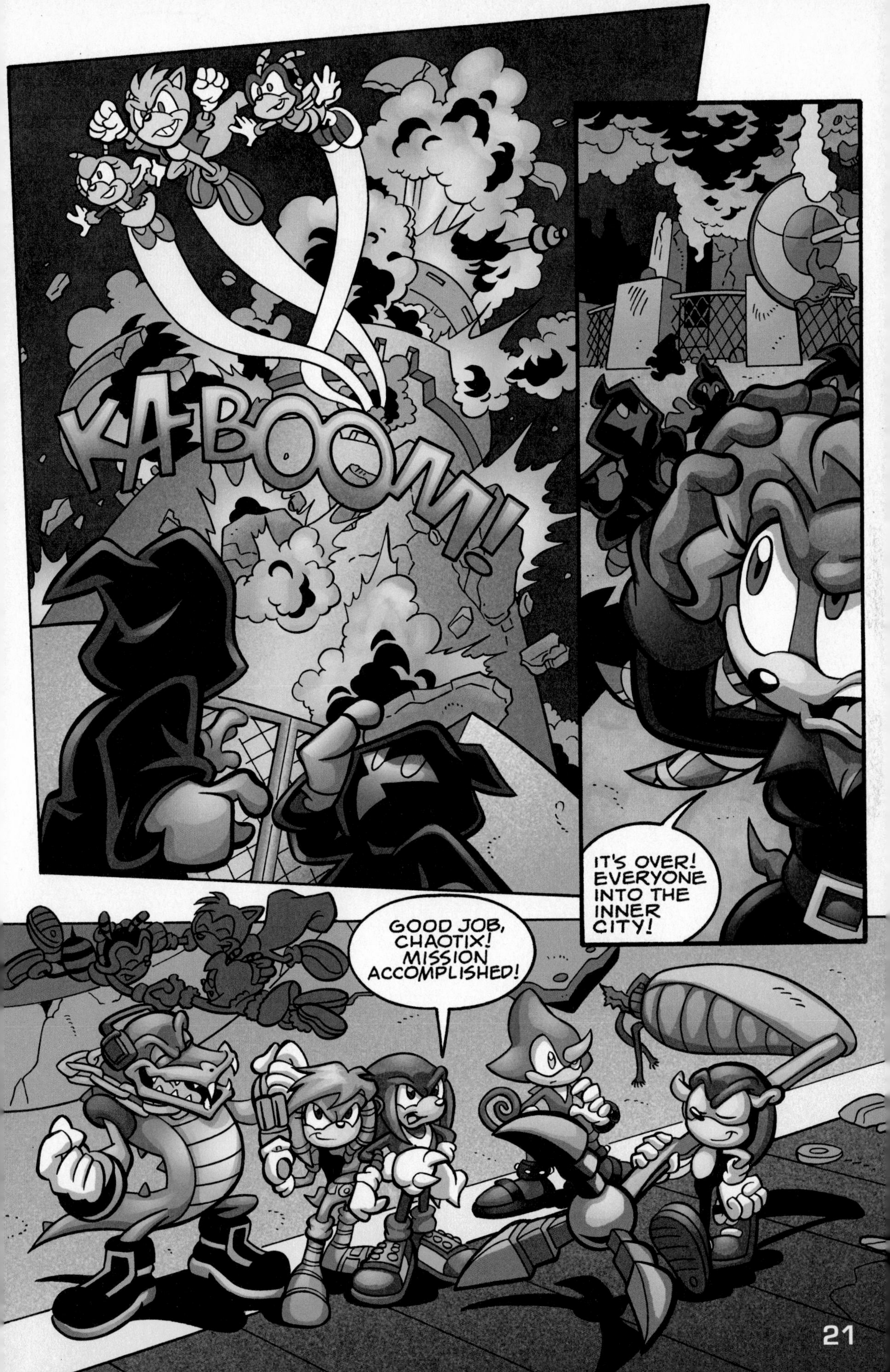
KA-BOOM!!
IT'S OVER! EVERYONE INTO THE INNER CITY!
GOOD JOB, CHAOTIX! MISSION ACCOMPLISHED!

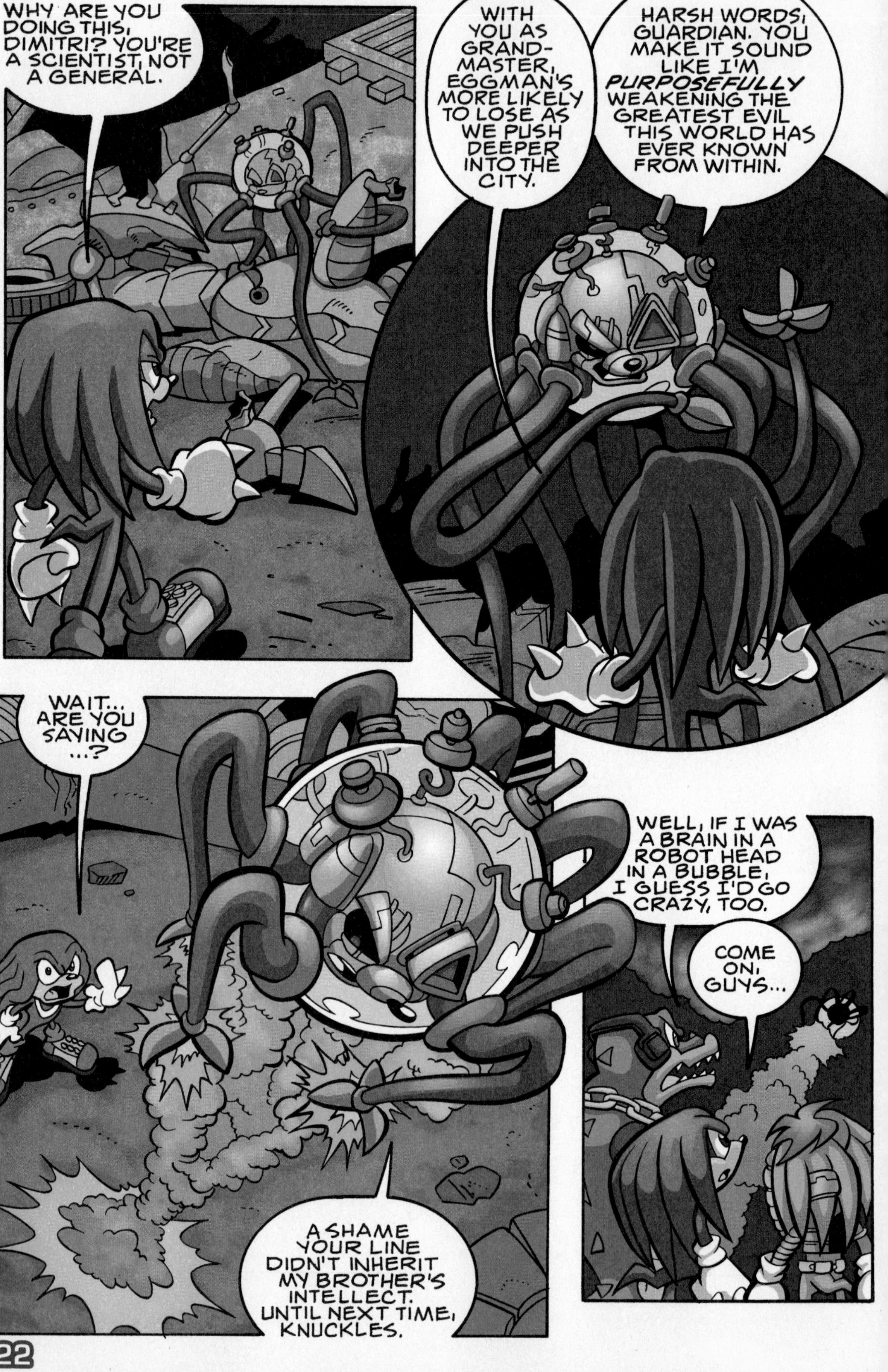
WHY ARE YOU DOING THIS, DIMITRI? YOU'RE A SCIENTIST, NOT A GENERAL.
WITH YOU AS GRAND-MASTER, EGGMAN'S MORE LIKELY TO LOSE AS WE PUSH DEEPER INTO THE CITY.
HARSH WORDS, GUARDIAN. YOU MAKE IT SOUND LIKE I'M *PURPOSEFULLY* WEAKENING THE GREATEST EVIL THIS WORLD HAS EVER KNOWN FROM WITHIN.
WAIT... ARE YOU SAYING ...?
A SHAME YOUR LINE DIDN'T INHERIT MY BROTHER'S INTELLECT. UNTIL NEXT TIME, KNUCKLES.
WELL, IF I WAS A BRAIN IN A ROBOT HEAD IN A BUBBLE, I GUESS I'D GO CRAZY, TOO.
COME ON, GUYS...

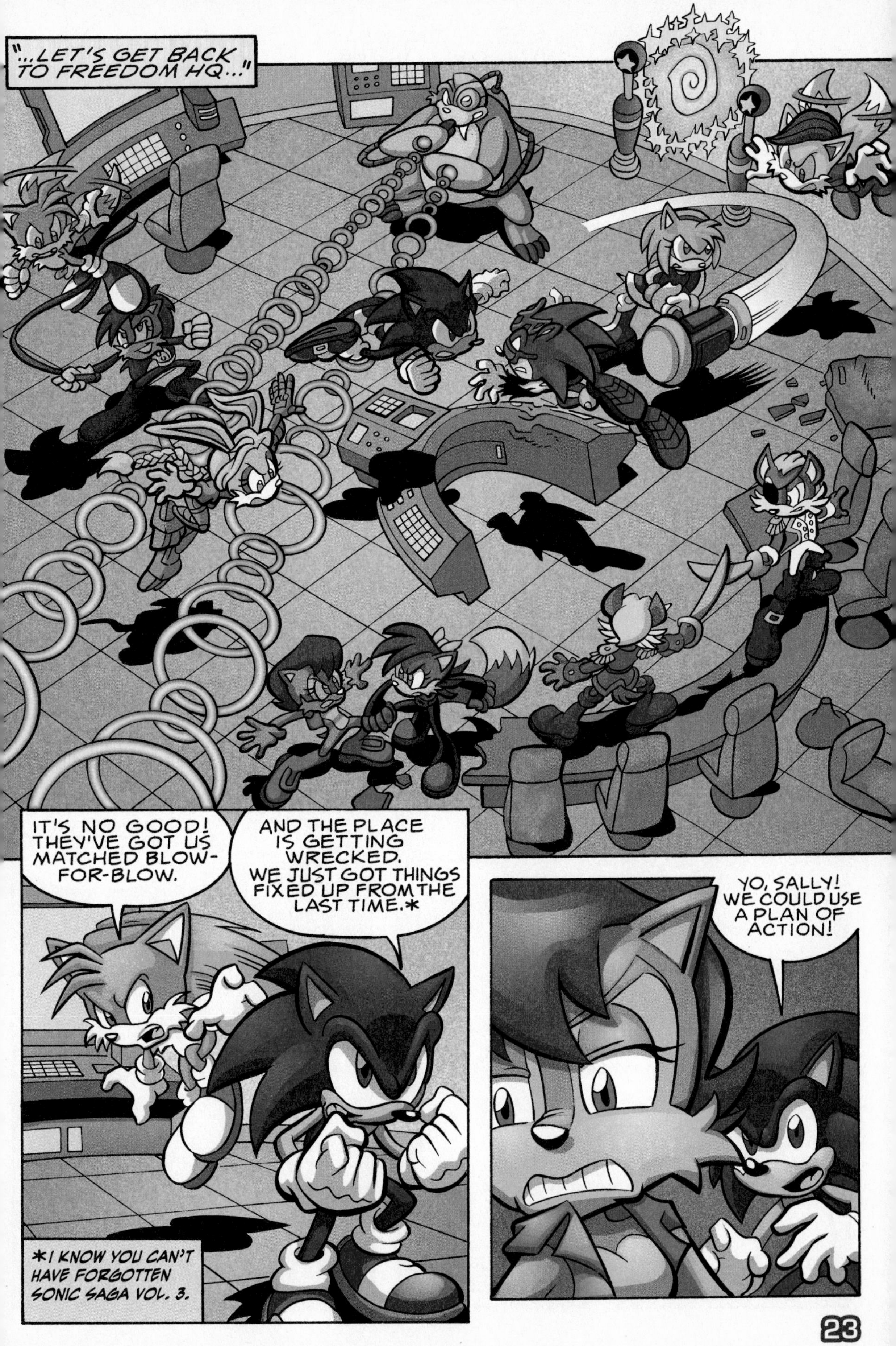
"...LET'S GET BACK TO FREEDOM HQ..."
IT'S NO GOOD! THEY'VE GOT US MATCHED BLOW-FOR-BLOW.
AND THE PLACE IS GETTING WRECKED. WE JUST GOT THINGS FIXED UP FROM THE LAST TIME.*
*I KNOW YOU CAN'T HAVE FORGOTTEN SONIC SAGA VOL. 3.
YO, SALLY! WE COULD USE A PLAN OF ACTION!

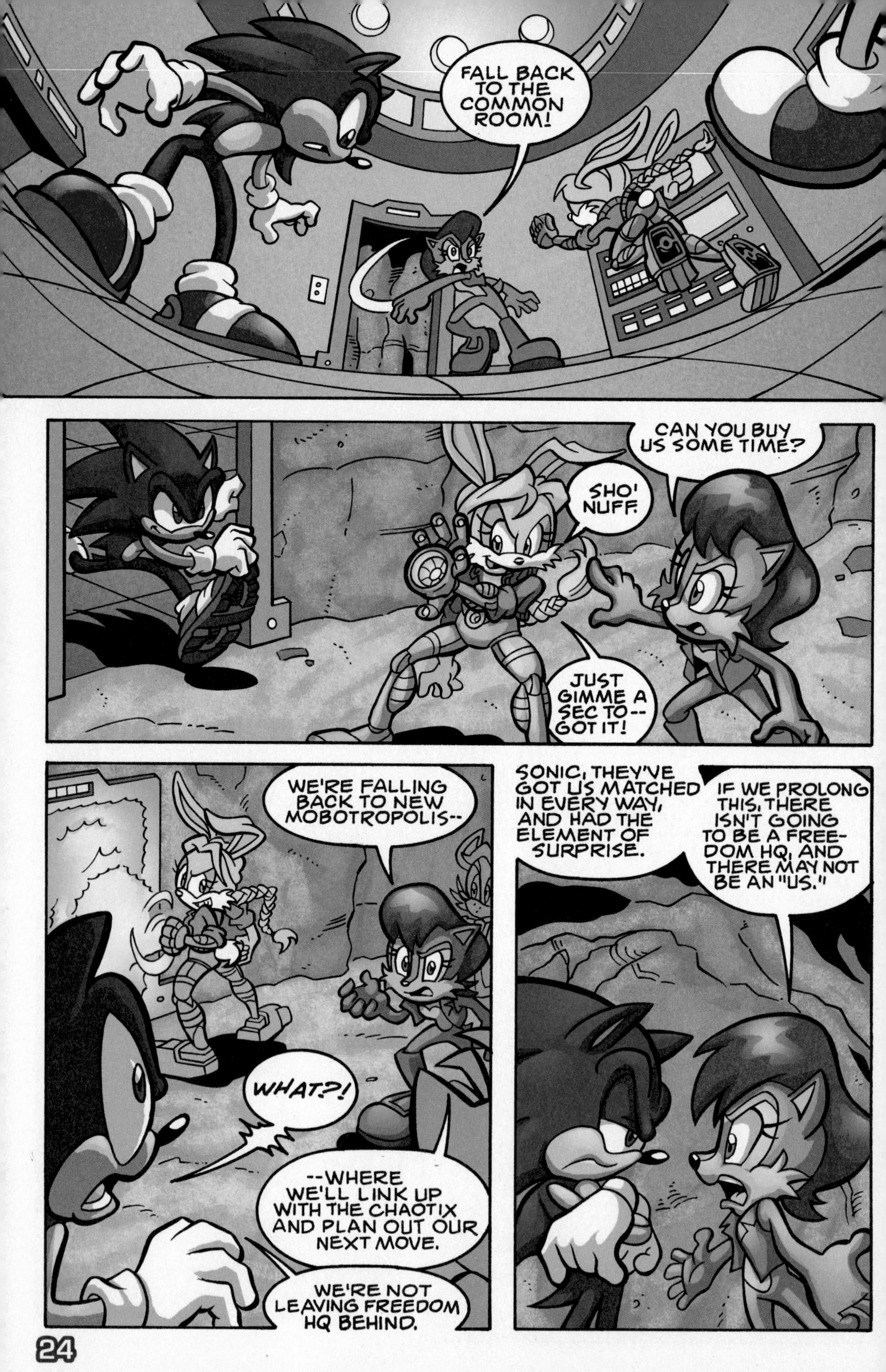
FALL BACK TO THE COMMON ROOM!
CAN YOU BUY US SOME TIME?
SHO' NUFF.
JUST GIMME A SEC TO-- GOT IT!
WE'RE FALLING BACK TO NEW MOBOTROPOLIS--
WHAT?!
--WHERE WE'LL LINK UP WITH THE CHAOTIX AND PLAN OUT OUR NEXT MOVE.
WE'RE NOT LEAVING FREEDOM HQ BEHIND.
SONIC, THEY'VE GOT US MATCHED IN EVERY WAY, AND HAD THE ELEMENT OF SURPRISE.
IF WE PROLONG THIS, THERE ISN'T GOING TO BE A FREEDOM HQ, AND THERE MAY NOT BE AN "US."

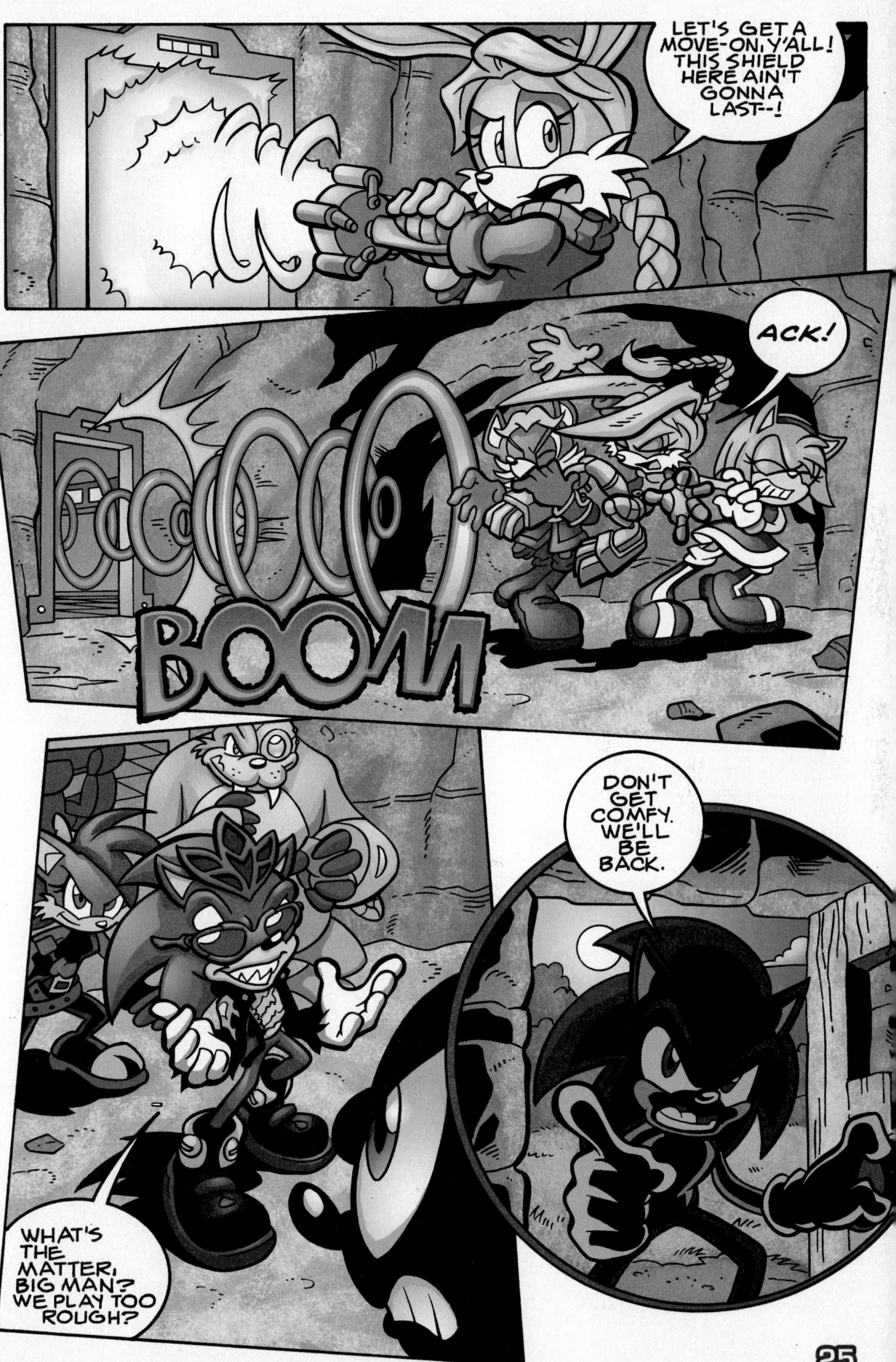
LET'S GET A MOVE-ON, Y'ALL! THIS SHIELD HERE AIN'T GONNA LAST--!
ACK!
BOOM
DON'T GET COMFY. WE'LL BE BACK.
WHAT'S THE MATTER, BIG MAN? WE PLAY TOO ROUGH?

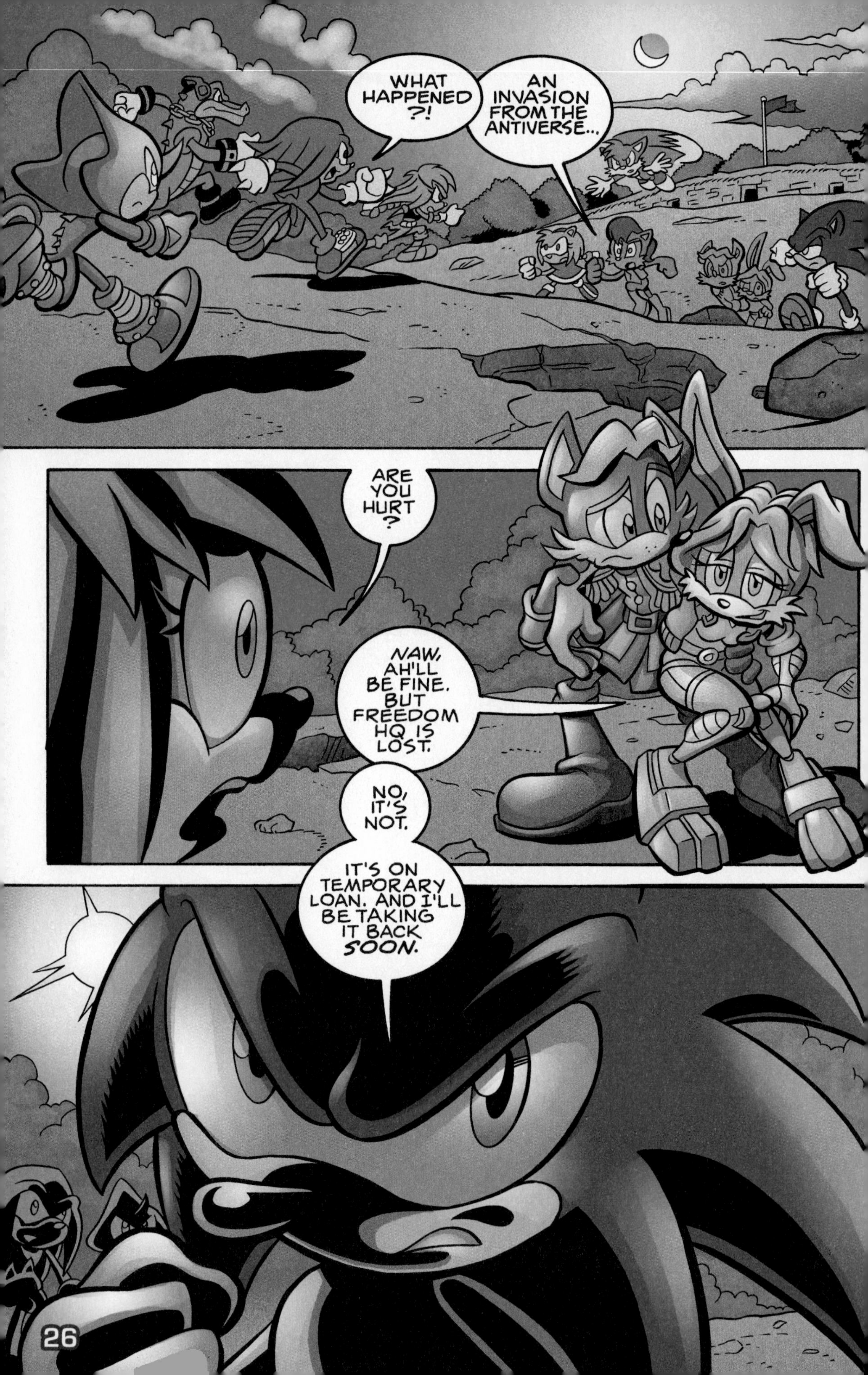
WHAT HAPPENED ?!
AN INVASION FROM THE ANTIVERSE...
ARE YOU HURT ?
NAW, AH'LL BE FINE. BUT FREEDOM HQ IS LOST.
NO, IT'S NOT.
IT'S ON TEMPORARY LOAN. AND I'LL BE TAKING IT BACK SOON.

CHAPTER 2

SONIC THE HEDGEHOG 191
COVER BY TRACY YARDLEY AND JASON JENSEN

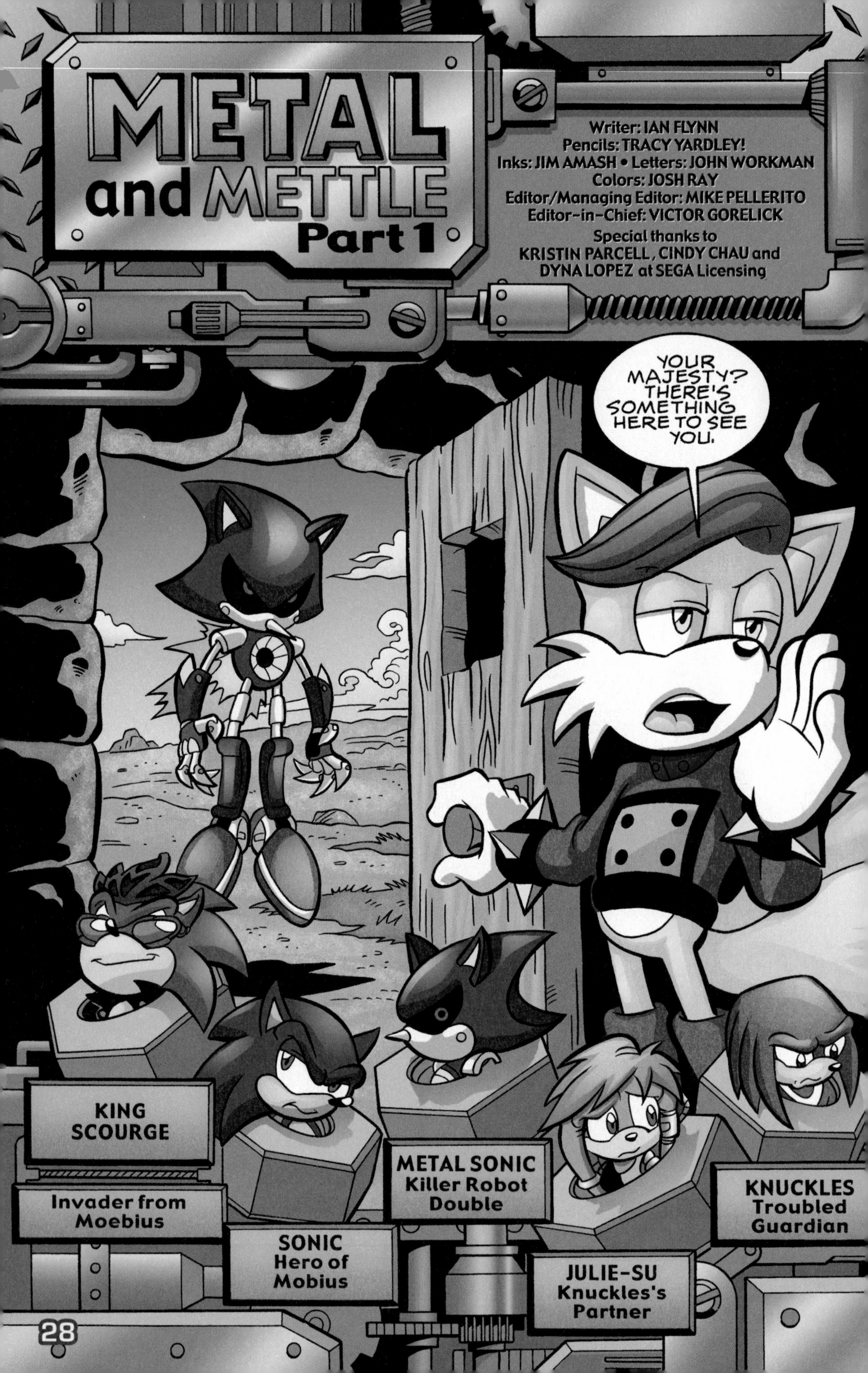
METAL and METTLE Part 1
Writer: IAN FLYNN
Pencils: TRACY YARDLEY!
Inks: JIM AMASH • Letters: JOHN WORKMAN
Colors: JOSH RAY
Editor/Managing Editor: MIKE PELLERITO
Editor-in-Chief: VICTOR GORELICK
Special thanks to KRISTIN PARCELL, CINDY CHAU and DYNA LOPEZ at SEGA Licensing
YOUR MAJESTY? THERE'S SOMETHING HERE TO SEE YOU.
KING SCOURGE
Invader from Moebius
SONIC Hero of Mobius
METAL SONIC Killer Robot Double
JULIE-SU Knuckles's Partner
KNUCKLES Troubled Guardian
28

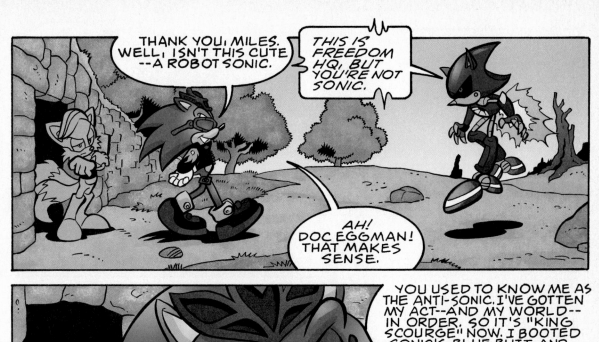

THANK YOU, MILES. WELL, ISN'T THIS CUTE --A ROBOT SONIC.

THIS IS FREEDOM HQ, BUT YOU'RE NOT SONIC.

AH! DOC EGGMAN! THAT MAKES SENSE.

YOU USED TO KNOW ME AS THE ANTI-SONIC. I'VE GOTTEN MY ACT--AND MY WORLD-- IN ORDER. SO IT'S "KING SCOURGE" NOW. I BOOTED SONIC'S BLUE BUTT, AND HIS BUDDIES, OUT A COUPLE OF DAYS BACK.

OH-HO! I WASN'T AWARE. WELL, THAT CHANGES MY PLANS FOR TODAY.

HONEST MISTAKE. I'LL LET YOU KNOW WHEN I'M READY TO CONQUER YOUR PARTS OF THE PLANET.

THEN AGAIN, WHY PASS UP ONE UPPITY HEDGEHOG FOR ANOTHER?

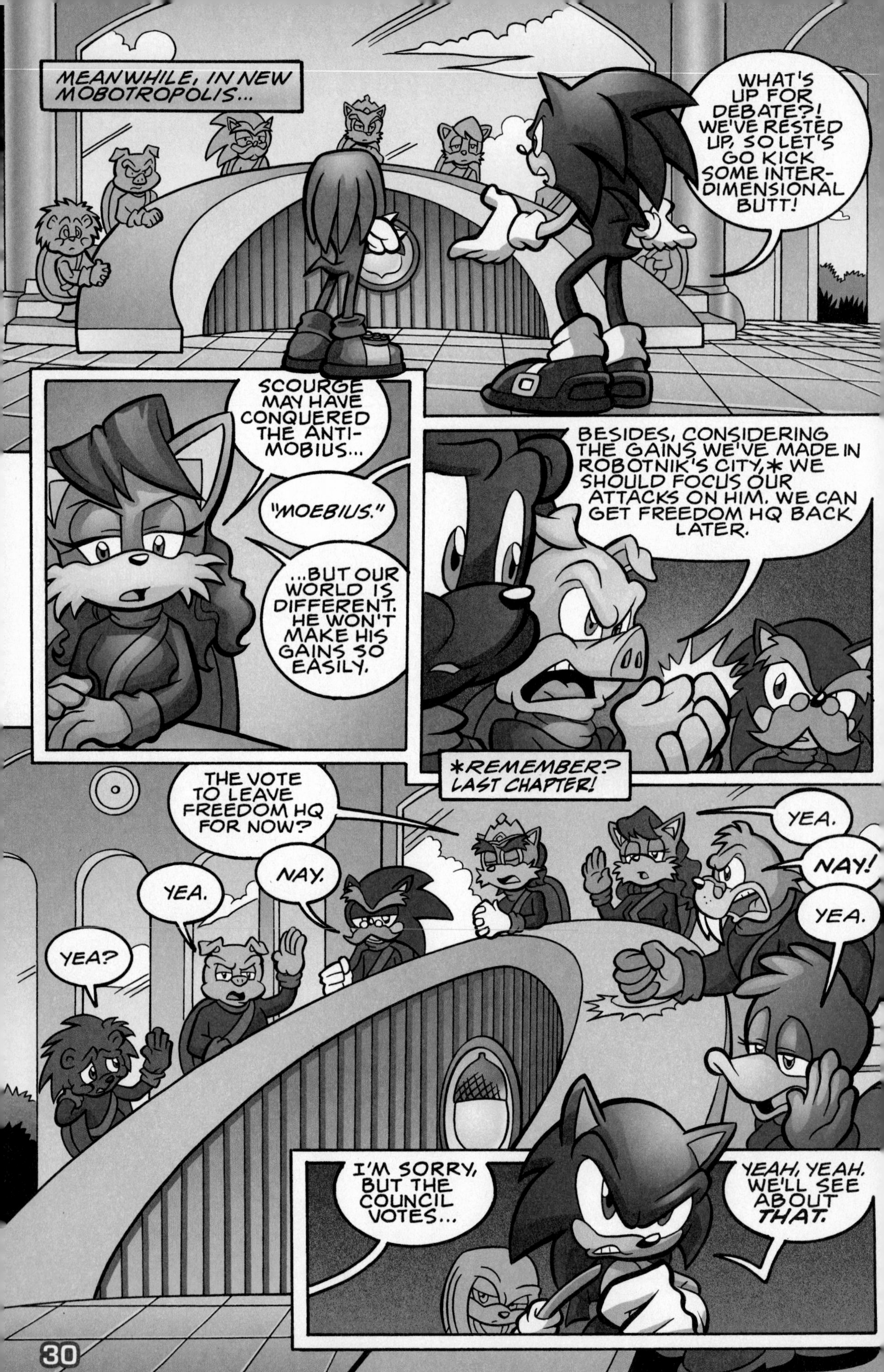
MEANWHILE, IN NEW MOBOTROPOLIS...
WHAT'S UP FOR DEBATE?! WE'VE RESTED UP, SO LET'S GO KICK SOME INTER-DIMENSIONAL BUTT!
SCOURGE MAY HAVE CONQUERED THE ANTI-MOBIUS...
"MOEBIUS."
...BUT OUR WORLD IS DIFFERENT. HE WON'T MAKE HIS GAINS SO EASILY.
BESIDES, CONSIDERING THE GAINS WE'VE MADE IN ROBOTNIK'S CITY,* WE SHOULD FOCUS OUR ATTACKS ON HIM. WE CAN GET FREEDOM HQ BACK LATER.
*REMEMBER? LAST CHAPTER!
THE VOTE TO LEAVE FREEDOM HQ FOR NOW?
YEA?
YEA.
NAY.
YEA.
NAY!
YEA.
I'M SORRY, BUT THE COUNCIL VOTES...
YEAH, YEAH. WE'LL SEE ABOUT THAT.

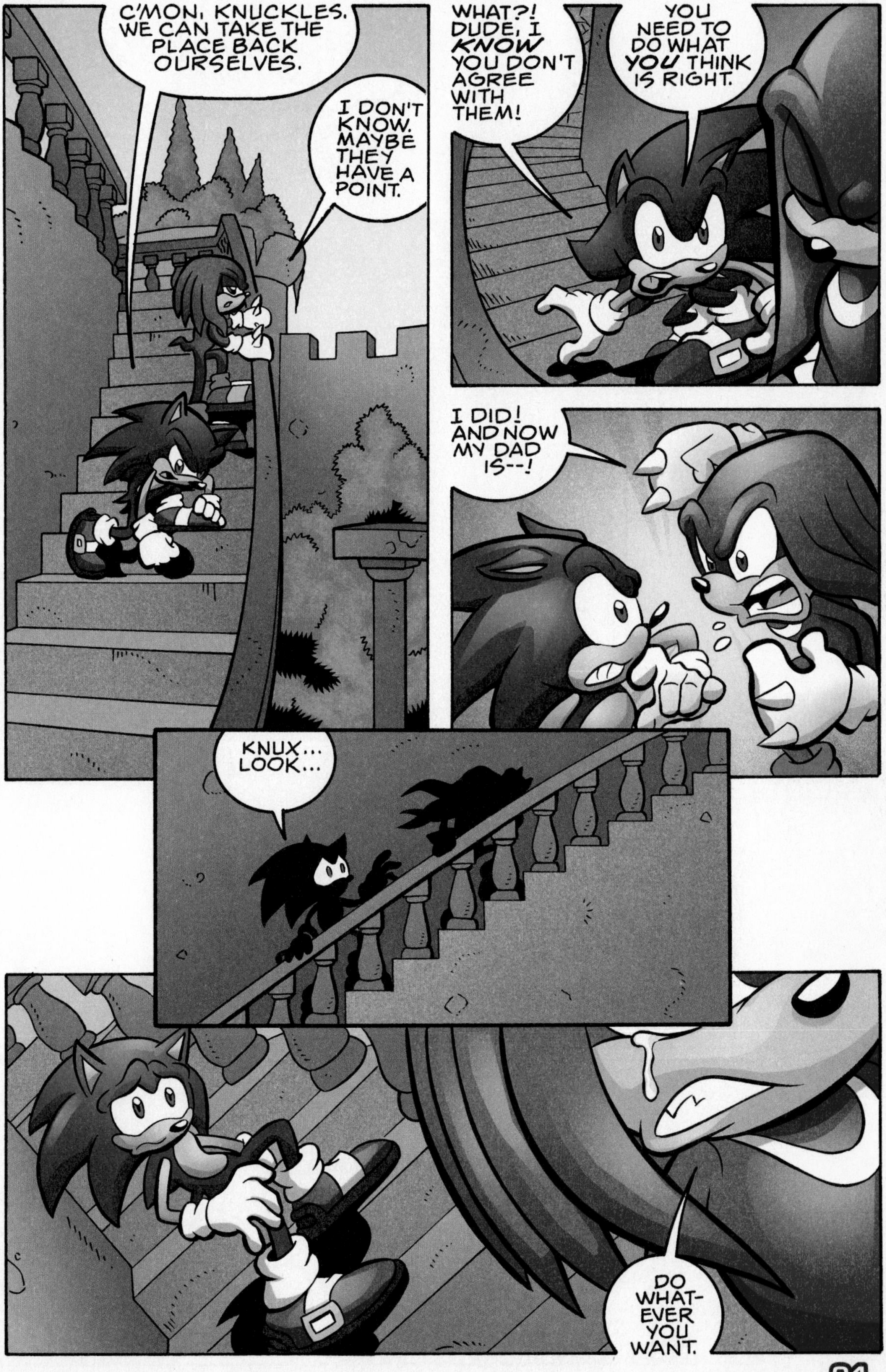

C'MON, KNUCKLES. WE CAN TAKE THE PLACE BACK OURSELVES.
I DON'T KNOW. MAYBE THEY HAVE A POINT.
WHAT?! DUDE, I KNOW YOU DON'T AGREE WITH THEM!
YOU NEED TO DO WHAT YOU THINK IS RIGHT.
I DID! AND NOW MY DAD IS--!
KNUX... LOOK...
DO WHAT-EVER YOU WANT.

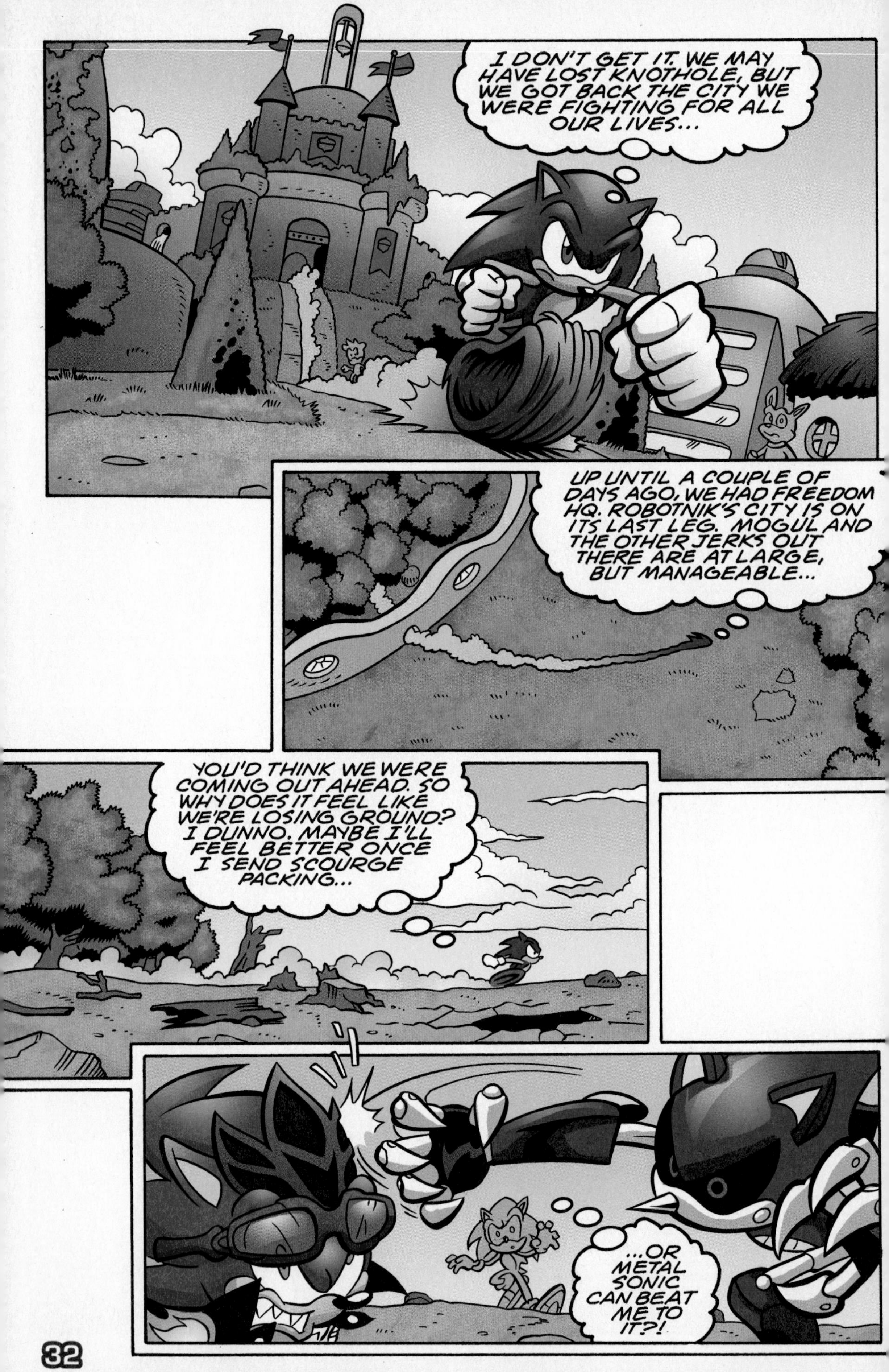
I DON'T GET IT. WE MAY HAVE LOST KNOTHOLE, BUT WE GOT BACK THE CITY WE WERE FIGHTING FOR ALL OUR LIVES...
UP UNTIL A COUPLE OF DAYS AGO, WE HAD FREEDOM HQ. ROBOTNIK'S CITY IS ON ITS LAST LEG. MOGUL AND THE OTHER JERKS OUT THERE ARE AT LARGE, BUT MANAGEABLE...
YOU'D THINK WE WERE COMING OUT AHEAD. SO WHY DOES IT FEEL LIKE WE'RE LOSING GROUND? I DUNNO. MAYBE I'LL FEEL BETTER ONCE I SEND SCOURGE PACKING...
...OR METAL SONIC CAN BEAT ME TO IT?!

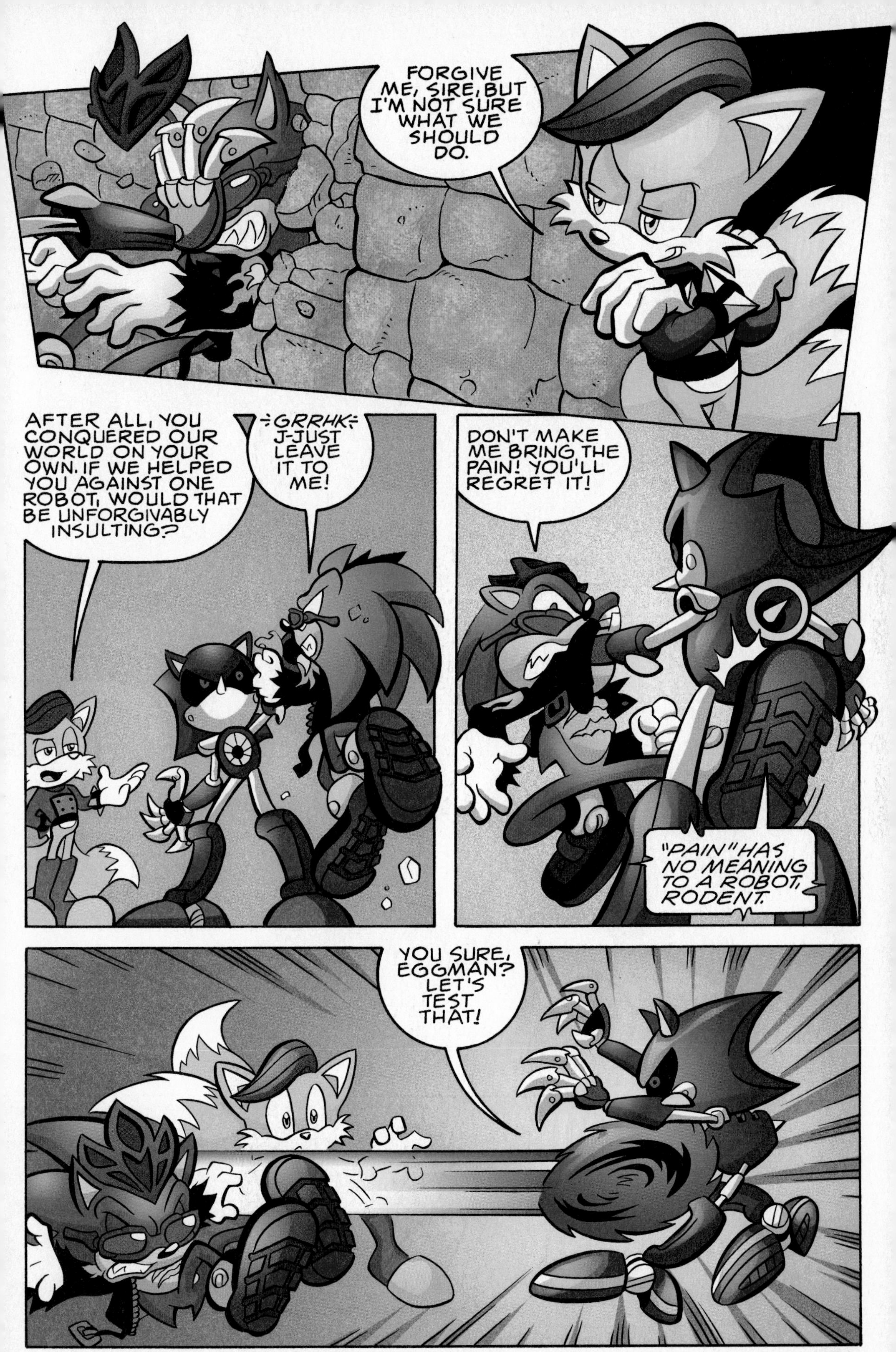
FORGIVE ME, SIRE, BUT I'M NOT SURE WHAT WE SHOULD DO.
AFTER ALL, YOU CONQUERED OUR WORLD ON YOUR OWN. IF WE HELPED YOU AGAINST ONE ROBOT, WOULD THAT BE UNFORGIVABLY INSULTING?
GRRHK J-JUST LEAVE IT TO ME!
DON'T MAKE ME BRING THE PAIN! YOU'LL REGRET IT!
"PAIN" HAS NO MEANING TO A ROBOT, RODENT.
YOU SURE, EGGMAN? LET'S TEST THAT!

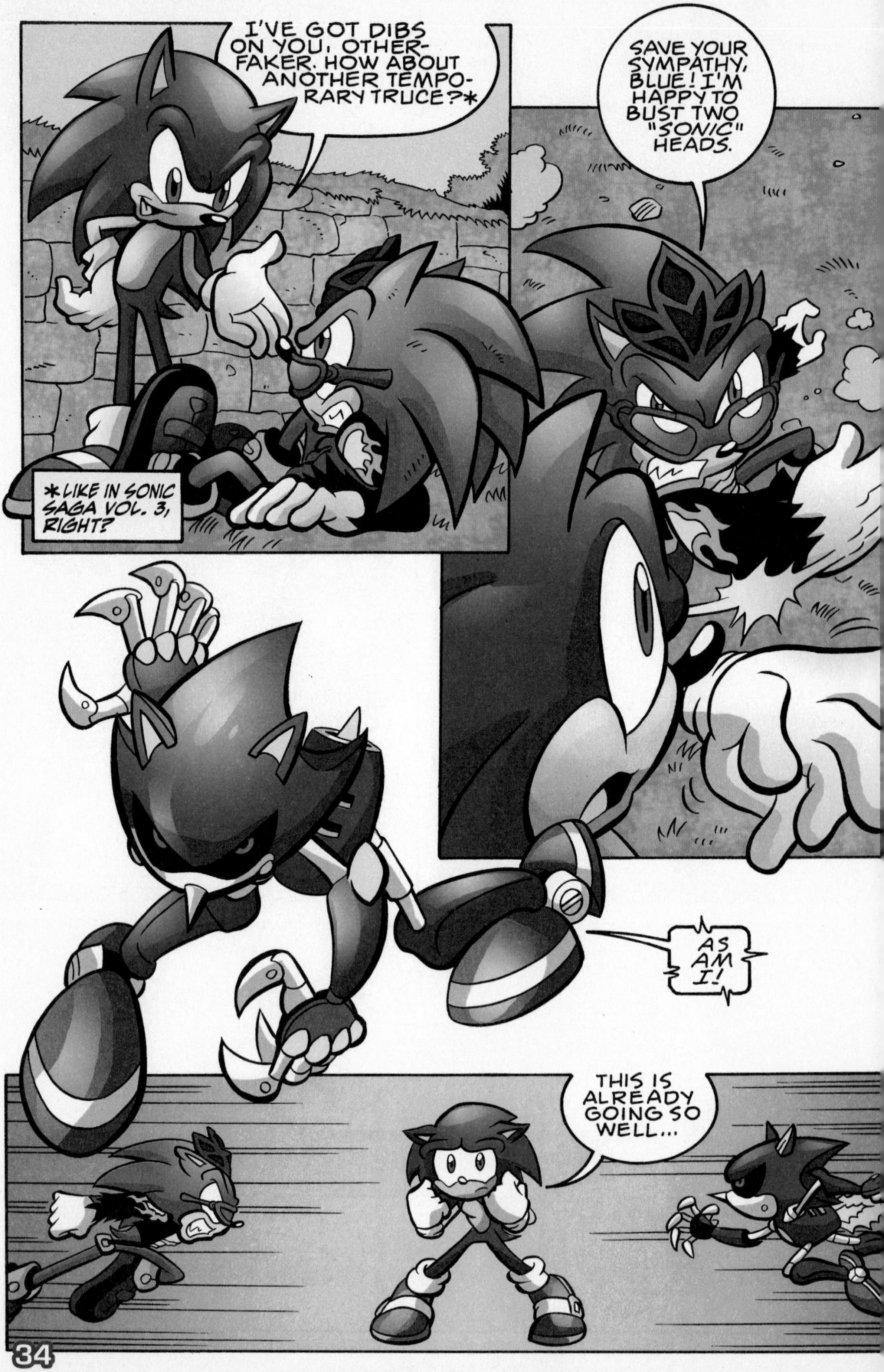
I'VE GOT DIBS ON YOU, OTHER-FAKER. HOW ABOUT ANOTHER TEMPO-RARY TRUCE?*
*LIKE IN SONIC SAGA VOL. 3, RIGHT?
SAVE YOUR SYMPATHY, BLUE! I'M HAPPY TO BUST TWO "SONIC" HEADS.
AS AM I!
THIS IS ALREADY GOING SO WELL...

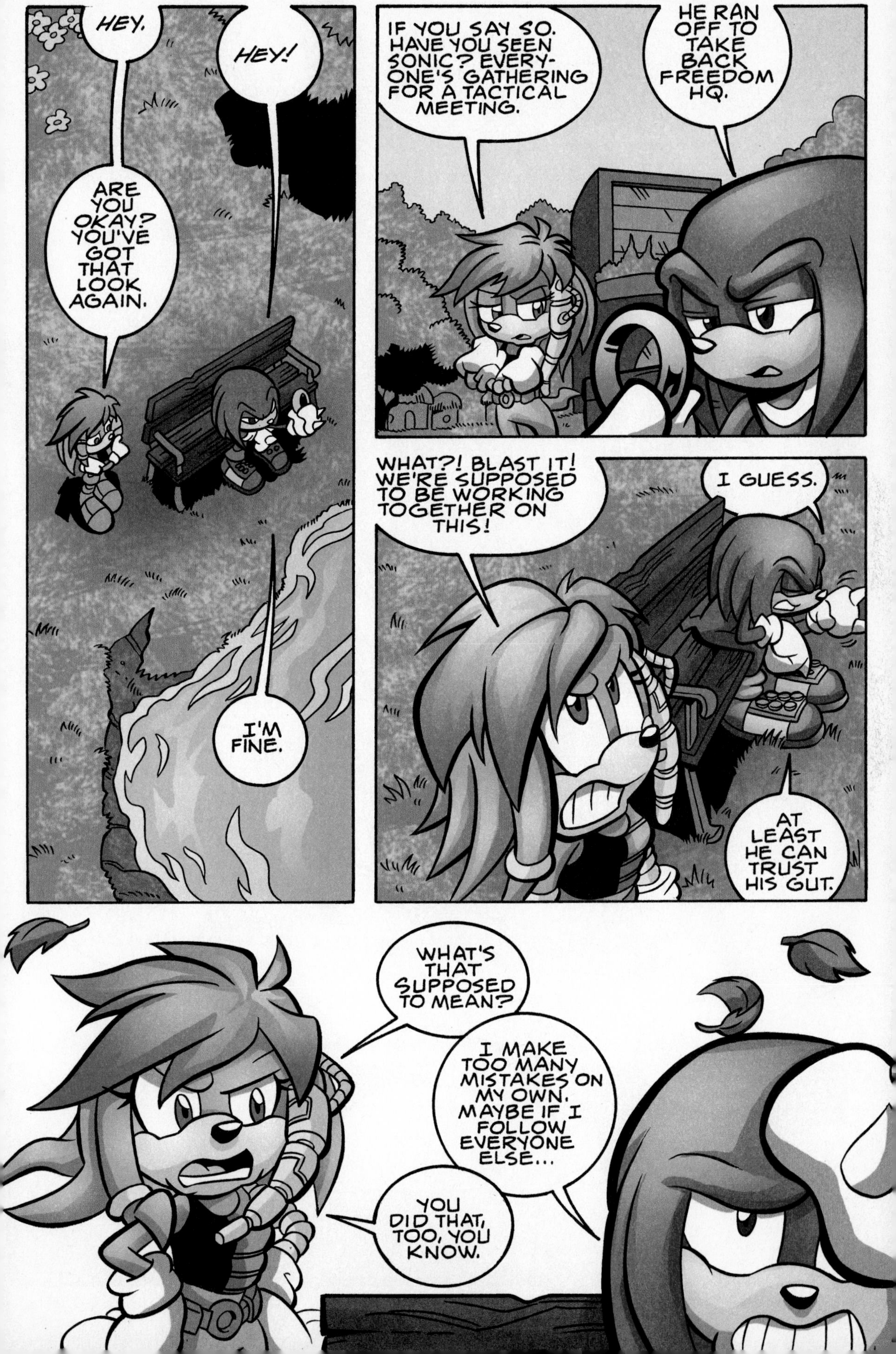
HEY.
HEY!
ARE YOU OKAY? YOU'VE GOT THAT LOOK AGAIN.
I'M FINE.
IF YOU SAY SO. HAVE YOU SEEN SONIC? EVERY-ONE'S GATHERING FOR A TACTICAL MEETING.
HE RAN OFF TO TAKE BACK FREEDOM HQ.
WHAT?! BLAST IT! WE'RE SUPPOSED TO BE WORKING TOGETHER ON THIS!
I GUESS.
AT LEAST HE CAN TRUST HIS GUT.
WHAT'S THAT SUPPOSED TO MEAN?
I MAKE TOO MANY MISTAKES ON MY OWN. MAYBE IF I FOLLOW EVERYONE ELSE...
YOU DID THAT, TOO, YOU KNOW.

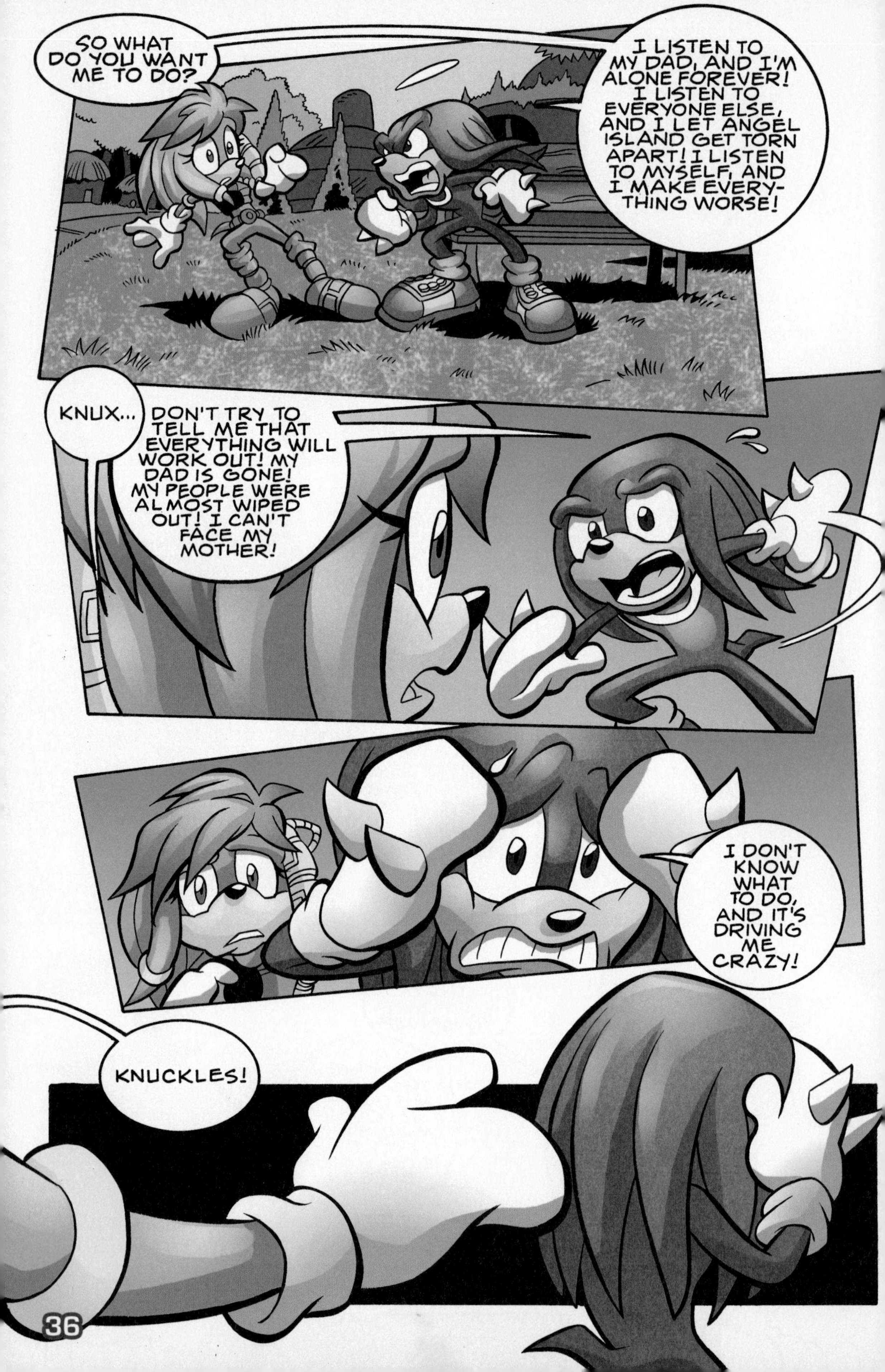
SO WHAT DO YOU WANT ME TO DO?
I LISTEN TO MY DAD, AND I'M ALONE FOREVER! I LISTEN TO EVERYONE ELSE, AND I LET ANGEL ISLAND GET TORN APART! I LISTEN TO MYSELF, AND I MAKE EVERY-THING WORSE!
KNUX...
DON'T TRY TO TELL ME THAT EVERYTHING WILL WORK OUT! MY DAD IS GONE! MY PEOPLE WERE ALMOST WIPED OUT! I CAN'T FACE MY MOTHER!
I DON'T KNOW WHAT TO DO, AND IT'S DRIVING ME CRAZY!
KNUCKLES!

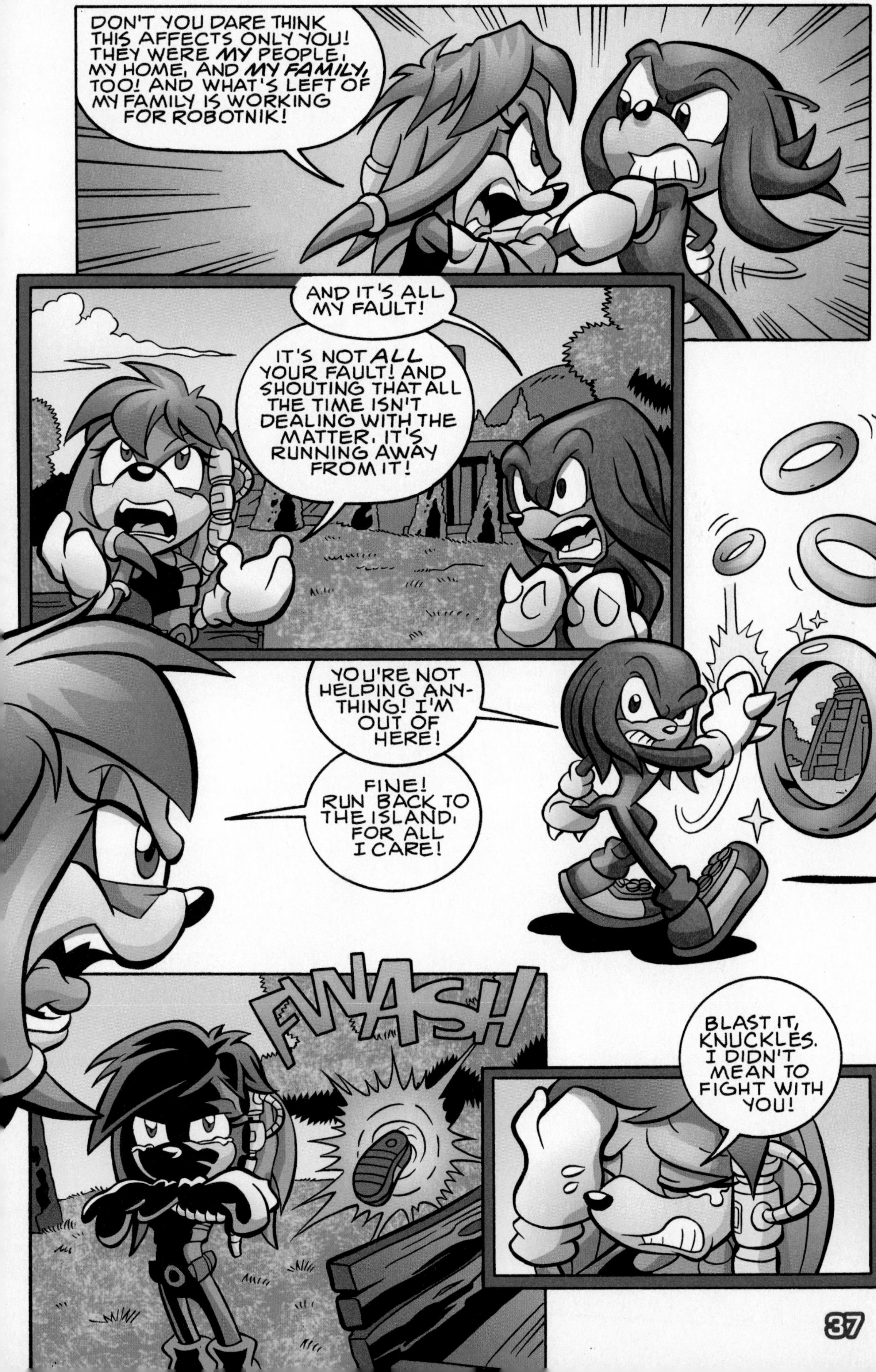
DON'T YOU DARE THINK THIS AFFECTS ONLY YOU! THEY WERE MY PEOPLE, MY HOME, AND MY FAMILY, TOO! AND WHAT'S LEFT OF MY FAMILY IS WORKING FOR ROBOTNIK!
AND IT'S ALL MY FAULT!
IT'S NOT ALL YOUR FAULT! AND SHOUTING THAT ALL THE TIME ISN'T DEALING WITH THE MATTER, IT'S RUNNING AWAY FROM IT!
YOU'RE NOT HELPING ANY-THING! I'M OUT OF HERE!
FINE! RUN BACK TO THE ISLAND, FOR ALL I CARE!
FWASH
BLAST IT, KNUCKLES. I DIDN'T MEAN TO FIGHT WITH YOU!

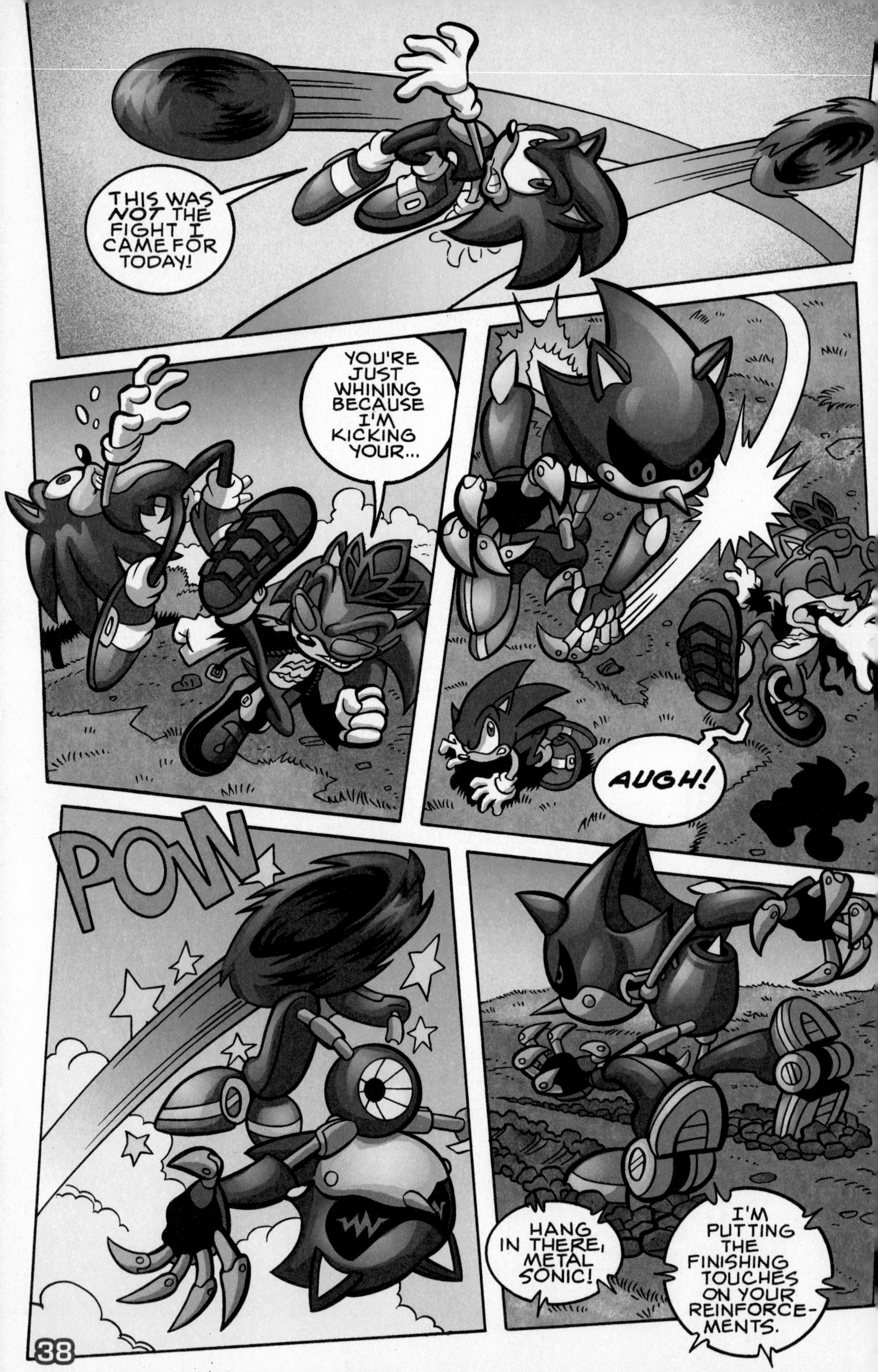
THIS WAS NOT THE FIGHT I CAME FOR TODAY!
YOU'RE JUST WHINING BECAUSE I'M KICKING YOUR...
AUGH!
POW
HANG IN THERE, METAL SONIC!
I'M PUTTING THE FINISHING TOUCHES ON YOUR REINFORCE-MENTS.

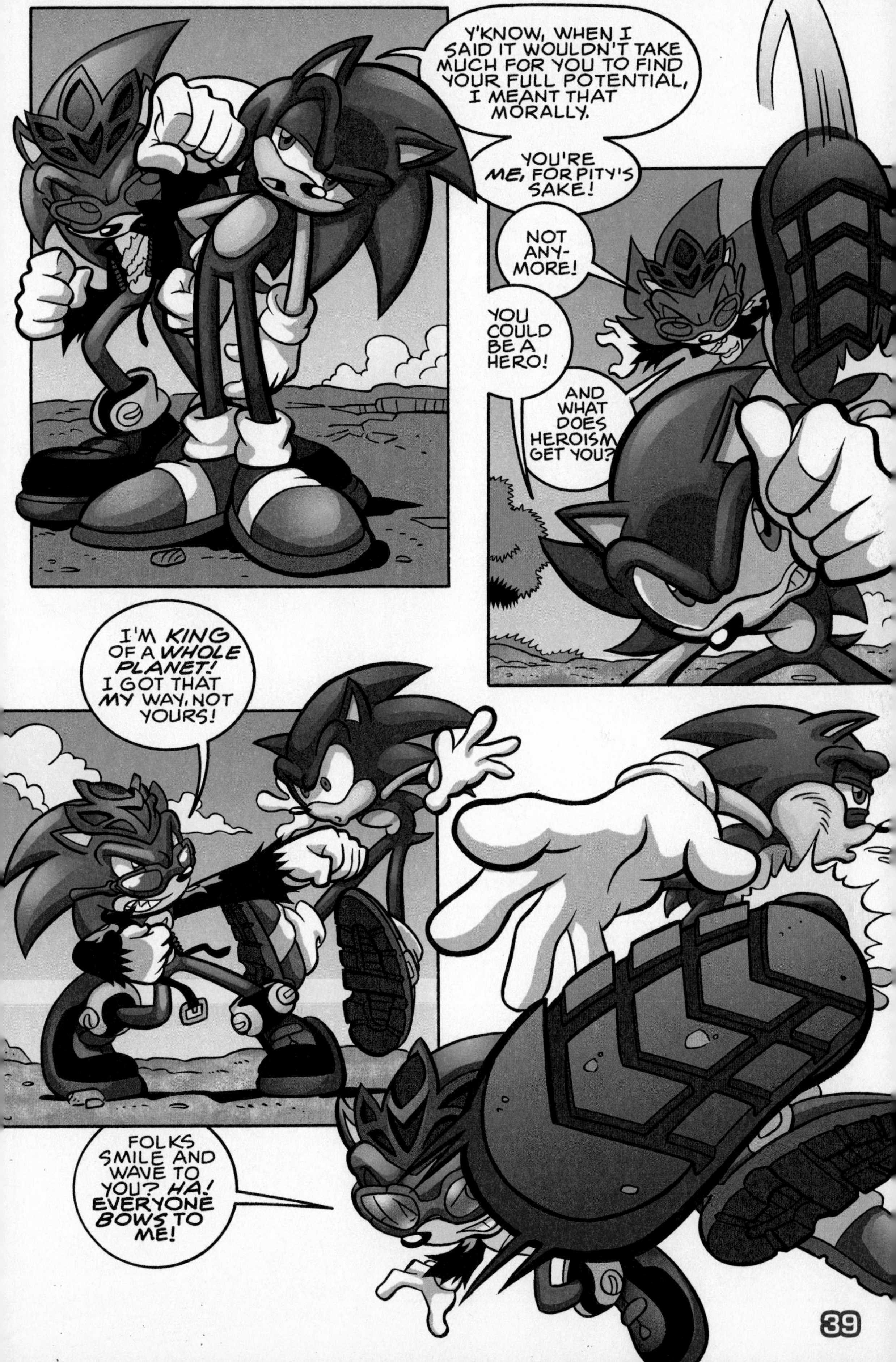
Y'KNOW, WHEN I SAID IT WOULDN'T TAKE MUCH FOR YOU TO FIND YOUR FULL POTENTIAL, I MEANT THAT MORALLY.
YOU'RE ME, FOR PITY'S SAKE!
NOT ANY-MORE!
YOU COULD BE A HERO!
AND WHAT DOES HEROISM GET YOU?
I'M KING OF A WHOLE PLANET! I GOT THAT MY WAY, NOT YOURS!
FOLKS SMILE AND WAVE TO YOU? HA! EVERYONE BOWS TO ME!

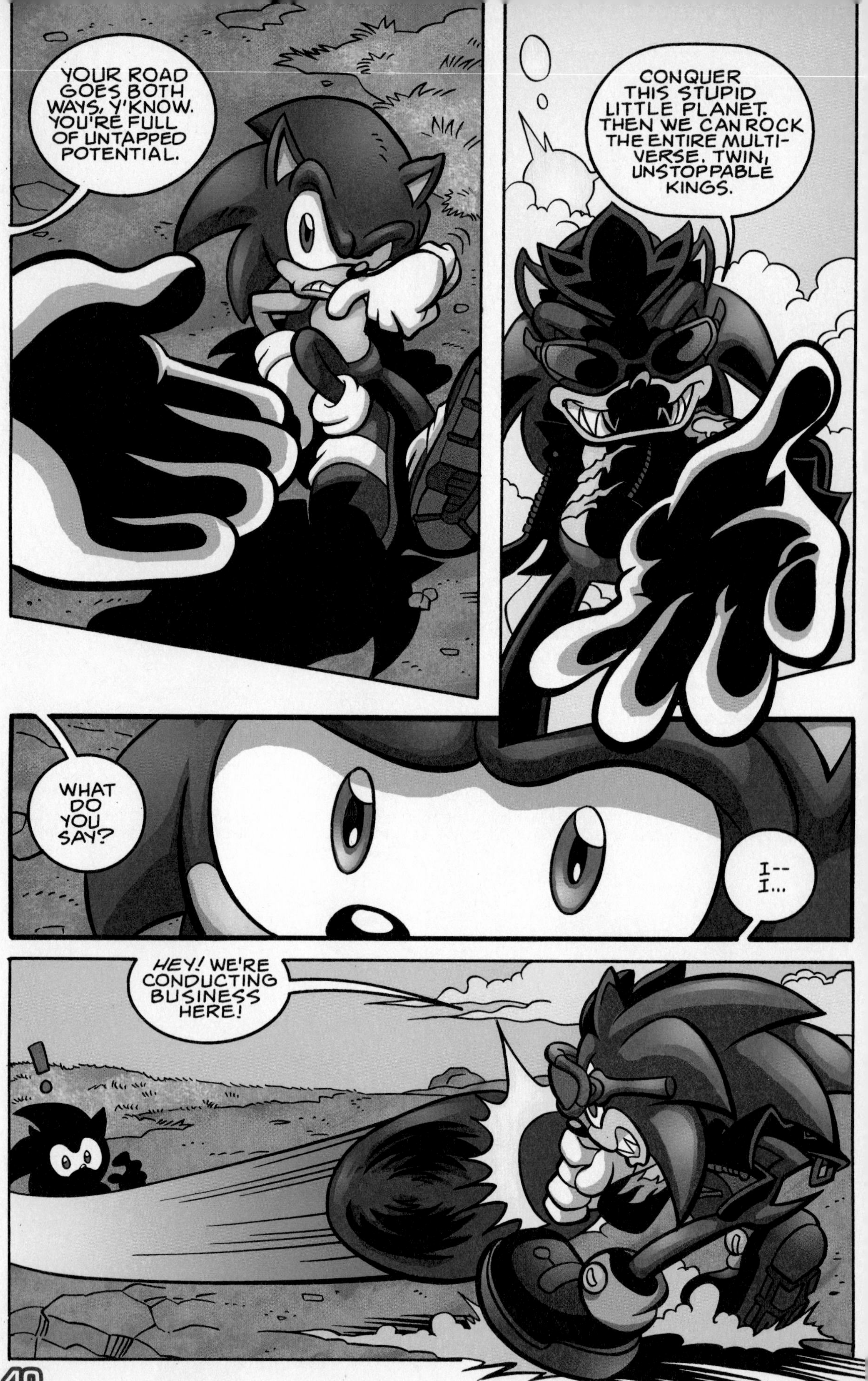
YOUR ROAD GOES BOTH WAYS, Y'KNOW. YOU'RE FULL OF UNTAPPED POTENTIAL.
CONQUER THIS STUPID LITTLE PLANET. THEN WE CAN ROCK THE ENTIRE MULTI-VERSE. TWIN, UNSTOPPABLE KINGS.
WHAT DO YOU SAY?
I-- I...
HEY! WE'RE CONDUCTING BUSINESS HERE!

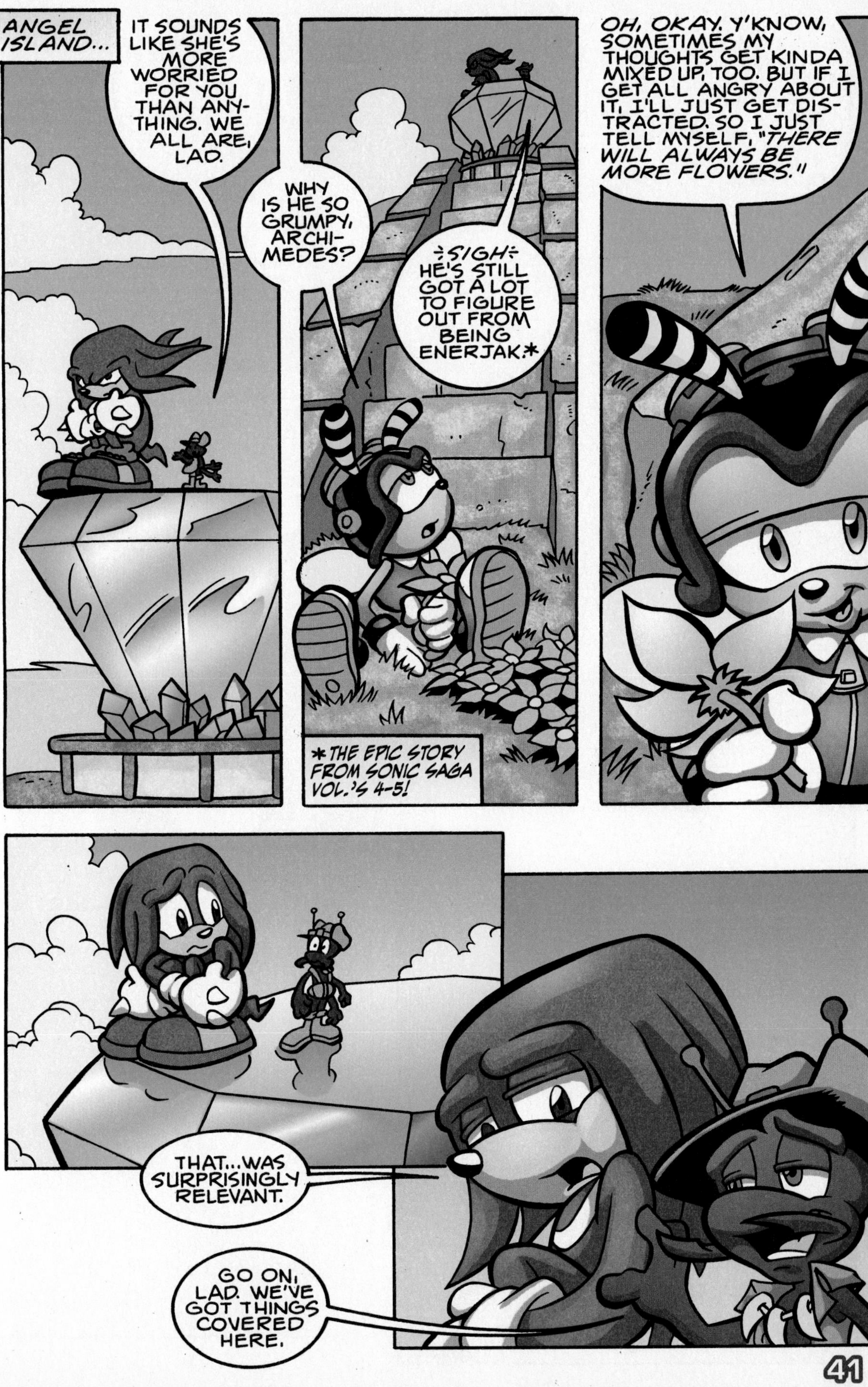

ANGEL ISLAND...
IT SOUNDS LIKE SHE'S MORE WORRIED FOR YOU THAN ANYTHING. WE ALL ARE, LAD.
WHY IS HE SO GRUMPY, ARCHIMEDES?
⁘SIGH⁘ HE'S STILL GOT A LOT TO FIGURE OUT FROM BEING ENERJAK.*
*THE EPIC STORY FROM SONIC SAGA VOL.'S 4-5!
OH, OKAY. Y'KNOW, SOMETIMES MY THOUGHTS GET KINDA MIXED UP, TOO. BUT IF I GET ALL ANGRY ABOUT IT, I'LL JUST GET DISTRACTED. SO I JUST TELL MYSELF, "THERE WILL ALWAYS BE MORE FLOWERS."
THAT...WAS SURPRISINGLY RELEVANT.
GO ON, LAD. WE'VE GOT THINGS COVERED HERE.

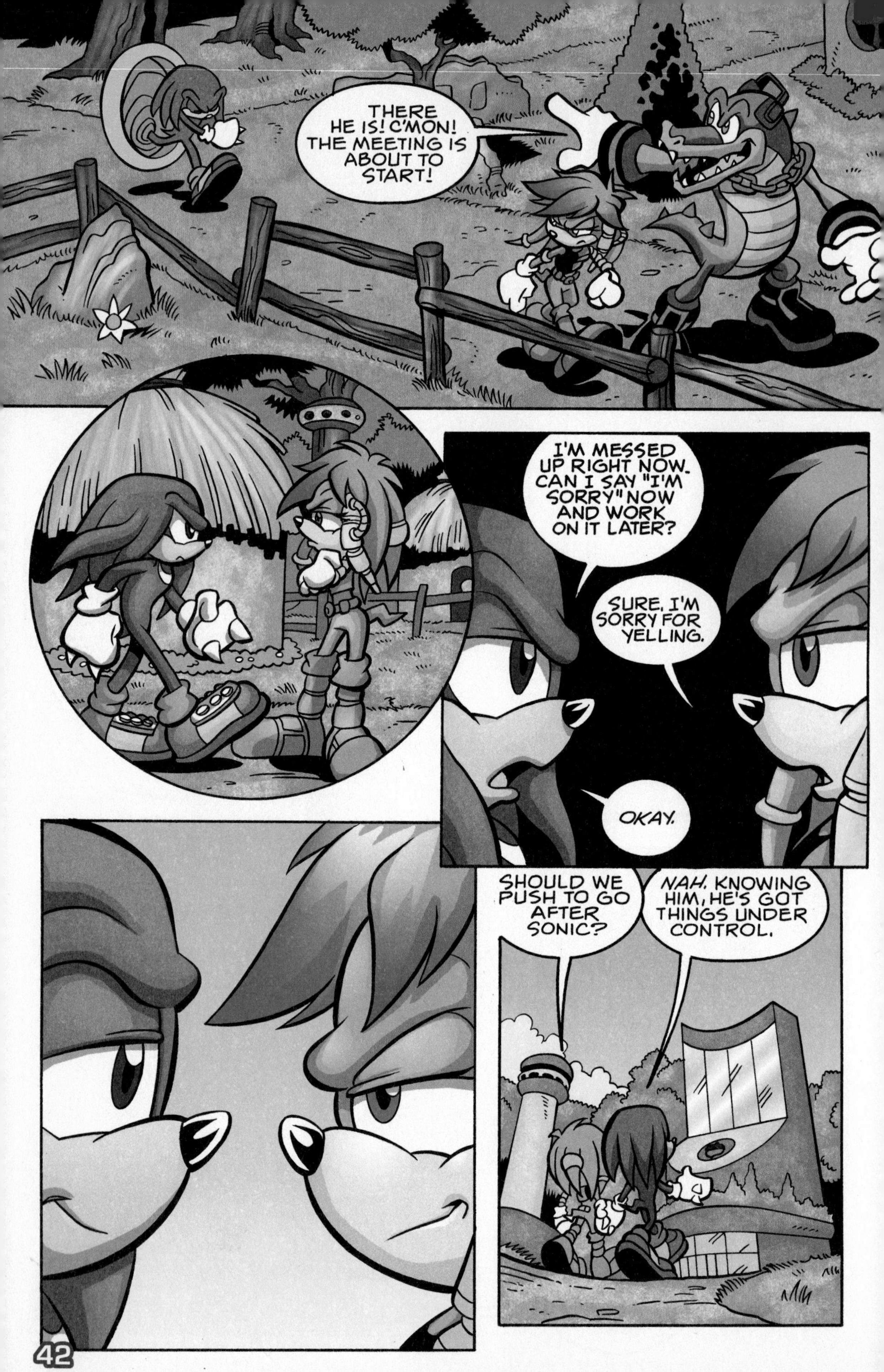
THERE HE IS! C'MON! THE MEETING IS ABOUT TO START!
I'M MESSED UP RIGHT NOW. CAN I SAY "I'M SORRY" NOW AND WORK ON IT LATER?
SURE. I'M SORRY FOR YELLING.
OKAY.
SHOULD WE PUSH TO GO AFTER SONIC?
NAH. KNOWING HIM, HE'S GOT THINGS UNDER CONTROL.

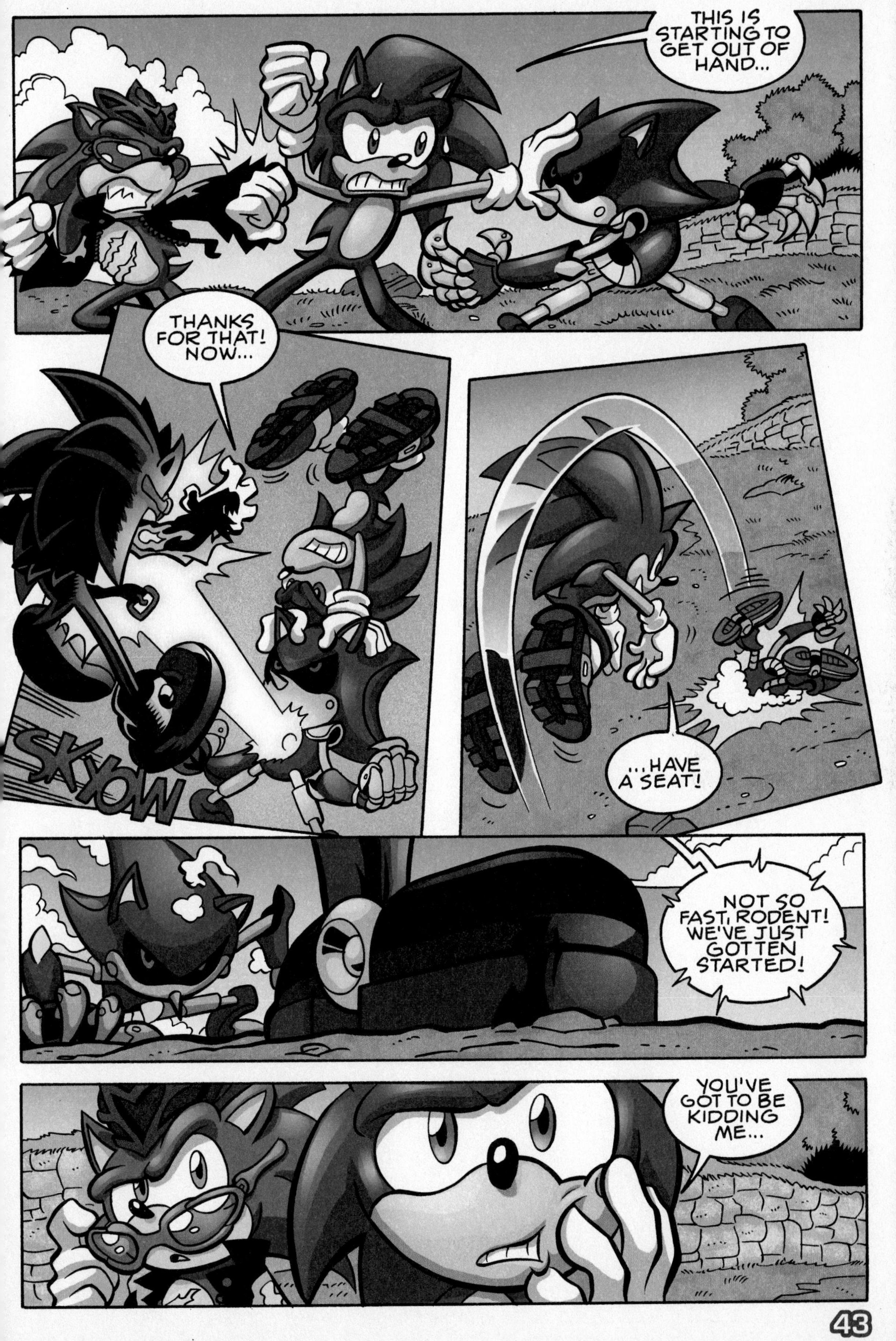

THIS IS STARTING TO GET OUT OF HAND...
THANKS FOR THAT! NOW...
SKYOW
...HAVE A SEAT!
NOT SO FAST, RODENT! WE'VE JUST GOTTEN STARTED!
YOU'VE GOT TO BE KIDDING ME...

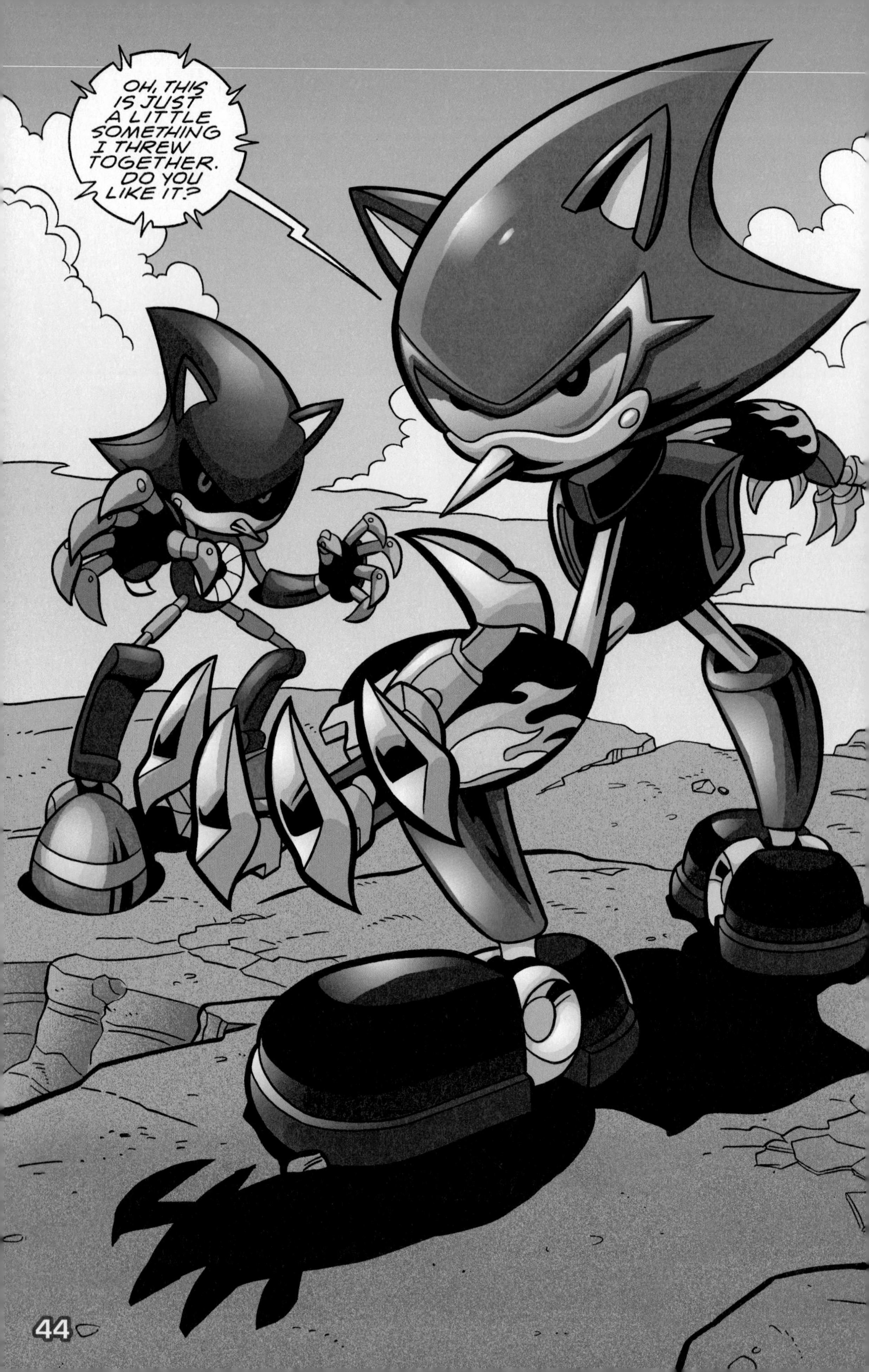
OH, THIS IS JUST A LITTLE SOMETHING I THREW TOGETHER. DO YOU LIKE IT?

CHAPTER 3

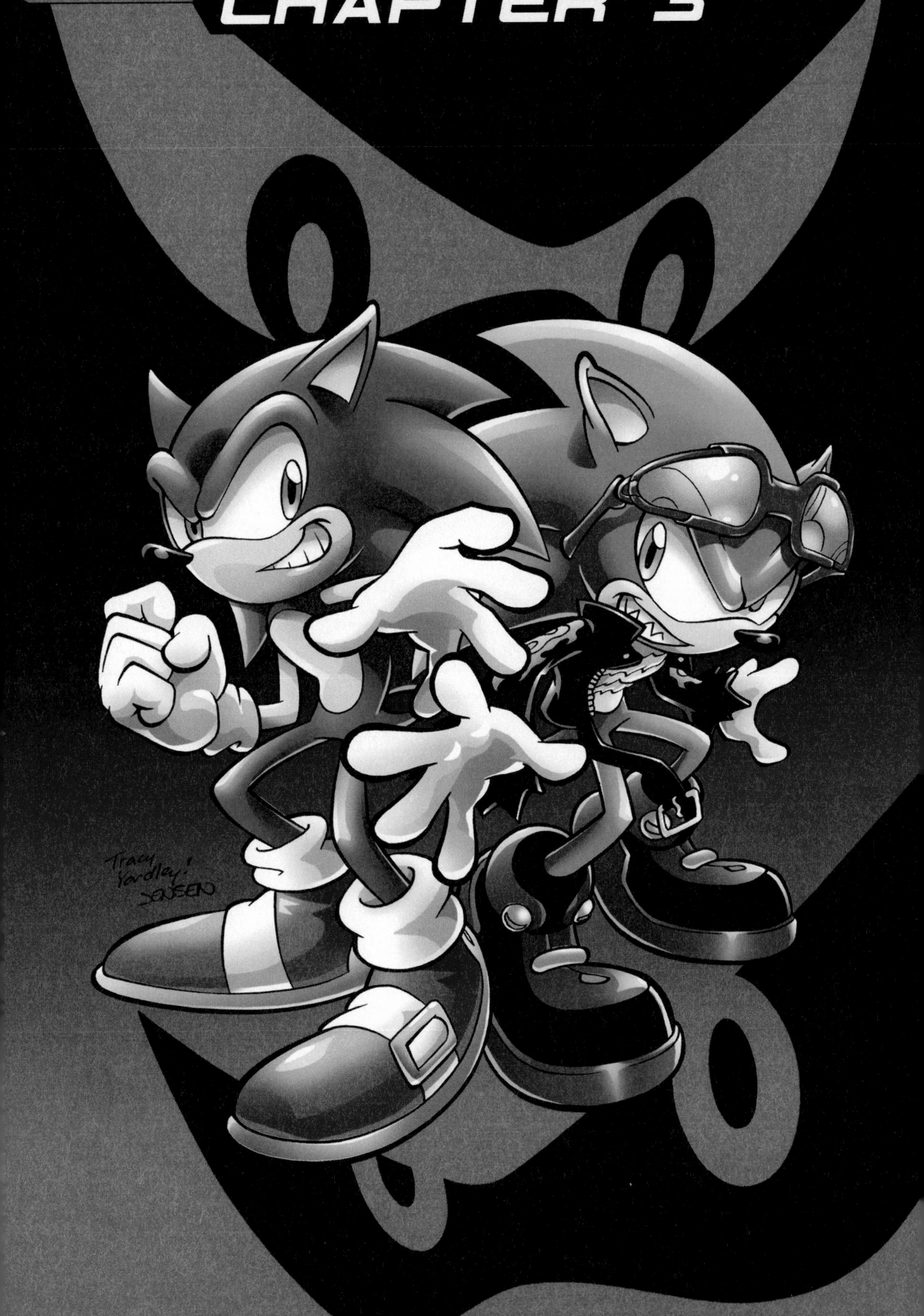
Tracy Yardley! JENSEN

SONIC THE HEDGEHOG 192
COVER BY TRACY YARDLEY AND JASON JENSEN

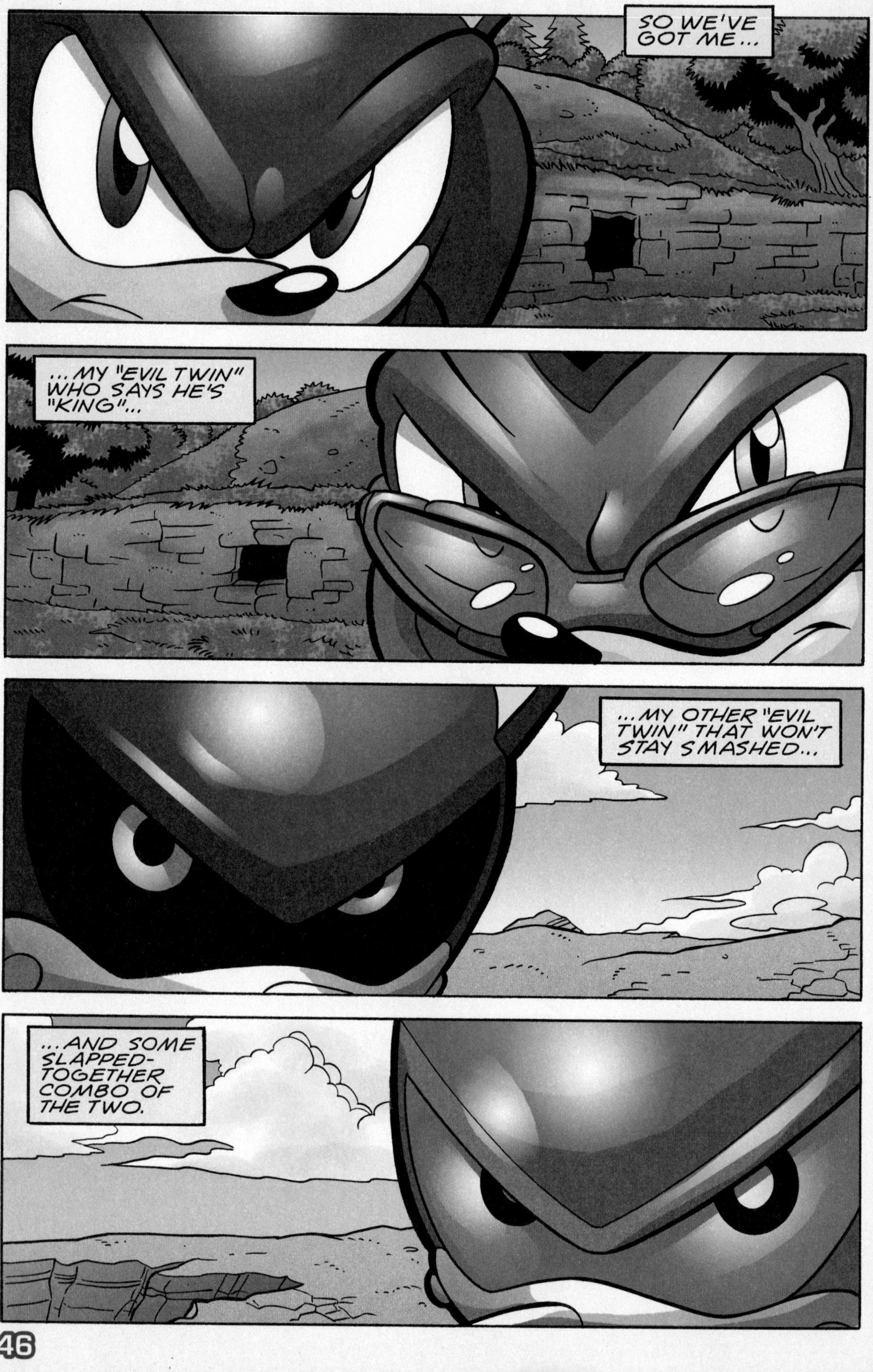
SO WE'VE GOT ME...
...MY "EVIL TWIN" WHO SAYS HE'S "KING"...
...MY OTHER "EVIL TWIN" THAT WON'T STAY SMASHED...
...AND SOME SLAPPED-TOGETHER COMBO OF THE TWO.

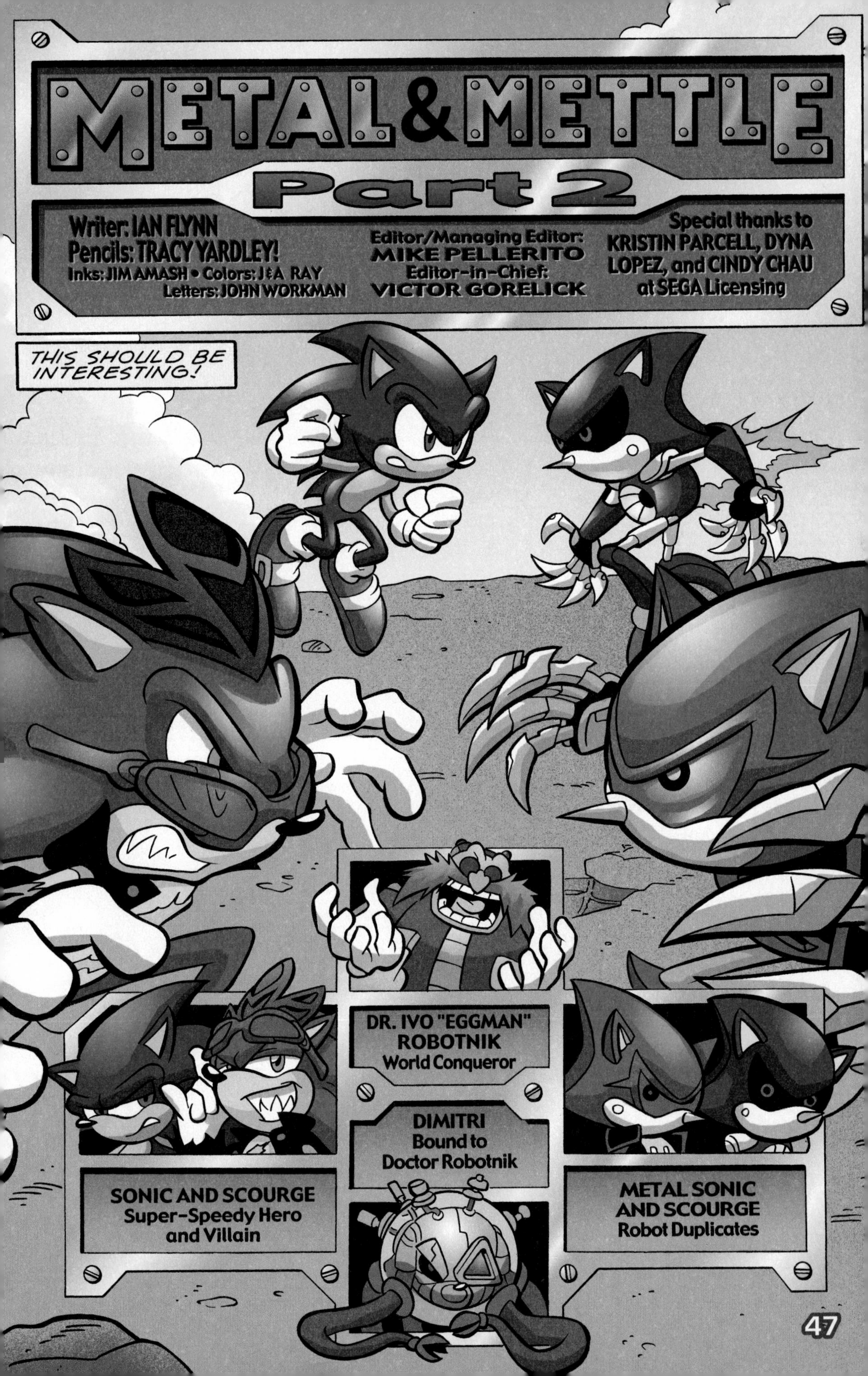

METAL & METTLE
Part 2
Writer: IAN FLYNN
Pencils: TRACY YARDLEY!
Inks: JIM AMASH • Colors: J&A RAY
Letters: JOHN WORKMAN
Editor/Managing Editor:
MIKE PELLERITO
Editor-in-Chief:
VICTOR GORELICK
Special thanks to
KRISTIN PARCELL, DYNA LOPEZ, and CINDY CHAU
at SEGA Licensing
THIS SHOULD BE INTERESTING!
DR. IVO "EGGMAN" ROBOTNIK
World Conqueror
DIMITRI
Bound to Doctor Robotnik
SONIC AND SCOURGE
Super-Speedy Hero and Villain
METAL SONIC AND SCOURGE
Robot Duplicates
47

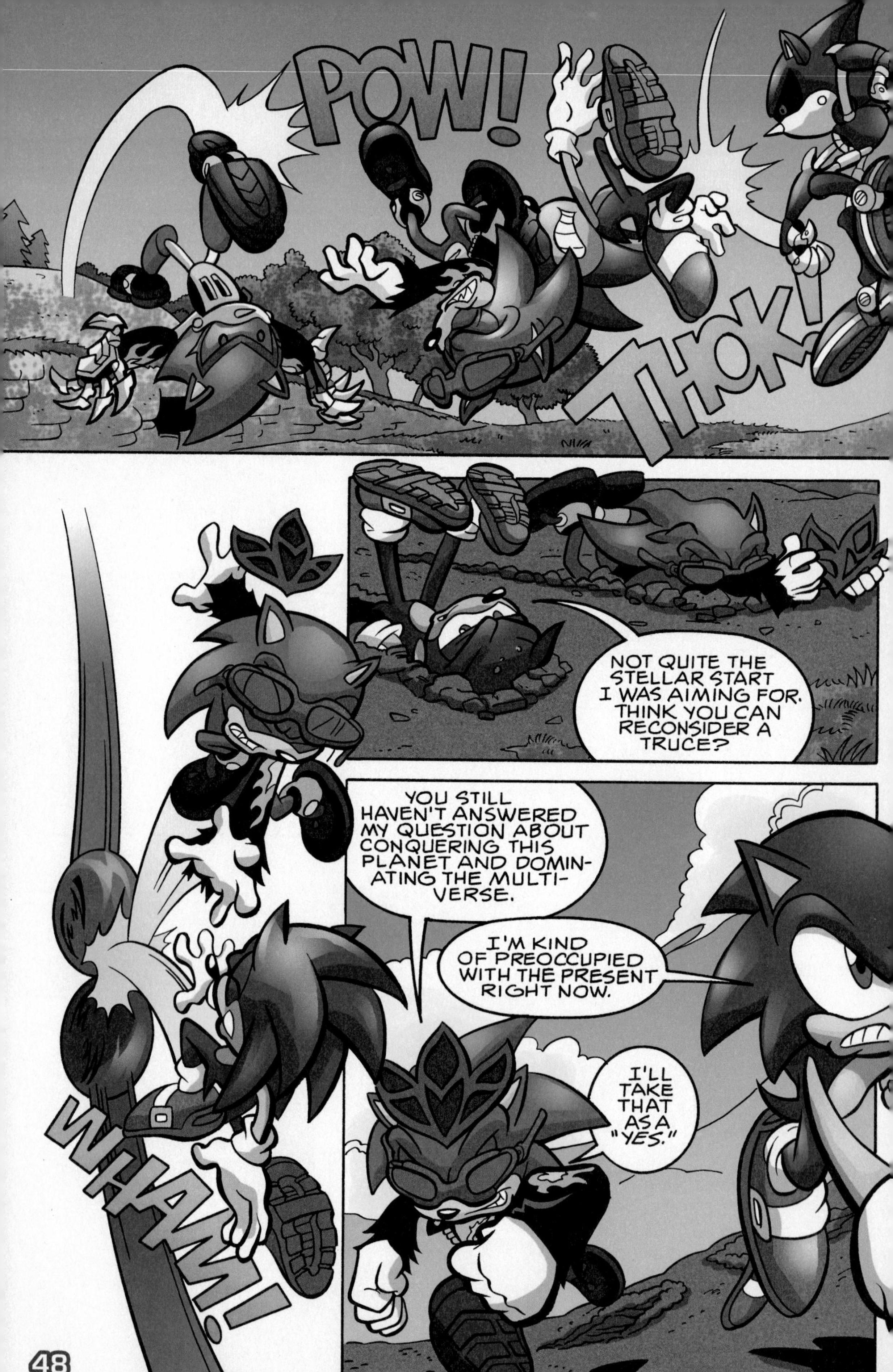
POW!
THOK!
NOT QUITE THE STELLAR START I WAS AIMING FOR. THINK YOU CAN RECONSIDER A TRUCE?
WHAM!
YOU STILL HAVEN'T ANSWERED MY QUESTION ABOUT CONQUERING THIS PLANET AND DOMINATING THE MULTIVERSE.
I'M KIND OF PREOCCUPIED WITH THE PRESENT RIGHT NOW.
I'LL TAKE THAT AS A "YES."

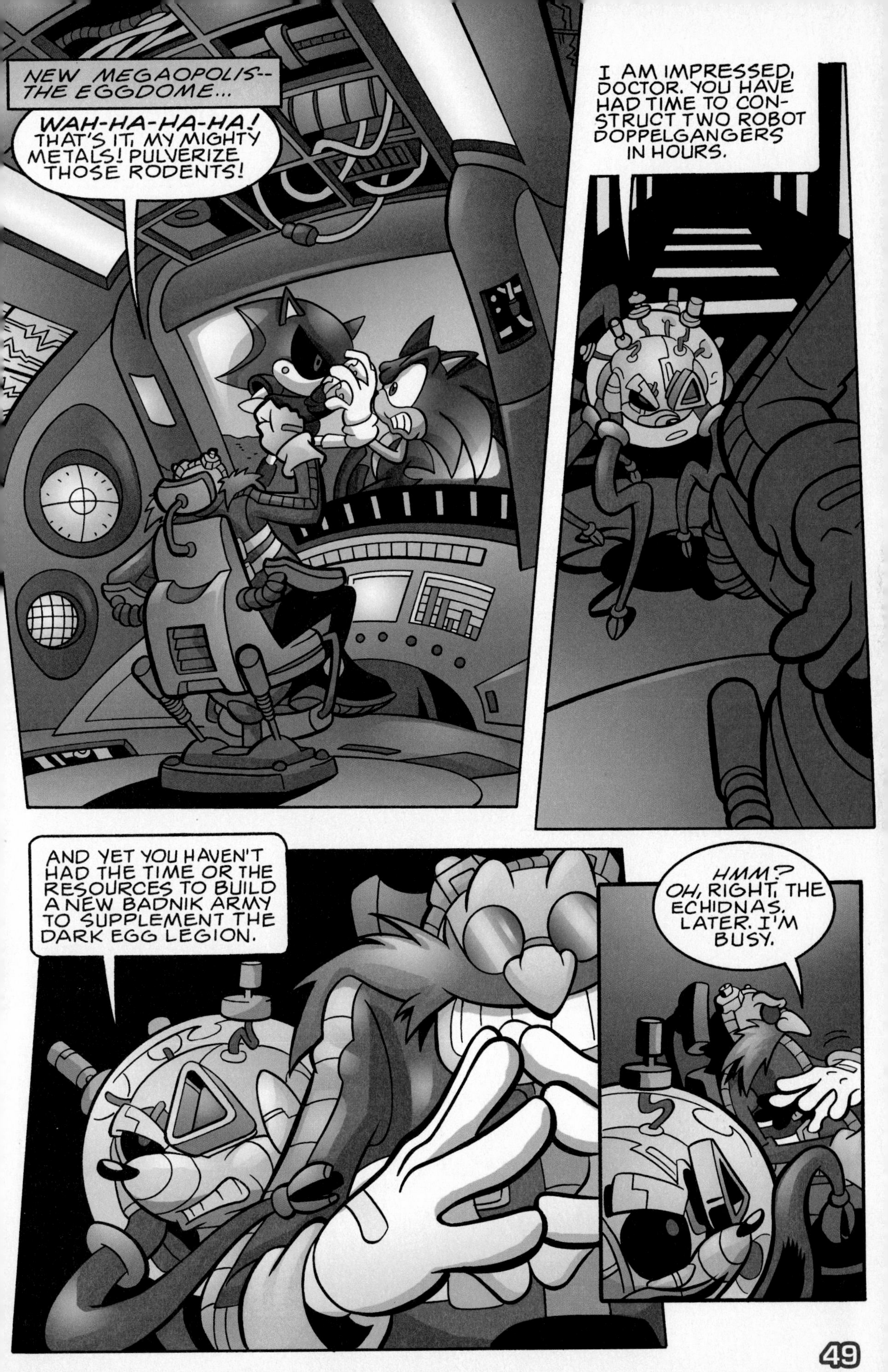
NEW MEGAOPOLIS-- THE EGGDOME...
WAH-HA-HA-HA! THAT'S IT, MY MIGHTY METALS! PULVERIZE THOSE RODENTS!
I AM IMPRESSED, DOCTOR. YOU HAVE HAD TIME TO CONSTRUCT TWO ROBOT DOPPELGANGERS IN HOURS.
AND YET YOU HAVEN'T HAD THE TIME OR THE RESOURCES TO BUILD A NEW BADNIK ARMY TO SUPPLEMENT THE DARK EGG LEGION.
HMM? OH, RIGHT, THE ECHIDNAS. LATER. I'M BUSY.

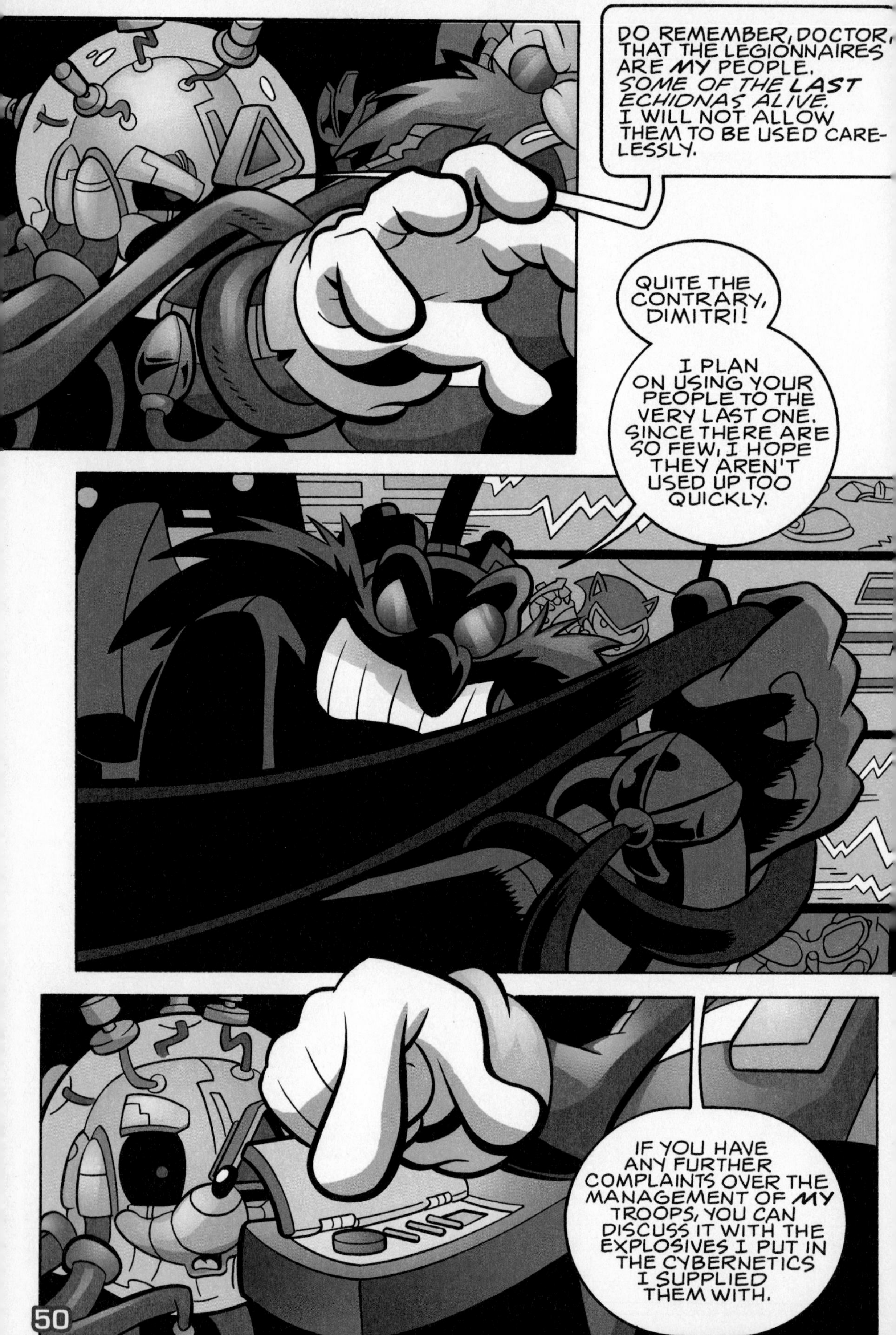
DO REMEMBER, DOCTOR, THAT THE LEGIONNAIRES ARE *MY* PEOPLE. *SOME OF THE LAST ECHIDNAS ALIVE.* I WILL NOT ALLOW THEM TO BE USED CARE-LESSLY.
QUITE THE CONTRARY, DIMITRI!
I PLAN ON USING YOUR PEOPLE TO THE VERY LAST ONE. SINCE THERE ARE SO FEW, I HOPE THEY AREN'T USED UP TOO QUICKLY.
IF YOU HAVE ANY FURTHER COMPLAINTS OVER THE MANAGEMENT OF *MY* TROOPS, YOU CAN DISCUSS IT WITH THE EXPLOSIVES I PUT IN THE CYBERNETICS I SUPPLIED THEM WITH.

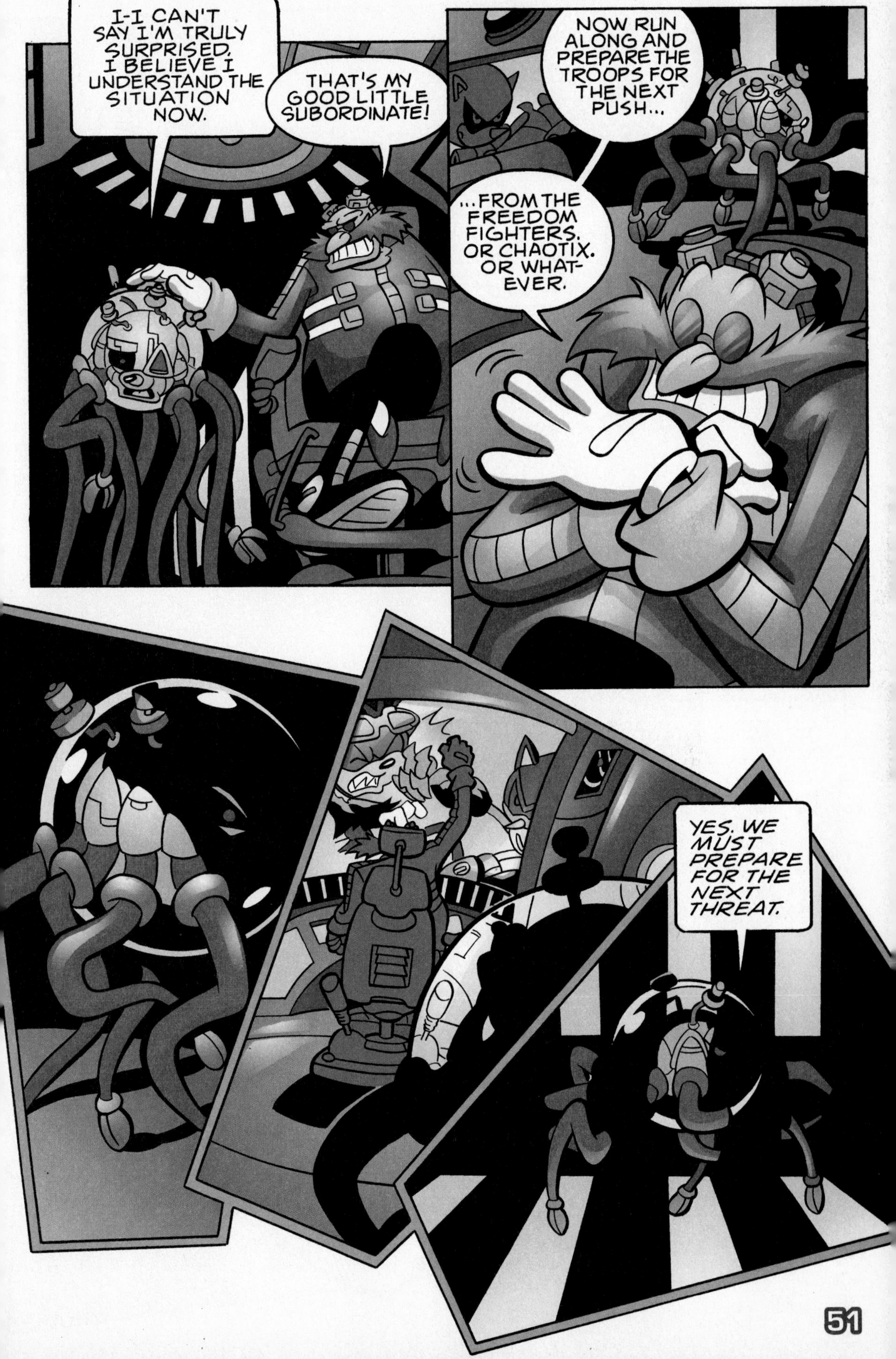
I-I CAN'T SAY I'M TRULY SURPRISED. I BELIEVE I UNDERSTAND THE SITUATION NOW.
THAT'S MY GOOD LITTLE SUBORDINATE!
NOW RUN ALONG AND PREPARE THE TROOPS FOR THE NEXT PUSH...
...FROM THE FREEDOM FIGHTERS. OR CHAOTIX. OR WHAT-EVER.
YES. WE MUST PREPARE FOR THE NEXT THREAT.

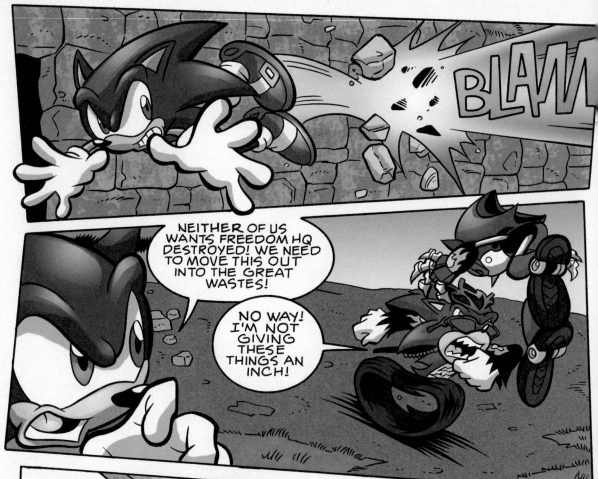

NEITHER OF US WANTS FREEDOM HQ DESTROYED! WE NEED TO MOVE THIS OUT INTO THE GREAT WASTES!

NO WAY! I'M NOT GIVING THESE THINGS AN INCH!

SCOURGE? HON? DO YOU WANT US TO STEP IN?

YOU SAYIN' I CAN'T HANDLE THIS?

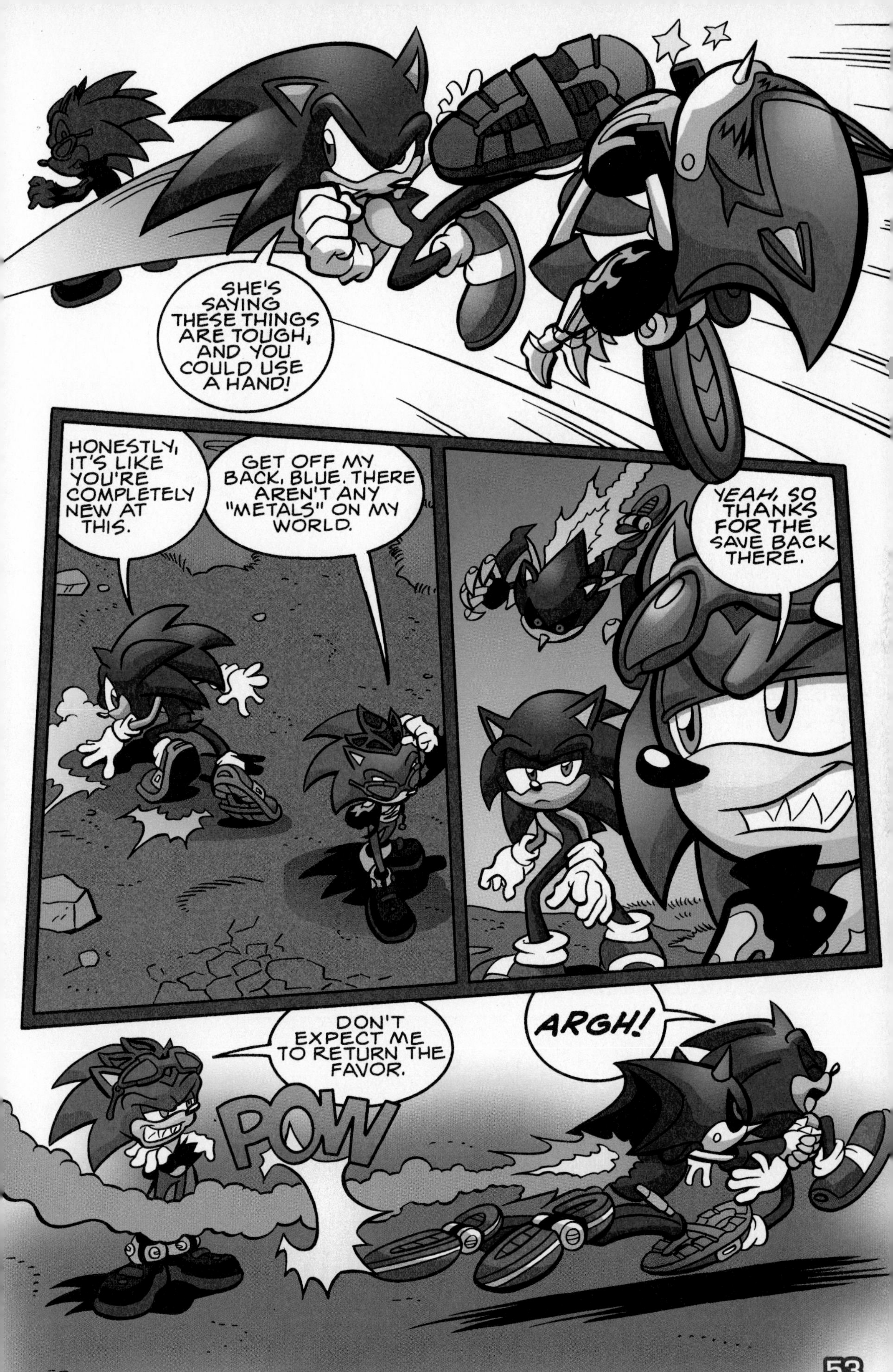
SHE'S SAYING THESE THINGS ARE TOUGH, AND YOU COULD USE A HAND!
HONESTLY, IT'S LIKE YOU'RE COMPLETELY NEW AT THIS.
GET OFF MY BACK, BLUE. THERE AREN'T ANY "METALS" ON MY WORLD.
YEAH, SO THANKS FOR THE SAVE BACK THERE.
DON'T EXPECT ME TO RETURN THE FAVOR.
POW
ARGH!

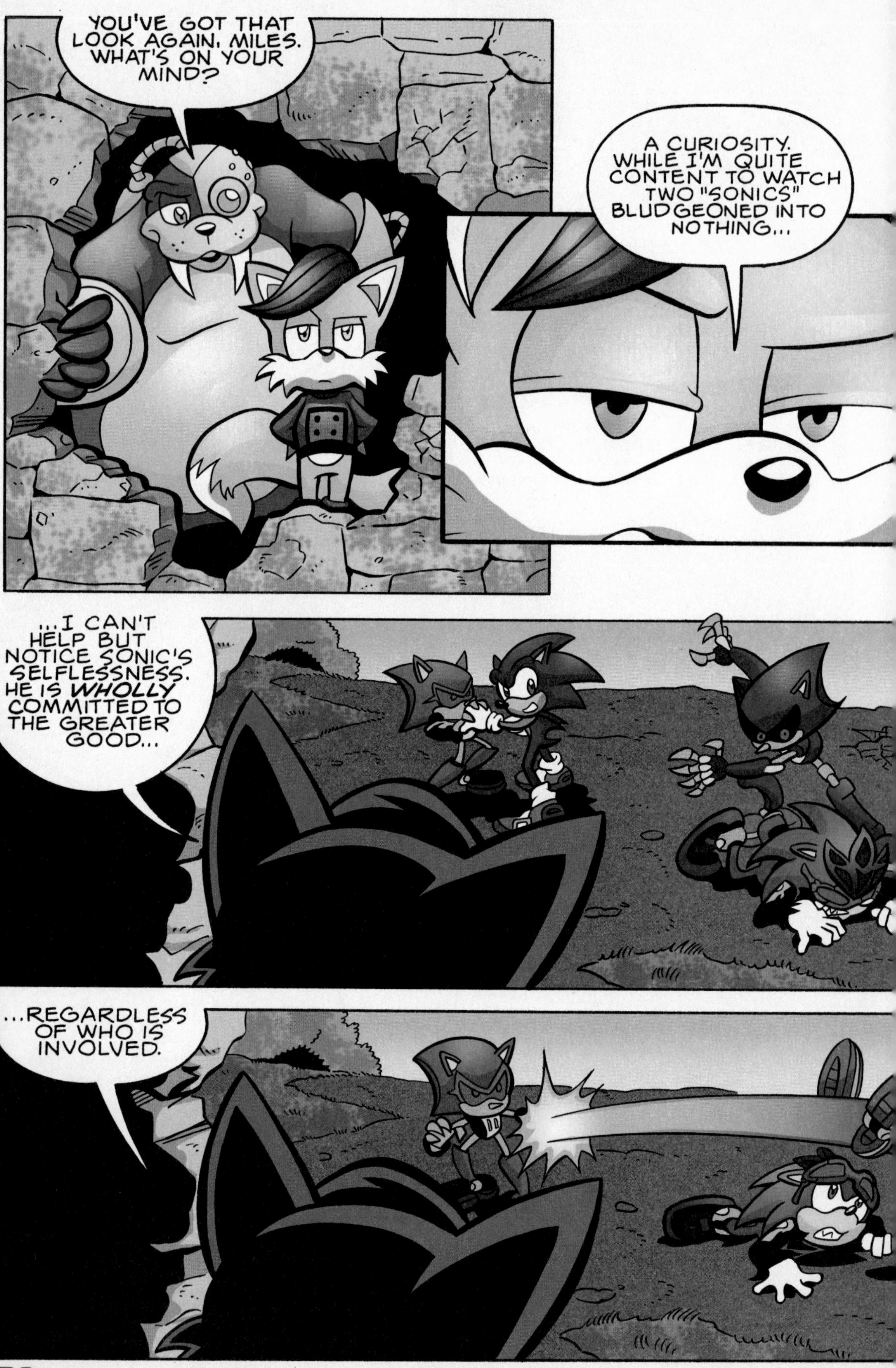
YOU'VE GOT THAT LOOK AGAIN, MILES. WHAT'S ON YOUR MIND?
A CURIOSITY. WHILE I'M QUITE CONTENT TO WATCH TWO "SONICS" BLUDGEONED INTO NOTHING...
...I CAN'T HELP BUT NOTICE SONIC'S SELFLESSNESS. HE IS *WHOLLY* COMMITTED TO THE GREATER GOOD...
...REGARDLESS OF WHO IS INVOLVED.

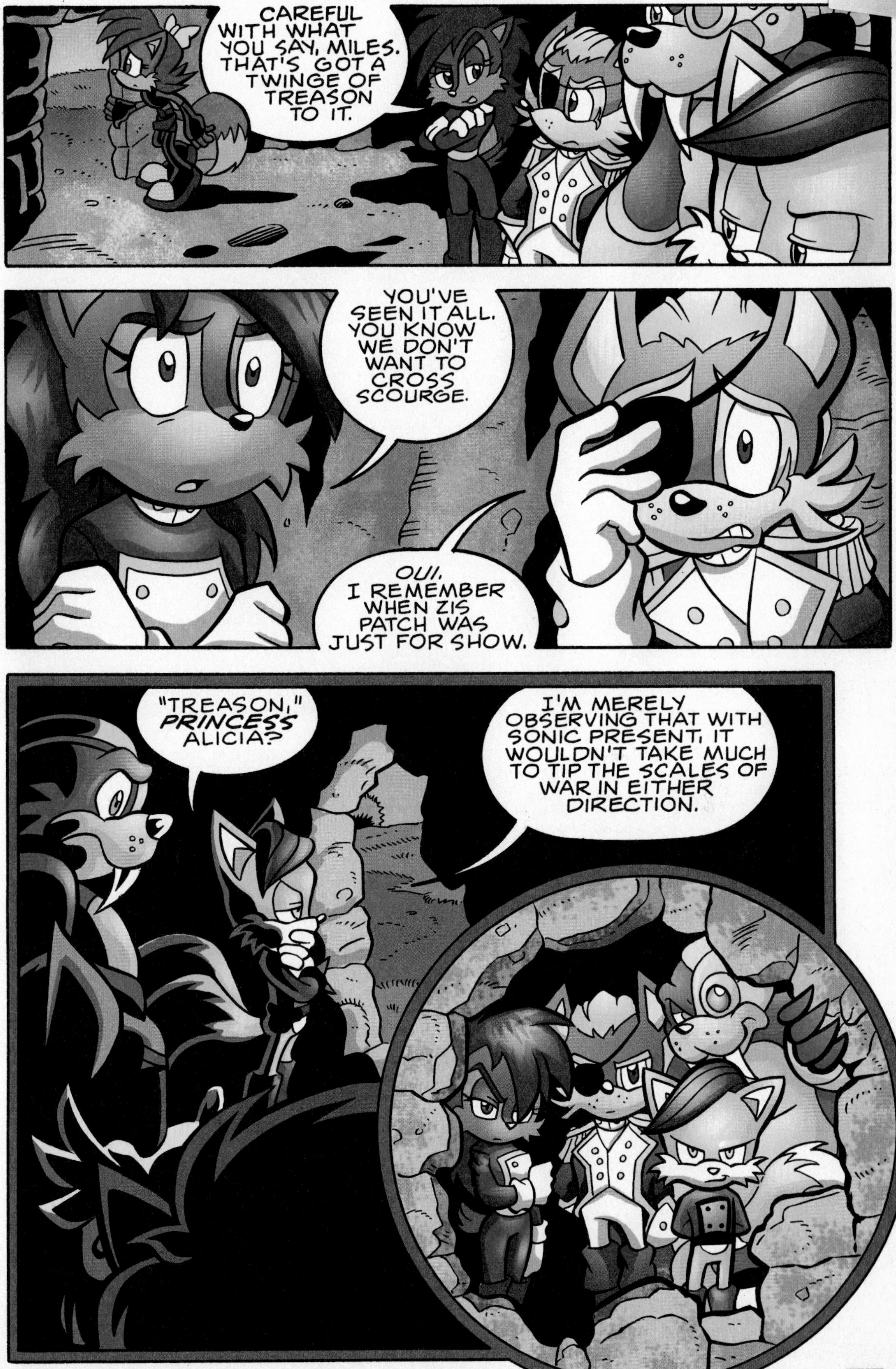
CAREFUL WITH WHAT YOU SAY, MILES. THAT'S GOT A TWINGE OF TREASON TO IT.
YOU'VE SEEN IT ALL. YOU KNOW WE DON'T WANT TO CROSS SCOURGE.
OUI. I REMEMBER WHEN ZIS PATCH WAS JUST FOR SHOW.
"TREASON," PRINCESS ALICIA?
I'M MERELY OBSERVING THAT WITH SONIC PRESENT, IT WOULDN'T TAKE MUCH TO TIP THE SCALES OF WAR IN EITHER DIRECTION.

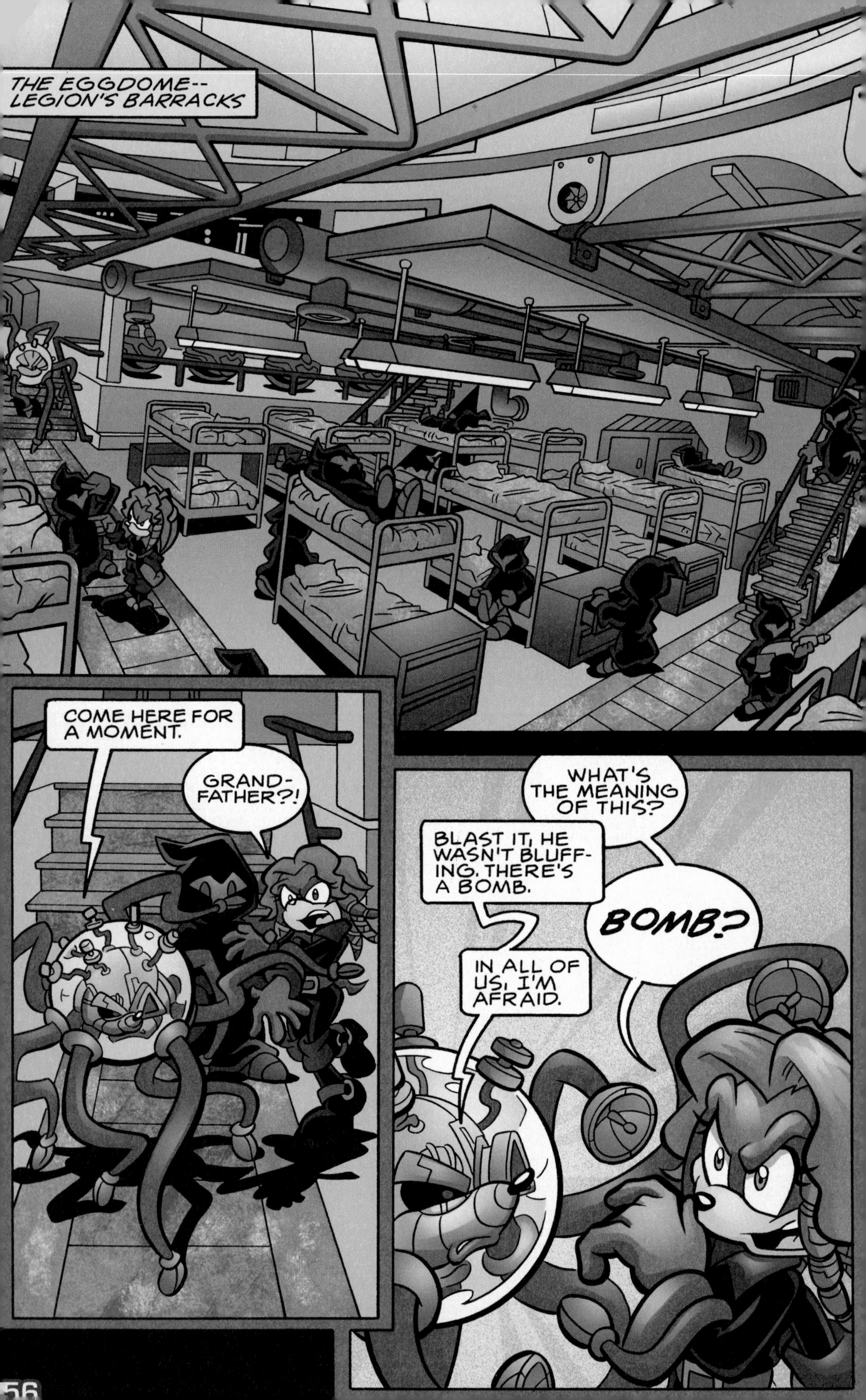
THE EGGDOME--
LEGION'S BARRACKS
COME HERE FOR A MOMENT.
GRAND-FATHER?!
WHAT'S THE MEANING OF THIS?
BLAST IT, HE WASN'T BLUFF-ING. THERE'S A BOMB.
BOMB?
IN ALL OF US, I'M AFRAID.

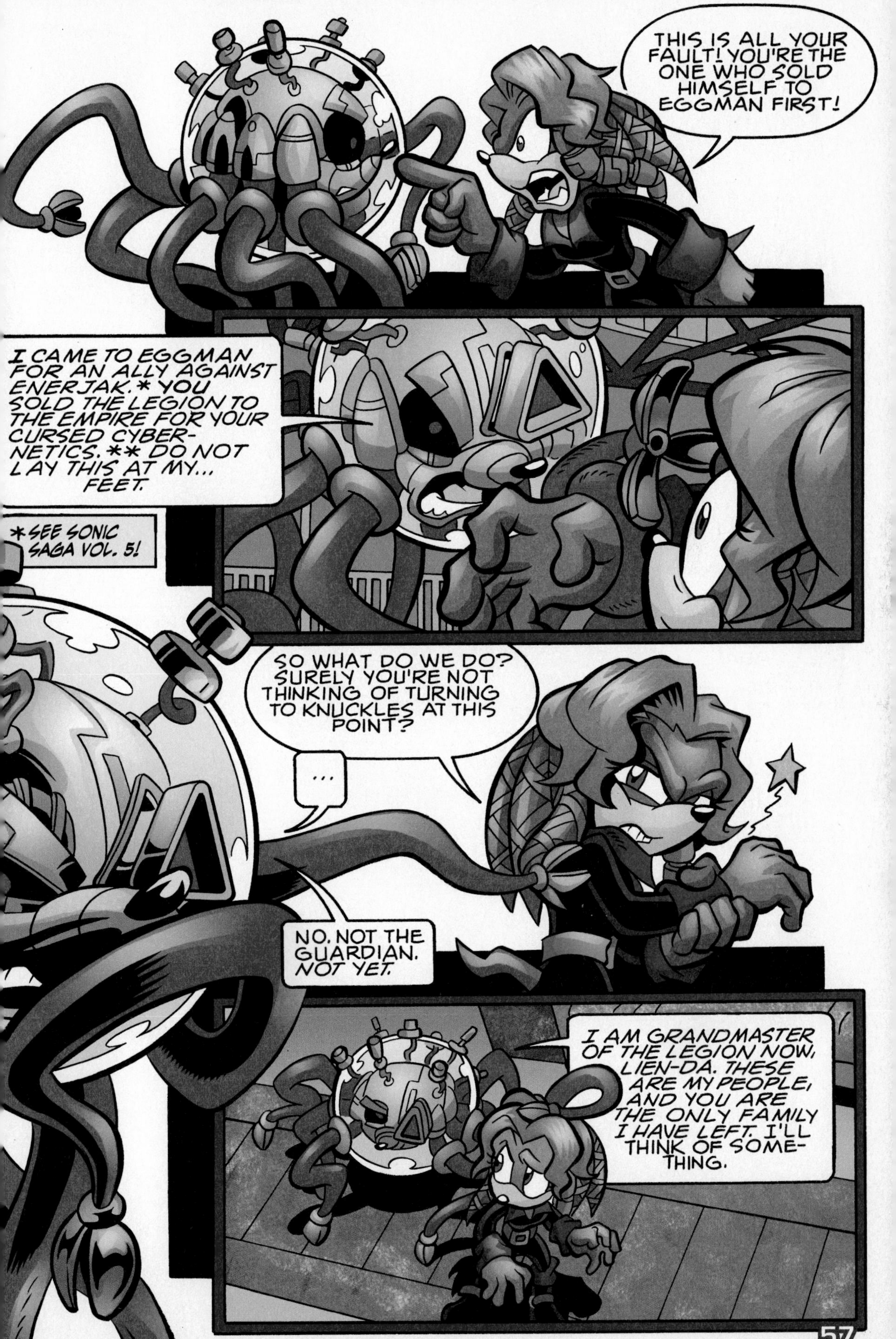
THIS IS ALL YOUR FAULT! YOU'RE THE ONE WHO SOLD HIMSELF TO EGGMAN FIRST!
I CAME TO EGGMAN FOR AN ALLY AGAINST ENERJAK.* YOU SOLD THE LEGION TO THE EMPIRE FOR YOUR CURSED CYBERNETICS.** DO NOT LAY THIS AT MY... FEET.
*SEE SONIC SAGA VOL. 5!
SO WHAT DO WE DO? SURELY YOU'RE NOT THINKING OF TURNING TO KNUCKLES AT THIS POINT?
...
NO, NOT THE GUARDIAN. NOT YET.
I AM GRANDMASTER OF THE LEGION NOW, LIEN-DA. THESE ARE MY PEOPLE, AND YOU ARE THE ONLY FAMILY I HAVE LEFT. I'LL THINK OF SOMETHING.

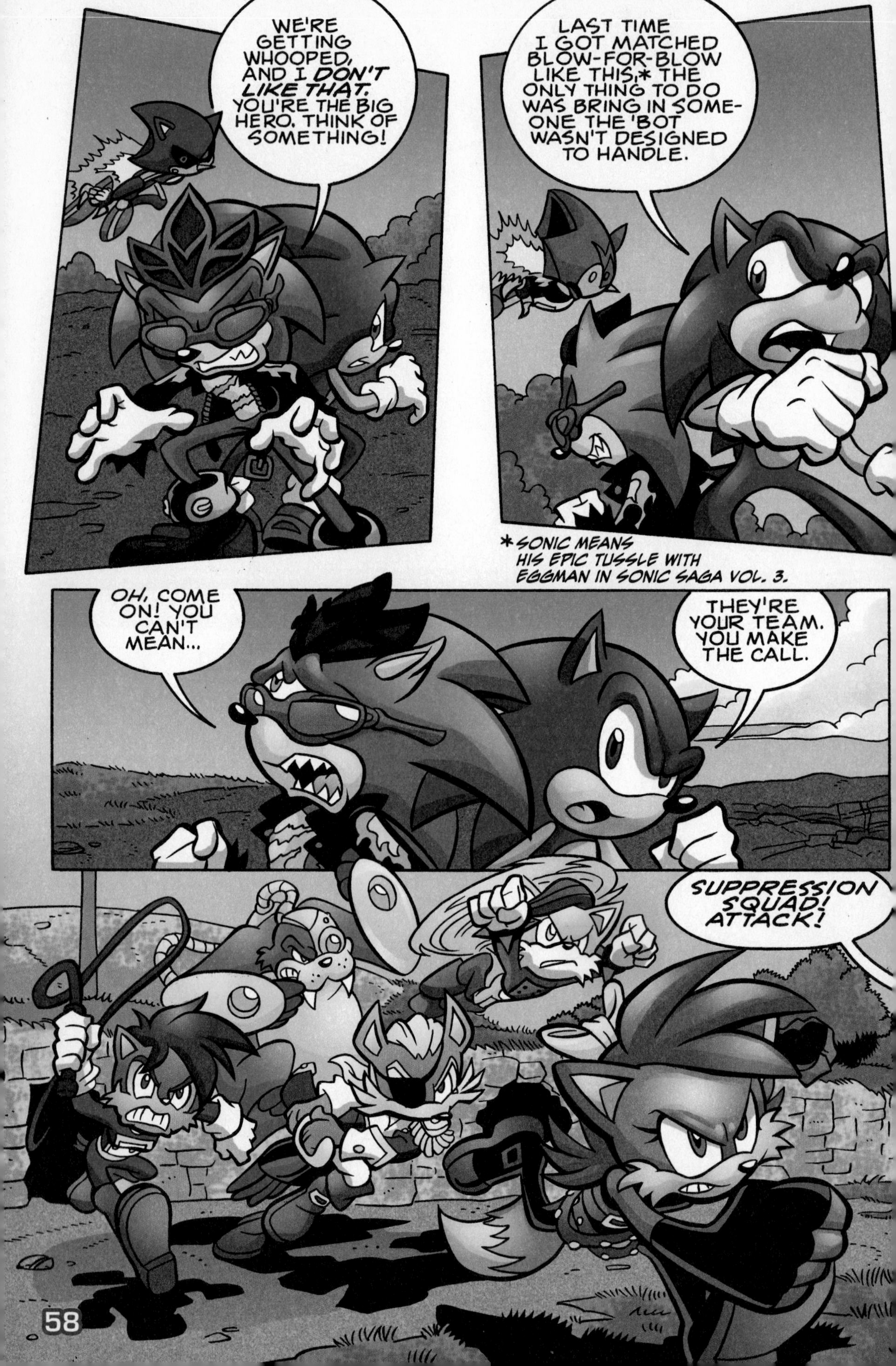
WE'RE GETTING WHOOPED, AND I DON'T LIKE THAT. YOU'RE THE BIG HERO. THINK OF SOMETHING!
LAST TIME I GOT MATCHED BLOW-FOR-BLOW LIKE THIS,* THE ONLY THING TO DO WAS BRING IN SOME-ONE THE 'BOT WASN'T DESIGNED TO HANDLE.
*SONIC MEANS HIS EPIC TUSSLE WITH EGGMAN IN SONIC SAGA VOL. 3.
OH, COME ON! YOU CAN'T MEAN...
THEY'RE YOUR TEAM. YOU MAKE THE CALL.
SUPPRESSION SQUAD! ATTACK!

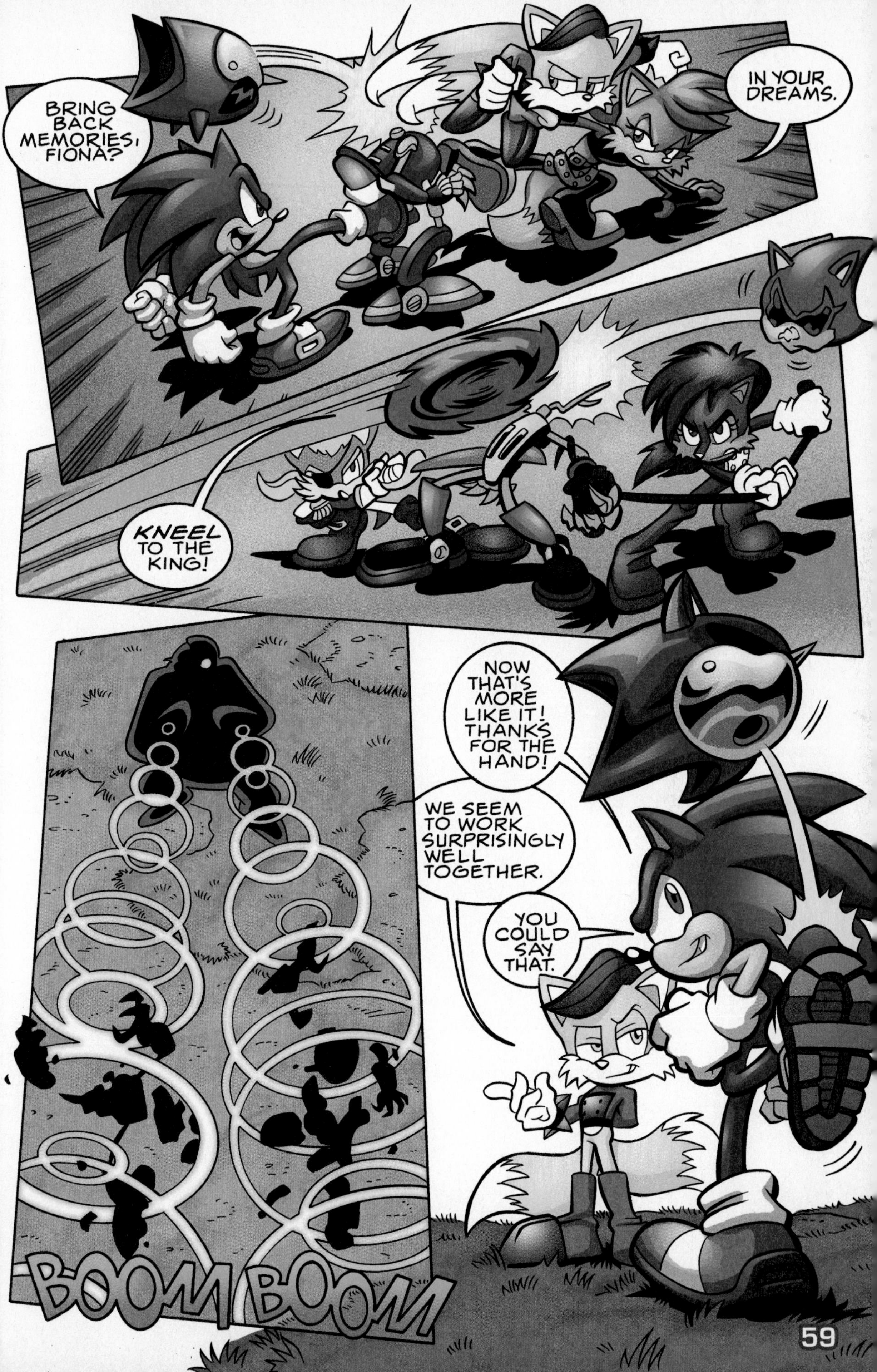
BRING BACK MEMORIES, FIONA?
IN YOUR DREAMS.
KNEEL TO THE KING!
BOOM BOOM
NOW THAT'S MORE LIKE IT! THANKS FOR THE HAND!
WE SEEM TO WORK SURPRISINGLY WELL TOGETHER.
YOU COULD SAY THAT.

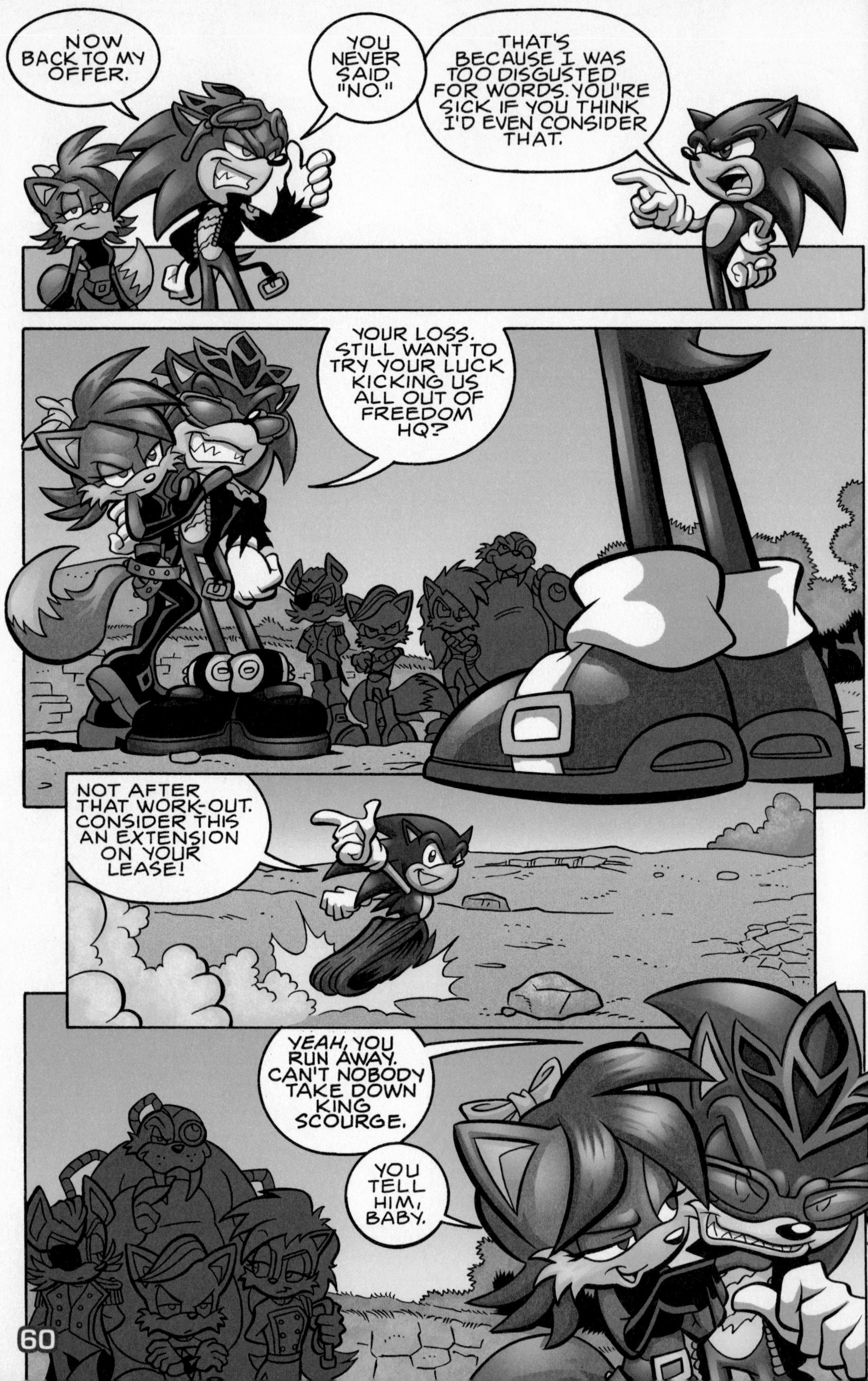
NOW BACK TO MY OFFER.
YOU NEVER SAID "NO."
THAT'S BECAUSE I WAS TOO DISGUSTED FOR WORDS. YOU'RE SICK IF YOU THINK I'D EVEN CONSIDER THAT.
YOUR LOSS. STILL WANT TO TRY YOUR LUCK KICKING US ALL OUT OF FREEDOM HQ?
NOT AFTER THAT WORK-OUT. CONSIDER THIS AN EXTENSION ON YOUR LEASE!
YEAH, YOU RUN AWAY. CAN'T NOBODY TAKE DOWN KING SCOURGE.
YOU TELL HIM, BABY.

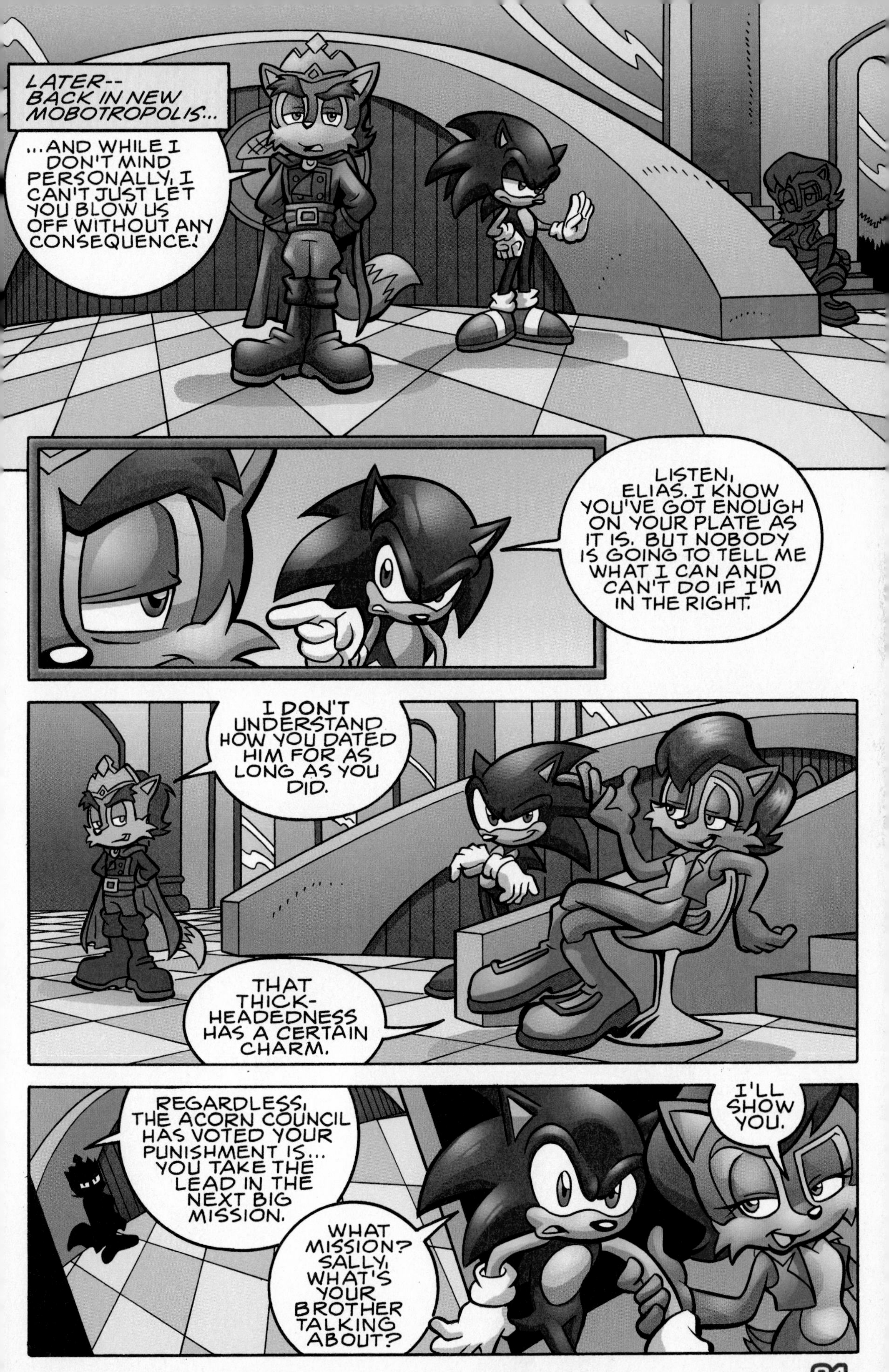
LATER-- BACK IN NEW MOBOTROPOLIS...
...AND WHILE I DON'T MIND PERSONALLY, I CAN'T JUST LET YOU BLOW US OFF WITHOUT ANY CONSEQUENCE!
LISTEN, ELIAS. I KNOW YOU'VE GOT ENOUGH ON YOUR PLATE AS IT IS. BUT NOBODY IS GOING TO TELL ME WHAT I CAN AND CAN'T DO IF I'M IN THE RIGHT.
I DON'T UNDERSTAND HOW YOU DATED HIM FOR AS LONG AS YOU DID.
THAT THICK-HEADEDNESS HAS A CERTAIN CHARM.
REGARDLESS, THE ACORN COUNCIL HAS VOTED YOUR PUNISHMENT IS... YOU TAKE THE LEAD IN THE NEXT BIG MISSION.
WHAT MISSION? SALLY, WHAT'S YOUR BROTHER TALKING ABOUT?
I'LL SHOW YOU.

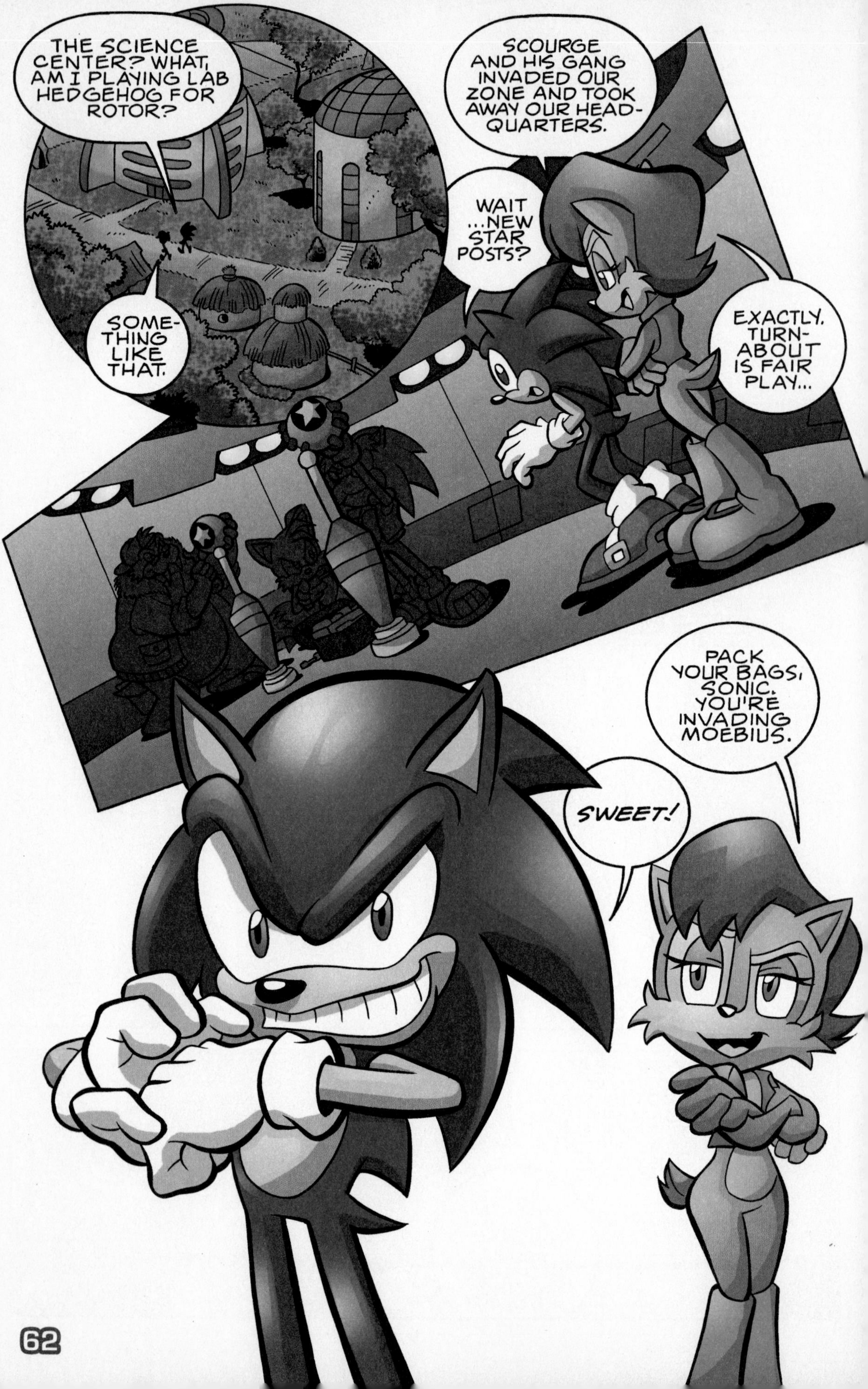
THE SCIENCE CENTER? WHAT, AM I PLAYING LAB HEDGEHOG FOR ROTOR?
SOMETHING LIKE THAT.
SCOURGE AND HIS GANG INVADED OUR ZONE AND TOOK AWAY OUR HEADQUARTERS.
WAIT ...NEW STAR POSTS?
EXACTLY. TURN-ABOUT IS FAIR PLAY...
PACK YOUR BAGS, SONIC. YOU'RE INVADING MOEBIUS.
SWEET!

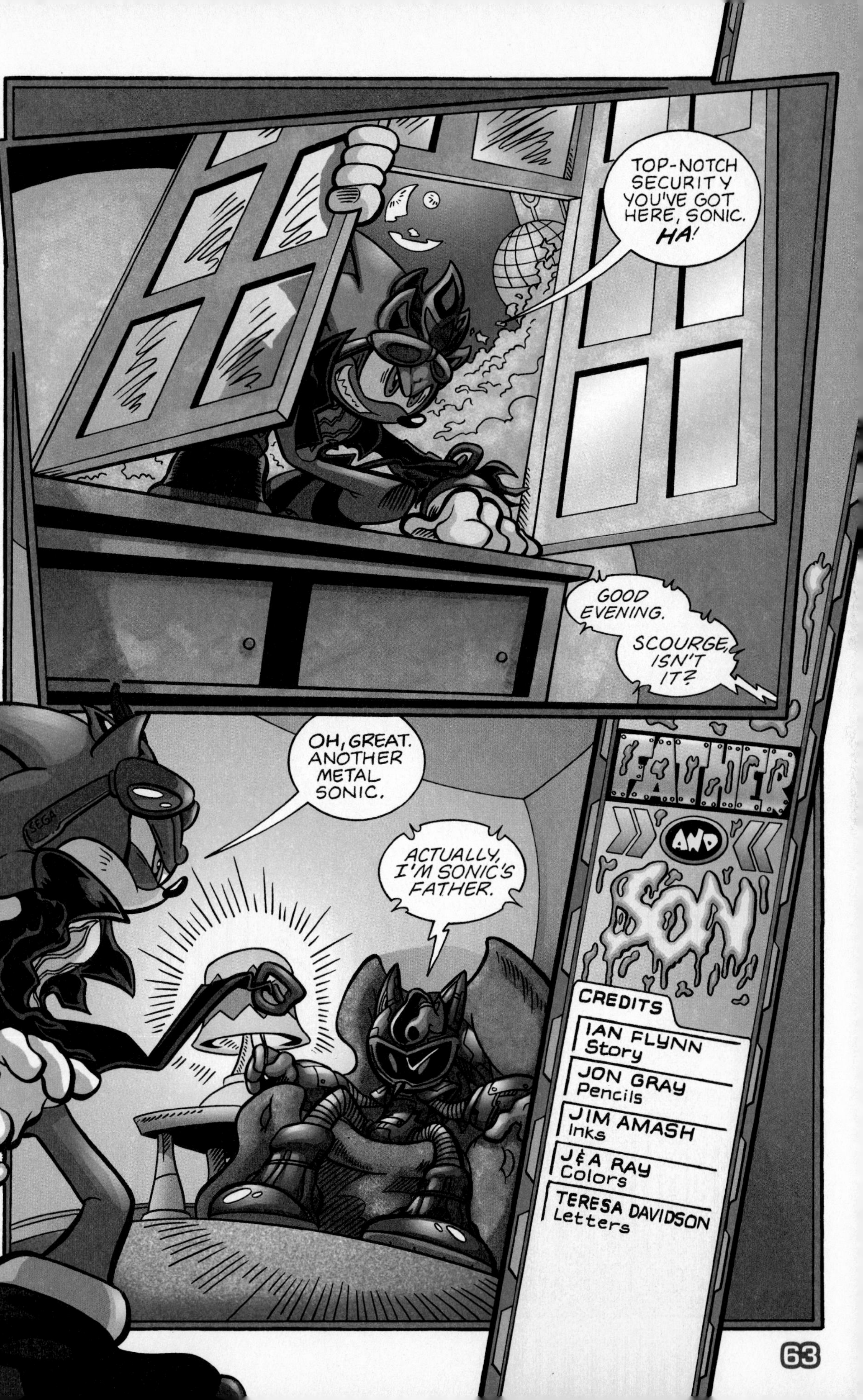
TOP-NOTCH SECURITY YOU'VE GOT HERE, SONIC. HA!
GOOD EVENING.
SCOURGE, ISN'T IT?
OH, GREAT. ANOTHER METAL SONIC.
ACTUALLY, I'M SONIC'S FATHER.
FATHER AND SON
CREDITS
IAN FLYNN Story
JON GRAY Pencils
JIM AMASH Inks
J&A RAY Colors
TERESA DAVIDSON Letters

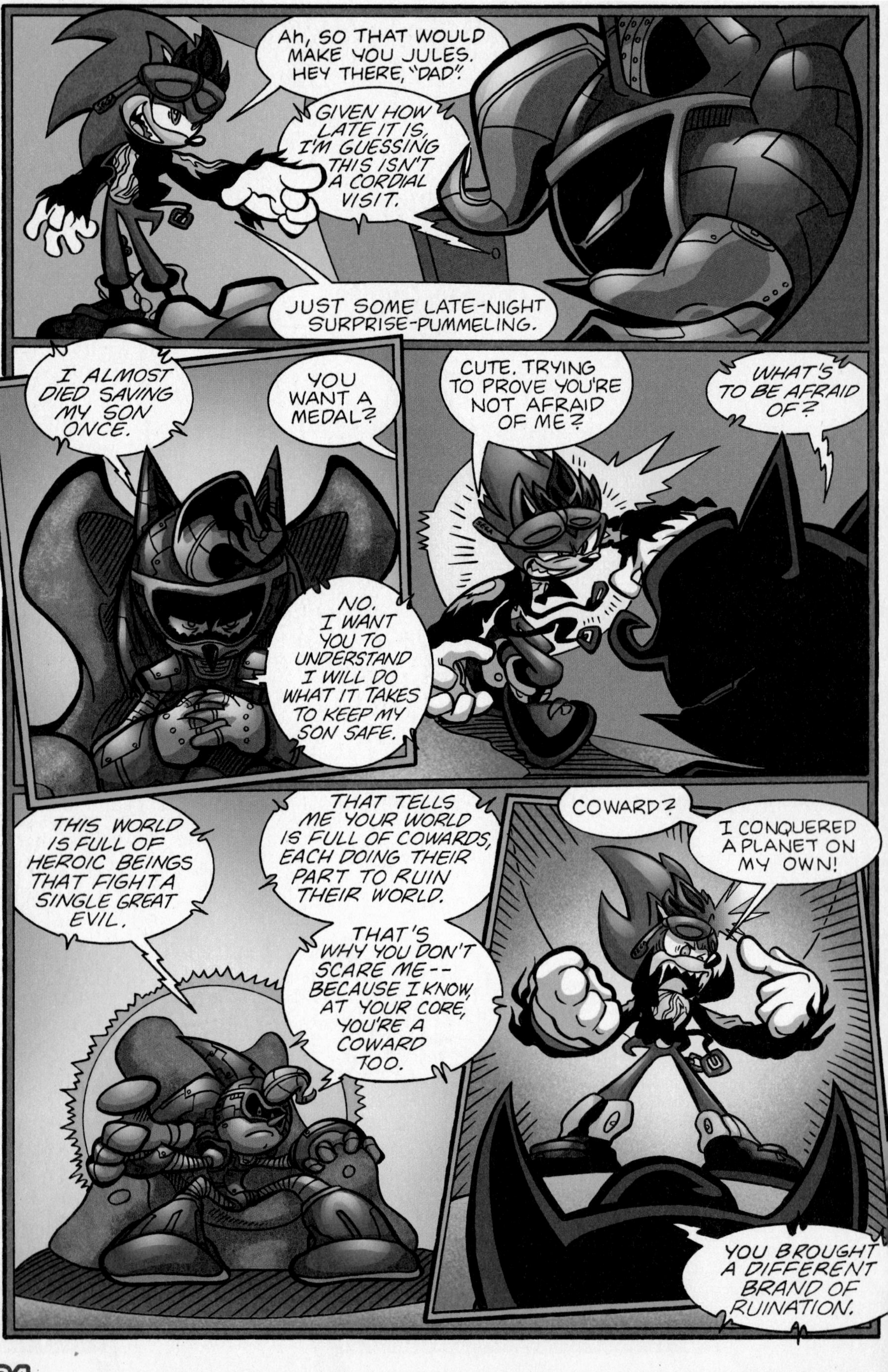
Ah, SO THAT WOULD MAKE YOU JULES. HEY THERE, "DAD".
GIVEN HOW LATE IT IS, I'M GUESSING THIS ISN'T A CORDIAL VISIT.
JUST SOME LATE-NIGHT SURPRISE-PUMMELING.
I ALMOST DIED SAVING MY SON ONCE.
YOU WANT A MEDAL?
NO. I WANT YOU TO UNDERSTAND I WILL DO WHAT IT TAKES TO KEEP MY SON SAFE.
CUTE. TRYING TO PROVE YOU'RE NOT AFRAID OF ME?
WHAT'S TO BE AFRAID OF?
THIS WORLD IS FULL OF HEROIC BEINGS THAT FIGHT A SINGLE GREAT EVIL.
THAT TELLS ME YOUR WORLD IS FULL OF COWARDS, EACH DOING THEIR PART TO RUIN THEIR WORLD.
THAT'S WHY YOU DON'T SCARE ME-- BECAUSE I KNOW, AT YOUR CORE, YOU'RE A COWARD TOO.
COWARD?
I CONQUERED A PLANET ON MY OWN!
YOU BROUGHT A DIFFERENT BRAND OF RUINATION.

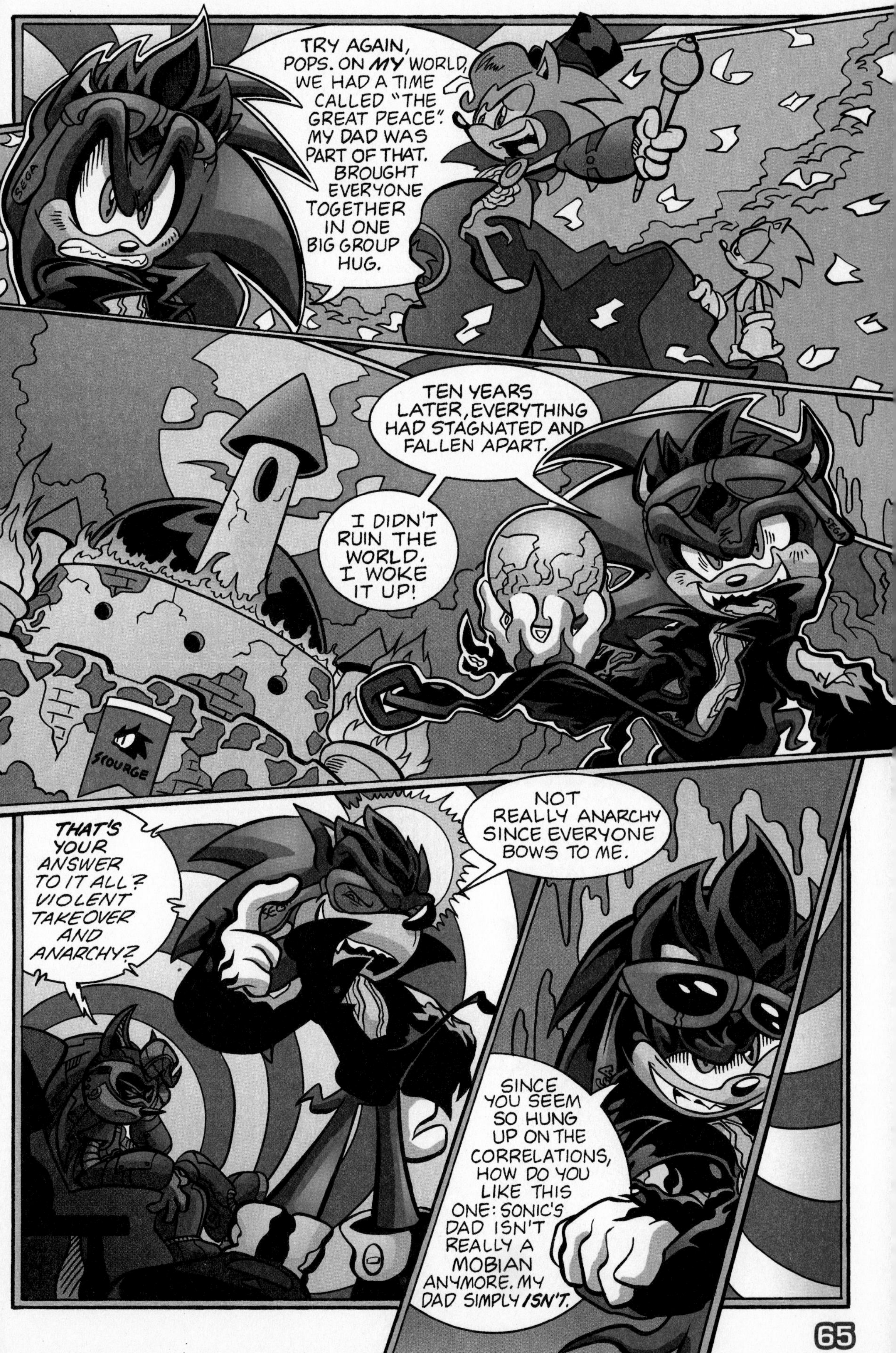
TRY AGAIN, POPS. ON MY WORLD, WE HAD A TIME CALLED "THE GREAT PEACE". MY DAD WAS PART OF THAT. BROUGHT EVERYONE TOGETHER IN ONE BIG GROUP HUG.
TEN YEARS LATER, EVERYTHING HAD STAGNATED AND FALLEN APART.
I DIDN'T RUIN THE WORLD. I WOKE IT UP!
SCOURGE
THAT'S YOUR ANSWER TO IT ALL? VIOLENT TAKEOVER AND ANARCHY?
NOT REALLY ANARCHY SINCE EVERYONE BOWS TO ME.
SINCE YOU SEEM SO HUNG UP ON THE CORRELATIONS, HOW DO YOU LIKE THIS ONE: SONIC'S DAD ISN'T REALLY A MOBIAN ANYMORE. MY DAD SIMPLY ISN'T.

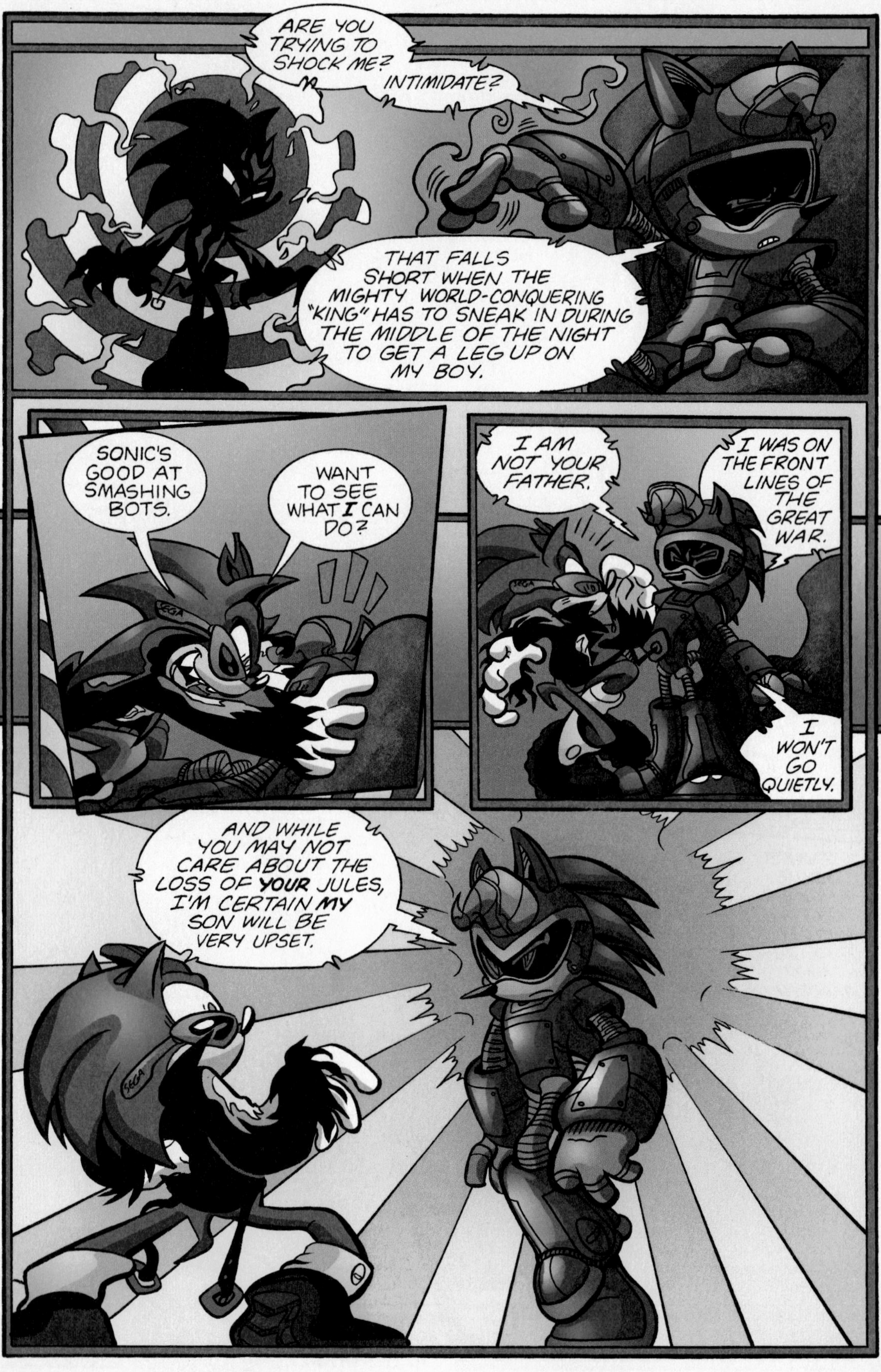
ARE YOU TRYING TO SHOCK ME? INTIMIDATE?
THAT FALLS SHORT WHEN THE MIGHTY WORLD-CONQUERING "KING" HAS TO SNEAK IN DURING THE MIDDLE OF THE NIGHT TO GET A LEG UP ON MY BOY.
SONIC'S GOOD AT SMASHING BOTS.
WANT TO SEE WHAT I CAN DO?
I AM NOT YOUR FATHER.
I WAS ON THE FRONT LINES OF THE GREAT WAR.
I WON'T GO QUIETLY.
AND WHILE YOU MAY NOT CARE ABOUT THE LOSS OF YOUR JULES, I'M CERTAIN MY SON WILL BE VERY UPSET.

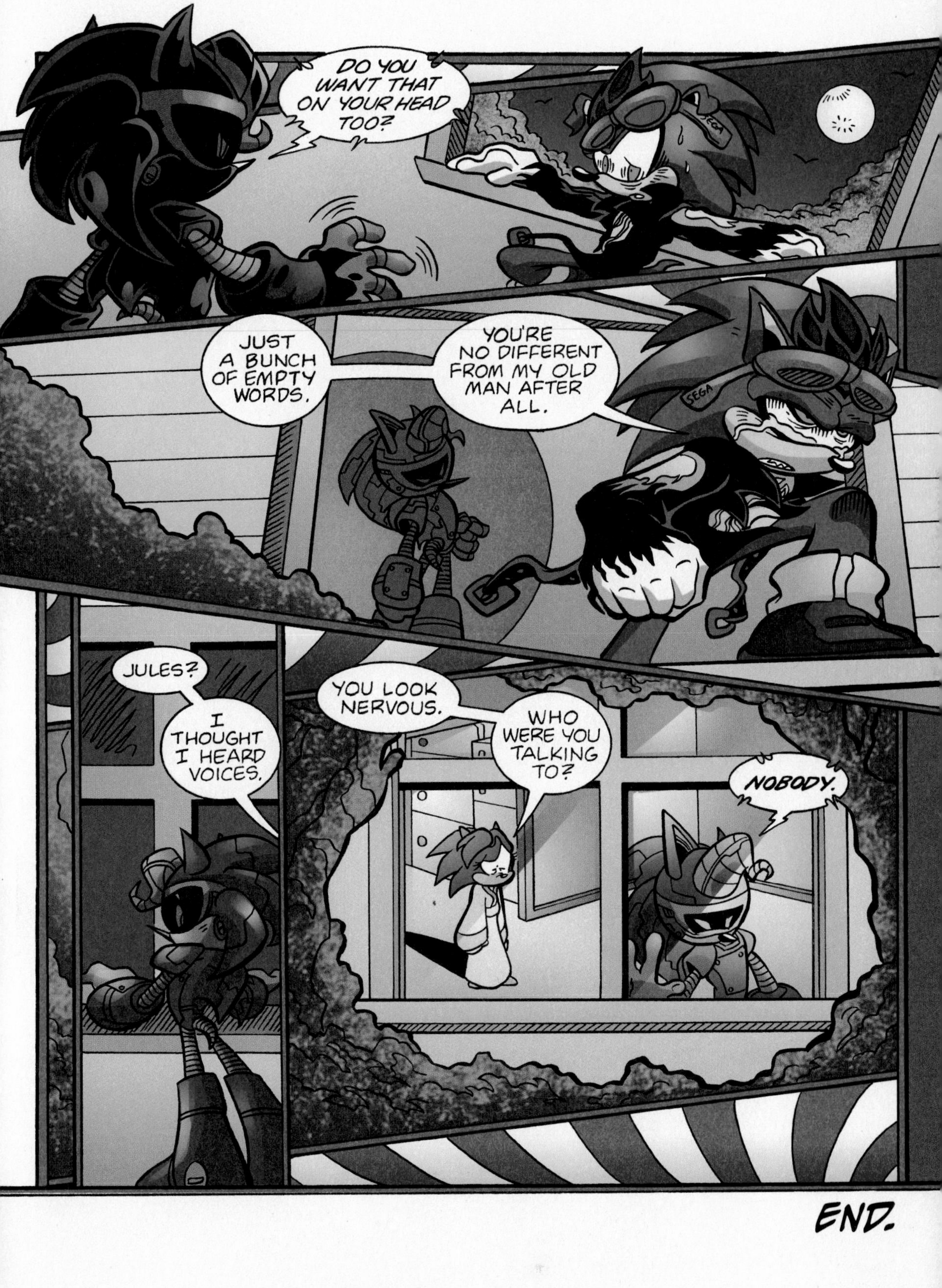
DO YOU WANT THAT ON YOUR HEAD TOO?
JUST A BUNCH OF EMPTY WORDS.
YOU'RE NO DIFFERENT FROM MY OLD MAN AFTER ALL.
JULES?
I THOUGHT I HEARD VOICES.
YOU LOOK NERVOUS.
WHO WERE YOU TALKING TO?
NOBODY.

END.

CHAPTER 4

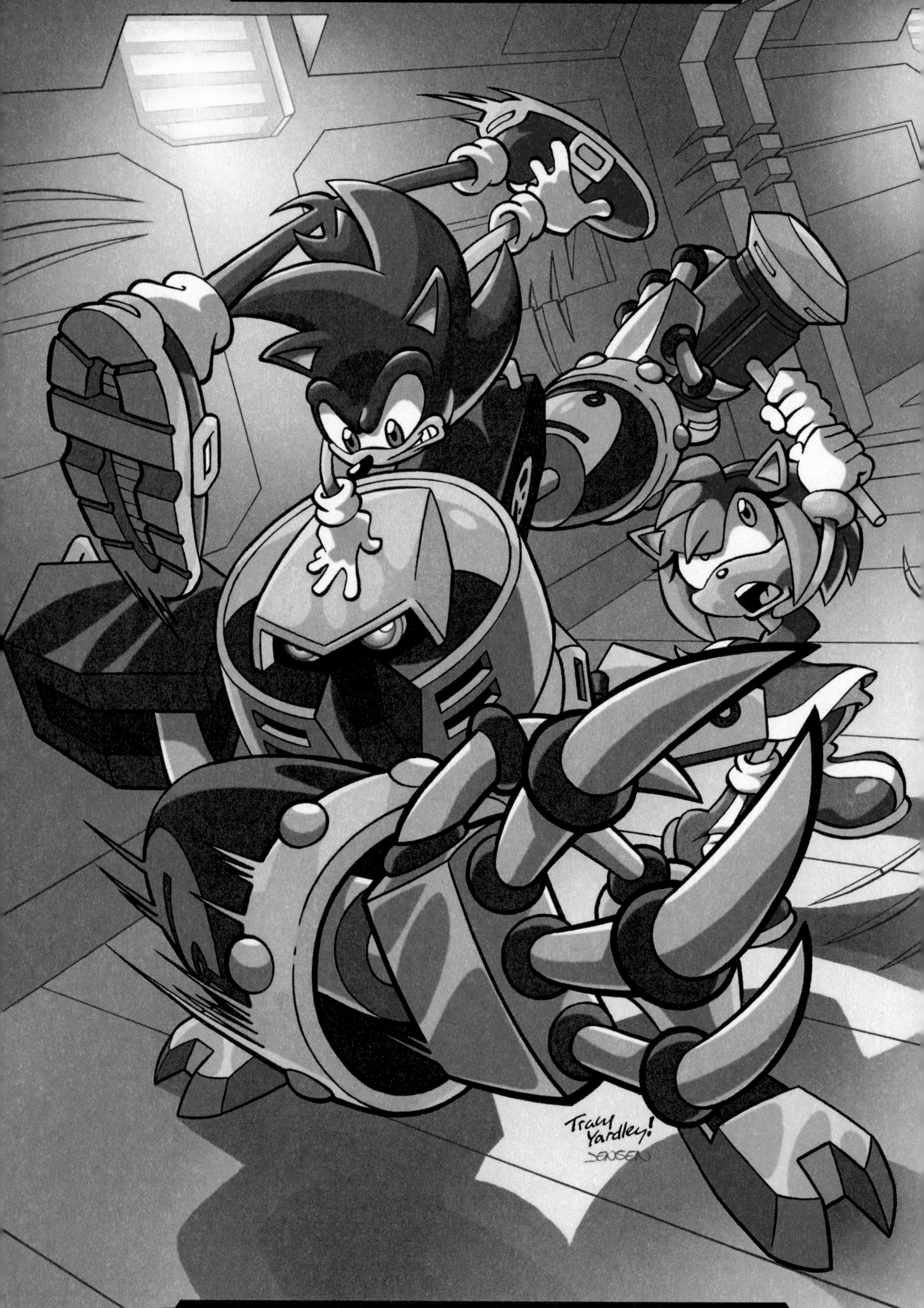
Tracy Yardley!
JENSEN

SONIC THE HEDGEHOG 193
COVER BY TRACY YARDLEY AND JASON JENSEN

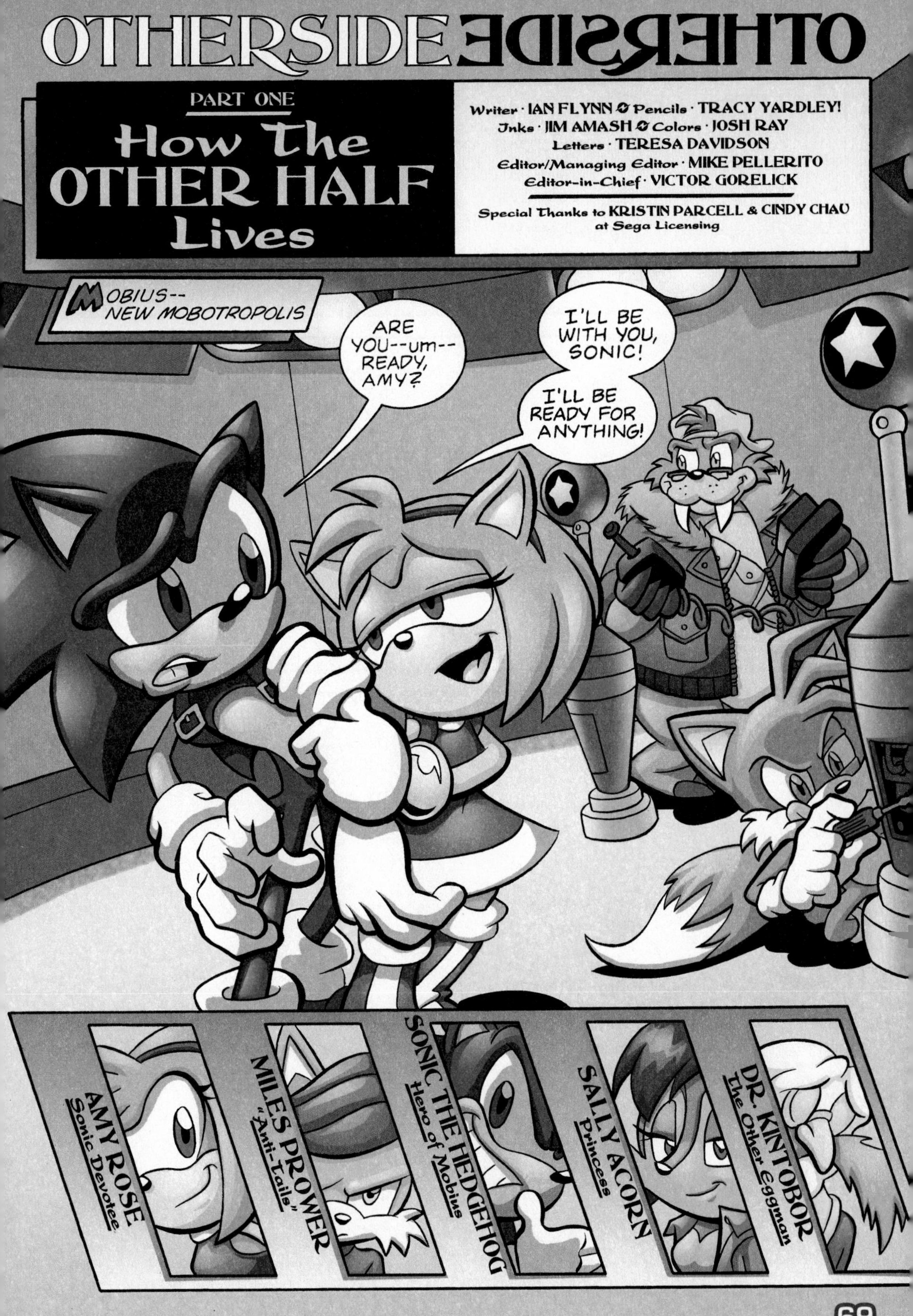
OTHERSIDE OTHERSIDE
PART ONE
How The OTHER HALF Lives
Writer · IAN FLYNN Pencils · TRACY YARDLEY!
Inks · JIM AMASH Colors · JOSH RAY
Letters · TERESA DAVIDSON
Editor/Managing Editor · MIKE PELLERITO
Editor-in-Chief · VICTOR GORELICK
Special Thanks to KRISTIN PARCELL & CINDY CHAU at Sega Licensing
MOBIUS-- NEW MOBOTROPOLIS
ARE YOU--um-- READY, AMY?
I'LL BE WITH YOU, SONIC!
I'LL BE READY FOR ANYTHING!
AMY ROSE Sonic Devotee
MILES PROWER "Anti-Tails"
SONIC THE HEDGEHOG Hero of Mobius
SALLY ACORN Princess
DR. KINTOBOR The Other Eggman

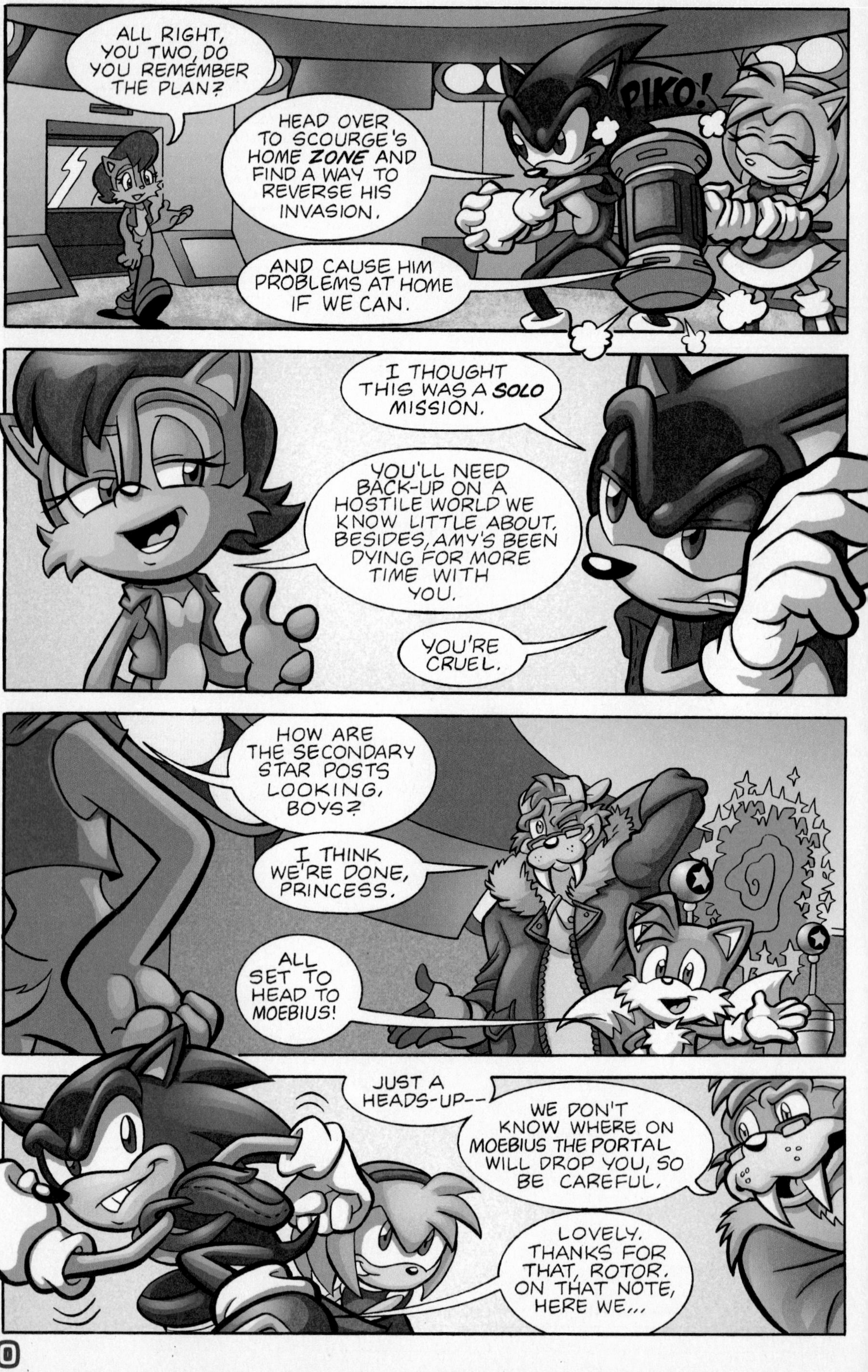
ALL RIGHT, YOU TWO, DO YOU REMEMBER THE PLAN?
HEAD OVER TO SCOURGE'S HOME *ZONE* AND FIND A WAY TO REVERSE HIS INVASION.
AND CAUSE HIM PROBLEMS AT HOME IF WE CAN.
PIKO!
I THOUGHT THIS WAS A *SOLO* MISSION.
YOU'LL NEED BACK-UP ON A HOSTILE WORLD WE KNOW LITTLE ABOUT. BESIDES, AMY'S BEEN DYING FOR MORE TIME WITH YOU.
YOU'RE CRUEL.
HOW ARE THE SECONDARY STAR POSTS LOOKING, BOYS?
I THINK WE'RE DONE, PRINCESS.
ALL SET TO HEAD TO MOEBIUS!
JUST A HEADS-UP--
WE DON'T KNOW WHERE ON MOEBIUS THE PORTAL WILL DROP YOU, SO BE CAREFUL.
LOVELY. THANKS FOR THAT, ROTOR. ON THAT NOTE, HERE WE...

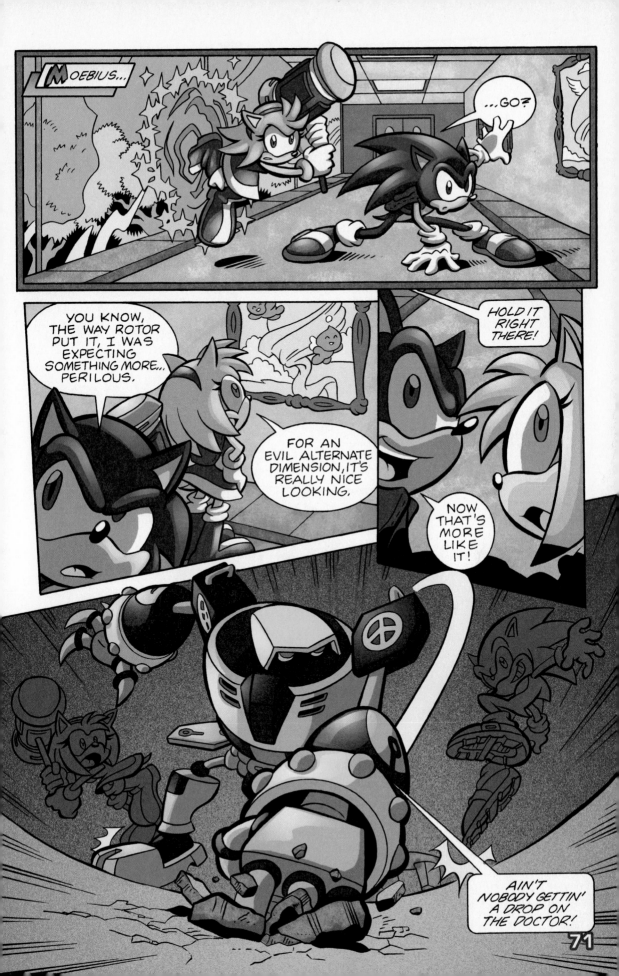

MOEBIUS...

...GO?

YOU KNOW, THE WAY ROTOR PUT IT, I WAS EXPECTING SOMETHING MORE... PERILOUS.

FOR AN EVIL ALTERNATE DIMENSION, IT'S REALLY NICE LOOKING.

HOLD IT RIGHT THERE!

NOW THAT'S MORE LIKE IT!

AIN'T NOBODY GETTIN' A DROP ON THE DOCTOR!

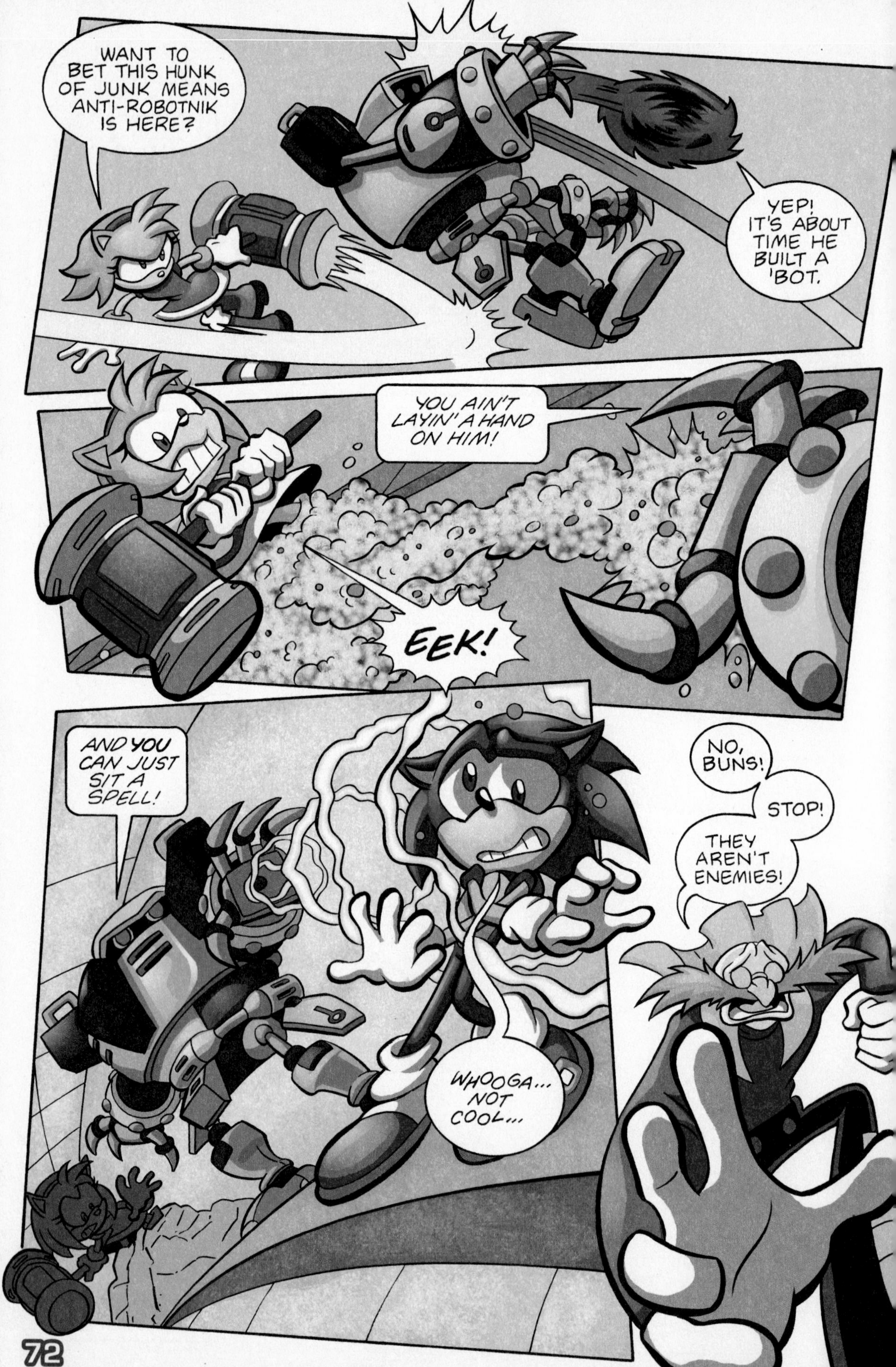
WANT TO BET THIS HUNK OF JUNK MEANS ANTI-ROBOTNIK IS HERE?
YEP! IT'S ABOUT TIME HE BUILT A 'BOT.
YOU AIN'T LAYIN' A HAND ON HIM!
EEK!
AND YOU CAN JUST SIT A SPELL!
NO, BUNS!
STOP!
THEY AREN'T ENEMIES!
WHOOGA... NOT COOL...

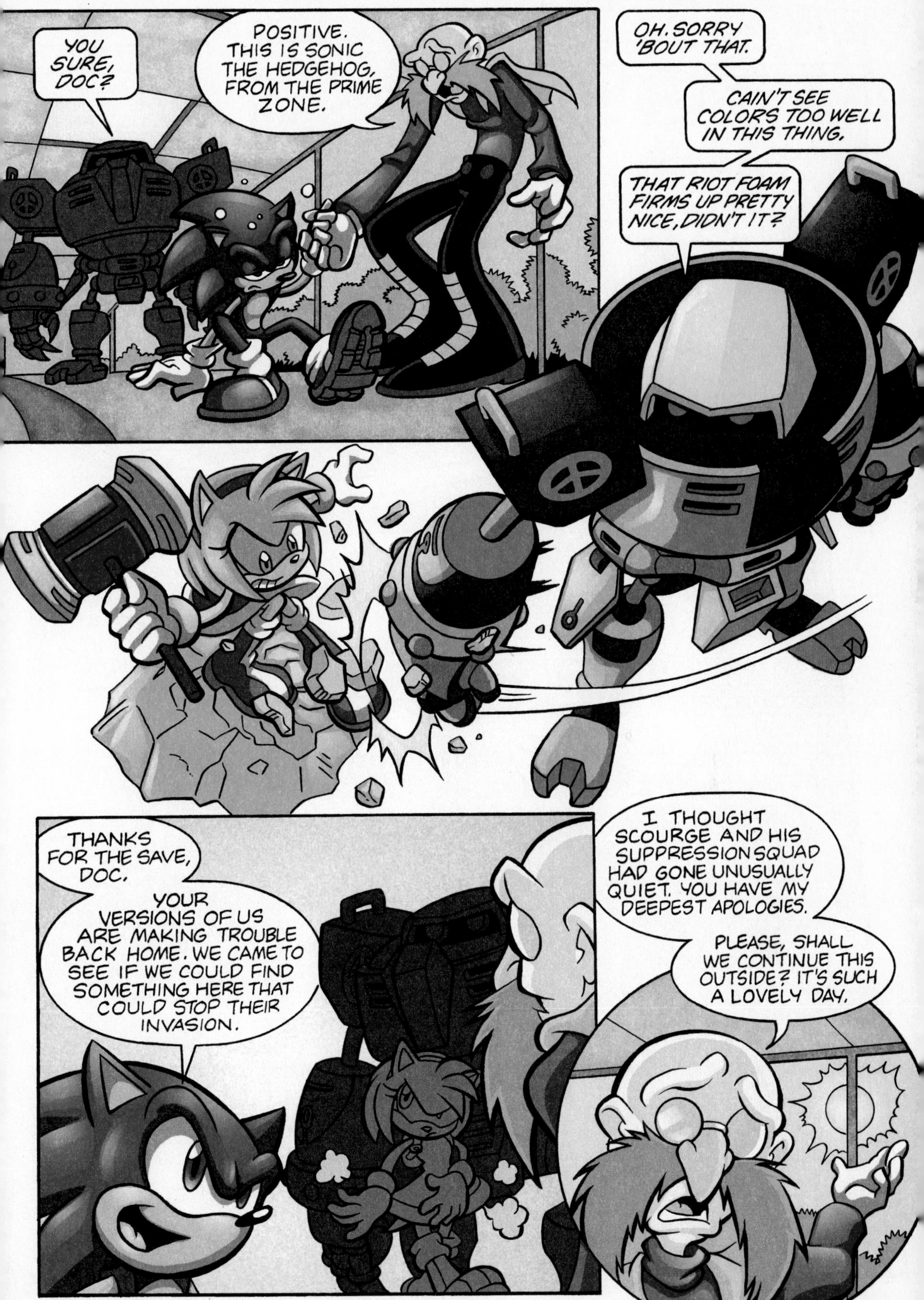
YOU SURE, DOC?
POSITIVE. THIS IS SONIC THE HEDGEHOG, FROM THE PRIME ZONE.
OH. SORRY 'BOUT THAT.
CAIN'T SEE COLORS TOO WELL IN THIS THING.
THAT RIOT FOAM FIRMS UP PRETTY NICE, DIDN'T IT?
THANKS FOR THE SAVE, DOC.
YOUR VERSIONS OF US ARE MAKING TROUBLE BACK HOME. WE CAME TO SEE IF WE COULD FIND SOMETHING HERE THAT COULD STOP THEIR INVASION.
I THOUGHT SCOURGE AND HIS SUPPRESSION SQUAD HAD GONE UNUSUALLY QUIET. YOU HAVE MY DEEPEST APOLOGIES.
PLEASE, SHALL WE CONTINUE THIS OUTSIDE? IT'S SUCH A LOVELY DAY.

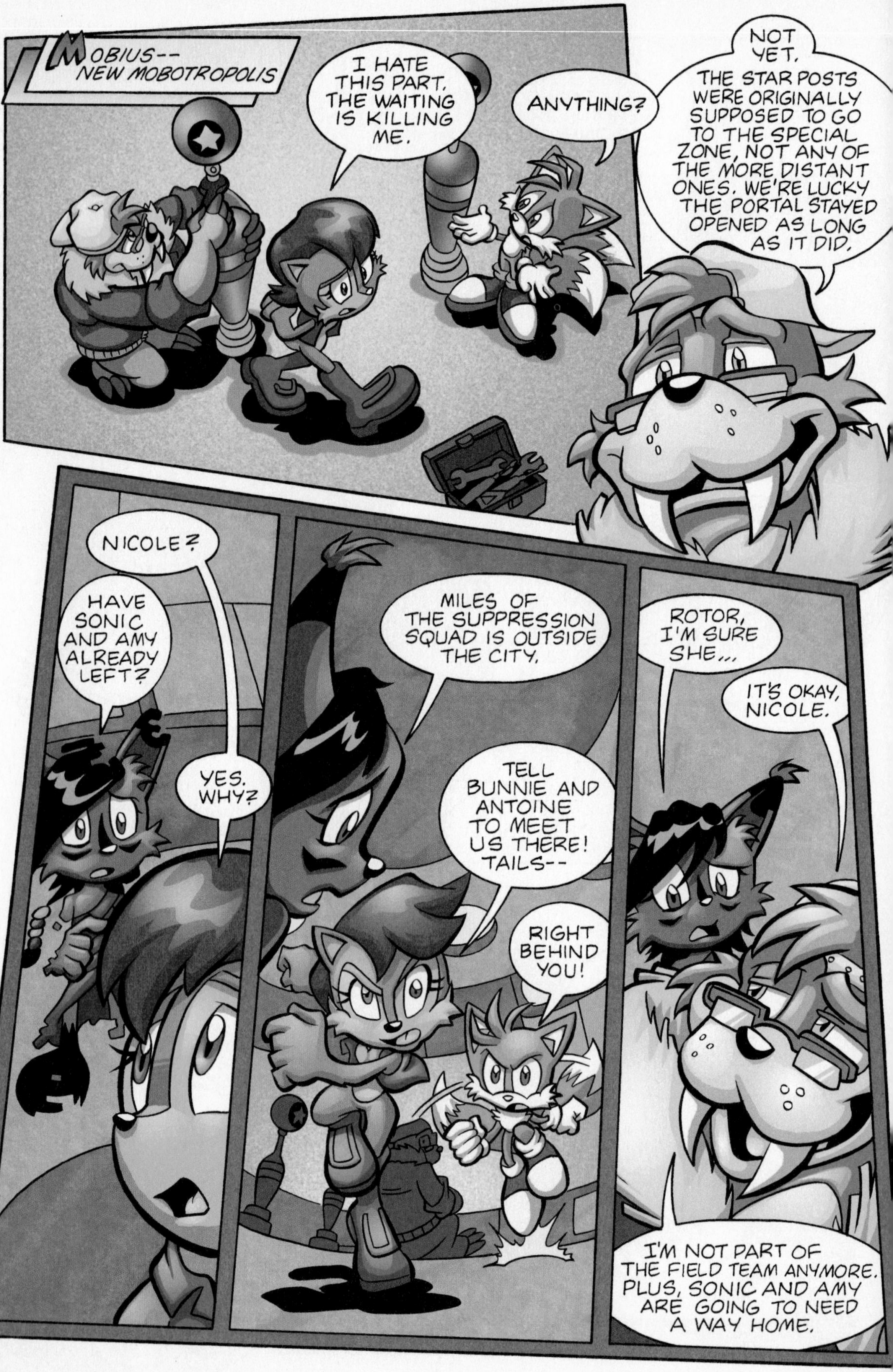
MOBIUS--
NEW MOBOTROPOLIS
I HATE THIS PART. THE WAITING IS KILLING ME.
ANYTHING?
NOT YET.
THE STAR POSTS WERE ORIGINALLY SUPPOSED TO GO TO THE SPECIAL ZONE, NOT ANY OF THE MORE DISTANT ONES. WE'RE LUCKY THE PORTAL STAYED OPENED AS LONG AS IT DID.
NICOLE?
HAVE SONIC AND AMY ALREADY LEFT?
YES. WHY?
MILES OF THE SUPPRESSION SQUAD IS OUTSIDE THE CITY.
TELL BUNNIE AND ANTOINE TO MEET US THERE! TAILS--
RIGHT BEHIND YOU!
ROTOR, I'M SURE SHE...
IT'S OKAY, NICOLE.
I'M NOT PART OF THE FIELD TEAM ANYMORE. PLUS, SONIC AND AMY ARE GOING TO NEED A WAY HOME.

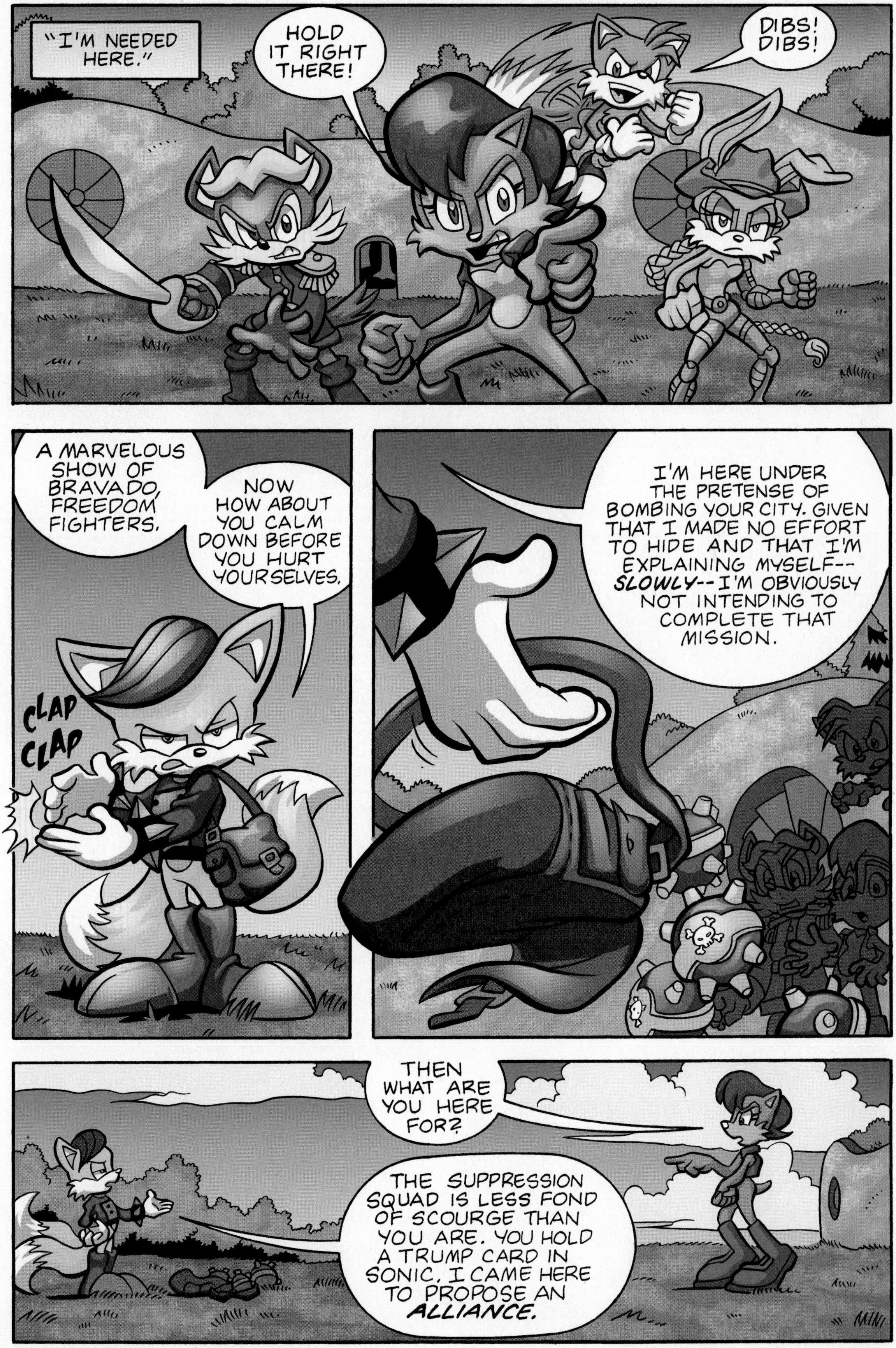
"I'M NEEDED HERE."
HOLD IT RIGHT THERE!
DIBS! DIBS!
A MARVELOUS SHOW OF BRAVADO, FREEDOM FIGHTERS.
NOW HOW ABOUT YOU CALM DOWN BEFORE YOU HURT YOURSELVES.
CLAP CLAP
I'M HERE UNDER THE PRETENSE OF BOMBING YOUR CITY. GIVEN THAT I MADE NO EFFORT TO HIDE AND THAT I'M EXPLAINING MYSELF-- SLOWLY-- I'M OBVIOUSLY NOT INTENDING TO COMPLETE THAT MISSION.
THEN WHAT ARE YOU HERE FOR?
THE SUPPRESSION SQUAD IS LESS FOND OF SCOURGE THAN YOU ARE. YOU HOLD A TRUMP CARD IN SONIC. I CAME HERE TO PROPOSE AN ALLIANCE.

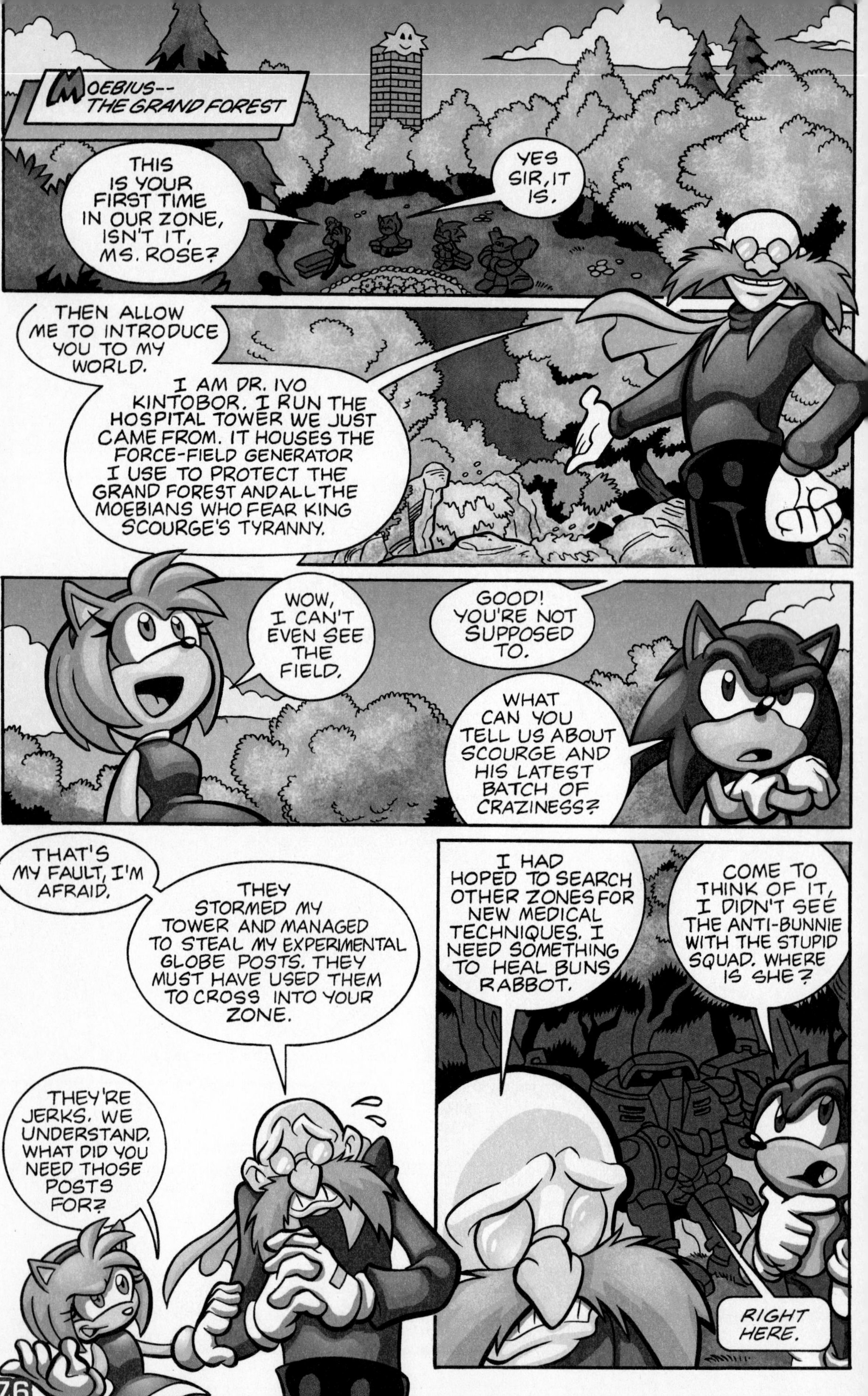
MOEBIUS-- THE GRAND FOREST
THIS IS YOUR FIRST TIME IN OUR ZONE, ISN'T IT, MS. ROSE?
YES SIR, IT IS.
THEN ALLOW ME TO INTRODUCE YOU TO MY WORLD.
I AM DR. IVO KINTOBOR. I RUN THE HOSPITAL TOWER WE JUST CAME FROM. IT HOUSES THE FORCE-FIELD GENERATOR I USE TO PROTECT THE GRAND FOREST AND ALL THE MOEBIANS WHO FEAR KING SCOURGE'S TYRANNY.
WOW, I CAN'T EVEN SEE THE FIELD.
GOOD! YOU'RE NOT SUPPOSED TO.
WHAT CAN YOU TELL US ABOUT SCOURGE AND HIS LATEST BATCH OF CRAZINESS?
THAT'S MY FAULT, I'M AFRAID.
THEY STORMED MY TOWER AND MANAGED TO STEAL MY EXPERIMENTAL GLOBE POSTS. THEY MUST HAVE USED THEM TO CROSS INTO YOUR ZONE.
THEY'RE JERKS. WE UNDERSTAND. WHAT DID YOU NEED THOSE POSTS FOR?
I HAD HOPED TO SEARCH OTHER ZONES FOR NEW MEDICAL TECHNIQUES. I NEED SOMETHING TO HEAL BUNS RABBOT.
COME TO THINK OF IT, I DIDN'T SEE THE ANTI-BUNNIE WITH THE STUPID SQUAD. WHERE IS SHE?
RIGHT HERE.

NOT LONG AGO, I DEVELOPED N.I.D.S. STARTED IN THE BASE OF MAH SPINE. SCOURGE KICKED ME OUT AND LEFT ME FOR DEAD.

THE DOC HERE TOOK ME IN AND BUILT ME THIS SUIT.

IT WAS THE LEAST I COULD DO. MY OMEGA CARE UNIT CREATES A STASIS FIELD THAT PREVENTS HER CONDITION FROM PROGRESSING AND SUPPORTS HER IMMUNE SYSTEM.

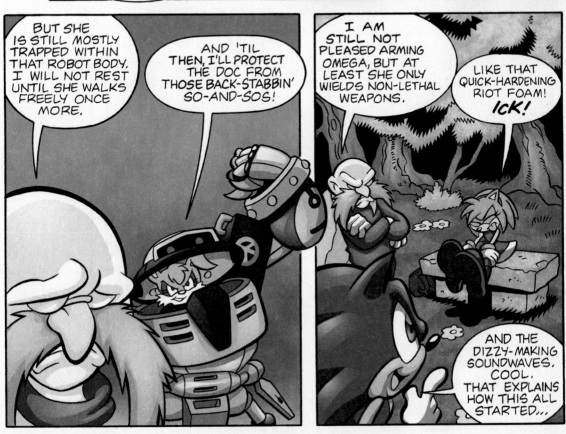

BUT SHE IS STILL MOSTLY TRAPPED WITHIN THAT ROBOT BODY. I WILL NOT REST UNTIL SHE WALKS FREELY ONCE MORE.

AND 'TIL THEN, I'LL PROTECT THE DOC FROM THOSE BACK-STABBIN' SO-AND-SOS!

I AM STILL NOT PLEASED ARMING OMEGA, BUT AT LEAST SHE ONLY WIELDS NON-LETHAL WEAPONS.

LIKE THAT QUICK-HARDENING RIOT FOAM! *ICK!*

AND THE DIZZY-MAKING SOUNDWAVES. COOL. THAT EXPLAINS HOW THIS ALL STARTED...

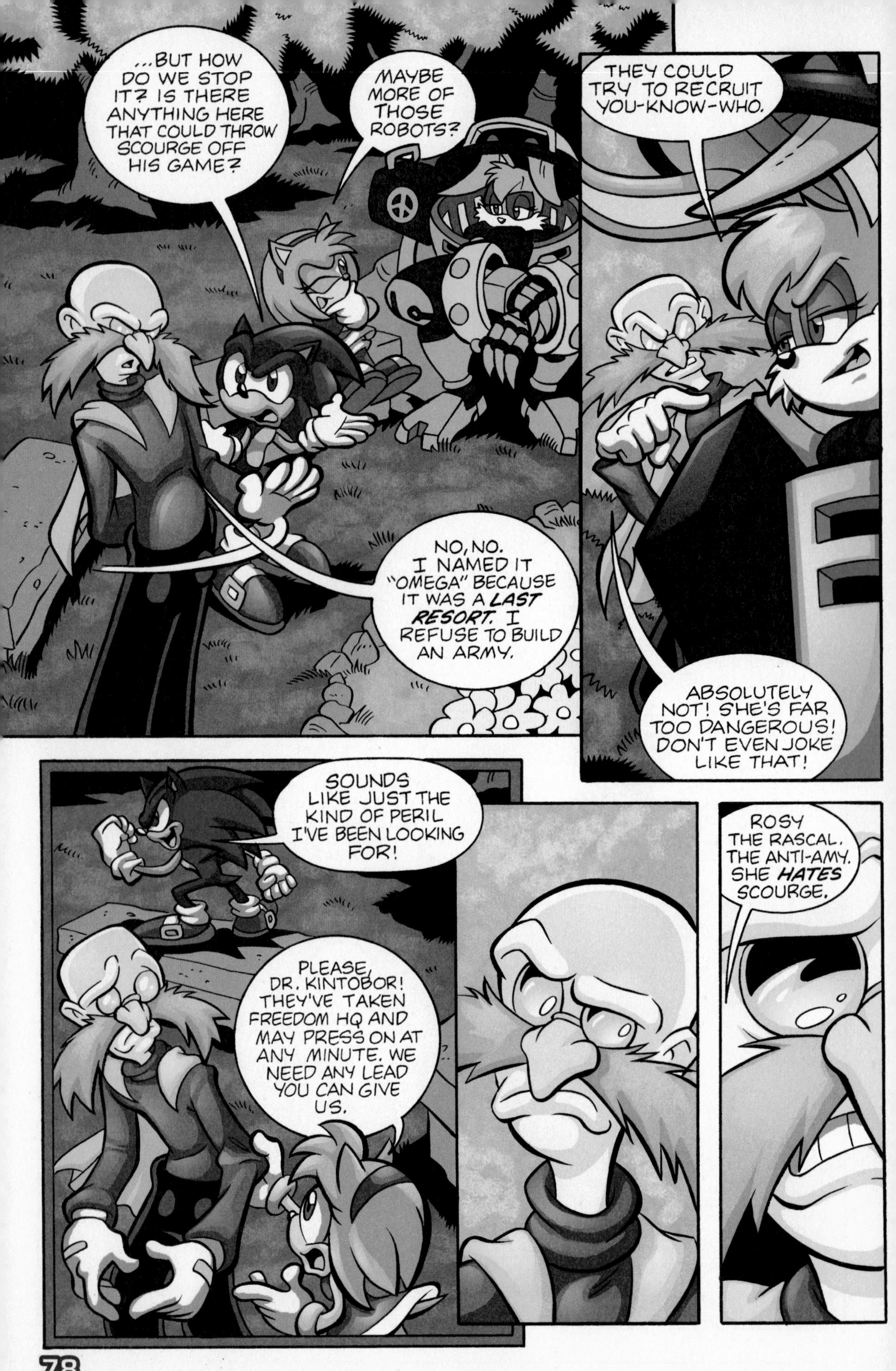
...BUT HOW DO WE STOP IT? IS THERE ANYTHING HERE THAT COULD THROW SCOURGE OFF HIS GAME?
MAYBE MORE OF THOSE ROBOTS?
NO, NO. I NAMED IT "OMEGA" BECAUSE IT WAS A LAST RESORT. I REFUSE TO BUILD AN ARMY.
THEY COULD TRY TO RECRUIT YOU-KNOW-WHO.
ABSOLUTELY NOT! SHE'S FAR TOO DANGEROUS! DON'T EVEN JOKE LIKE THAT!
SOUNDS LIKE JUST THE KIND OF PERIL I'VE BEEN LOOKING FOR!
PLEASE, DR. KINTOBOR! THEY'VE TAKEN FREEDOM HQ AND MAY PRESS ON AT ANY MINUTE. WE NEED ANY LEAD YOU CAN GIVE US.
ROSY THE RASCAL. THE ANTI-AMY. SHE HATES SCOURGE.

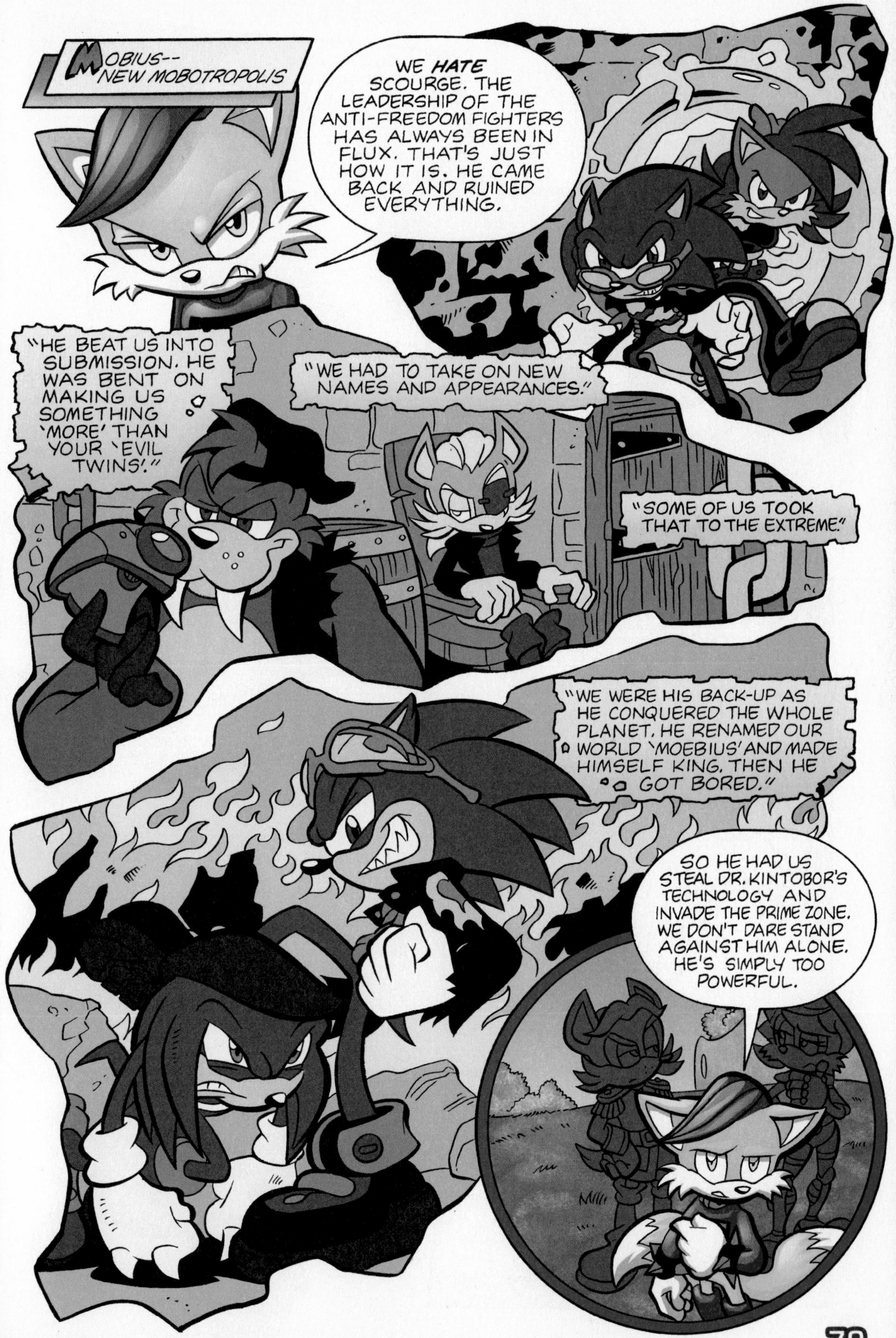
MOBIUS--
NEW MOBOTROPOLIS
WE **HATE** SCOURGE. THE LEADERSHIP OF THE ANTI-FREEDOM FIGHTERS HAS ALWAYS BEEN IN FLUX. THAT'S JUST HOW IT IS. HE CAME BACK AND RUINED EVERYTHING.
"HE BEAT US INTO SUBMISSION. HE WAS BENT ON MAKING US SOMETHING 'MORE' THAN YOUR 'EVIL TWINS'."
"WE HAD TO TAKE ON NEW NAMES AND APPEARANCES."
"SOME OF US TOOK THAT TO THE EXTREME."
"WE WERE HIS BACK-UP AS HE CONQUERED THE WHOLE PLANET. HE RENAMED OUR WORLD 'MOEBIUS' AND MADE HIMSELF KING. THEN HE GOT BORED."
SO HE HAD US STEAL DR. KINTOBOR'S TECHNOLOGY AND INVADE THE PRIME ZONE. WE DON'T DARE STAND AGAINST HIM ALONE. HE'S SIMPLY TOO POWERFUL.

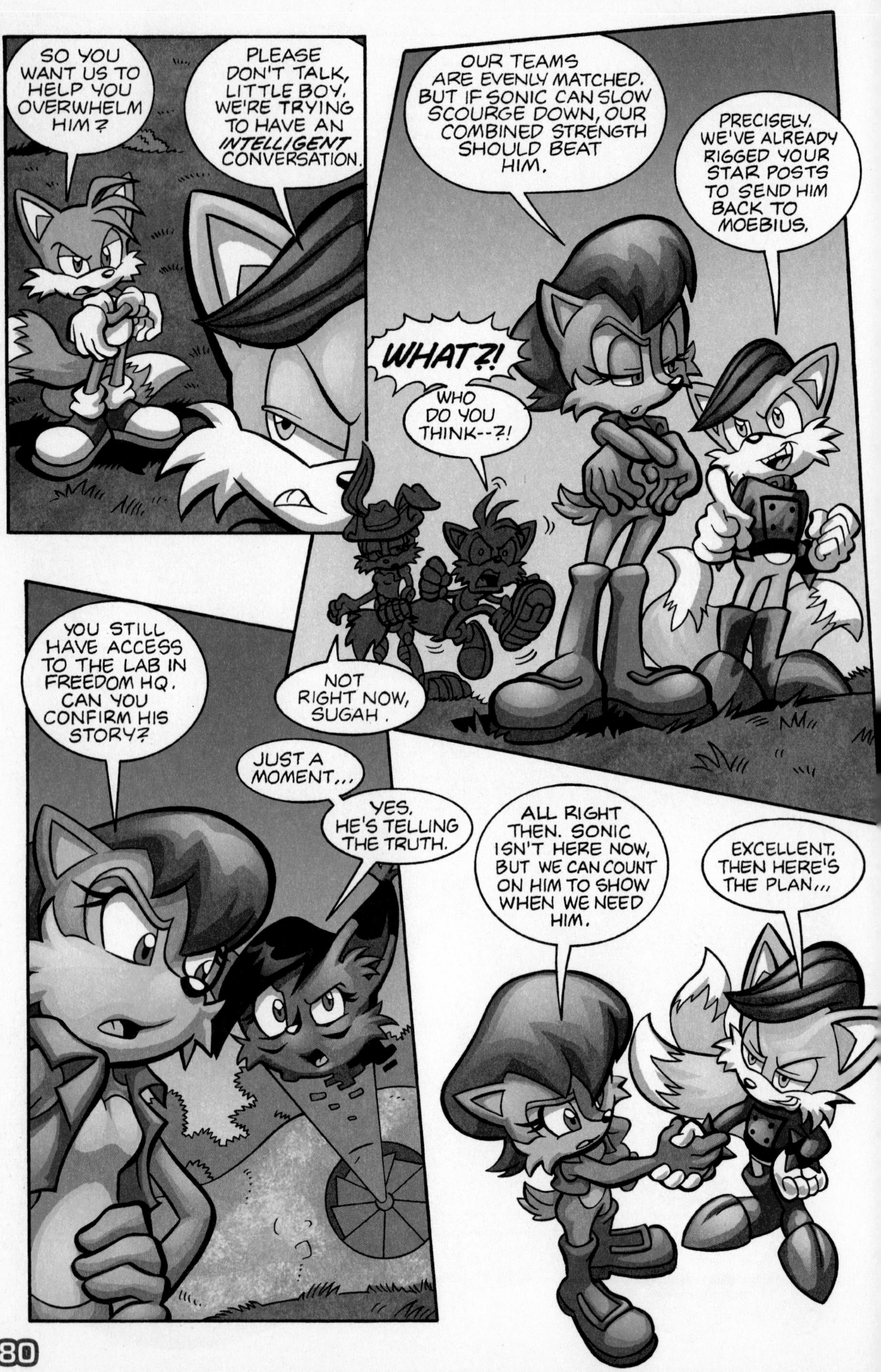
SO YOU WANT US TO HELP YOU OVERWHELM HIM?
PLEASE DON'T TALK, LITTLE BOY. WE'RE TRYING TO HAVE AN *INTELLIGENT* CONVERSATION.
OUR TEAMS ARE EVENLY MATCHED. BUT IF SONIC CAN SLOW SCOURGE DOWN, OUR COMBINED STRENGTH SHOULD BEAT HIM.
PRECISELY. WE'VE ALREADY RIGGED YOUR STAR POSTS TO SEND HIM BACK TO MOEBIUS.
WHAT?!
WHO DO YOU THINK--?!
NOT RIGHT NOW, SUGAH.
YOU STILL HAVE ACCESS TO THE LAB IN FREEDOM HQ. CAN YOU CONFIRM HIS STORY?
JUST A MOMENT...
YES. HE'S TELLING THE TRUTH.
ALL RIGHT THEN. SONIC ISN'T HERE NOW, BUT WE CAN COUNT ON HIM TO SHOW WHEN WE NEED HIM.
EXCELLENT. THEN HERE'S THE PLAN...

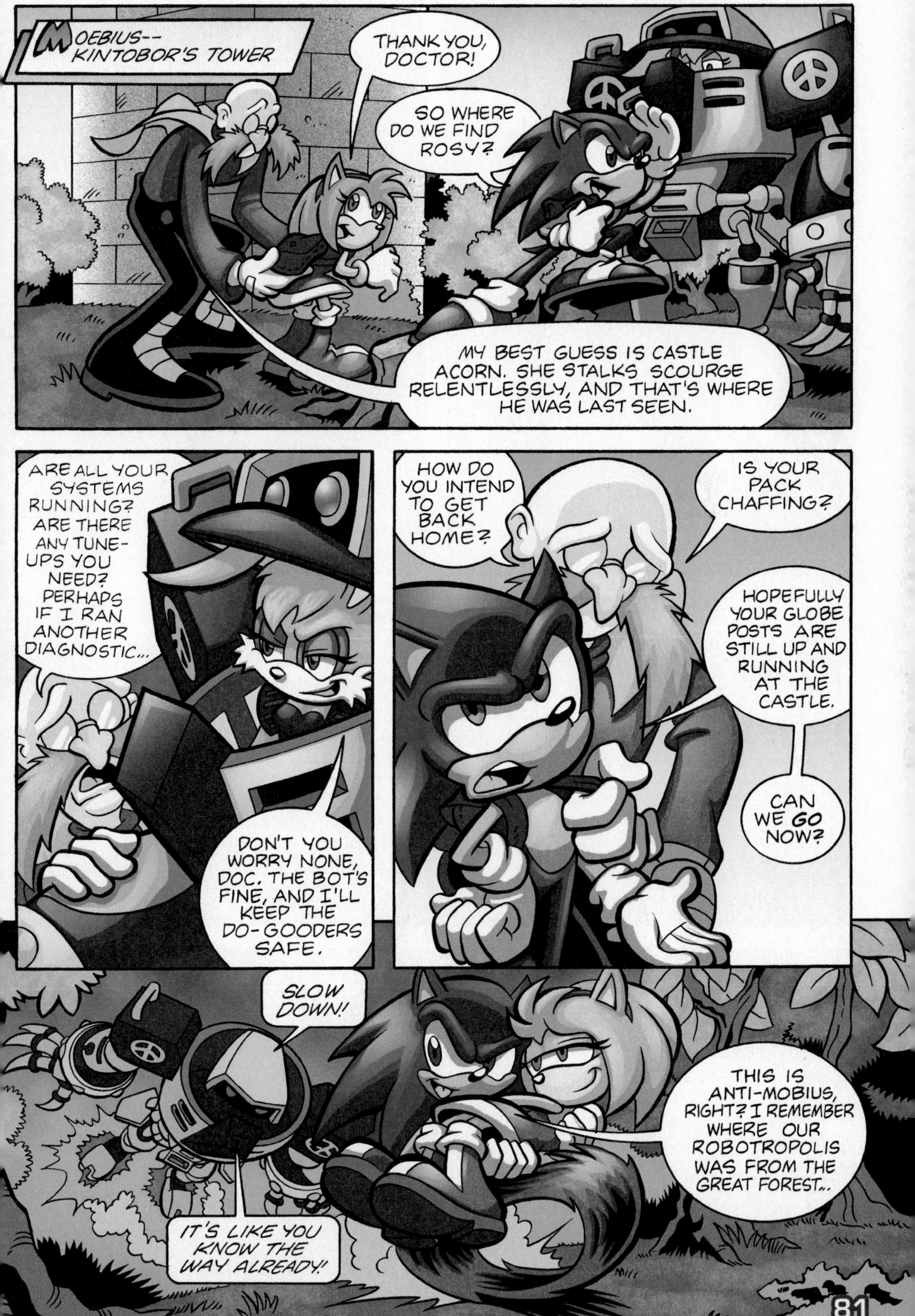
MOEBIUS--
KINTOBOR'S TOWER
THANK YOU, DOCTOR!
SO WHERE DO WE FIND ROSY?
MY BEST GUESS IS CASTLE ACORN. SHE STALKS SCOURGE RELENTLESSLY, AND THAT'S WHERE HE WAS LAST SEEN.
ARE ALL YOUR SYSTEMS RUNNING? ARE THERE ANY TUNE-UPS YOU NEED? PERHAPS IF I RAN ANOTHER DIAGNOSTIC...
DON'T YOU WORRY NONE, DOC. THE BOT'S FINE, AND I'LL KEEP THE DO-GOODERS SAFE.
HOW DO YOU INTEND TO GET BACK HOME?
IS YOUR PACK CHAFFING?
HOPEFULLY YOUR GLOBE POSTS ARE STILL UP AND RUNNING AT THE CASTLE.
CAN WE GO NOW?
SLOW DOWN!
THIS IS ANTI-MOBIUS, RIGHT? I REMEMBER WHERE OUR ROBOTROPOLIS WAS FROM THE GREAT FOREST...
IT'S LIKE YOU KNOW THE WAY ALREADY!

...WHICH PUTS YOUR CASTLE ACORN THE SAME DISTANCE FROM THE GRAND FOREST.

CRIPES... HOW COULD YOU STAND TO LIVE IN SUCH A DUMP?

NEVER WAS A FAN OF YOUR CUSHY LIFESTYLE. 'SIDES, IT'S A CASTLE.

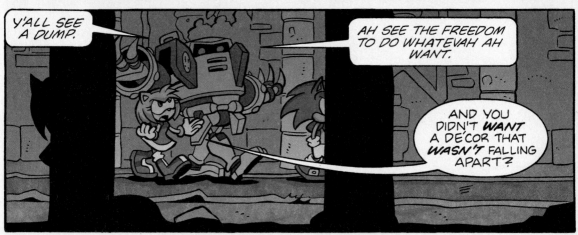

Y'ALL SEE A DUMP.

AH SEE THE FREEDOM TO DO WHATEVAH AH WANT.

AND YOU DIDN'T WANT A DE'COR THAT WASN'T FALLING APART?

IT'S SYMBOLIC!

IT'S DEPRESSING!

YO, LADIES! DID ANYBODY SEE THAT?

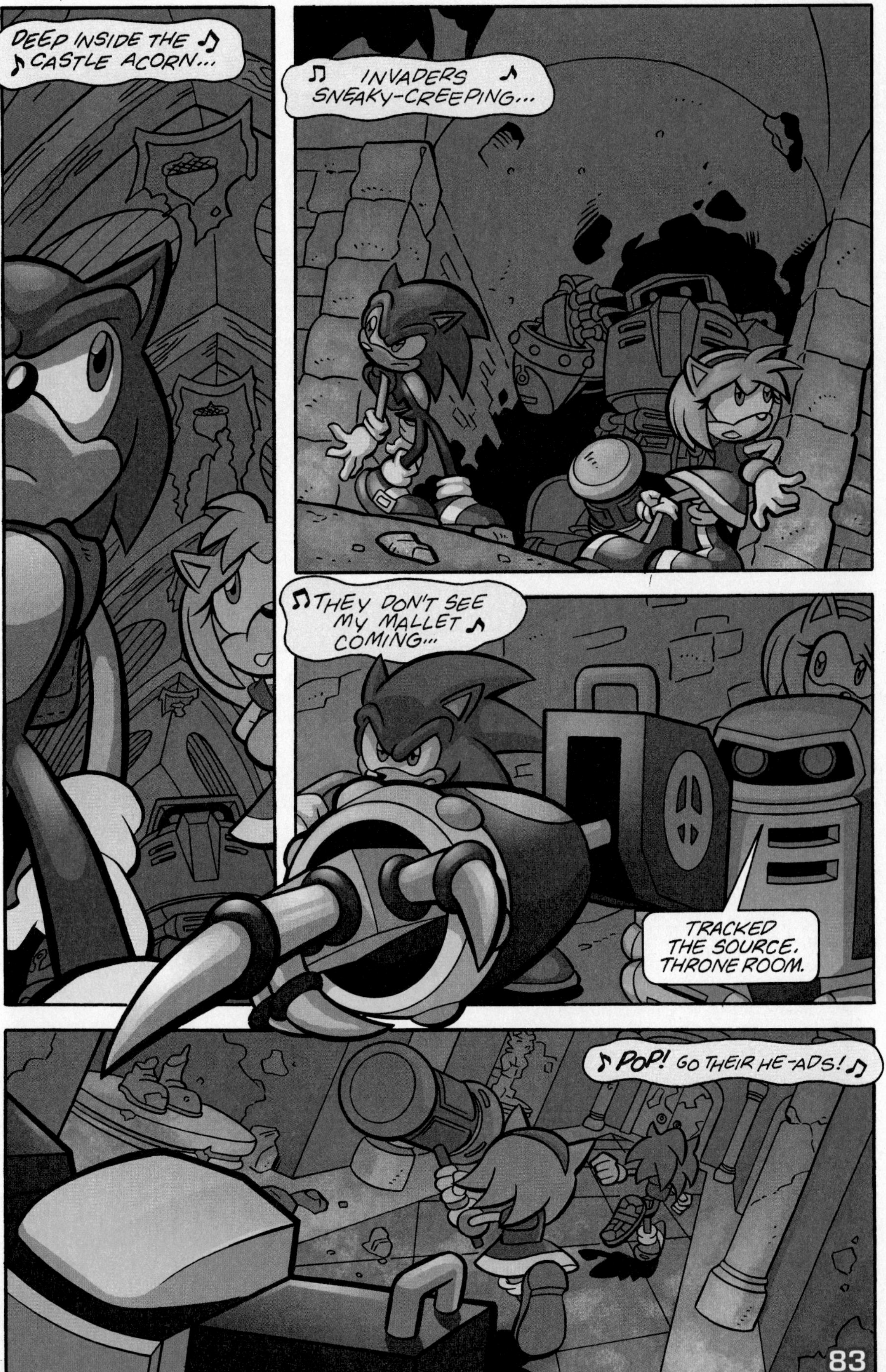
♪ DEEP INSIDE THE ♪ CASTLE ACORN...
♫ INVADERS ♪ SNEAKY-CREEPING...
♫ THEY DON'T SEE MY MALLET ♪ COMING...
TRACKED THE SOURCE. THRONE ROOM.
♪ POP! GO THEIR HE-ADS! ♫

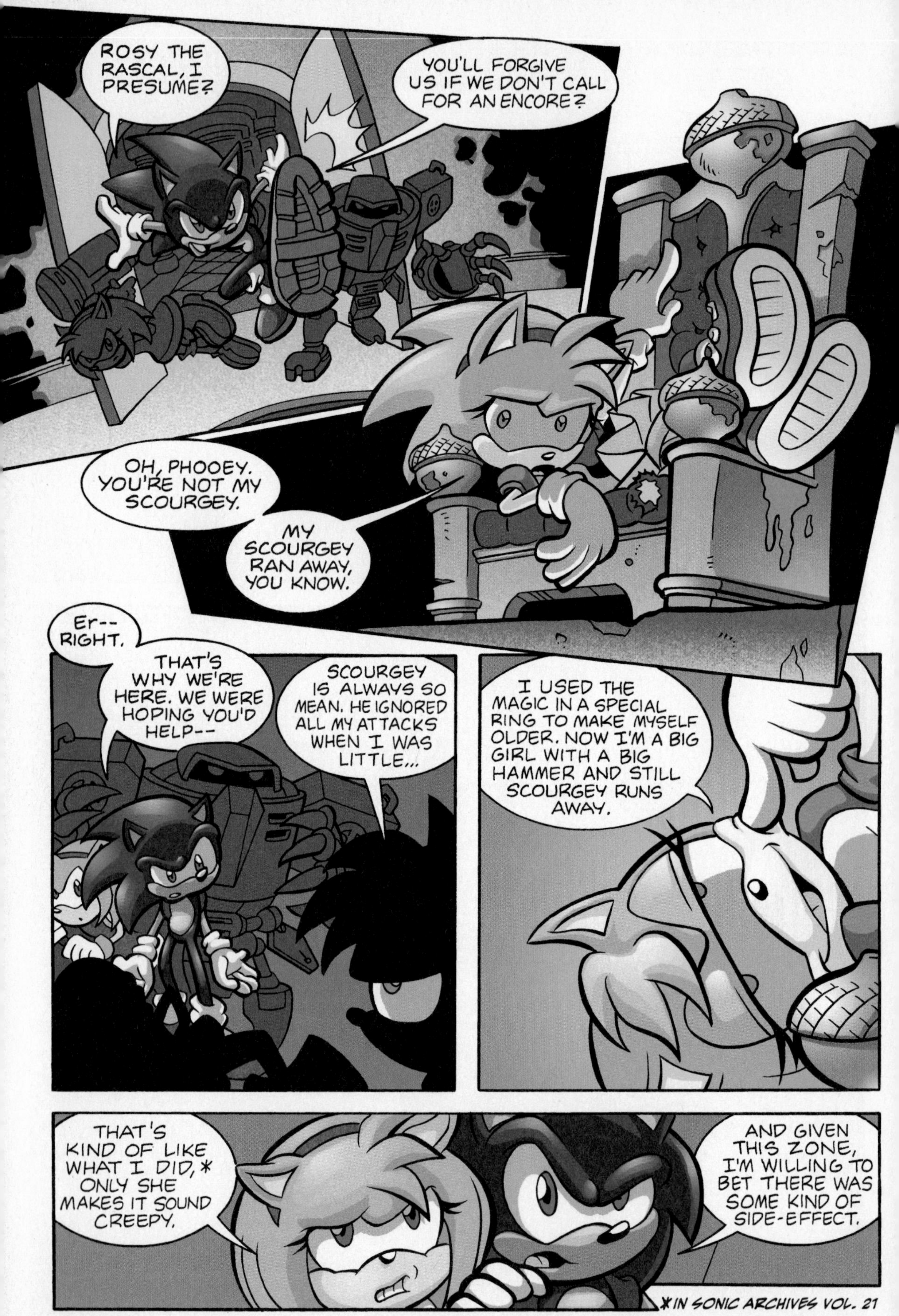
ROSY THE RASCAL, I PRESUME?
YOU'LL FORGIVE US IF WE DON'T CALL FOR AN ENCORE?
OH, PHOOEY. YOU'RE NOT MY SCOURGEY.
MY SCOURGEY RAN AWAY, YOU KNOW.
Er-- RIGHT.
THAT'S WHY WE'RE HERE. WE WERE HOPING YOU'D HELP--
SCOURGEY IS ALWAYS SO MEAN. HE IGNORED ALL MY ATTACKS WHEN I WAS LITTLE...
I USED THE MAGIC IN A SPECIAL RING TO MAKE MYSELF OLDER. NOW I'M A BIG GIRL WITH A BIG HAMMER AND STILL SCOURGEY RUNS AWAY.
THAT'S KIND OF LIKE WHAT I DID,* ONLY SHE MAKES IT SOUND CREEPY.
AND GIVEN THIS ZONE, I'M WILLING TO BET THERE WAS SOME KIND OF SIDE-EFFECT.
*IN SONIC ARCHIVES VOL. 21

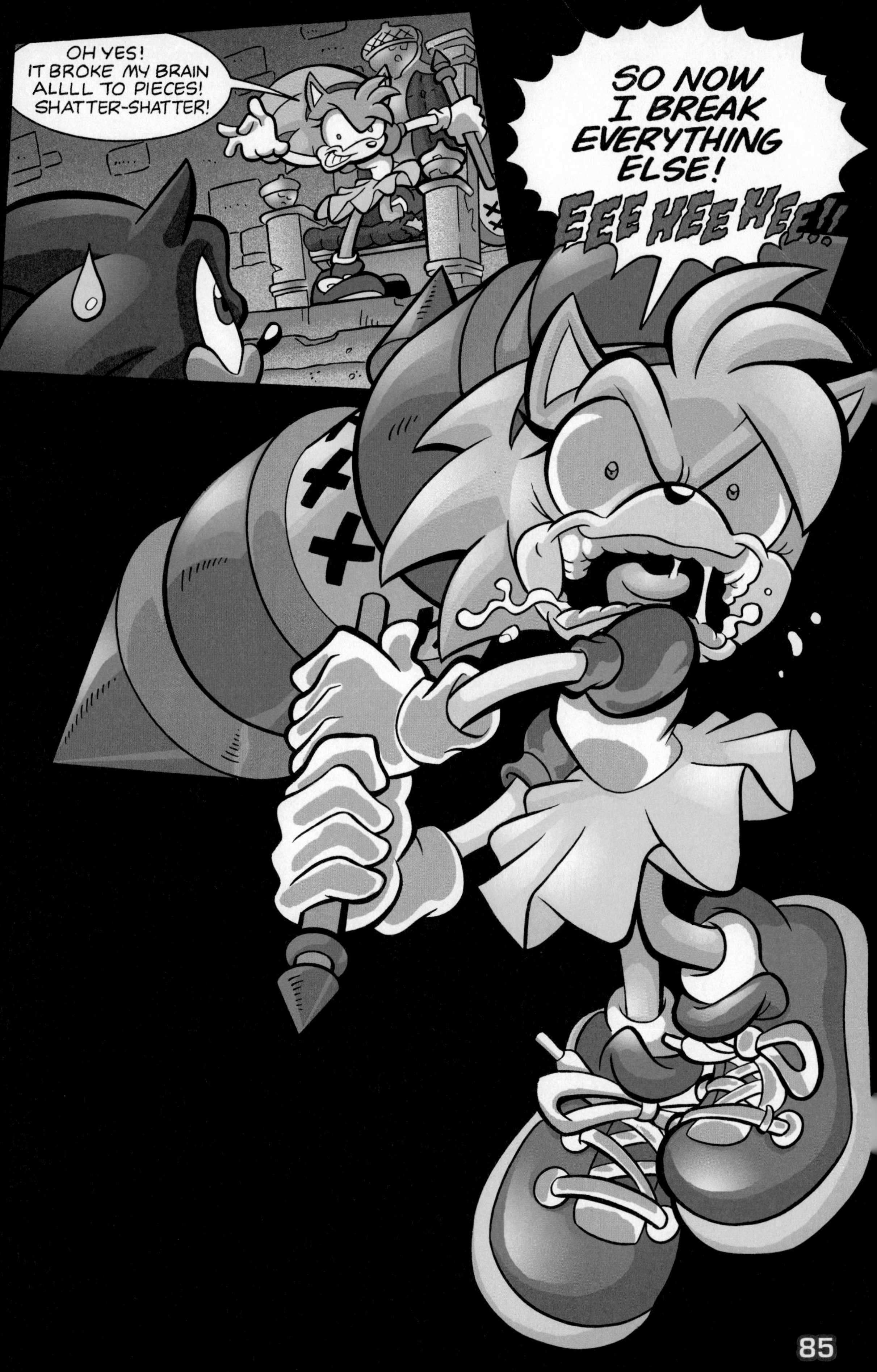
OH YES! IT BROKE MY BRAIN ALLLL TO PIECES! SHATTER-SHATTER!
SO NOW I BREAK EVERYTHING ELSE!
EEE HEE HEE!!

CHAPTER 5

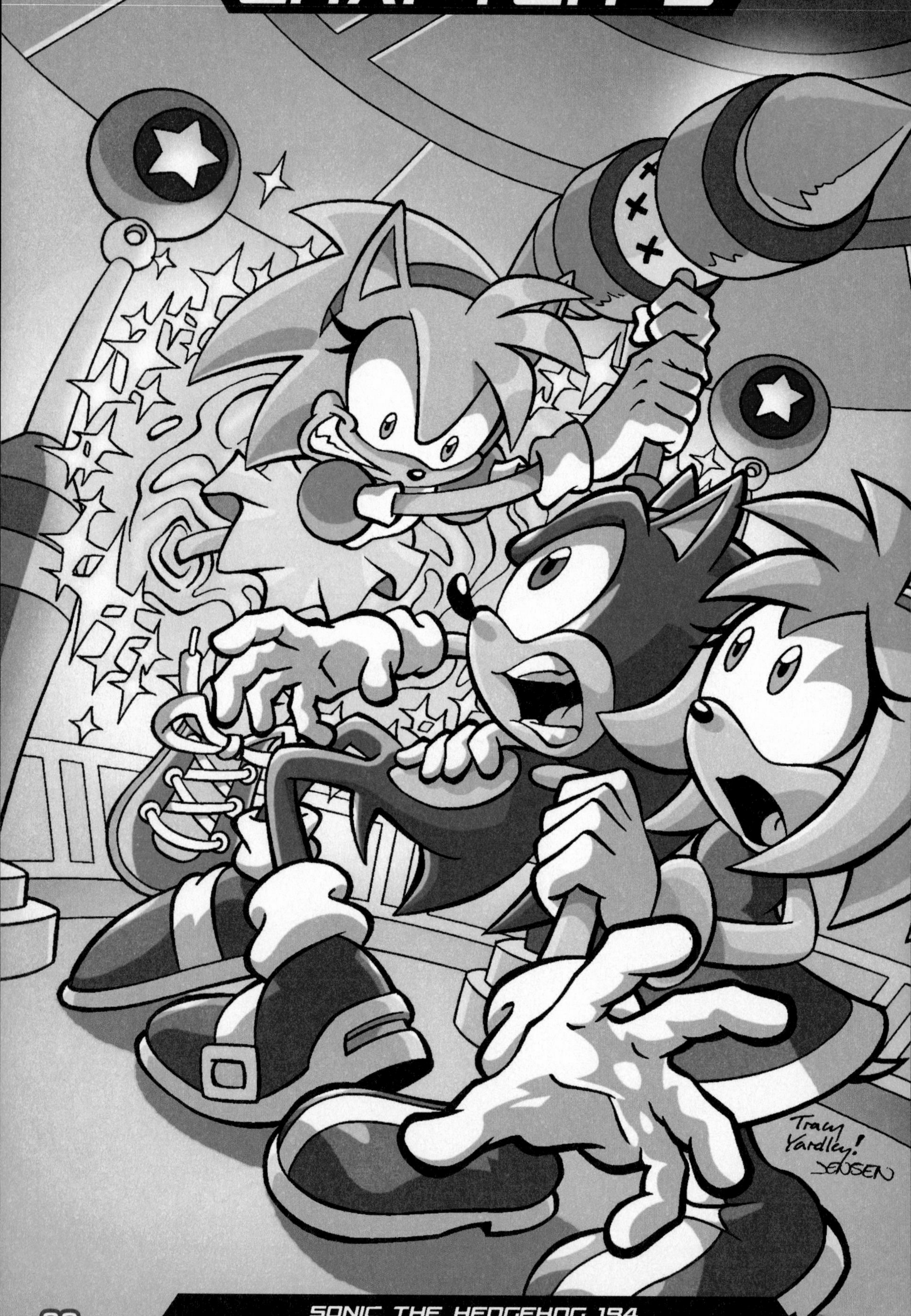
Tracy Yardley! JENSEN

SONIC THE HEDGEHOG 194
COVER BY TRACY YARDLEY AND JASON JENSEN

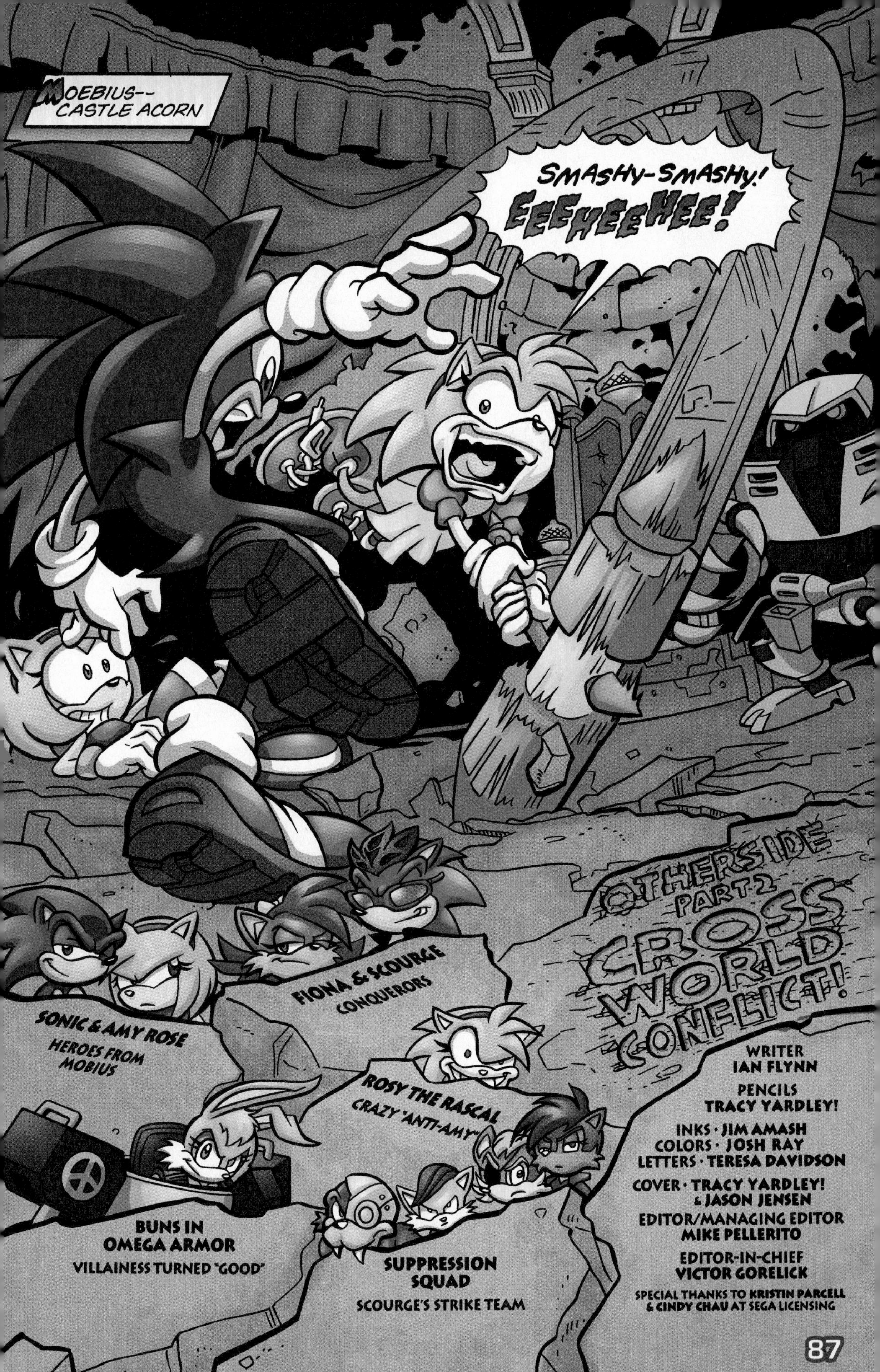
MOEBIUS--
CASTLE ACORN
SMASHY-SMASHY!
EEEHEEHEE!
OTHERSIDE
PART 2
CROSS WORLD CONFLICT!
SONIC & AMY ROSE
HEROES FROM MOBIUS
FIONA & SCOURGE
CONQUERORS
ROSY THE RASCAL
CRAZY "ANTI-AMY"
BUNS IN OMEGA ARMOR
VILLAINESS TURNED "GOOD"
SUPPRESSION SQUAD
SCOURGE'S STRIKE TEAM
WRITER
IAN FLYNN
PENCILS
TRACY YARDLEY!
INKS · JIM AMASH
COLORS · JOSH RAY
LETTERS · TERESA DAVIDSON
COVER · TRACY YARDLEY!
& JASON JENSEN
EDITOR/MANAGING EDITOR
MIKE PELLERITO
EDITOR-IN-CHIEF
VICTOR GORELICK
SPECIAL THANKS TO KRISTIN PARCELL
& CINDY CHAU AT SEGA LICENSING

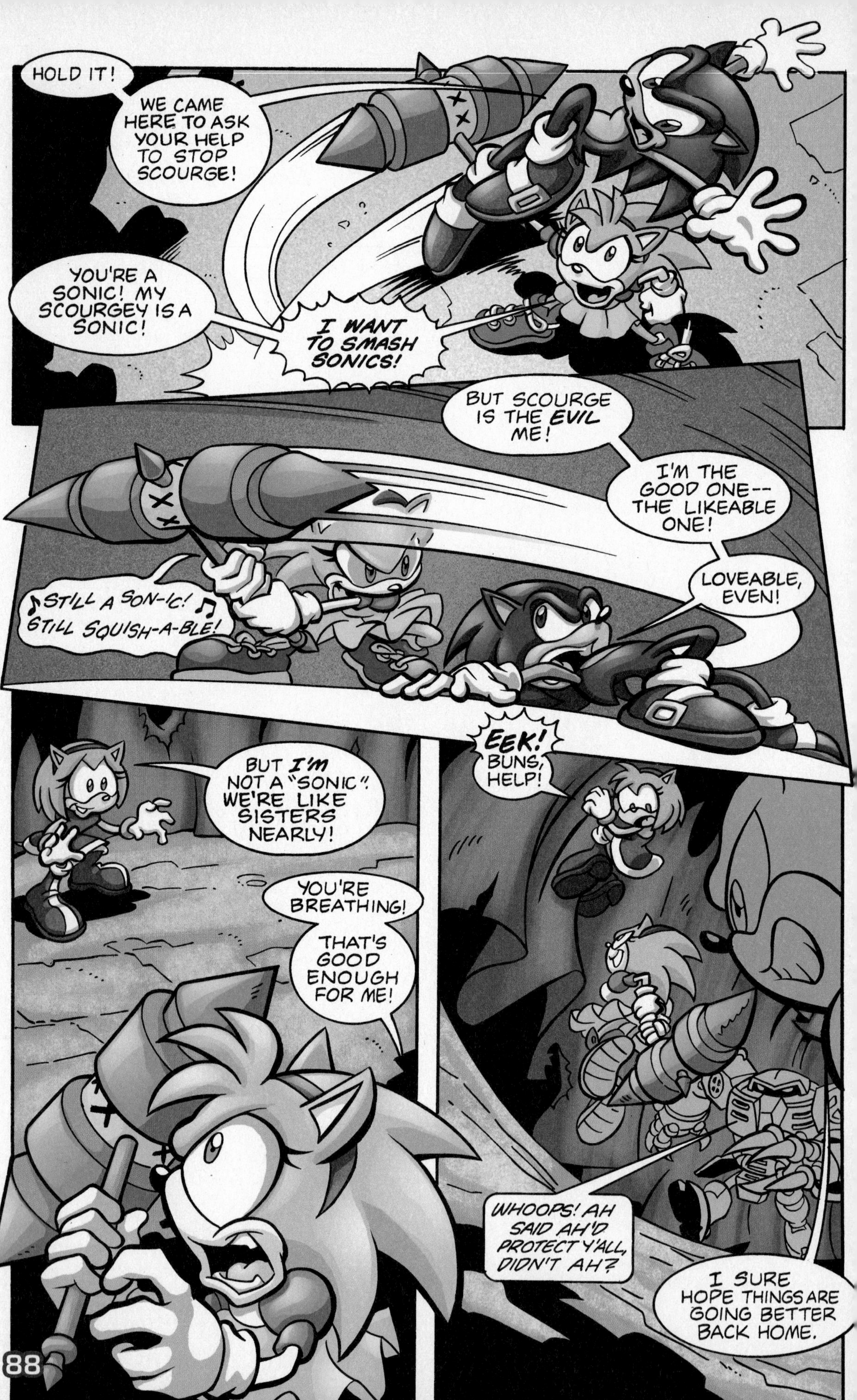
HOLD IT!
WE CAME HERE TO ASK YOUR HELP TO STOP SCOURGE!
YOU'RE A SONIC! MY SCOURGEY IS A SONIC!
I WANT TO SMASH SONICS!
BUT SCOURGE IS THE EVIL ME!
I'M THE GOOD ONE-- THE LIKEABLE ONE!
LOVEABLE, EVEN!
♪STILL A SON-IC! ♫ STILL SQUISH-A-BLE!
BUT I'M NOT A "SONIC". WE'RE LIKE SISTERS NEARLY!
YOU'RE BREATHING!
THAT'S GOOD ENOUGH FOR ME!
EEK! BUNS, HELP!
WHOOPS! AH SAID AH'D PROTECT Y'ALL, DIDN'T AH?
I SURE HOPE THINGS ARE GOING BETTER BACK HOME.

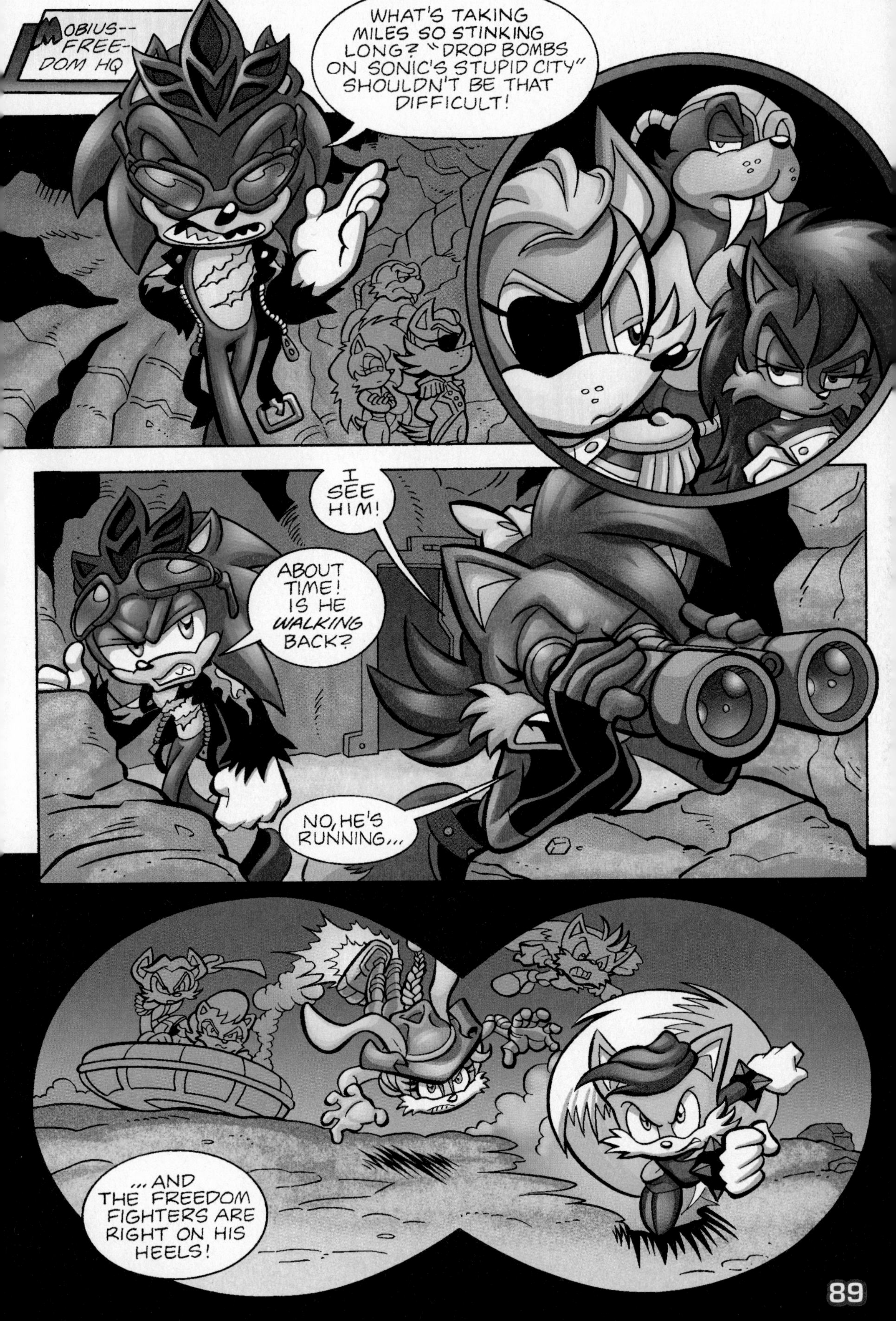
MOBIUS-- FREE-DOM HQ
WHAT'S TAKING MILES SO STINKING LONG? "DROP BOMBS ON SONIC'S STUPID CITY" SHOULDN'T BE THAT DIFFICULT!
I SEE HIM!
ABOUT TIME! IS HE *WALKING* BACK?
NO, HE'S RUNNING...
...AND THE FREEDOM FIGHTERS ARE RIGHT ON HIS HEELS!

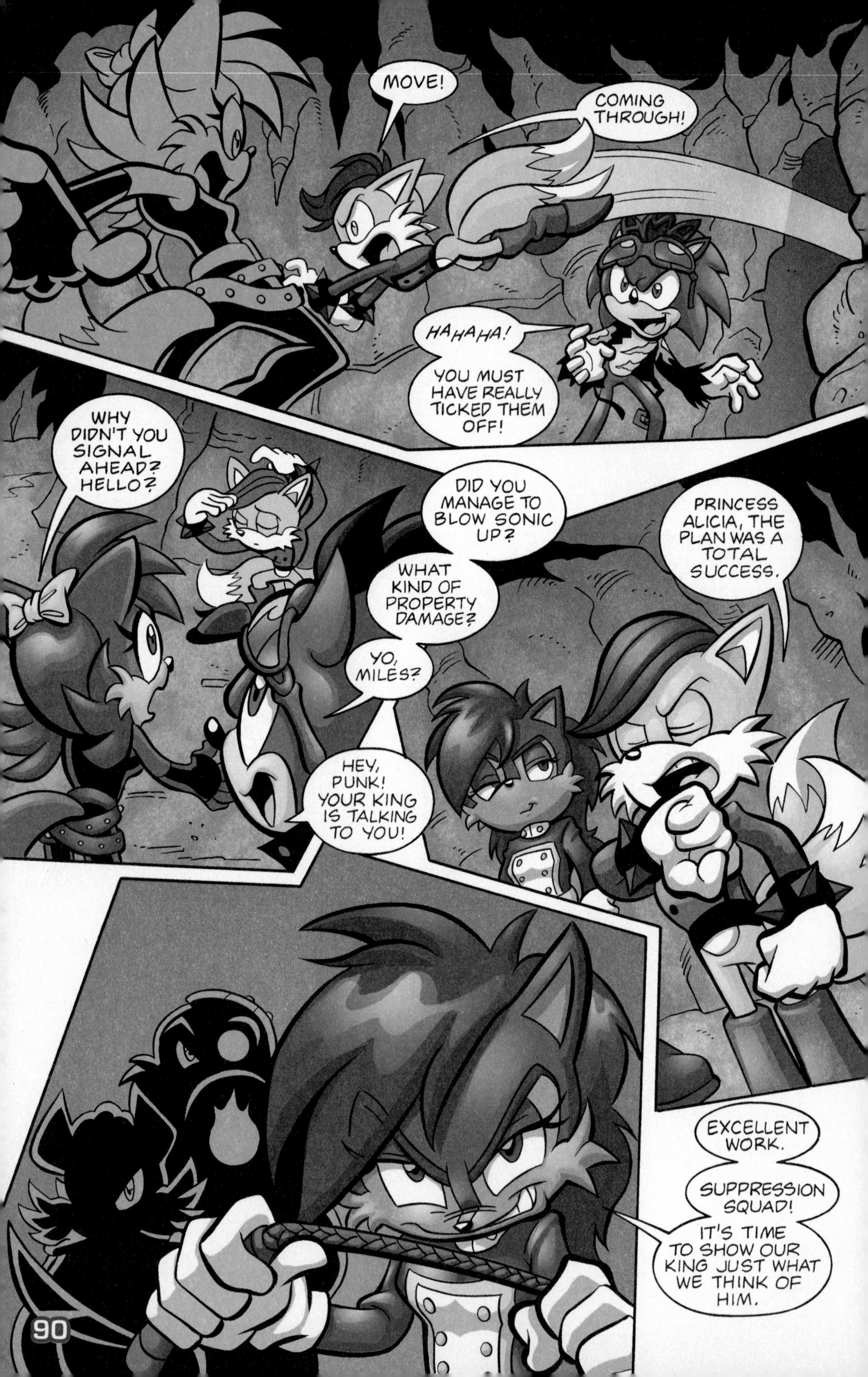
MOVE!
COMING THROUGH!
HAHAHA!
YOU MUST HAVE REALLY TICKED THEM OFF!
WHY DIDN'T YOU SIGNAL AHEAD? HELLO?
DID YOU MANAGE TO BLOW SONIC UP?
WHAT KIND OF PROPERTY DAMAGE?
YO, MILES?
HEY, PUNK! YOUR KING IS TALKING TO YOU!
PRINCESS ALICIA, THE PLAN WAS A TOTAL SUCCESS.
EXCELLENT WORK.
SUPPRESSION SQUAD!
IT'S TIME TO SHOW OUR KING JUST WHAT WE THINK OF HIM.

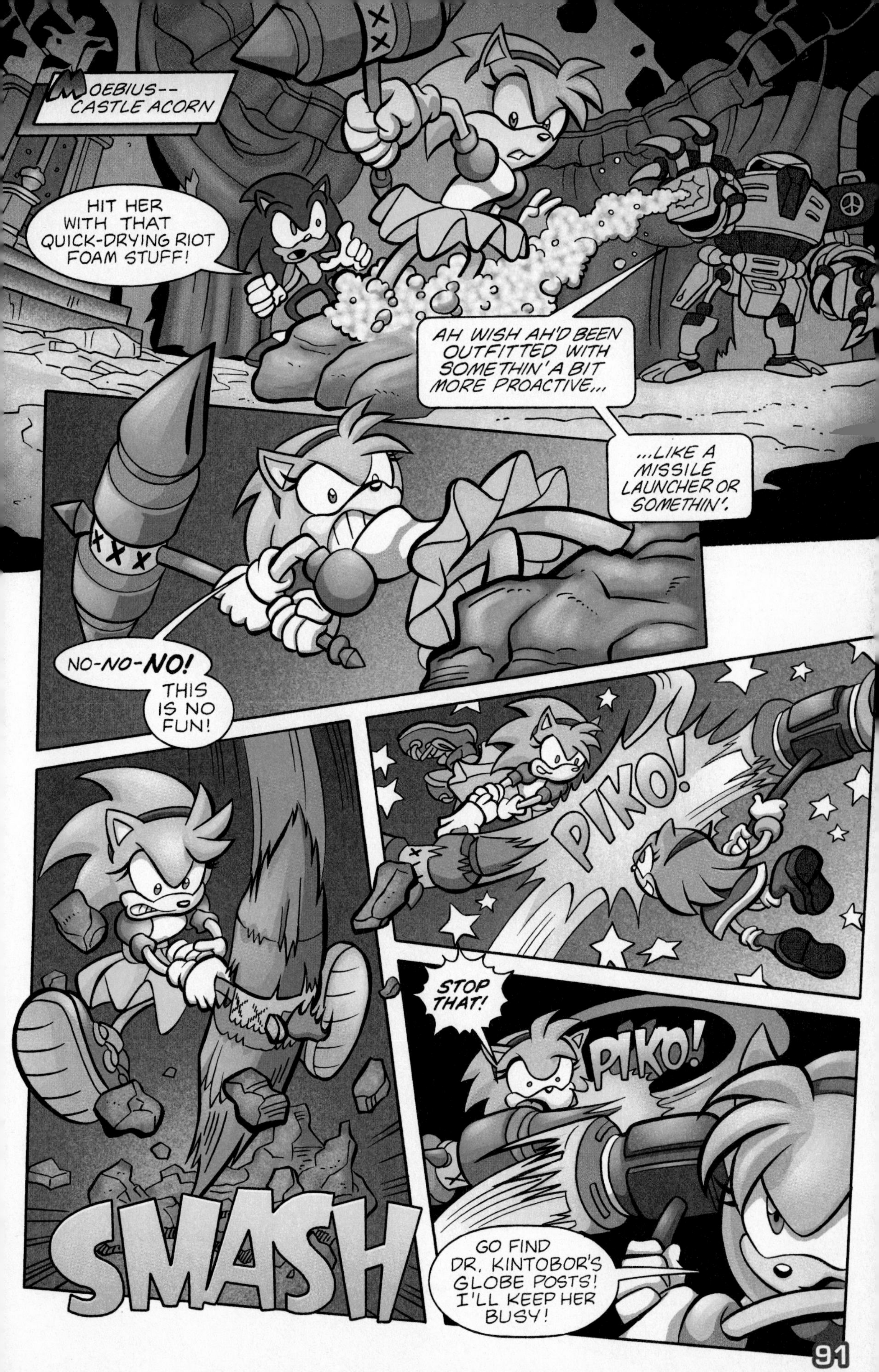
MOEBIUS--
CASTLE ACORN
HIT HER WITH THAT QUICK-DRYING RIOT FOAM STUFF!
AH WISH AH'D BEEN OUTFITTED WITH SOMETHIN' A BIT MORE PROACTIVE...
...LIKE A MISSILE LAUNCHER OR SOMETHIN'.
NO-NO-NO! THIS IS NO FUN!
PIKO!
SMASH
STOP THAT!
PIKO!
GO FIND DR. KINTOBOR'S GLOBE POSTS! I'LL KEEP HER BUSY!

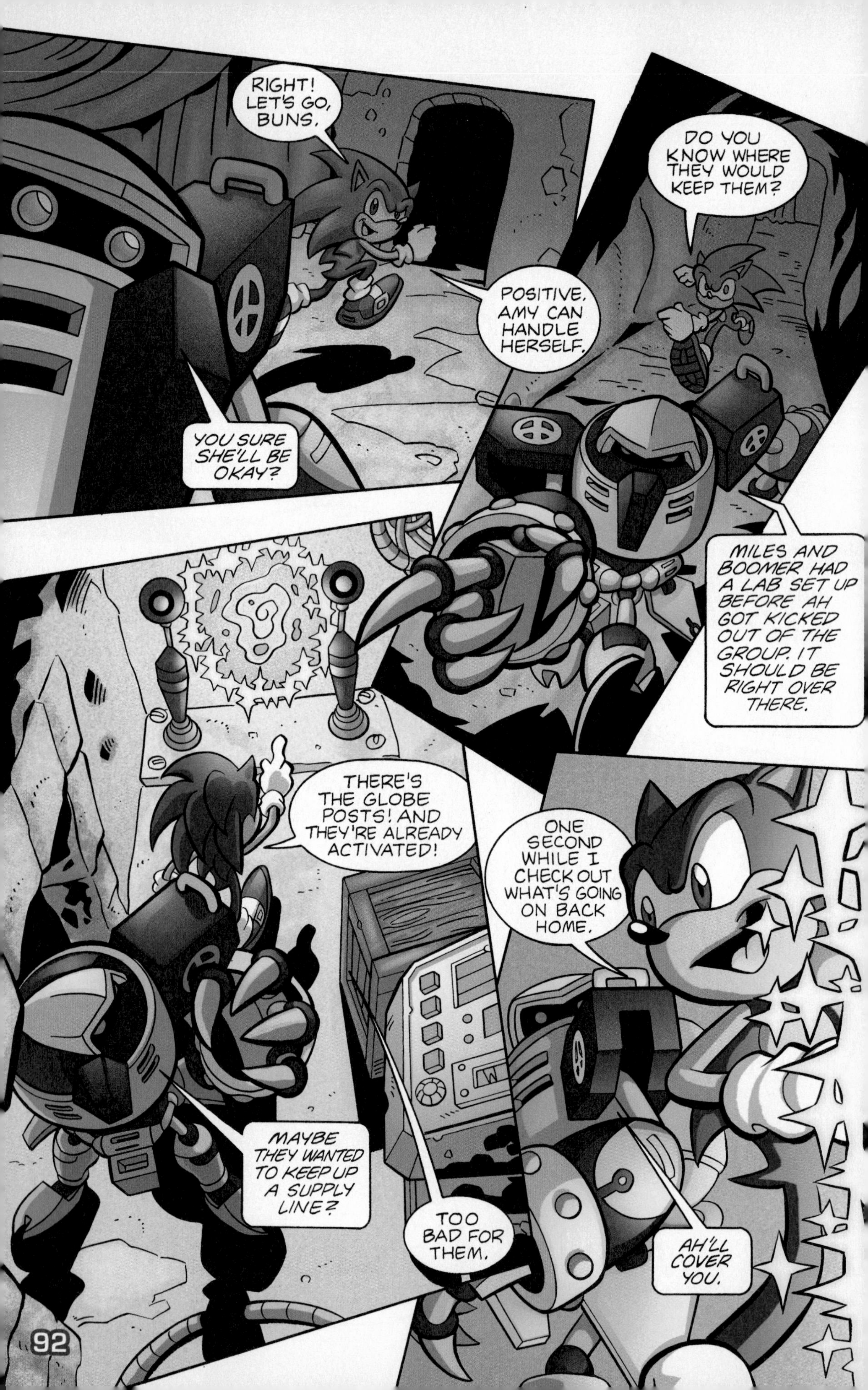
RIGHT! LET'S GO, BUNS.
YOU SURE SHE'LL BE OKAY?
POSITIVE. AMY CAN HANDLE HERSELF.
DO YOU KNOW WHERE THEY WOULD KEEP THEM?
MILES AND BOOMER HAD A LAB SET UP BEFORE AH GOT KICKED OUT OF THE GROUP. IT SHOULD BE RIGHT OVER THERE.
THERE'S THE GLOBE POSTS! AND THEY'RE ALREADY ACTIVATED!
MAYBE THEY WANTED TO KEEP UP A SUPPLY LINE?
TOO BAD FOR THEM.
ONE SECOND WHILE I CHECK OUT WHAT'S GOING ON BACK HOME.
AH'LL COVER YOU.

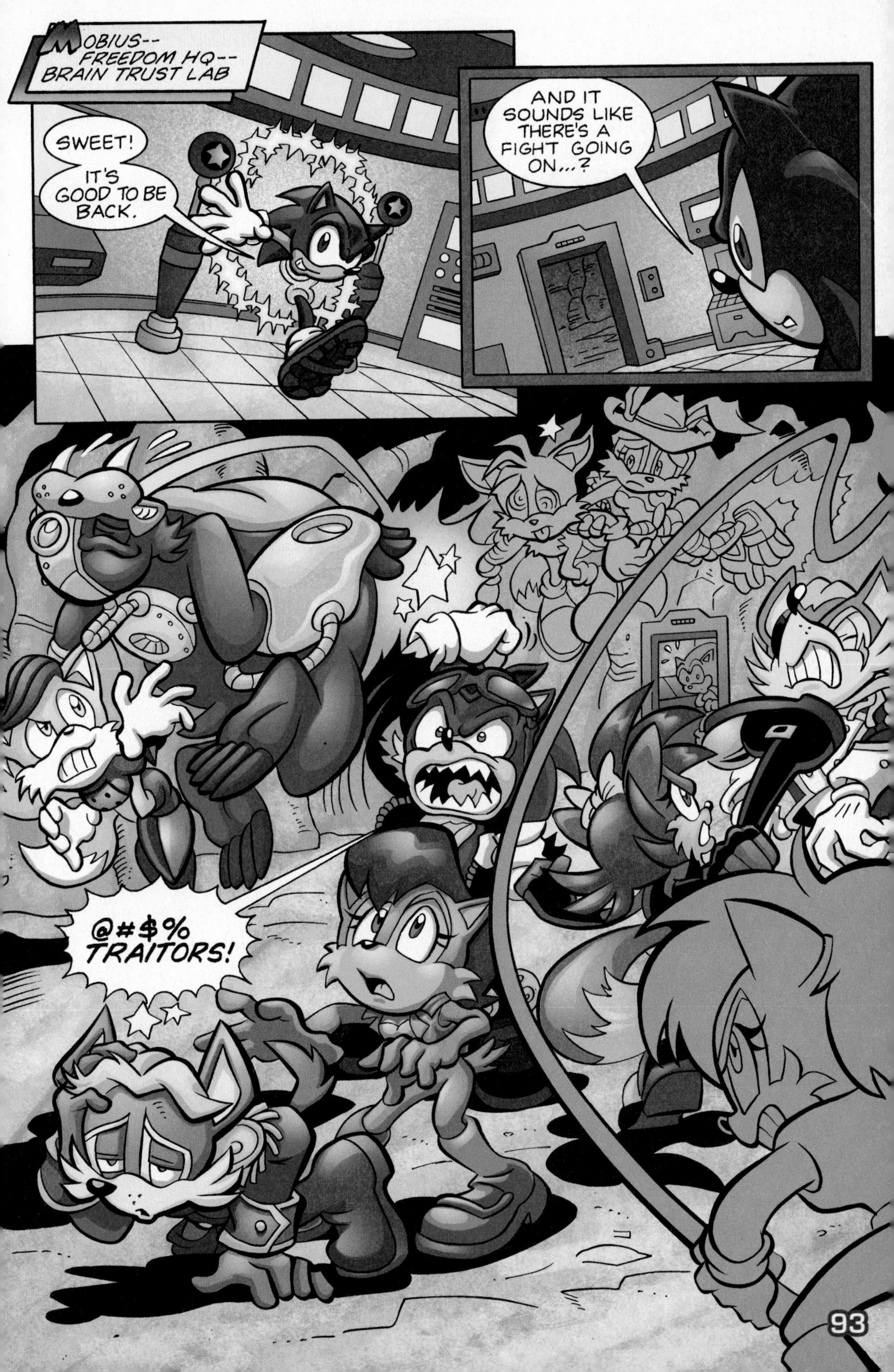

MOBIUS--
FREEDOM HQ--
BRAIN TRUST LAB
SWEET!
IT'S GOOD TO BE BACK.
AND IT SOUNDS LIKE THERE'S A FIGHT GOING ON...?
@#$% TRAITORS!

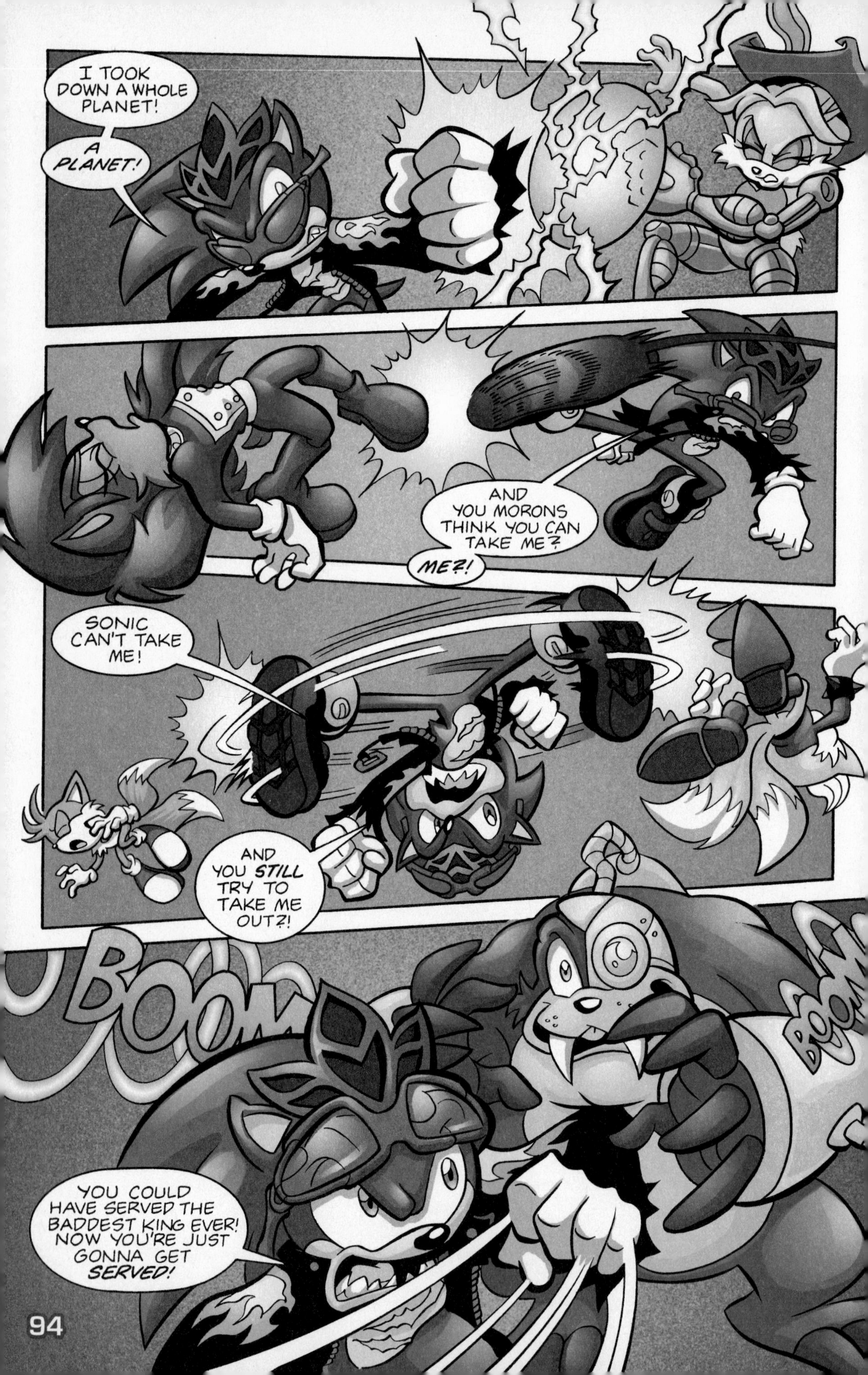
I TOOK DOWN A WHOLE PLANET!
A PLANET!
AND YOU MORONS THINK YOU CAN TAKE ME?
ME?!
SONIC CAN'T TAKE ME!
AND YOU STILL TRY TO TAKE ME OUT?!
BOOM
BOOM
YOU COULD HAVE SERVED THE BADDEST KING EVER! NOW YOU'RE JUST GONNA GET SERVED!

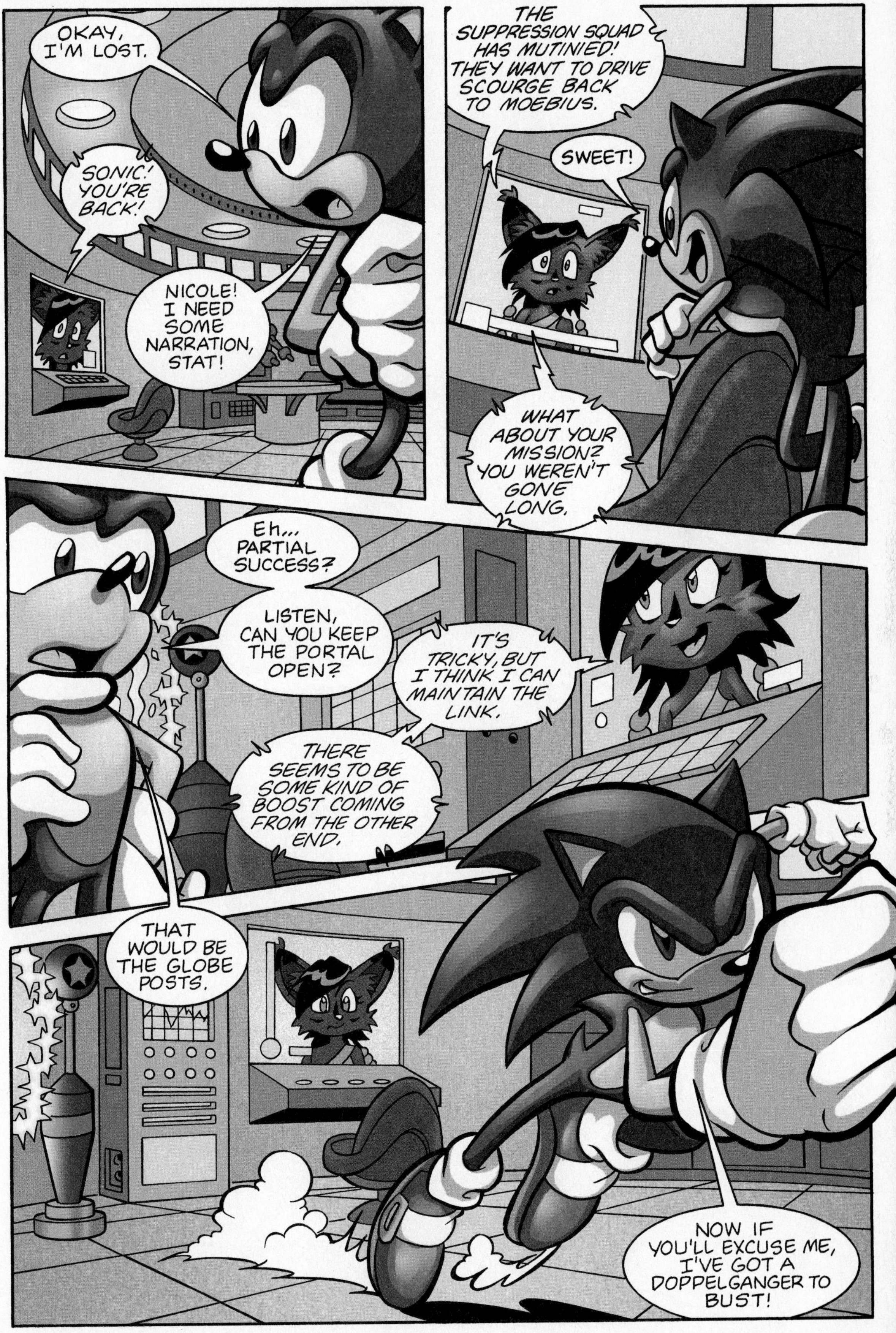
OKAY, I'M LOST.
SONIC! YOU'RE BACK!
NICOLE! I NEED SOME NARRATION, STAT!
THE SUPPRESSION SQUAD HAS MUTINIED! THEY WANT TO DRIVE SCOURGE BACK TO MOEBIUS.
SWEET!
WHAT ABOUT YOUR MISSION? YOU WEREN'T GONE LONG.
Eh... PARTIAL SUCCESS?
LISTEN, CAN YOU KEEP THE PORTAL OPEN?
IT'S TRICKY, BUT I THINK I CAN MAINTAIN THE LINK.
THERE SEEMS TO BE SOME KIND OF BOOST COMING FROM THE OTHER END.
THAT WOULD BE THE GLOBE POSTS.
NOW IF YOU'LL EXCUSE ME, I'VE GOT A DOPPELGANGER TO BUST!

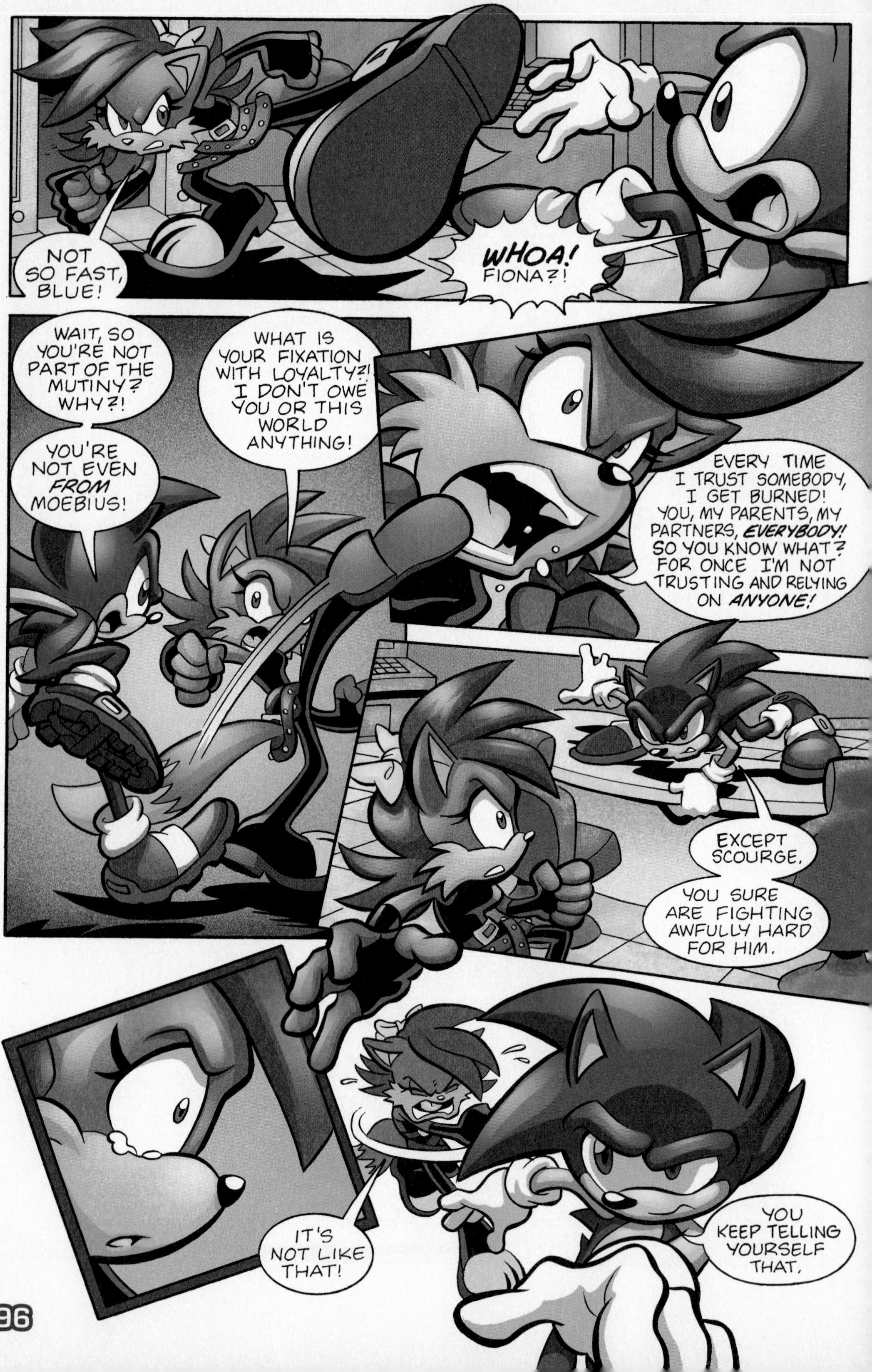
NOT SO FAST, BLUE!
WHOA! FIONA?!
WAIT, SO YOU'RE NOT PART OF THE MUTINY? WHY?!
YOU'RE NOT EVEN FROM MOEBIUS!
WHAT IS YOUR FIXATION WITH LOYALTY?! I DON'T OWE YOU OR THIS WORLD ANYTHING!
EVERY TIME I TRUST SOMEBODY, I GET BURNED! YOU, MY PARENTS, MY PARTNERS, EVERYBODY! SO YOU KNOW WHAT? FOR ONCE I'M NOT TRUSTING AND RELYING ON ANYONE!
EXCEPT SCOURGE.
YOU SURE ARE FIGHTING AWFULLY HARD FOR HIM.
IT'S NOT LIKE THAT!
YOU KEEP TELLING YOURSELF THAT.

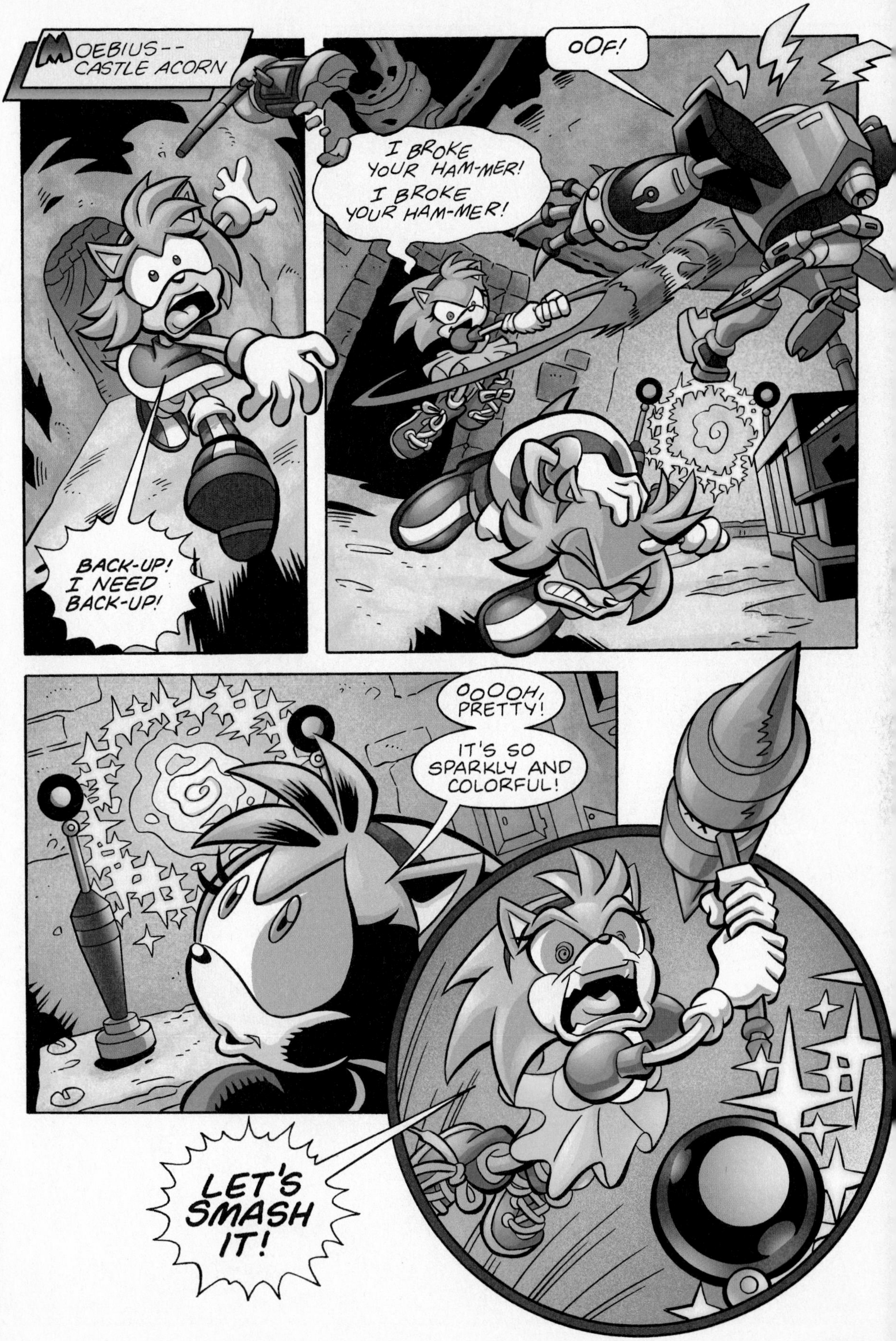
MOEBIUS-- CASTLE ACORN
BACK-UP! I NEED BACK-UP!
OOF!
I BROKE YOUR HAM-MER! I BROKE YOUR HAM-MER!
OOOOH, PRETTY!
IT'S SO SPARKLY AND COLORFUL!
LET'S SMASH IT!

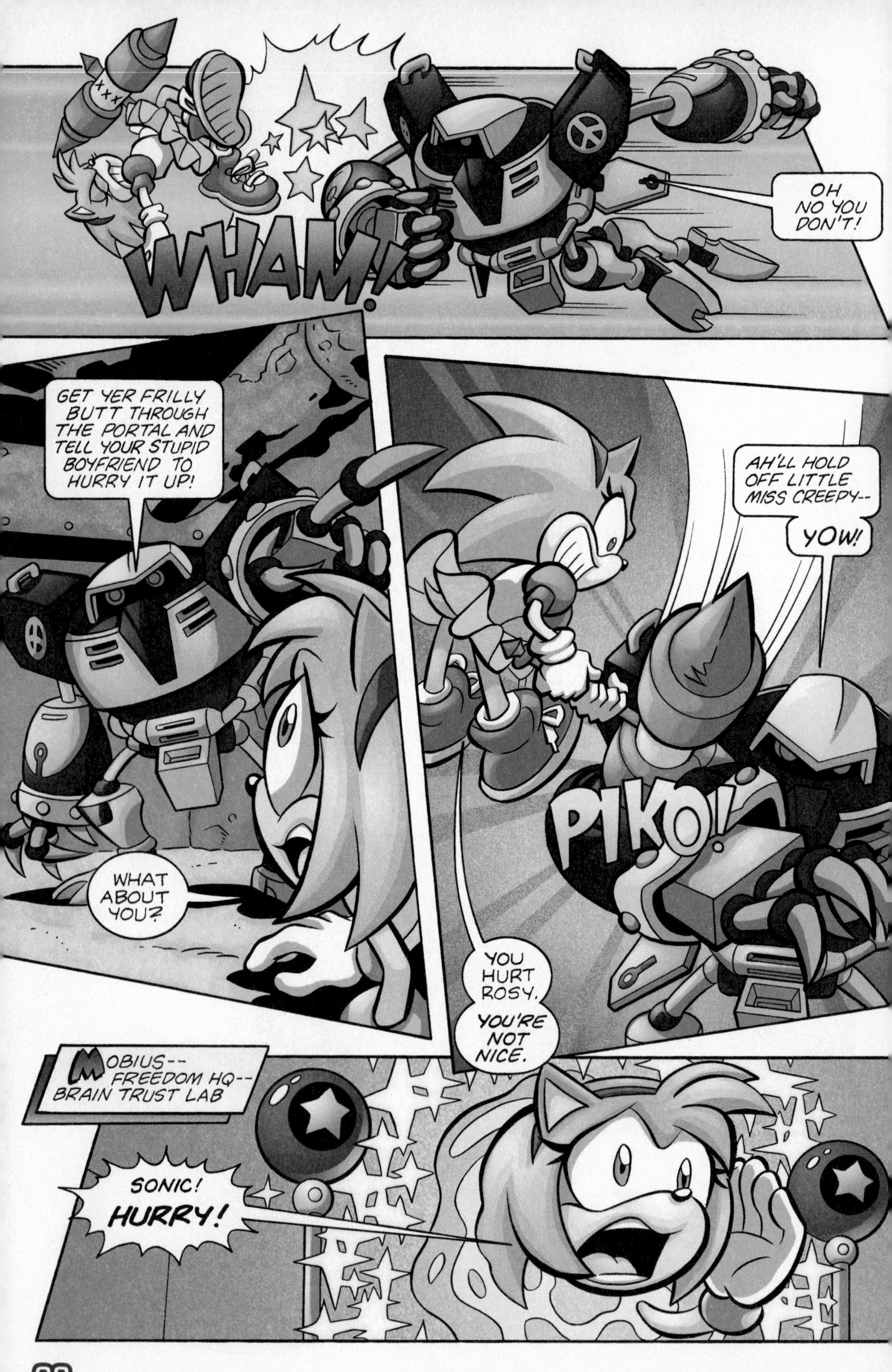
WHAM!
OH NO YOU DON'T!
GET YER FRILLY BUTT THROUGH THE PORTAL AND TELL YOUR STUPID BOYFRIEND TO HURRY IT UP!
WHAT ABOUT YOU?
AH'LL HOLD OFF LITTLE MISS CREEPY--
YOW!
PIKO!
YOU HURT ROSY.
YOU'RE NOT NICE.
MOBIUS-- FREEDOM HQ-- BRAIN TRUST LAB
SONIC! HURRY!

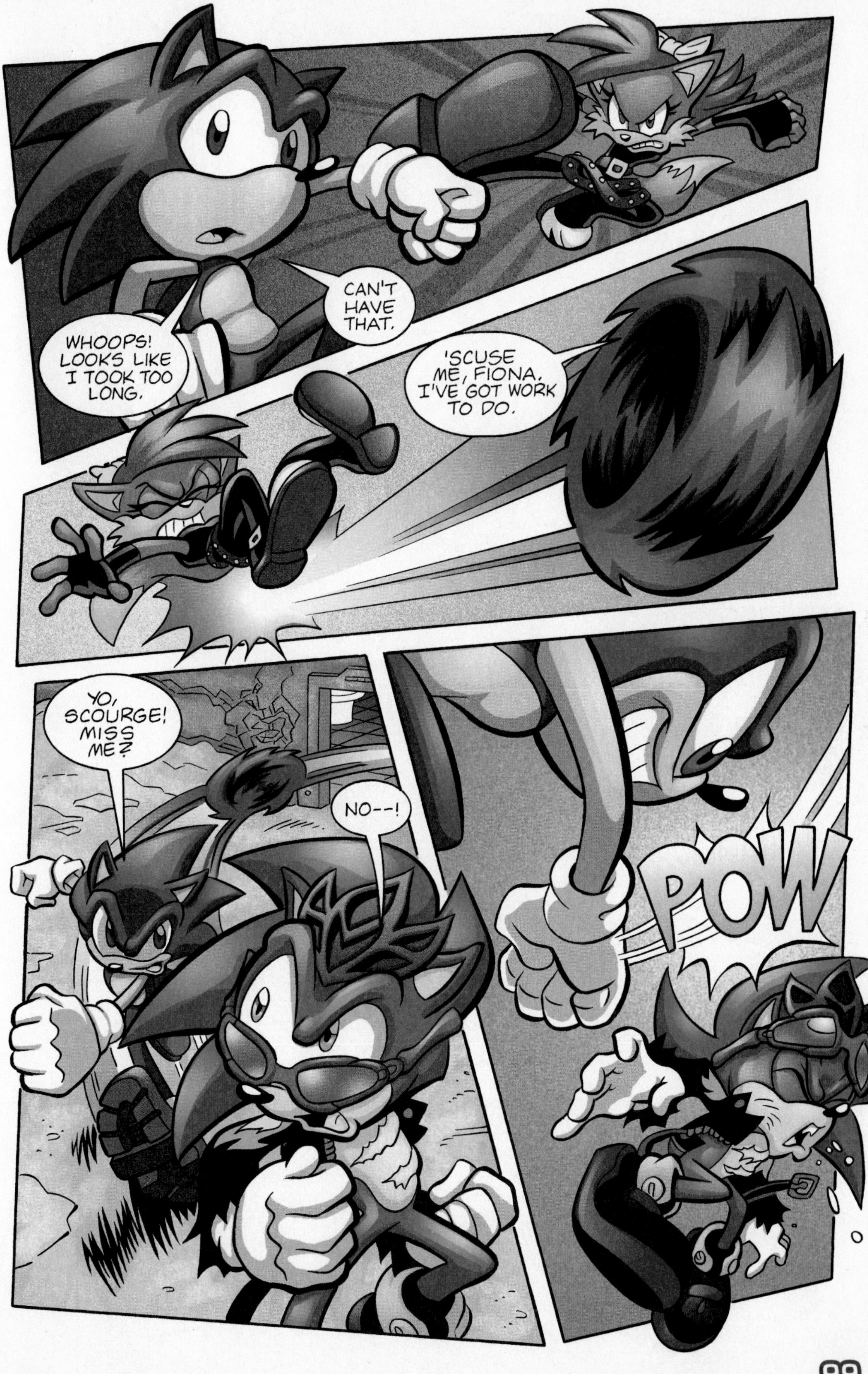

CAN'T HAVE THAT.
WHOOPS! LOOKS LIKE I TOOK TOO LONG.
'SCUSE ME, FIONA. I'VE GOT WORK TO DO.
YO, SCOURGE! MISS ME?
NO--!
POW

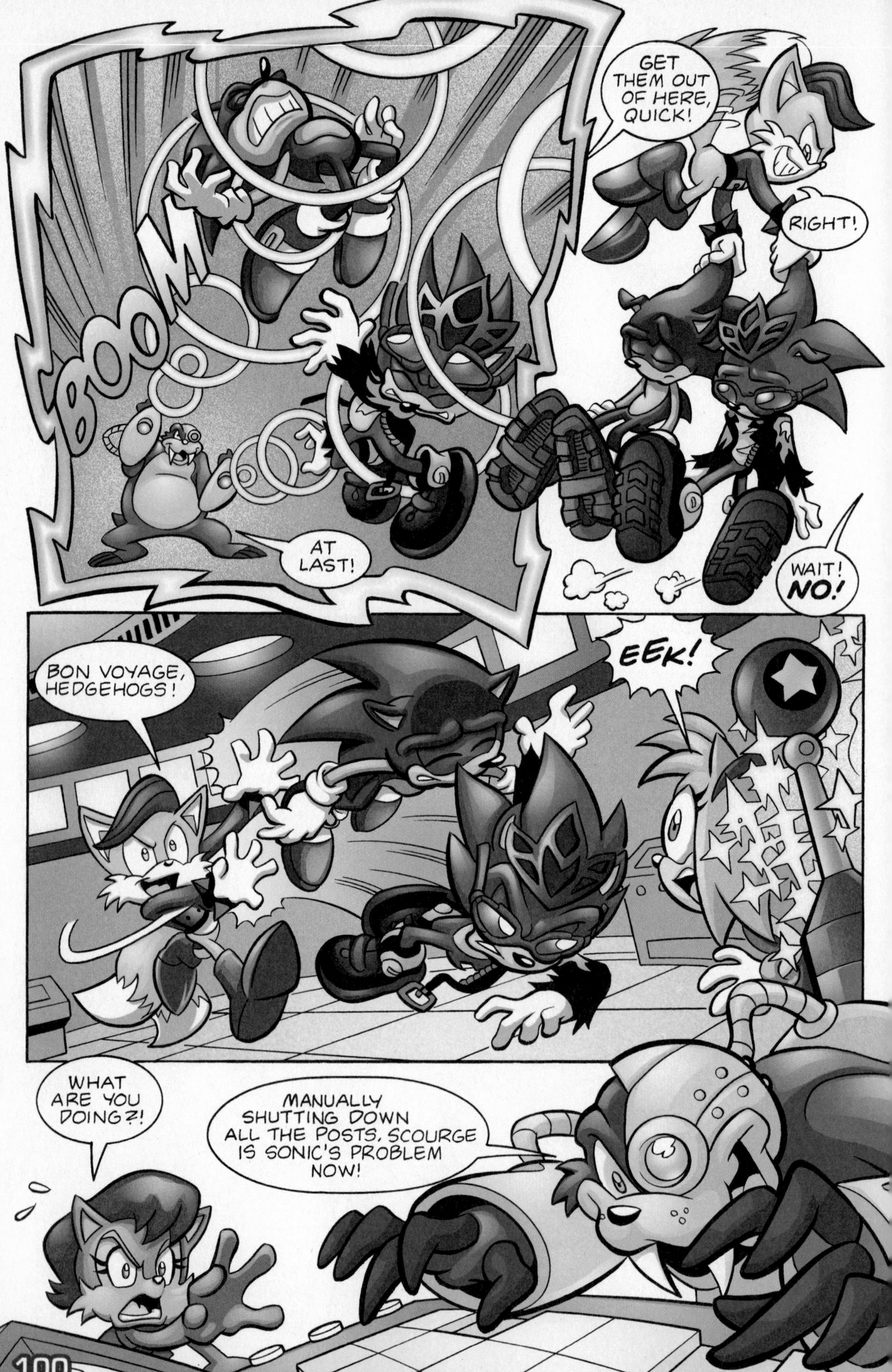
GET THEM OUT OF HERE, QUICK!
RIGHT!
BOOM
AT LAST!
WAIT! NO!
BON VOYAGE, HEDGEHOGS!
EEK!
WHAT ARE YOU DOING?!
MANUALLY SHUTTING DOWN ALL THE POSTS. SCOURGE IS SONIC'S PROBLEM NOW!

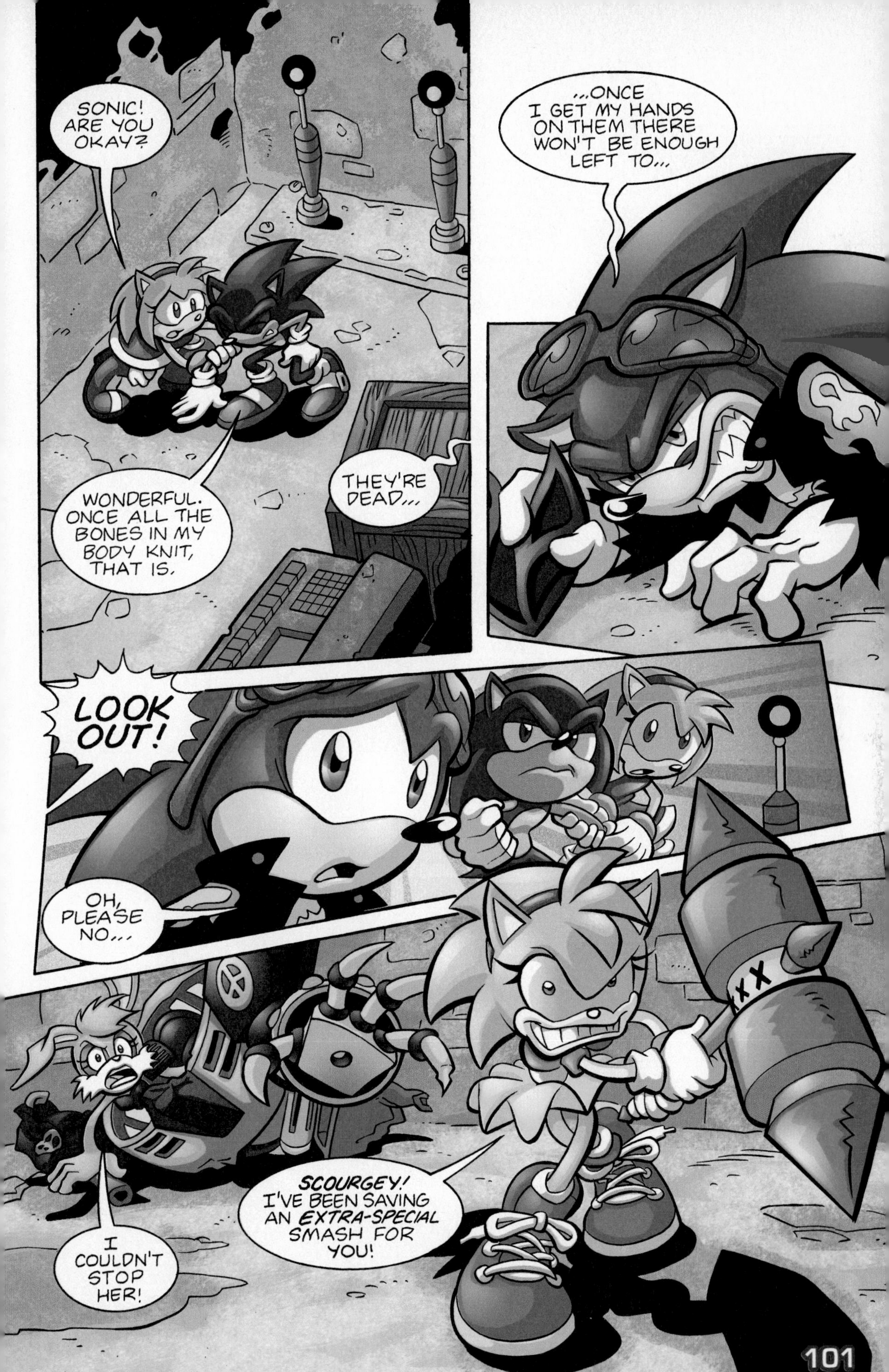

SONIC! ARE YOU OKAY?
WONDERFUL. ONCE ALL THE BONES IN MY BODY KNIT, THAT IS.
THEY'RE DEAD...
...ONCE I GET MY HANDS ON THEM THERE WON'T BE ENOUGH LEFT TO...
LOOK OUT!
OH, PLEASE NO...
SCOURGEY! I'VE BEEN SAVING AN EXTRA-SPECIAL SMASH FOR YOU!
I COULDN'T STOP HER!

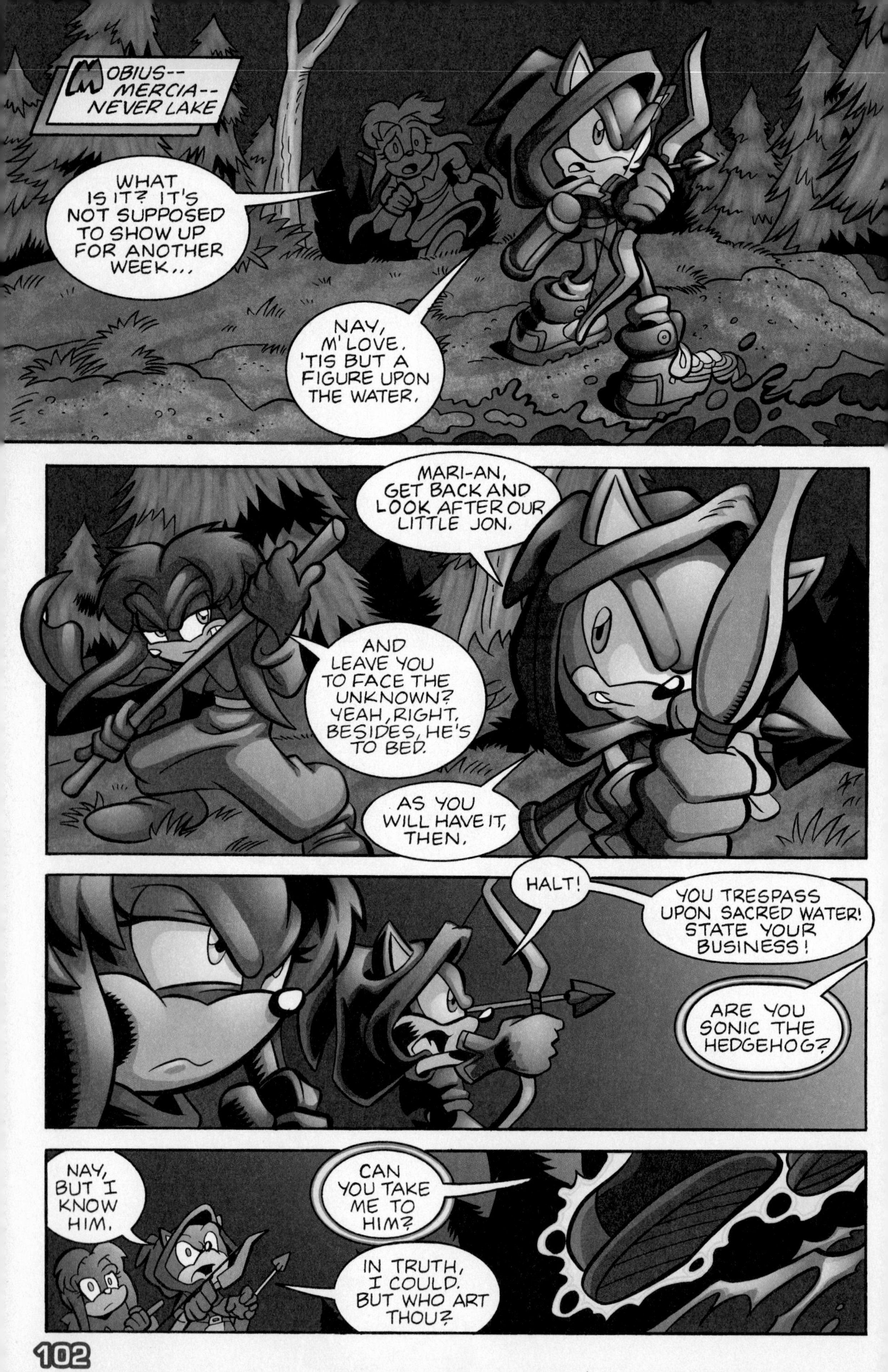
MOBIUS-- MERCIA-- NEVER LAKE
WHAT IS IT? IT'S NOT SUPPOSED TO SHOW UP FOR ANOTHER WEEK...
NAY, M' LOVE. 'TIS BUT A FIGURE UPON THE WATER.
MARI-AN, GET BACK AND LOOK AFTER OUR LITTLE JON.
AND LEAVE YOU TO FACE THE UNKNOWN? YEAH, RIGHT. BESIDES, HE'S TO BED.
AS YOU WILL HAVE IT, THEN.
HALT!
YOU TRESPASS UPON SACRED WATER! STATE YOUR BUSINESS!
ARE YOU SONIC THE HEDGEHOG?
NAY, BUT I KNOW HIM.
CAN YOU TAKE ME TO HIM?
IN TRUTH, I COULD. BUT WHO ART THOU?

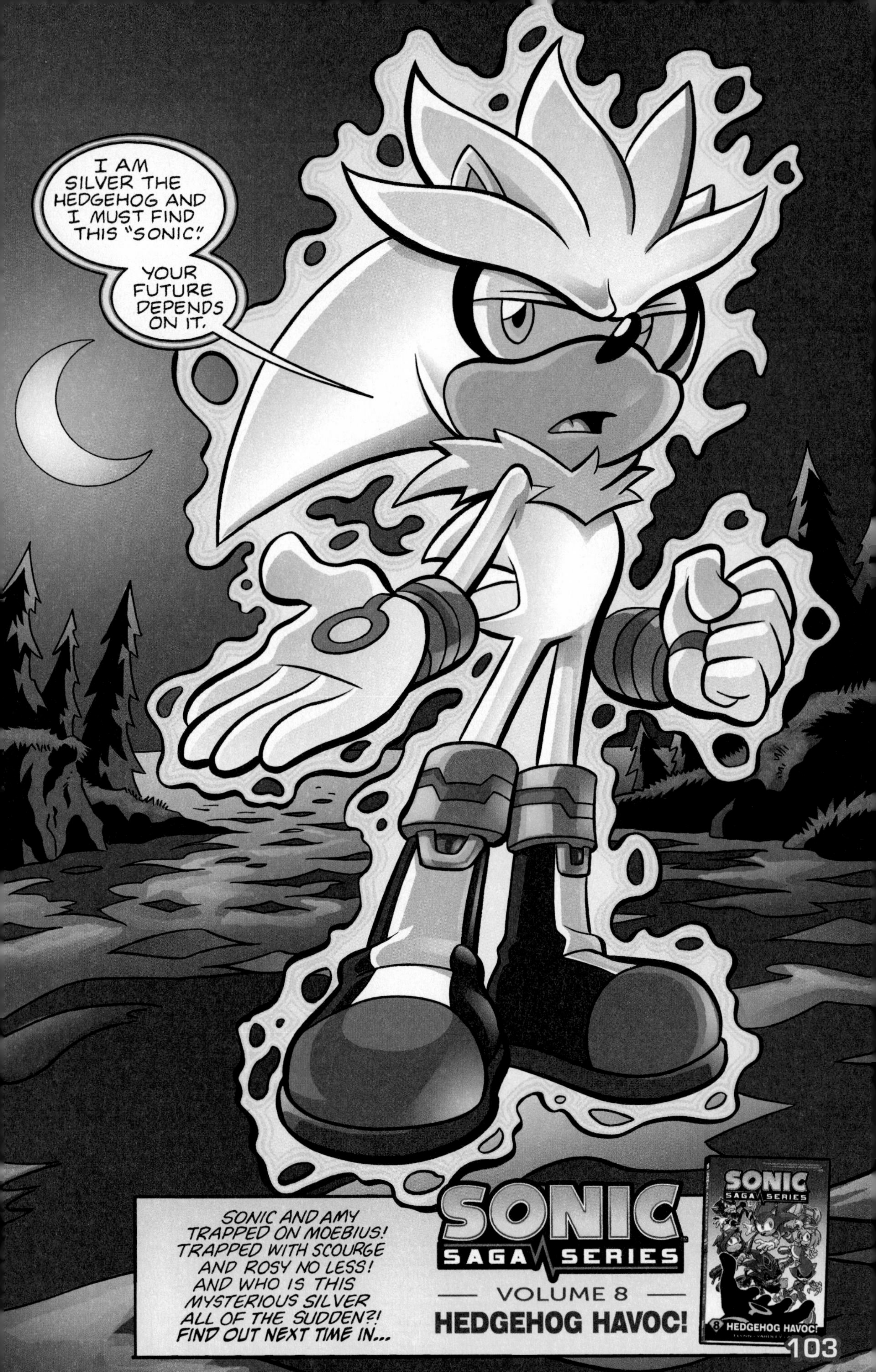
I AM SILVER THE HEDGEHOG AND I MUST FIND THIS "SONIC."
YOUR FUTURE DEPENDS ON IT.
SONIC AND AMY TRAPPED ON MOEBIUS! TRAPPED WITH SCOURGE AND ROSY NO LESS! AND WHO IS THIS MYSTERIOUS SILVER ALL OF THE SUDDEN?! FIND OUT NEXT TIME IN...
SONIC SAGA SERIES
VOLUME 8
HEDGEHOG HAVOC!
SONIC SAGA SERIES
8 HEDGEHOG HAVOC!

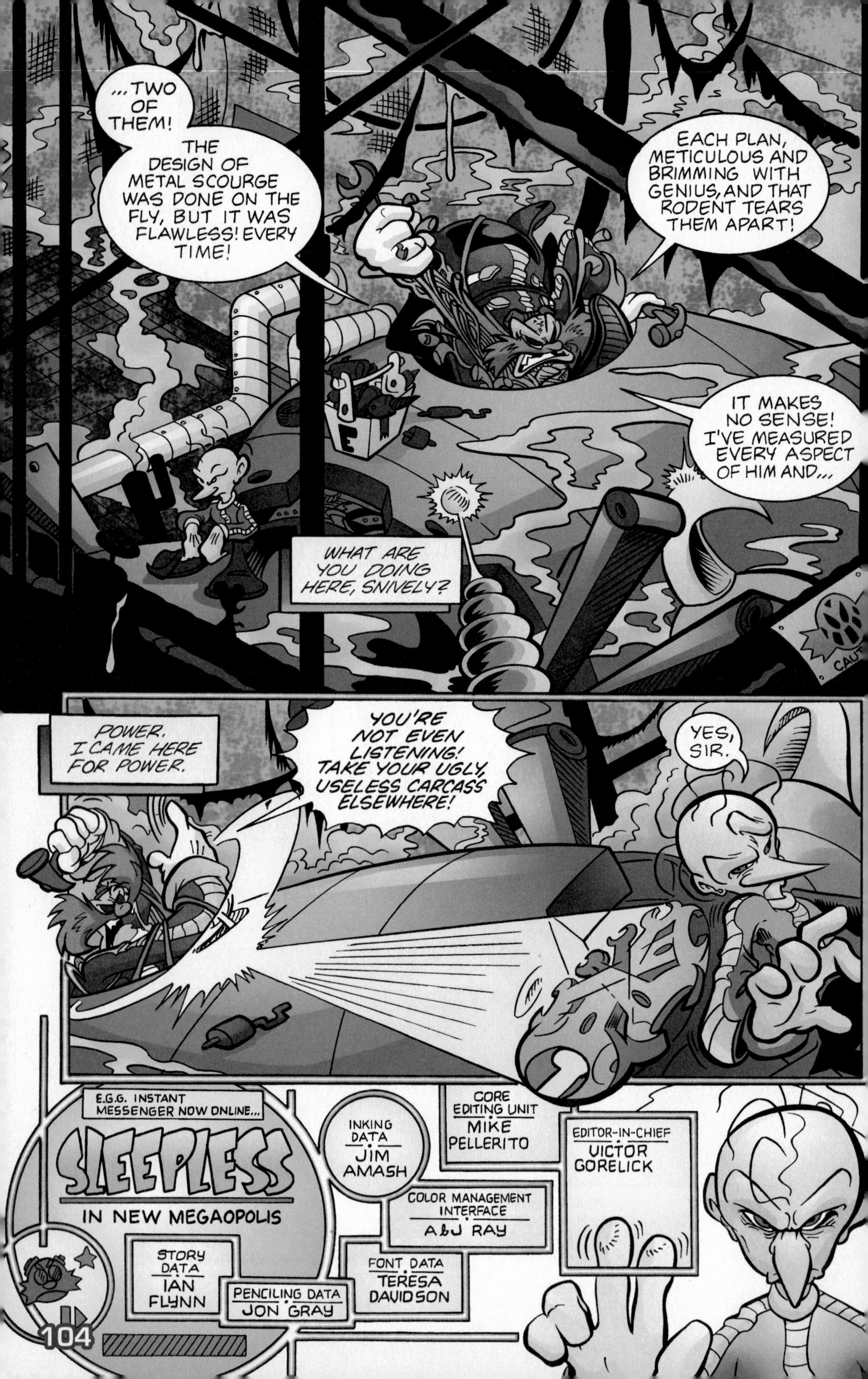
...TWO OF THEM!
THE DESIGN OF METAL SCOURGE WAS DONE ON THE FLY, BUT IT WAS FLAWLESS! EVERY TIME!
EACH PLAN, METICULOUS AND BRIMMING WITH GENIUS, AND THAT RODENT TEARS THEM APART!
IT MAKES NO SENSE! I'VE MEASURED EVERY ASPECT OF HIM AND...
WHAT ARE YOU DOING HERE, SNIVELY?
POWER. I CAME HERE FOR POWER.
YOU'RE NOT EVEN LISTENING! TAKE YOUR UGLY, USELESS CARCASS ELSEWHERE!
YES, SIR.
E.G.G. INSTANT MESSENGER NOW ONLINE...
SLEEPLESS
IN NEW MEGAOPOLIS
STORY DATA IAN FLYNN
PENCILING DATA JON GRAY
INKING DATA JIM AMASH
CORE EDITING UNIT MIKE PELLERITO
COLOR MANAGEMENT INTERFACE A&J RAY
FONT DATA TERESA DAVIDSON
EDITOR-IN-CHIEF VICTOR GORELICK

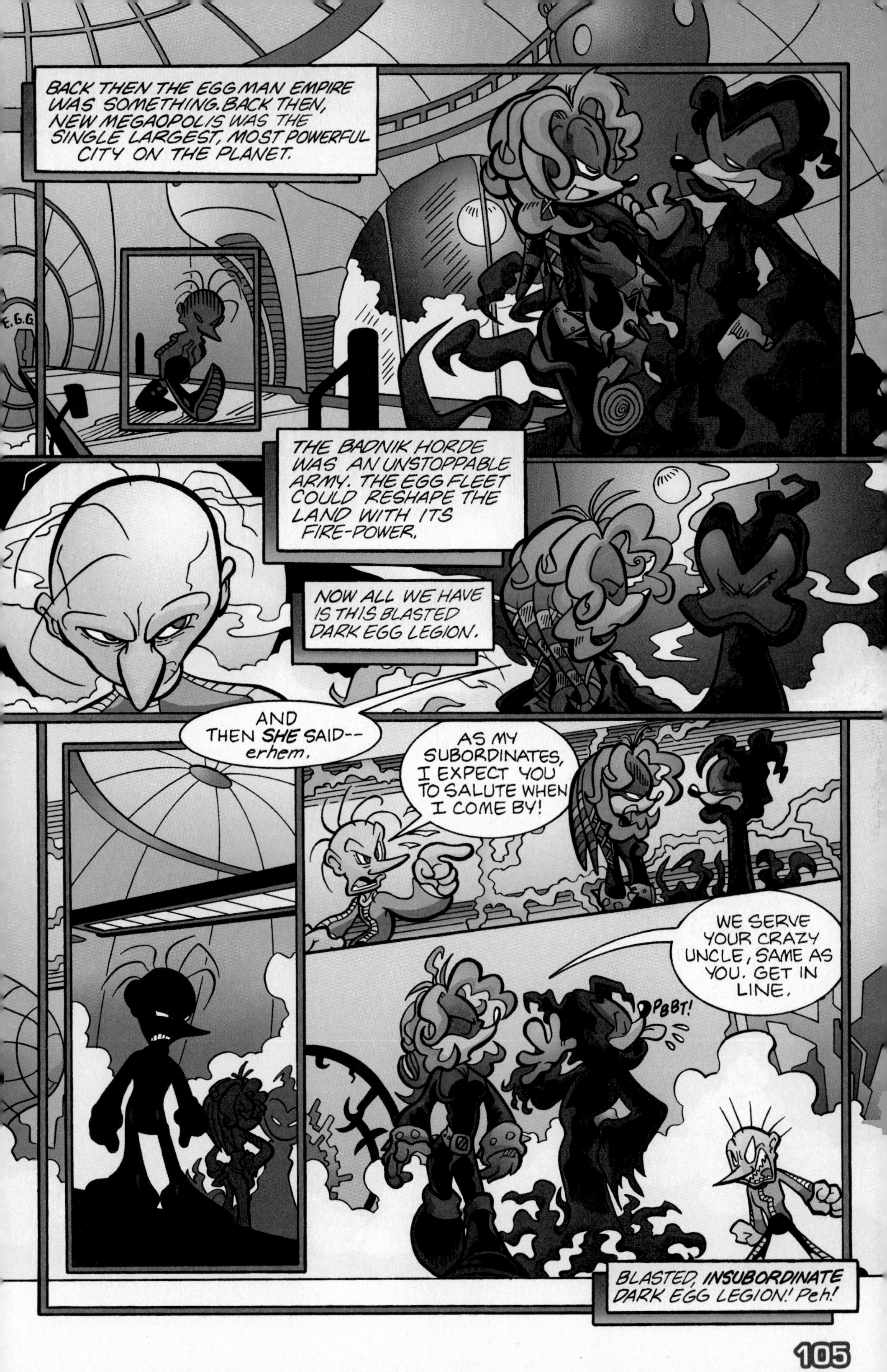
BACK THEN THE EGGMAN EMPIRE WAS SOMETHING. BACK THEN, NEW MEGAOPOLIS WAS THE SINGLE LARGEST, MOST POWERFUL CITY ON THE PLANET.
E.G.G.
THE BADNIK HORDE WAS AN UNSTOPPABLE ARMY. THE EGG FLEET COULD RESHAPE THE LAND WITH ITS FIRE-POWER.
NOW ALL WE HAVE IS THIS BLASTED DARK EGG LEGION.
AND THEN SHE SAID-- erhem.
AS MY SUBORDINATES, I EXPECT YOU TO SALUTE WHEN I COME BY!
WE SERVE YOUR CRAZY UNCLE, SAME AS YOU. GET IN LINE.
PBBT!
BLASTED, INSUBORDINATE DARK EGG LEGION! Peh!

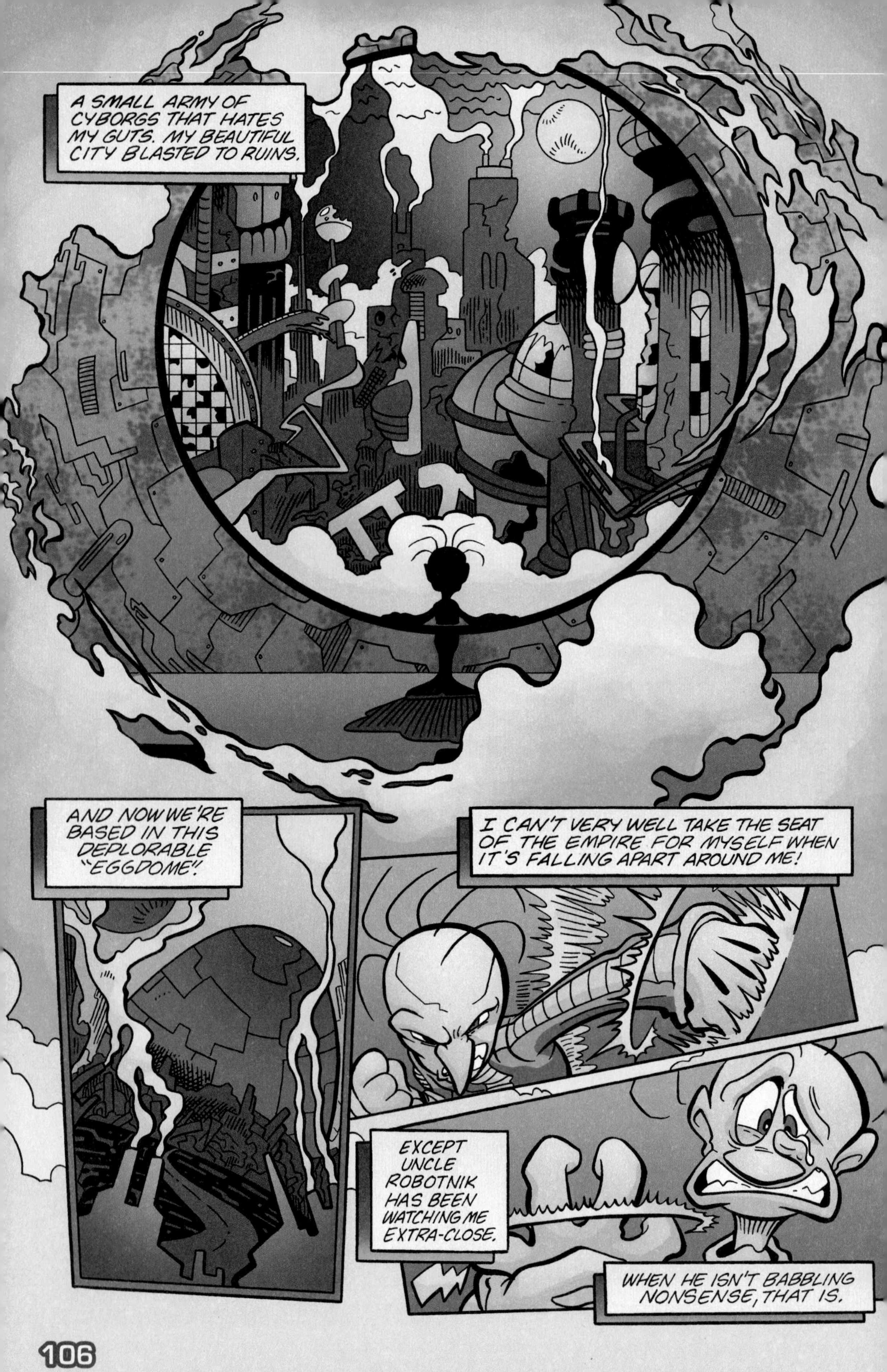
A SMALL ARMY OF CYBORGS THAT HATES MY GUTS. MY BEAUTIFUL CITY BLASTED TO RUINS.
AND NOW WE'RE BASED IN THIS DEPLORABLE "EGGDOME"!
I CAN'T VERY WELL TAKE THE SEAT OF THE EMPIRE FOR MYSELF WHEN IT'S FALLING APART AROUND ME!
EXCEPT UNCLE ROBOTNIK HAS BEEN WATCHING ME EXTRA-CLOSE.
WHEN HE ISN'T BABBLING NONSENSE, THAT IS.

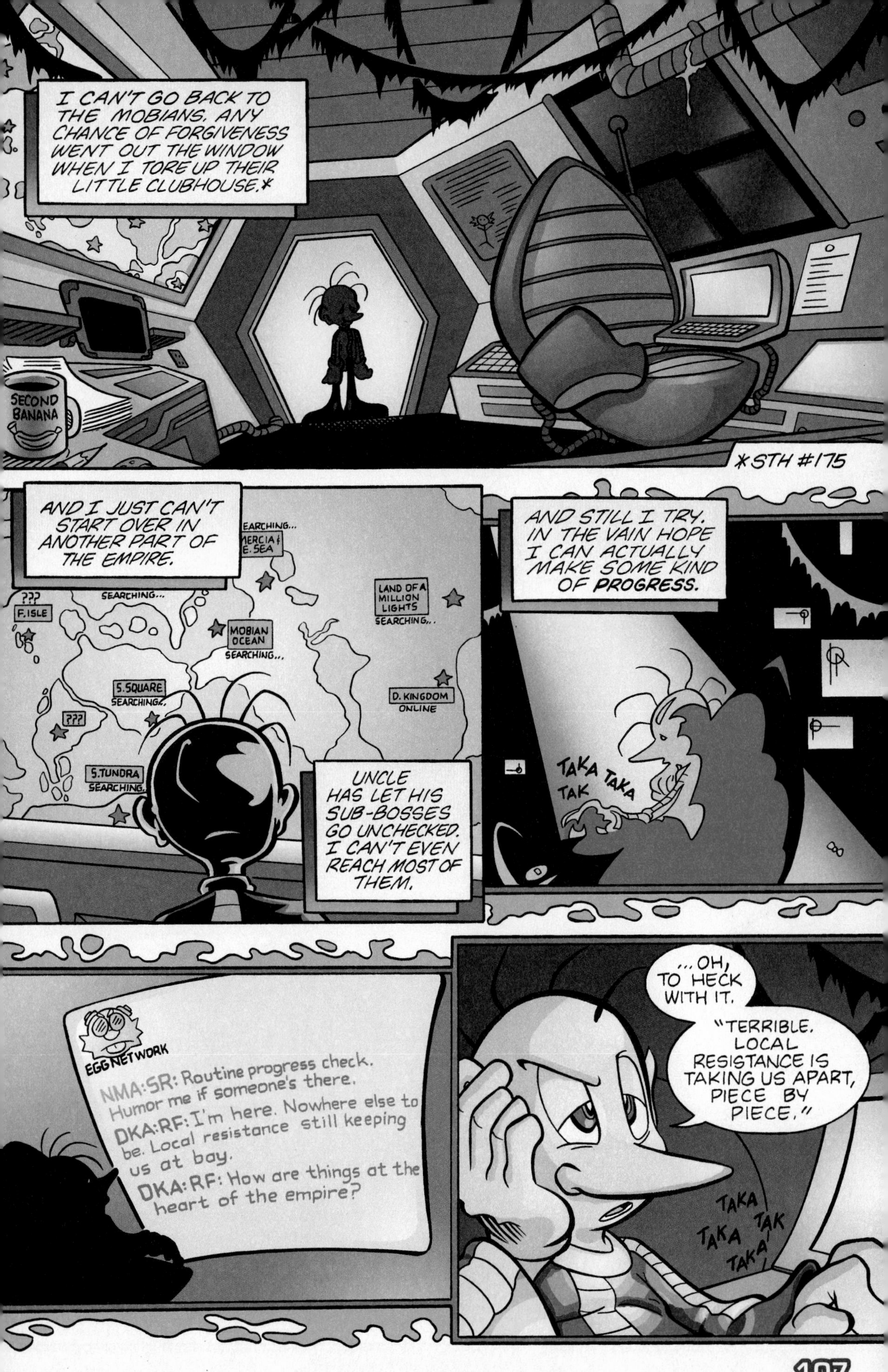

I CAN'T GO BACK TO THE MOBIANS. ANY CHANCE OF FORGIVENESS WENT OUT THE WINDOW WHEN I TORE UP THEIR LITTLE CLUBHOUSE.*
SECOND BANANA
*STH #175
AND I JUST CAN'T START OVER IN ANOTHER PART OF THE EMPIRE.
SEARCHING...
MERCIA & E. SEA
???
F. ISLE
SEARCHING...
MOBIAN OCEAN
SEARCHING...
LAND OF A MILLION LIGHTS
SEARCHING...
S. SQUARE
SEARCHING...
???
D. KINGDOM
ONLINE
S. TUNDRA
SEARCHING...
UNCLE HAS LET HIS SUB-BOSSES GO UNCHECKED. I CAN'T EVEN REACH MOST OF THEM.
AND STILL I TRY. IN THE VAIN HOPE I CAN ACTUALLY MAKE SOME KIND OF **PROGRESS.**
TAKA TAKA TAK
EGG NETWORK
NMA:SR: Routine progress check. Humor me if someone's there.
DKA:RF: I'm here. Nowhere else to be. Local resistance still keeping us at bay.
DKA:RF: How are things at the heart of the empire?
...OH, TO HECK WITH IT.
"TERRIBLE. LOCAL RESISTANCE IS TAKING US APART, PIECE BY PIECE."
TAKA TAKA TAK TAKA

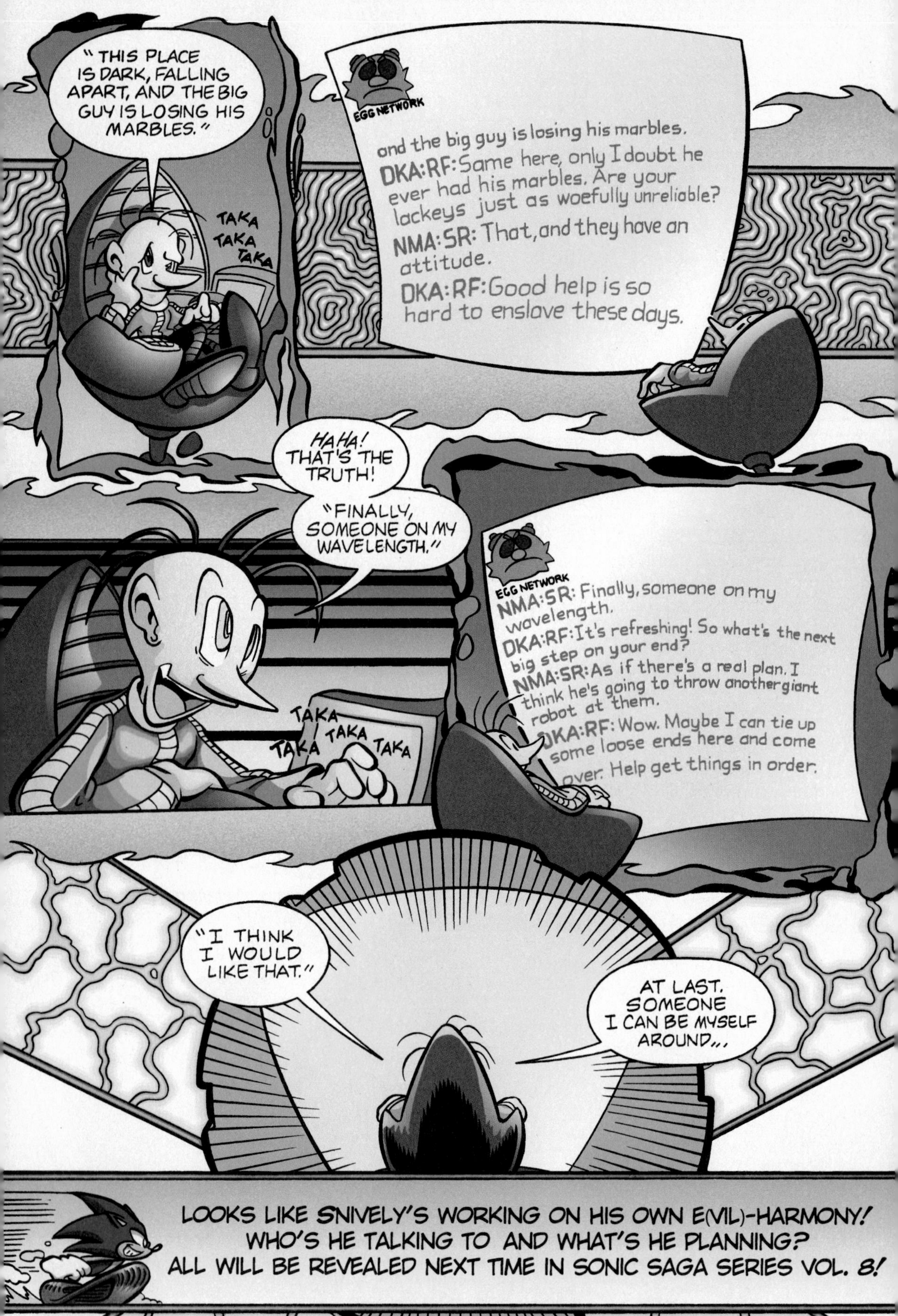

"THIS PLACE IS DARK, FALLING APART, AND THE BIG GUY IS LOSING HIS MARBLES."
EGG NETWORK
and the big guy is losing his marbles.
DKA:RF: Same here, only I doubt he ever had his marbles. Are your lackeys just as woefully unreliable?
NMA:SR: That, and they have an attitude.
DKA:RF: Good help is so hard to enslave these days.
TAKA TAKA TAKA
HAHA! THAT'S THE TRUTH!
"FINALLY, SOMEONE ON MY WAVELENGTH."
EGG NETWORK
NMA:SR: Finally, someone on my wavelength.
DKA:RF: It's refreshing! So what's the next big step on your end?
NMA:SR: As if there's a real plan. I think he's going to throw another giant robot at them.
DKA:RF: Wow. Maybe I can tie up some loose ends here and come over. Help get things in order.
TAKA TAKA TAKA TAKA
"I THINK I WOULD LIKE THAT."
AT LAST. SOMEONE I CAN BE MYSELF AROUND...
LOOKS LIKE SNIVELY'S WORKING ON HIS OWN E(VIL)-HARMONY! WHO'S HE TALKING TO AND WHAT'S HE PLANNING? ALL WILL BE REVEALED NEXT TIME IN SONIC SAGA SERIES VOL. 8!

SUPPRESSION SQUAD

PROFILE STATS:
First Appearance:
Sonic the Hedgehog #189

Originally just known as the **Anti-Freedom Fighters**, this group of thugs delighted in breaking the law and causing trouble for their virtuous counterparts on **Mobius Prime**. However, after being whipped into shape by **Scourge the Hedgehog**, the Suppression Squad became a force to be reckoned with.

Scourge the Hedgehog (1) – Their on-again, off-again leader. He's valued for his power, but the team hates his guts.

Fiona Fox (2) – Actually from Mobius Prime, she only held a ranking position because she was dating Scourge.

Princess Alicia Acorn (3) – Cold and unfeeling towards her comrades, she'll flirt with the man she sees as the most powerful to ensure she has someone close by to do her bidding – or to use as a shield. Her weapon of choice is a whip.

Miles Prower (4) – Smug and intelligent, Miles tries to appear mature despite his age and refuses to answer to "Tails." He often prefers to manipulate from behind the scenes, and to use magic before machinery.

Boomer Walrus (5) – The team's mechanic and heaviest hitter after Scourge. Disgusted with **Rotor's** "weakness," he cybernetically enhanced himself. He now has sonic cannons built into his arms.

Patch D'Coolette (6) – A back-stabbing rogue who managed to replace **Antoine** for months and did everything he could to ruin his life. Patch used to wear his eye-patch just for show until Scourge gave him a real reason to wear it. He's a viciously effective swordsman and often uses poison against his enemies.

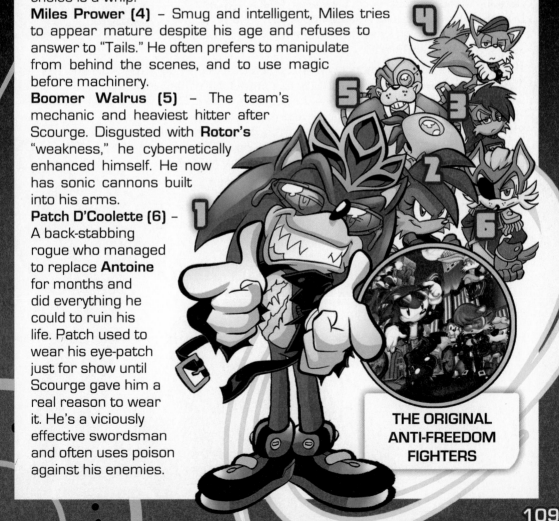

THE ORIGINAL ANTI-FREEDOM FIGHTERS

MOEBIUS

An alternate zone also known as **Anti-Mobius**, Moebius is a dark, twisted version of **Mobius Prime**. Instead of having a few powerful villains, the world is overrun with selfish, terrible people. Instead of being protected by many heroes, Moebius is barely protected by a few. Where there is bravery on Mobius Prime there is cowardice on Moebius, and so on. In this world there are hundreds of green gems called **Anarchy Beryl**. Like **Chaos Emeralds**, they have incredible magical properties, but their energies are negative and corrosive. A super-state (like **Super Sonic**) would wear out the user despite granting unlimited power. Power rings on Moebius are much rarer and the gifts they bestow often come with a twisted side-effect, as seen in the insane **Rosy the Rascal (3)**. During its **Great Peace**, Moebius culturally stagnated. Only when an early version of the Suppression Squad began causing trouble did things change, although not for the better.

Instead of the flying **Angel Island**, Moebius features the sunken **Demon Island** protected by **Overseer O'Nux (4)** and his **Orderix** enforcers. Its city **Atlantinopolis (5)** has a protective energy dome powered by six small pieces of Anarchy Beryl as opposed to **Master Emerald**.

The world suffered a shift in identity when Scourge the Hedgehog used the full extent of his power to conquer it. Bent on making his homeworld more than just a copy of Mobius, he invaded **Castle Acorn (6)** and forced the people to change their names and rebuild their identities. There is some hope. Kindly veterinarian and genius inventor **Dr. Ivo Kintobor (1)** keeps the **Grand Forest** protected from the pollution and chaos with an energy shield projected from his towering **clinic (7)**. He's assisted

by **Buns Rabbot (2)**, an ex-**Suppression Squad** member who was kicked out when it was discovered she had **N.I.D.S. (Neuro-Immune Deficiency Syndrome)**; her condition is kept in check inside the sterile environment of the **Omega Peace Unit** – a suit bearing non-lethal weaponry.

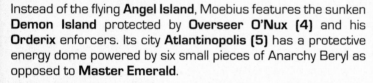

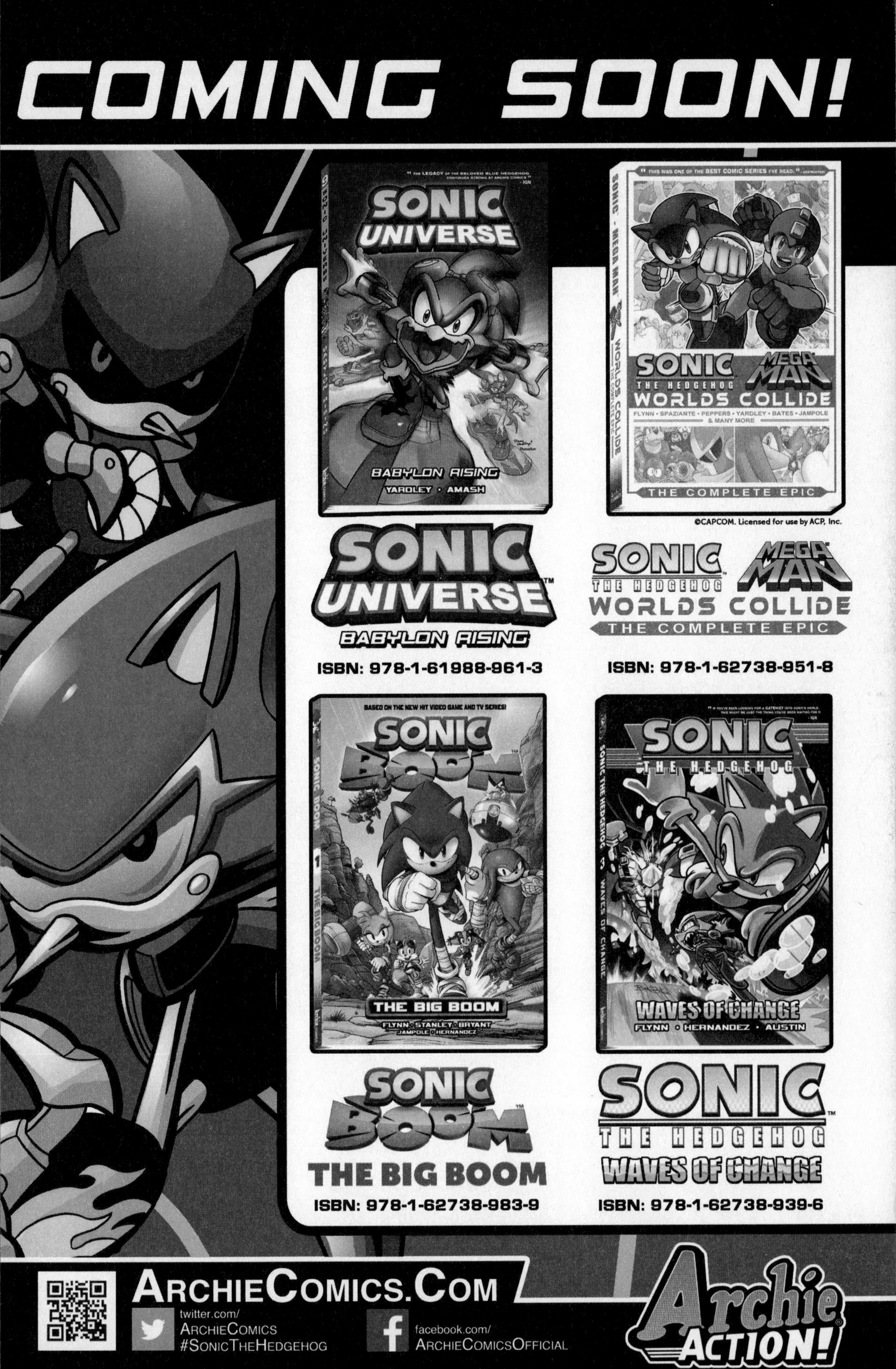
COMING SOON!
SONIC UNIVERSE
BABYLON RISING
YARDLEY • AMASH
SONIC THE HEDGEHOG MEGA MAN
WORLDS COLLIDE
FLYNN • SPAZIANTE • PEPPERS • YARDLEY • BATES • JAMPOLE & MANY MORE
THE COMPLETE EPIC
©CAPCOM. Licensed for use by ACP, Inc.
SONIC UNIVERSE™
BABYLON RISING
ISBN: 978-1-61988-961-3
SONIC THE HEDGEHOG MEGA MAN
WORLDS COLLIDE
THE COMPLETE EPIC
ISBN: 978-1-62738-951-8
BASED ON THE NEW HIT VIDEO GAME AND TV SERIES!
SONIC BOOM
THE BIG BOOM
FLYNN • STANLEY • BRYANT • JAMPOLE • HERNANDEZ
SONIC THE HEDGEHOG
WAVES OF CHANGE
FLYNN • HERNANDEZ • AUSTIN
SONIC BOOM™
THE BIG BOOM
ISBN: 978-1-62738-983-9
SONIC™ THE HEDGEHOG
WAVES OF CHANGE
ISBN: 978-1-62738-939-6
ARCHIECOMICS.COM
twitter.com/
ARCHIECOMICS
#SONICTHEHEDGEHOG
facebook.com/
ARCHIECOMICSOFFICIAL
Archie ACTION!

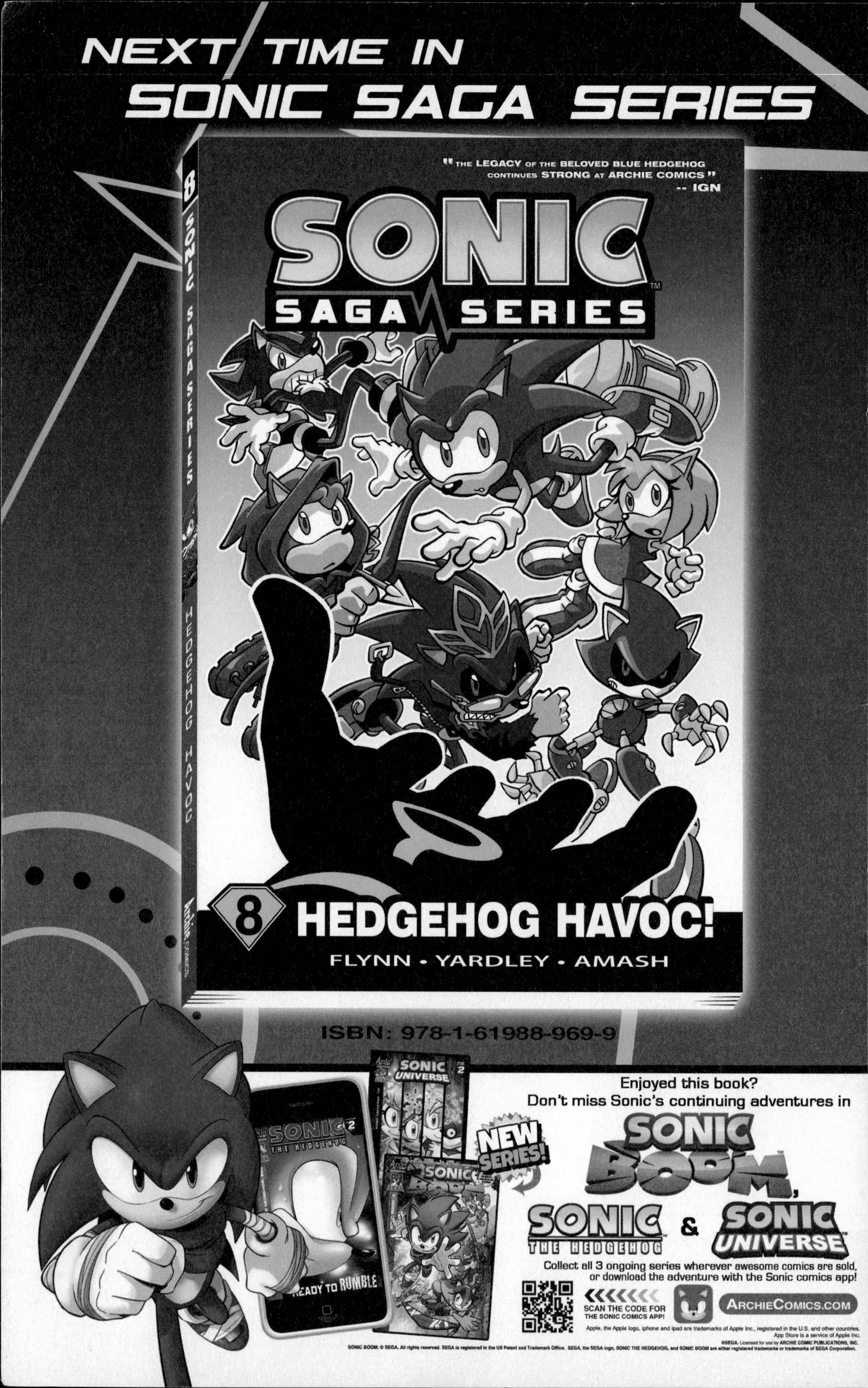

NEXT TIME IN
SONIC SAGA SERIES
"THE LEGACY OF THE BELOVED BLUE HEDGEHOG CONTINUES STRONG AT ARCHIE COMICS" -- IGN
SONIC SAGA SERIES
8 HEDGEHOG HAVOC!
FLYNN • YARDLEY • AMASH
ISBN: 978-1-61988-969-9
Enjoyed this book?
Don't miss Sonic's continuing adventures in
NEW SERIES!
SONIC BOOM,
SONIC THE HEDGEHOG & SONIC UNIVERSE
Collect all 3 ongoing series wherever awesome comics are sold,
or download the adventure with the Sonic comics app!
SCAN THE CODE FOR THE SONIC COMICS APP!
ARCHIECOMICS.COM
Apple, the Apple logo, iphone and ipad are trademarks of Apple Inc., registered in the U.S. and other countries. App Store is a service of Apple Inc.
©SEGA. Licensed for use by ARCHIE COMIC PUBLICATIONS, INC.
SONIC BOOM: © SEGA. All rights reserved. SEGA is registered in the US Patent and Trademark Office. SEGA, the SEGA logo, SONIC THE HEDGEHOG, and SONIC BOOM are either registered trademarks or trademarks of SEGA Corporation.